TALES O

"K'zarr's treasure," e
it's hid. Only I."

Even for us, K'zarr was a name of vague dread. There had been many kzin freebooters, outside the disciplined armed forces of the Patriarchy (who in all good faith had been more than bad enough!), but he had been the worst. Even kzin-occupied villages and asteroids had not been safe from him, and he had slain men and kzin who crossed him or stood in his way with impartial cruelty. He was one of the few beings who had had a reward placed on his head by kzin and humans both, a distinction in which, it was said, his crew took some pride.

"I was the first mate, I was, d'ye see, K'zarr's first mate, an' I'm the on'y one what knows where his treasure is. He gave it t'me, K'zarr did, when he lay dying, out there where the purple nebulae lit the sky, where ancient suns go to die, that's when K'zarr got his. The suns died and so did K'zarr. But not before he gave me the directions, so he did. An' the scum wants them, they wants them bad. An' it's the death claw fer me, 'tes so."

"What is this death claw, Captain?" I asked.

"Ah, 'tes the summons, the last one a freebooter iver gets. But keep yer eyes open, Peter, my lady, an' I'll share it all wi' ye both, in memory o' the last noggin. 'Tes on'y fair. You helped me face down the horrors, Peter."

He pronounced my name carefully, as he always did: Names are important to a kzin. But he was wandering, it was plain to see, and his voice trailed off and he lapsed back into sleep. When we heard him snoring, we tiptoed out.

BAEN BOOKS

THE MAN-KZIN WARS SERIES

Created by Larry Niven

The Man-Kzin Wars
The Houses of the Kzinti
Man-Kzin Wars V
Man-Kzin WarsVI
Man-Kzin Wars VII
Choosing Names: Man-Kzin Wars VIII
Man-Kzin Wars IX
Man-Kzin Wars X: The Wunder War
Man-Kzin Wars XI

The Best of All Possible Wars

Destiny's Forge by Paul Chafe

Treasure Planet by Hal Colebatch & Jessica Q. Fox

TREASURE PLANET

A MAN-KZIN NOVEL

SERIES CREATED BY
LARRY NIVEN

BY
HAL COLEBATCH
AND
JESSICA Q. FOX

TREASURE PLANET

A Baen Books Original

Baen Publishing Enterprises
P.O. Box 1403
Riverdale, NY 10471
www.baen.com

ISBN: 978-1-4767-8070-2

Cover art by Sam Kennedy

First Baen paperback printing, August 2015

Distributed by Simon & Schuster
1230 Avenue of the Americas
New York, NY 10020

Library of Congress Cataloging-in-Publication Data

Colebatch, Hal, 1945 –
Treasure Planet / created by Larry Niven ; Hal Colebatch, Jessica Q. Fox.
Pages cm. – (Man-kzin wars ; 16)
ISBN 978-1-4767-3640-2 {pbk.)
1. Kzin (Imaginary place)--Fiction. 2. Life on other planets—Fiction. 3. Space warfare—Fiction. I. Fox, Jessica Q. , author. II. Niven, Larry. III. Title.
PR9619.3.C5648T44 2014
813'.54—dc23
2013049453

Printed in the United States of America

10 9 8 7 6 5 4 3 2 1

murders and treachery. Hopes we'll forget about them, perhaps. Well, I shan't."

Why leave the message? What did he hope to gain? I just didn't understand him.

After days of careful checking, lest Silver had left some booby traps on *Valiant*, S'maak-Captain pronounced himself reasonably satisfied and steered the *Valiant* towards the outer edges of the Tamburlaine system, and off the ecliptic. This took another three days. Then we swung around and aimed for the Alpha Centauri system, with little Proxima out on the edge, and Wunderland close in.

It took us weeks to get back, and when we did, we needed tugs and hired crew to bring her back to ground. But we did it, and it was good to be home. Redroar was close to launching the relief vessel.

Getting into the old routine felt strange. Mother hugged me and cried and told me she'd never expected to see me again. Then she asked me if I'd bought her a present in foreign parts, and I was glad that I'd remembered to get her a roll of fabric from Tamburlaine five. I'd chosen it because it had the color of the nebulae streaming silently through it. Mother had never seen anything like it and, I suspect, had no idea what to do with it, but she kissed me and hugged me and cried all over again.

Orion had rewarded our crew generously; those loyal Kzin who had died in the course of duty had their families looked after too. I suppose that being a member of a Kzin family headed by a spacer seldom brought rewards and the risks were great, but at least these would never have to worry about money ever again.

Marthar and I often look into the night sky to see the direction of the swirl-rift and the treasure planet, although, of course, it's much too far to see with the naked eye. But imagination and memory bring back the sight of those dark towers rising against an indigo sky, lit by a green oval sun with red dirt and stones underfoot. And when night falls, I can imagine the purple nebulae like the dresses of women a million light-years tall, dancing, frozen, swirling but stopped in time by sheer vastness.

Bengar is happy in his role as head of the security detail for Marthar, and although it's been an easy job so far, that could change. Orion is happy with him, and lets him accompany Marthar to school.

We are both officially back at school, but unofficially we are trying to understand some of the alien science. Marthar still has the sunny optimism that we shall crack it one day. We have some help: Orion is hiring scholars of all sorts to make sense of it. Many seem even slower than we are and absorbed by minutiae. This vexes Marthar considerably; she does not have the academic temperament.

"Why can't they see the wood and not get disabled by the trees?" she asked fiercely once. "Oh, well, if they had really good minds, they would be competition, I suppose, so I guess we just use them."

Dimity Carmody had been fascinated by the mathematics. She cracked the whole thing overnight and was translating it by hand into something we could understand, then she wrote a program to do it. I gave up trying to understand the original, but I could make vague sense out of the translation. Marthar was using it to crack the problem of the transfer discs and was cursing a good deal.

And in time we will crack it, I believe, no doubt with a lot of help. And one day, we shall return to the treasure planet, with a much better idea of what we want from it. Both Marthar and I are determined, and we will never give up while we live.

I often think about Silver, and wonder if we shall ever see him again. It doesn't seem impossible, and I don't know how I feel about it. I am sure he would have returned to the treasure planet by now, and tried to extract wealth from it somehow, which isn't at all an easy matter. Yet he has a first-rate mind, as even Marthar admits, and a fund of ingenuity. So he may well think of something.

So one day, not too far off, we shall go to that ancient world and perhaps see once again the dark towers and the relics of a race that died before my own was born. Trying, so hard, as they did, to pass on something of what they had learned of this universe to those who came later. I still don't really know anything about them save that: They had a certain nobility and a need to leave a record. I can understand that and admire it. There's a determination to defy time and destiny there, and it resonates with something inside me. Whatever comes of their knowledge, I shall feel grateful to them for trying. And I would like to go back one day and know them a little better.

But that's another story.

TREASURE PLANET

A MAN-KZIN NOVEL

Under the wide and starry sky,
Dig the grave and let me lie.
Glad did I live and gladly die,
And I laid me down with a will.
This be the verse you graved for me:
Here he lies where he longed to be;
Home is the sailor, home from sea,
And the hunter home from the hill.

ACKNOWLEDGEMENT

Thanks are due to Mrs. Alexandra Colebatch for much editorial help and to Larry Niven for his encouragement.

DEDICATION

We dedicate this book to the memory of
Robert Louis Stevenson, gentleman, traveller, poet,
conservative (after a brief experiment with socialism),
and master story-teller, whose story lines, characterization
and dialogue have survived, in our view unsurpassed,
for nearly a century-and-a-half so far,
and have a long way to go. An' ye may lay to that!

AUTHOR'S NOTE

Previous adventures of Rarrgh,
The Judge, Dimity Carmody, Vaemar-Riit and certain other characters are to be found in earlier volumes of *The Man-Kzin Wars*, especially Vols. IX, X, XI and XII.

CONTENTS

Part One:
The Kzin Pirate
1

Part Two:
The Space Tutor
87

Part Three:
The Planet-Fall Adventure
167

Part Four:
A Defensive Position
207

Part Five:
Return to the Valiant
263

PART ONE

THE KZIN PIRATE

CHAPTER ONE

My name is Peter Cartwright, and I was raised in Thoma'stown on Wunderland. It is East of the ranges and named after our first Judge, Jorg von Thoma,[1] who is still alive and an important man in the town and for miles around. He is pretty old by now, and sure looks it. I hear he objected to having the town named after him when the surveyor came from München, but everybody else voted against him, so it was not quite unanimous. I guess the surveyor must have grinned when he pencilled in the name and made it official.

I have been told to write this account by him and the Doctor, who I knew from childhood. It is a true account of what happened to us when we went to the Treasure Planet, and is as complete as I can make it, though there's a bit of misdirection in where the Treasure Planet actually *is*, because one day we're going back there, and we don't want to find that any other human or kzin has got to it first.

[1] For the previous history of Jorg von Thoma see His Sergeant's Honor in Man-Kzin Wars IX.

There is still lots of treasure left, a whole world of the stuff, and when I'm older I plan to go back again with my friend, Marthar.

We live in the back-blocks of Wunderland. Thoma'stown is still in quite wild country. We share the town with some of the kzin.

Before I was born, there was a long, long war between men and kzin, and kzin occupied the whole planet of Wunderland as masters.

Humans had control only of the Solar System four-and-a-bit light-years away, Earth, Sol's asteroid belt, and a few scattered settlements in outlying Goldilocks planets which the early ramrobots had found. (We live under Alpha Centauri A. Its twin, Alpha Centauri B, is about twenty-five AUs away). After more than sixty years of war, kzin were breaking through Sol's defenses. The Kzin Empire was very big, and their gravity drives were better than anything we had. Kzin are described as felinoids. They look something like tigers, but are much, much bigger and quicker—fiercer, too, say those who know both. And they look different in silhouette, also, for their brain-cases are far bigger. They fight with fangs and claws, and personal knives called *wtsais* and other blades (cutlasses, too, now, as you'll hear); but they can also fight with laser-cannon, beam-weapons, rail-guns, mass-drivers, needlers, blasters, heat-induction rays, anemones and other things. Fortunately we can, too. The Kzin Empire has a ruler called The Patriarch, and over a long time the kzin have occupied many worlds.

It seems that most civilized, space-travelling species they came across had forgotten how to fight. As humans nearly had. But one thing this meant was that, apart from fighting among themselves, of which they had done a lot, the kzin had little experience of war.

They landed on and occupied Wunderland and the asteroids of the Serpent Swarm, getting some human collaborators to run them for them, collect taxes and organize the other humans as slaves or monkey-meat.

Those who disobeyed were eaten, either on the spot or in the public hunts. Fortunately, a lot of Wunderland is unsettled, and there were big caves, swamps and forests, so the humans who resisted had some hiding places. Some humans fought the kzin, on the ground and even in space, but as the Occupation wore on, the human resistance was being ground down.

The Kzin built fleets and sent them against Earth and the asteroids of the old Solar System. One fleet after another failed to break through Earth's defenses in strength, but, as I said, the humans were gradually losing.

Then the Sol humans got an FTL—a faster-than-light drive—thanks to Dimity Carmody, who had been put on a ship out of Wunderland, and the Hyperdrive Armada came sweeping in from Earth to liberate us. But that's a long story.

Most of the kzin and humans are at peace now. The most important kzin on Wunderland is Vaemar-Riit. You know from his name, Riit, that he is one of the Royal Family. His Sire, as the kzin call their fathers, Chuut-Riit, was Planetary Governor during the kzin Occupation, but was killed towards the end of it. I gather no one, kzin or human, likes talking about how he was killed.

When we learned the Kzin had a few hyperdrives (the

technology was given to them by a treacherous human), many humans were afraid the war would start again and this time the humans would lose. But it turned out differently: it meant there were new planets accessible for everyone, though some say the kzin are waiting their chance to start another war. I hope that's not true, for a lot of reasons. At one time some humans, especially some who had lived through the Occupation, wanted to kill all the kzin on Wunderland, but it was felt, I am told, that if that happened, the war would go on forever, or until everyone was dead and all the planets were smoking radioactive craters. Besides, there is no doubt that some kzin, led by the Lord Vaemar-Riit, want peace. And there are both humans and kzin who believe the two can learn from each other. The kzin who live in our village are friendly, anyway. They run the security force and a lot of other things. Female kzin, or kzinretti, except for a few like Lord Vaemar-Riit's mate, the Lady Karan, are stupid unless they are given special treatments.

My mother used to run the *Lord Templemount*, which she called a hotel, though it was just an inn, with a few spare rooms that were rarely hired out. There are only two inns in the town, and ours was the smaller, out towards the wall on the southern side, and we didn't make a lot of money. My father died two years before my story begins. It was a bit of a struggle, I see now, although I didn't notice much at the time. I was just a lad with a taste for exploring the neighborhood with my friends. Particularly Marthar. In those days, she had to take some green pills every day. "If I don't, I'll get as stupid as you, or even worse," she explained to me once. Later, to replace the pills, she had some sort of implant which does the job for a year at a time. She is quite smart, but not so smart as to worry me. And she is brave and basically kind (though inclined to sarcasm), so I care for her a lot.

I wasn't particularly worried when the old kzin space-farer turned up at the inn one day. Of course, we had lots of kzin around the place, and the great war between men and kzin had been over for a long time. The sheriff and most of his deputies were kzin. They kept the Judge's Law East of the Ranges, and I admired them a lot. They were brave and strong, and stood for justice, something Marthar and I believed in. But at school, where Marthar and I first made friends, we did history classes and learned about the Occupation and the Liberation and it seemed strange that once upon a time, man and kzin were deadly enemies on this planet. Anyway, that happened years and years before I was born. I don't know what it's like elsewhere, but in Thoma'stown, we get on fine. Maybe far away in space, humans and kzin still fight, and maybe we will again one day on Wunderland, but I can't see it happening in Thoma'stown. There are some dangerous kzin in the wilds, but there are some dangerous humans too, and other things. I couldn't possibly hurt Marthar. We've been friends too long, and we've been through a lot together, although that's mostly in a part of my story that I'll get to later.

It was a morning in early spring when the space-farer came to us. He was not overtall for a kzin, and his fur was grizzled and poorly trimmed; once it had been *sable et or*, black and gold stripes, but now the colors had faded to dirty brown and dark gray. His eyes had the red lines and purple hue which tell of decompression and mark the space-farer, human or kzin. One of his claws was steel, while his right ear was little more than a stump. He carried a huge backpack on his shoulders and a stick, which he used to bang on the open door. A battered *wtsai* scabbard hung by his left side, with a few jewels still on it, and low down on his right thigh there was a needler with the big handle the kzin need on their guns. While all adult male kzin have their personal *wtsai*s, he also carried a great cutlass dangling on a cord down his back. A kzin cutlass, not a human one, with a blade at least seven feet long. I had heard they were becoming popular among kzin, especially since they still needed special permission on Wunderland to carry more sophisticated weapons. These various weapons were a give-away for a certain kind of spacer. You risk blowing a hole in a lightly built ship if you use a blaster, and you can run out of ammunition for a needler, so a *wtsai* or other blade-weapon is a sensible thing to have aboard a spaceship, assuming it's the kind of ship where you might need to kill another creature on board, plunder some other craft, or fight off pirates, like Gutfoot's Horde or some of the others who had not accepted the Armistice. Space is big enough for a lot of ships to hide, and the Serpent Swarm and other asteroids, as well as the planetoids of Alpha Centauri B and Proxima, made handy bases. Still, spacers have told me they prefer mounted laser-cannon to side-arms and it's pretty obvious why. Don't let an enemy ship get close, and don't let hostile kzin board.

The new arrival had two large ear-rings with a collection of kzin ears on them, but, from the gaps, I thought it likely that they had once also carried in other types of ears, ears that it would not be wise for a kzin to display on liberated Wunderland.

"Bit out of the way, here?" he asked my mother who was behind the bar. He had a foreign sort of accent as well as some strange ways with language which he rather mangled. Still, very few kzin spoke Wunderlander perfectly. He looked around appraisingly.

"Bit too far," my mother admitted. "We could do with some more customers, I will say."

"That suits me well enough," the kzin stated. "I don't go for socializing m'self. And what have you got that an old kzin could drink wi'out pizenin' 'imself?"

"We've got the very best beer, I brew it myself," my mother told him proudly. "And there's whisky and brandy and rum for them as like's it."

"Beer!" He growled disgustedly. "Monkey-piss! I'll have a big, big glass o' your rum, my lady. In a beer mug. A *big* beer mug. An' there's some coin will pay f'r it, I daresay." He threw a gold coin on the countertop. Mother poured him a generous quantity of the brown fluid, and he took it with a grunt, sniffed it and then sipped it.

I was a little surprised. Kzin are not strict tea-totalers, but as a rule, they are suspicious of alcohol, or anything else that makes them lose control. They generally drink, if at all, with small, cat-like sips of surprising daintiness, and brandy is a favorite drink.

"So there's not too many Heroes comes out this way, I'll wager?" the kzin asked.

"Most of the kzin in the town don't drink much, and there's a kzin bar for the others," Mother explained. "No, you're the first we've seen in a while."

The answered seemed to satisfy him. "Then this is the berth for me, I'll be bound," he said. "No dangers about, I take it?"

Now that was a *very* odd thing for a kzin to say. I had learned some kzinti etiquette from Marthar, and knew they were not supposed to notice danger, especially not scarred old warriors like this one. It was the height of bad manners to even mention it. And one look at any kzin was enough to indicate that bad manners were not a good idea.

"There are lesslocks outside," Mother said, "but we keep them under control—or the deputies do."

Lesslocks were a smaller, surface-dwelling variety of morlocks, the big, vaguely humanoid creatures at the top end of the food chain in the great caves. The kzin appeared to think little of lesslocks, though I knew well—too well—how deadly they could be. He went on:

"Ye have a room that will fit me though?"

"Of course," Mother replied. My father had hoped for both human and kzin customers, though truth to tell, there had been few of either. He'd had a few kzin-sized rooms installed, and a kzin kitchen. Since they ate mostly raw meat, the latter had not been difficult.

"Then I'll take your room, Manrett. And here's some further coin to pay for it." He threw down three or four gold coins. "Let me know when there's need for more. Ye may call me *Captain*, for I've a right to that name, if no others."

Another oddity. While most kzin were assigned rank-titles when young, most were desperate to acquire official Names and the respect and privileges they brought. Some had nicknames, though these were considered a poor substitute for the real thing. The etiquette of the matter was complex. But still, we knew that on liberated Wunderland many customs, especially kzin customs, were changing or being changed.

That was how the old space-farer came to stay at the *Lord Templemount*. Whether he had really captained a spacecraft I could not say, but he had the air of command despite his ragged appearance. If he'd ever kept a crew of kzin under control, with or without the fearsome disciplinary measures of the Patriarch's regular navy to back him, he would have needed that air of command, as well as a rapidly-swinging claw. I've seen the deputies deal with some bad-tempered kzin, and boy, it's scary.

The Captain would go out for a stroll every day, and he'd watch the news on a big phone he carried with him. Every evening he'd ask if there'd been any new kzin in town, and at first we thought he hungered for the company of his own kind, but we soon discovered that he wanted to avoid them. He had almost nothing to do with the kzin that lived there, once he had looked them over. I was his lookout, for he had promised me a silver three-neumark bit on the first of each month for reporting to him about any strangers. He cared little for human strangers, but was anxious to know of any kzin. "If you ever sees or hears of a red-furred Hero with a silver blaze on 'is chest an' one of his legs an arty-fish-al one, be sure to let me know quick as a wink, Peter, m' little *kz'zeerkt*," he had told me. "And there'll be another silver bit for ye, be sure of it." He was not much inclined to pay me when I went to him on the first of each month, and would growl at the back of his throat and stare at me from those bloodshot eyes, but he soon thought better of it and within a day or two he would pay up, with his reminder of the red-furred kzin with one leg natural and the other prosthetic. But I never saw such a creature in Thoma'stown. The Lord Vaemar-Riit came by on an inspection once to ceremonially open the new school and clinic extensions, accompanied by Professors Nils and Leonie Rykerman, a beautiful woman with golden hair who was pointed out to me as Dimity Carmody herself, and Rarrgh-Hero, who has a prosthetic arm and eye. I noticed our Captain kept well out of sight while they were here. Nobody said anything about him, but that did not surprise me. It's Wunderlanders' way to mind our own business, human or kzin.

Still, the Lord Vaemar spoke to me, and asked me about my schoolwork. He spoke rather longer with Marthar, but I suppose that was to be expected. "Remember you are my envoy here," I understood him say to her. The Judge and Rarrgh-Hero, I noticed, greeted each other like old acquaintances. "You seized your chances with both paws, I see," I heard Rarrgh-Hero say. "The chance that you gave me," the Judge replied. "I do not forget that I owe you a life." I wondered what they referred to. I left them with the Judge proudly showing Rarrgh the giant chessboard and pieces one of the kzin had carved for the little park beside the town square. Most kzin adore chess, though they have given the pieces their own names. They are liable to smash them when they lose, but consider it a point of honor to make new ones, better than the old.

Most of our regulars at the inn were afraid of the Captain, though I think he enjoyed their fear. He was fierce and overbearing to a degree. He didn't actually do anything violent, but he seemed to radiate menace. It gave me some faint shadow of a notion of how kzin must have appeared to humans during the Occupation, dread overlords, the humblest of whom had the power of life or death over any human. It made me realize the work Vaemar, The Rykermanns and others, kzin and human, had done to enable the two species to share a planet and live together, even if only in a few pockets like our village.

Of an evening, the Captain would recline on a *footch* we had for kzin visitors at the back of the room and drink his rum, and then he would tell stories, space stories, to the assembled crowd, stories to make the blood run cold. Of men and kzin in combat and in uneasy alliance, of both being spaced, ejected as exploded corpses into hard vacuum, with their lungs spewed out of their mouths (*eating a Christmas tree*); of planetfall on worlds that had atmospheres of corrosive poison, on others where his comrades had fallen in hundreds, victims of what he called the *green rot*; of monsters that had fought armed kzin to a standstill. Some of the young men actually seemed to admire him, and pointed out that a man-kzin alliance would make our kinds unbeatable if we ever encountered another foe. A couple of the younger kzin, still with traces of their kitten spots, listened too, and remarked proudly that he was the kind who made the name of kzin feared on countless worlds, until the sheriff took them aside for what he called a "talking to." What this consisted of I do not know, but they returned severely chastened, and we heard no more of such talk.

He spoke of beings with two heads; of others (or were

they the same?) with voices like sirens or mermaids, hauntingly beautiful and seductive; of warfare in space between every possible combination of man, kzin and alien. He told of rebellious Jotok, and of battles against the Chunquen and rumors of wars with other alien beings—mythical, perhaps—on the other side of the vast, irregular globe of space that was the Patriarchy, of relics of the ancient slavers; it occurred to me that an ARM agent might have picked up a good deal of useful information about the far-flung Kzin Empire from his ramblings, though how much of them were true was another matter.

He did have some discretion: he did not speak of the Occupation. At first I thought it was almost certain he had been involved, but Marthar suggested to me that perhaps he had kept away from Wunderland when it was called *Ka'ashi* and Chuut-Riit, Lord Vaemar's Sire, had ruled it on behalf of the Patriarchy. None of the men in the village remembered him from those days, but that did not prove anything; it was a long time ago and he would have been much younger then. Once the Judge spoke to me privately about his concern that the old pirate might stir up the kzin-human hatred that he and others had worked to eliminate in the village, but it did not seem to happen. Some of the men even seemed to enjoy his blood-curdling insults, his stories and his almost equally frightening rum-fueled good fellowship.

And he would sing, a gruff crooning voice that was half purr and which didn't seem to fit him, in some kzin patois, a dialect which only a few of us understood (the ordinary kzin languages are difficult enough). One night, Marthar had come to help in the bar, and she told me the song was about death and treachery and horrible things that she didn't want to talk about. I'd already worked out that much for myself! And he made the whole company sing it too, with little or no comprehension, but every one of them stumbling through it as loud as they could, for fear the captain would take it out on any who held back. Mother thought he would lose us every customer we had, but strange to say, the company got bigger than ever before. People like to be frightened a bit, and they would talk about it to each other, and so strangers came from all over the town to see our resident pirate-kzin (as we described him to ourselves). A deputy stuck his head in once or twice, looked around and vanished again. So long as it was only words, they didn't seem to care.

Once, when he was walking in the wild country outside the town walls, I accompanied him. It was as well he was there because we were attacked by a small troop of lesslocks. It could have been worse. It could have been Morlocks, driven out of the great caves of the High Kalkstein, though they were normally nocturnal on the surface. It was the first time I saw him in action with *wtsai* and cutlass, and it was breathtaking. He produced another knife, which he had concealed somewhere, and tossed it to me, with a cry of, "Now, Peter, young *Kz'zeerkt*, warrior, show them what a Man can do!" A blade flashing in each hand, too fast for my eyes to follow, he leapt on them, roaring. It was all over in a few minutes. I have heard it said that in hand-to-hand combat without beam or projectile weapons, one kzin was the equal of about forty fit men, and nothing I saw that day disproved that. When the slaughter was over, he seemed calmer and happier, even somehow more youthful. I had killed one of them, and he remarked jovially it was a pity I did not have an ear-ring of my own. He roared with laughter at a piece of lesslock I found dangling, wobbling from the brim of my hat.

There was another thing I found out about him: he openly despised Kdaptists. We had been told at school that in the last days of the Occupation, when the human counter-attacks from Sol had been beginning to bite on the kzin military machine, a strange set of religious beliefs called Kdaptism had made an appearance among some kzin. It owed its origin to the shocking, blasphemous realization, after the ecstatic joy of finding a species actually prepared to give them a fight, that this time, impossibly, blasphemously, the kzin might actually be defeated. The God, it was said, loved his humans, and gave them luck, whereas he honored his sons the kzin by giving them respect. Its baseline belief was that the God (precisely which god—the fanged or the bearded—it did not seem entirely clear), was coming to favor humans.

It had quickly split into several factions. Some, the high Kdaptists, saw the future as lying in cooperating with humans; others, the low Kdaptists, hoped to fool the God into granting them victory by dressing in garments made of human skin, and carrying out religious rites, which they had forced humans to teach them, with vessels made of human bone.

The K'daptists fought among themselves until Lord Vaemar and his followers and the Free Wunderland and UNSN forces imposed peace. Mind you, I never heard of a kzin trying to ingratiate himelf with humans by falsely claiming allegiance to K'daptism. kzin don't lie. At least, I thought then that kzin didn't lie, and certainly most don't, though some are capable of twisting the truth, particularly when talking to an enemy. Now and then when we talked, our conversation drifted into metaphysical areas, but it was plain that in his long, battle-scarred life, pity and mercy had played a negligible part. Whether he had voyaged with cut-throats of unusual brutality, or whether that had been standard behavior for kzin during the war, I was unsure.

Several of the men of the village had remarked how much most of the ordinary kzin on Wunderland had changed since those days, though of course the only ones we saw much of were those who had chosen to live with men in the village, or in the country nearby. The kzin remaining on Wunderland were not the very fiercest warriors—that was why they had survived—but any Kzin is fierce enough. There were, as I said, hold-out bands in the wild country. Wunderland, after all, was a whole world, much bigger than Mars, partially grown with forests and jungles as well as boasting ranges of hills, and there was no lack of refuges and hiding places.

Doctor Lemoine was in the neighborhood visiting some local woman with a liver condition, so he explained, and had gone into the parlor after taking a dinner from my mother, with a kindly "Thank-ee Mistress Cartwright, your servant, ma'am!" in his cold, clear voice. There he smoked a pipe and, in his neat, white lace and smart black suit, was a great contrast, with the old pirate-kzin in the corner, who had ragged fur and many belts and ear-rings so disarranged and multi-colored. The local tobacco crop was very fine and most human people, men and women, smoked cigars, so the long pipe of Doctor Lemoine was something of an oddity. Kzin seldom, and intelligent kzinretti never smoked cigars, possibly for fear of setting fire to their whiskers, and most claimed that the smell of tobacco disgusted them, so the Captain wrinkled his considerable nose, but took an interest in the pipe.

"And what be that contrivance, human? A machine for making a stink?" the captain asked truculently.

"It is a way of smoking tobacco that keeps the taste away from my palate and yet allows me to savor the scent of burning aromatic leaves," the Doctor explained with good humor. "They contain a little of the stimulant nicotine. It is known that small amounts of nicotine reduce certain common mental sicknesses, particularly neurosis and schizophrenia. There are minor carcinogenic side effects, but they are easily treated these days."

"So you would all go mad if you didn't sniff on a burning weed," the captain sneered.

"Some of us humans are prone to overlearning; you can mark us by the way we talk, a tendency to gabble too fast," the Doctor explained comfortably. "Sometimes this can get out of hand, the overlearning, not the gabbling, and we learn something which isn't so. And then we spread it around among others of our kind, transmitted much like a physical disease, a virus or bacterium. More of a problem in big cities, and we have only one real city after what happened to Neue Dresden, and Munchen is not overbig. But it afflicted some cultures on Old Earth a few centuries ago, with odd neuroses running rampant. So no, I don't fear adopting a neurosis or being attracted to some cult, I just like the smell. It is also addictive, I confess. You should try it."

"I've more than enough bad habits," the Captain growled. A small enough joke, but coming from him, it sounded funnier than perhaps it was.

"Indeed you have, and your drinking too much rum is one of them," the Doctor told him. "I can see from your eyes and tell from your voice and manner that you are far into choler, and it is affecting your maintenance drugs."

"What business is that of yours, monkey?" the Captain demanded.

"I'm a medical man, and have a duty to point out bad habits and their consequences. Maybe you *should* take up smoking, it might relax your choler. Although it may exacerbate your heart condition, so perhaps better not."

"What heart condition?" roared the kzin, bounding to his feet and towering over the Doctor in one stride. His claws extended and his jaws opened wide to show those great, curving incisors. My heart jumped within me as I watched.

"Why, the condition that you most clearly suffer from, and which may necessitate surgery if you persist in drinking rum every night. That's if we can get treatment to you in time." The Doctor looked up calmly, not the least overawed by the huge animal. "Not to mention the risk of blood clots which will lay you low. At least take some regular asprin to thin your blood, or you'll have a stroke within the year. Were you a human, your face would be purple and I'd give you less than six months unless you went in for a major reaming out of your arterial system. And cut down on the rum. I would guess that you need the rum to sleep, but the dependence is not good. Surely a Hero like you appreciates that. And your liver must be like an old black boot."

The Captain slumped and retreated. "Aarrgh, what would ye know of what troubles me, of what keeps me from sleep?"

"What in humans we would call a guilty conscience, at a guess. Bad memories, no doubt. Your brain is structured much like that of human beings. Two hemispheres joined by a corpus callosum, a dominant verbal one and a subdominant one where the ideas come from. And memories are thrown up, fears are transmitted from it and give you dreams. Bad dreams, I should judge. Alcohol is a powerful depressant and you drink enough for a fleet. Kzin and excessive alcohol don't mix well, and most of you have the sense to know it."

"Bad dreams," muttered the Captain, returning to his *footch*. "Aye, bad enough, I grant ye. And I've reason for them. But the future haunts me more than the past, human. 'Tes what the morrow may bring plagues me." He threw himself down and went back to his rum.

"Kzin have had very little concept of mercy, compassion or remorse," said the Doctor to me quietly. "Whatever he has done . . . well, it must have been pretty bad, that it should trouble him so. Or his fears for the future are terrible indeed."

Doctor Lemoine came back a few nights later to hear the gruesome stories and the strange wild song. He sat at the back and didn't join in the singing, but smoked his pipe and listened carefully. The Captain usually took it hard when anyone refused to join in the caterwauling, and roared at them, but he ignored the Doctor. They seemed to have some sort of uneasy truce. There was no doubt that the Doctor saw the Captain as a ruffian or worse, and I could not doubt that he was right to think so. He would tolerate a ruffian if the latter kept his behavior within the Doctor's capacious bounds. But there was steel in the Doctor that the Captain acknowledged, if reluctantly, and he never tried to compel the Doctor to his will as he did almost everyone else. I doubt he was aware that the Doctor had fought in the resistance, and more than that, had been decorated with the Centauri Cross.

CHAPTER TWO

Shortly after Doctor Lemoine had faced down the snarling Captain, the next event in the mystery occurred. It would mean the end of the captain, although not our involvement in his affairs.

The Captain had gone out early that morning, his breath making smoke as he strode up the hill, clutching his phone in one hand and a stick in the other. His *wtsai* swung from his left hip, his gun was down on his right thigh and his cutlass slung over his shoulder. I thought he looked as if he were going into battle.

Much of a year had passed since the Captain's arrival, and we were well into a bitter, cold winter when the kzin telepath turned up. The dust in the air from the war had left Wunderland's climate a mess. The newcomer was small and spindly for a kzin, though far bigger than me or any human. He, too, carried a cutlass. He had the tattoo on his forehead that marked some, not all, telepaths, and he walked with a telepath's stoop. (I had heard that we were trying to cure and rehabilitate the wretched creatures with new drugs, though evidently he was not of this number).

His pelt was dingy gray with darker gray spots as big as saucers, and he had two claws missing on his left paw. Mostly, a missing claw is replaced by a steel one, as in the case of the Captain or, if there was not enough to root it, by a prosthetic claw stronger than the original. I was all but alone in the inn at the time, my mother being at the markets. Marthar was doing her homework next door, and, truth to tell, mine too. She explains algebra and stuff to me until my head spins, and sometimes I almost understand it. But I can give her help on history, although I hear that there is algebra in *that* later on, so we'll have to work even closer if it is true, and not just a rumor made up to frighten us. Schoolteachers are capable of anything.

Working counts as being part of school of course; we get credit for economics if we know how businesses work, and I should by now. So I was planning, for the millionth time, what to do to make the inn more attractive to customers and laying the breakfast table in the parlor for the Captain's return when I heard the outside door creak, and turned to see a fanged and whiskered face look in. Seeing I was alone, the kzin entered, not in the usual lope, but in a sort of sidle like a mudcrawler.

I've nothing against kzin. Several of the younger ones, not only Marthar, are friends with the young humans in the village. But something about this one struck me as bad before he spoke. Another thing: there are a myriad of small matters—postures, gestures, a special quickness and neatness of movement, even of the part of the shabby old Captain, that, in human or kzin, signal an experienced spacer. This one didn't have those things, yet he had an air of a spacer about him.

"Well, man, what are you then, the waiter? Some sort of servant? Speak up." He had a strangely sibilant voice, a sort of perpetual whine. Even the way he said 'man' somehow recalled instantly the sixty-plus years of war and Occupation well before my birth (the marks of which were still with us), and sent invisible things running up and down my spine. It suddenly made me aware of how friendly our own kzin in the village were, and how lucky I was to have been born when I was. He would never have made a living as a servant or a waiter, such unappealing company would have lost us every customer we had. I've been brought up to feel that there is no shame in any work so it is done well and honestly, and doing someone a service in exchange for money is honorable employ. This kzin clearly felt quite differently about it. Perhaps it is what happens when people are raised to value honor and confuse respect with deference.

"I serve here, true enough. Who are you, sir kzin," (I thought as I said it that in the days of the Occupation, any human-to-kzin address less obsequious than 'Noble Hero' could have been fatal. He had a way of making me think of things like that), "and what may I do for you?" I asked boldly, for a servant is not a slave, least of all in a family business; he trades his skills, and a pleasant and agreeable manner is an asset to be counted, one our visitor plainly lacked.

"Information, man, I need information. Do you have a kzin here, a space-farer? One with an ear missing and a steel claw? Striped black and gold?" Why didn't he use his telepath power? I wondered briefly. Perhaps he had lost it. I have heard that can happen.

I looked at him. Male kzin generally refer to one another as "Hero"—something like *kzintosh* in their own language. That was an oddity in his expression. Information is often traded, but what would I get for this? And I was being paid by the Captain, so I owed him the information of this present kzin's existence, while I owed this one nothing. He saw my hesitation.

"Come little monkey," he crooned, and seized my arm. His claws pinched, not yet drawing blood, but clearly capable of doing so with only a little more pressure. "Be a good boy, a talkative *kz'zeerkt*, an open and friendly little gossip of a *kz'zeerkt*, and no harm will come to ye." No ambiguity about that. *Kz'zeerkt* is the kzin word for "monkey," occasionally used affectionately between friends, but as a rule much more insulting than "Man," though, as I said, the kzin can make that sound like an insult too. Unless affectionately, and among intimate equals, *Kz'zeerkt* is not used in the village, just as we don't say "ratcat."

I was getting angry. "Let me go this instant, you ratc. . . ." I shouted at him, but not struggling against those claws. I had to look up at him. He did not look like a great warrior, but against me he did not need to be.

"Yes. Let him go, Addict. Or I will have your heart's blood. Count on it." Marthar's voice, strangely flat, spoke from the doorway. She was as big as the telepath, bigger, and a whole lot more alive. It was as if she radiated power; she always did, but usually it was just sort of *life.* Now, suddenly, it was death too. I saw his eyes go to her ear-tattoos. I had seen kzin pay attention to them before. Her lips drew back in a grimace and her fangs shone. She took a step forward, a prowling step with her eyes fixed on the telepath as if he were magnetic. He let me go as if I were red hot and retreated with something like panic in his eyes.

"No offense, no offense i' the world, your grace," he said to Marthar. It's true that Marthar's father is some sort of big buzz among the kzin—just how big I learned later—and it's true she held herself like a very princess, one of the sort that drove chariots with slashing blades on the wheels and threw spears clean through the enemy soldiers, armor and all. The kzin have such stories as well as do humans; I guess we're about equally ferocious when you get right down to it. They say their god punished the females long ago for rebellion by taking away their intelligence, but I know that is not true. I had seen her talking with Vaemar-Riit and Karan, standing tall and proud. I'd seen the Captain looking crosswise at Marthar when she served the drinks of an evening, but he'd never said anything.

It crossed my mind to wonder if the Captain wasn't maybe a little afraid of Marthar. Or at least, afraid of what she represented.

"Go. Now." Marthar told him and turned back without waiting to see whether he would obey. Homework called, and Marthar heard it. The telepath wasn't game to face Marthar if he interrupted her from something she obviously thought a lot more important than him, and he slunk out, his tail quite literally between his legs. He didn't look at me once.

As he opened the door, I saw that the Captain was coming down the hill. He saw us, and the telepath saw him at the same time. The telepath went out quickly and closed the door behind him, and I went to it and opened it slightly so I could hear the conversation. I believe in getting information. Makes all the difference in combat and also in commerce.

"You know an old shipmate, Skel, I hope?" the telepath said whiningly. But under the whine the tone was not pleasant, and the Captain's face had changed with something very like fear. After growing up with kzin, I could read their expressions, although not as well as Marthar could read mine.

"So 'tes the Dog hisself," the Captain said with what was almost a gasp. *Dog* when used by a kzin makes *Kz'zeerkt* seem almost a compliment by comparison. There were no dogs in the village now, though I was told that in the bad time we had needed them to make insulin.

"Surely, and I've come t'see me old shipmate Skel, as was with me for so long a time. Recall, Skel, when I lost these two talons?" He held up his left paw to show the gaps. "Ah, it's been many a long year since then, old companion."

"I'll grant ye that ye've run me down, Dog; well, what is it that ye want o' me?"

"Why nothing more than a little conversation. Why do we not go inside this little inn and join in a jug of rum? Then we can talk of old times, and even a little of what the future holds for either of us, mayhap."

The Captain was less than gracious, but capitulated, so I pulled back hurriedly behind the bar as they came in, Dog first, and the Captain, Skel was his name apparently, behind.

"Ah, the young servant monkey"—there was no affection in the term—"the one I took such a fancy to and treated so gently," Dog said, with a quick glance at the door from which Marthar had come. "Fetch us a jug of rum, me bully manling, and leave us for a little talking." He spoke civilly and quietly, evidently not wishing to attract the attention of Marthar again. I got them a jug of rum.

"Off ye go *kz'zeerkt*, and close the door behind ye; I know what young *kz'zeerkti* are, inquisitive and wanting to find out all they can of other people's business which they don't have no right to do, dear me, no they doesn't," said Dog. I went to join Marthar after tapping on the door. She looked up at me. She was lying on the floor besides a fire of burning logs which crackled energetically.

I closed the door behind me. "I think I'd like to know what they are saying, but it will be hard through the keyhole," I explained to her in a whisper as I bent down on her side of the door. She came and stood by me as I knelt, and I glimpsed a thoughtful look in her eye and her ears come erect before I lost sight of her behind me.

"A fool," I heard her whisper. "A closed door hides and protects us as an open door would not." I caught a wild ginger-like scent coming from her, and knew what it signified. Fortunately the two adult male kzin were pouring out too much of it themselves to detect it. I remembered Dog was a telepath, and was glad he was concentrating everything on the Captain, not on searching for eavesdroppers' thoughts.

I could hear very little. Just a rattling and growling in the Heroes' Tongue that was hard to understand. But the tempers frayed quickly. "I urinate on the shrines of your ancestors from a height!" That was an old-fashioned kzin curse. "*And* excrete partly-digested vegetable material on them!" So was that. I had seen enough of kzin being disciplined by other kzin to know that at any moment might come a scream and leap from one of them.

I heard the Captain say something I translated as, "One dies, we all die," though the word he used for "die" (there are many words for "die" in the Heroes' Tongue), had a suggestion of death by torture in it, something no longer permitted for judicial execution under Vaemar-Riit's rule. Then there was an explosion of curses, something for which the Heroes' Tongue is so well suited, and the crash of furniture together with a clash of steel, mono-molecular-edged with osmium, and I stood up to feel Marthar's warm breath on my neck. We opened the door and looked out to see the Captain waving his *wtsai* and cutlass, one in each hand, screaming at Dog, who had drawn his own weapons and parried the blows. The energy of the old Captain was astonishing, he swung again and again and drove the other to the door, from which he ran. The Captain followed Dog outside, and the fighting continued. At the same time as this flashing combat, with sparks coming off the blades and a clanging that smote the ear, there were curses and screams of rage from both parties.

Once outside, it did not take the telepath long to decide he would lose if he continued. He had neither the height nor the mass nor yet the total ferocity of the older kzin, so he threw his *wtsai* at the captain and ran. The Captain swept the flying weapon aside contemptuously, and ran after him, cursing as he went. Telepaths are reputed to have a sort of mind-weapon of their own, but if so, I did not see this one use it.

It did not take the Captain long to see that the telepath

had the legs to outrun him, so he gave up reluctantly and after shouting further curses, turned and descended the hill. He got to the door before his face turned gray. He passed his paw over his face, looked bewildered and saw me. "Peter, rum," he said, and fell forward. Marthar and I tried to help him stand up, and got him as far as the *footch*, where he lay making some terrible noises. Marthar got him some rum and tried to force it between his lips, while I ran to call the Doctor, who fortunately was back with the woman with the liver problem again, and followed me around immediately.

"Is it alright to give him rum? He begged for it," Marthar asked, anxiously.

"Oh, one won't harm him. The trouble is, once he's had one he'll want another, and then another. Weakens the will, which is never much anyway for the older kzin with a long habit of drinking, unless you know the right triggers to invoke. Impulsive beggars. Earthcats can't taste sugar, and rum's full of it, but he's no Earthcat."

"There doesn't seem to be any blood," Marthar said, puzzled. "He hit the telepath, I saw blood running from his shoulder, although it didn't slow him down much, and it was only venous blood." (Kzin's venous blood is orange-colored. Arterial blood is purple.) "I thought the telepath must have got in a cut somewhere, but I can't see it."

"Ha, he's got too much blood, not too little," Doctor Lemoine explained. "He's had an internal aneurysm maybe, most likely a simple stroke. I warned him of that. Let's see . . ." He fished in his little black bag and pulled out a syringe and an ampoule with a purple top. "Three hundred years ago they'd have given him rat poison.

Warfarin, a blood thinner. Enough to kill a rat would have just given a human being a few liver spots, and had no detectable effect on a kzin, except to bypass the brain blockage. Three centuries before that, they'd cup him, take out about two pints of blood. Both would have had some beneficial effects, though the warfarin was much better. Nowadays we can do a lot better again. He'll still be vulnerable, though, unless he changes his lifestyle. Which he won't. People prefer death to change. Goes for kzin too, young lady. Think about it. And never forget, like all cats, your kidneys are your weak point. Care for them and you'll never need a transplant."

He injected the ampoule into the moaning kzin. "Nannites to ream out his arterial system. There, he'll recover now. Give him a day of resting if you can make him do it. Two days would be better. Best of luck with that."

He stood and looked down at the kzin. Then he turned to Marthar. "I hope you have your implant updated regularly. I don't want to see you turn into a vegetable."

"No chance of that," Marthar told him. She shivered. "My mother was born before they invented the little green pills, and it is horrible. She likes to rub herself against my father and be petted, like pictures I've seen of housecats on Earth. She hardly has the sense to talk even. I would rather die than be like her."

The Doctor looked grim for a moment. "Yes, the male kzin has slightly more neuro-transmitters than humans do, and the kzinretti have two less. It's not a development one can explain by reference to evolution. We theorize that some evil shits did some genetic manipulations a long time ago so that females couldn't metabolize some vital transmitters that are used mainly in the dominant hemisphere. Left for human beings, right for kzin, you don't have the lunatic cross-over human beings have. Hence the little green pills. One day we'll repair the damage with genetic surgery, but we are too backward on Wunderland to be able to do it yet. We're working on it."

"Why did they do something so horrible?" Marthar demanded.

"Because the culture was male-dominated and because a smart kzinrett could twist a male kzin around her finger if she wanted to. That didn't sit well with some of the older kzin. They wanted to keep their harems and their dominance. From what little we humans know of kzin history, we think the priesthood were chiefly responsible. You don't hear much of the fanged demons these days, but they were all female. Tells you how they saw the kzinretti."

"That's terrible," I exclaimed. "How could anyone be so vile?"

"Mark you, the males lost by it as well. A male lacking a mate who can also be a companion is diminished in more ways than I can go into. My own theory—and it is not mine alone—is that kzin males who never come into contact with intelligent females—or at least never knowingly so—live in a permanent state of loss and black rage. Fortunately, the Lord Vaemar understands this and has supported our program to boost the kzinretti' brainpower.

"And there have been human cultures that did much the same sort of thing. Not by genetic manipulation, they didn't have the technology. But three centuries ago there was a culture which kept their women at home and wouldn't let them go out into the world and learn about it, so they stayed as children. And we in the west weren't much better a hundred years earlier. The playwright George Bernard Shaw pointed out that the Chinese had the horrid practice of binding female babies' feet, after breaking the bones, so they would grow up to have small feet, which were considered attractive. It also displayed the fact that they were of such high position that they did not have to walk. While the English of that time, he pointed out, would bind the females' minds instead to keep *them* small and stunted. Which, he declared, was far worse. And the English, from my reading, were actually among the more enlightened. That was only four hundred years ago. If you grew up in such a society, it all seemed natural. Women never went to university, not even to school in most cases. People can be persuaded to anything, no matter how repulsive, if they are accustomed to it. And if you change slowly enough, you can get to anywhere from anywhere. Do you know that in the Earth city of London in 2011, there was an official called the Head of Behavior Change? Changing behavior might be a good thing, but not when governments do it for you. That was one of the things that came together in ARM's great 'Project' to turn humans into sheep. That was when many people thought space flight was a waste of money, and having landed a few men on the Moon, decades before, thought that there was no more to be done in space! A politician in the richest country who proposed a Moon colony was laughed at."

"That's ridiculous!" I protested.

"Yes. Yet that was in the culture from which many of our notions of freedom had once originated. We were lucky to grow out of that phase, or to have been pushed out of it. To have all the challenge and adventure of space travel before us, and to have turned away from it, that would have murdered something in the human spirit. We might easily have remained mired in medievalism, using up Earth's resources without replacing them, with our technology slowly regressing until our population collapsed upon itself, and certainly until the kzin arrived. We could never have met them as we did, beyond the orbit of Saturn. We would never even have been warned they were coming from a deep-space colony ship . . ."

I'd done some of this in history lessons, but I'd never seen before how custom is king of everything. It was my first lesson, too, on free Wunderland, how subtly and pervasively bad governments can control the way people think. It made me feel slightly sick when I contemplated it. But it was followed by a less depressing thought: for all the horrors of the decades-long war and the occupation of Wunderland which followed, the kzin had saved us from turning ourselves into herd animals.

"Right, now I have other people to see. Until we can afford autodocs in Thoma'stown, I'm the next best thing. You kids be good, and look after each other."

I didn't see that I could look after Marthar very much, but I would certainly do my best. She had looked after me, and I was grateful.

Marthar and I sat with Captain Skel until he recovered consciousness. He sat up with a jerk, almost jumping out of the *footch*. "Where is Dog?" he wanted to know. He had come gradually to accept Marthar, though he was a kzin of the old school if ever there was one.

"Dog is gone. You chased him away and wounded him in the shoulder," Marthar told him. "And the Doctor says you must rest for a day. But we can help you up to your room, I expect."

The Captain groaned, but agreed to be helped up, and leaned on Marthar as she patiently helped him to his room. I went with them, although I was not much use.

The room was a mess. The backpack was on the floor and some of its contents strewn around. There was a half-full bottle of rum, which the Captain grabbed greedily.

"You're not supposed to have that," Marthar told him sternly. He answered her by taking off the top and swigging it like lemonade. Then he lowered himself onto the bigger *footch* that was his bed with another groan. "I must get away," he said to himself, and then dropped the bottle, which Marthar caught before it hit the floor. She put the top back and carried it out of the room. The Captain's eyes rolled up and he fell back and started snoring almost immediately.

CHAPTER THREE

I passed by the Captain's room an hour later, and the snoring had stopped so, rather frightened, I knocked and went in. The Captain was half-up and out of the *footch*, and nodding groggily.

"Har, Peter, there, help me up, boy. Or that kzinrett of yours. And get me a noggin o' rum."

Marthar wasn't *my* kzinrett, and the Doctor had forbidden more drink, I told him.

"Just the one, lad, just the one. A single one can't do me harm. Now yer a good one for a *Kz'zeerkt*, Peter, and the on'y one I can trust. And haven't I paid ye regular, a silver thruppenny, once a month? And doctors is quacks and knows nothing o' the world. Why, I've been in places where wi'out rum, I'd ha' died o' the fever. I been places where the swamps were fuller of disease than o' mud, where the birds died on the wing from the insex, an' where the insex bit worse than what ye call crocodilians or zeitungers here. An' 'twas the rum saved me then, an' it'll be the rum saves me now, d'ye see? For I'm startin' t' get the shakes, d'ye see?" He held up his paw, and it trembled right enough. I felt torn. The Doctor had said that one wouldn't hurt him. And he did look terrible.

He saw me weaken. "Why, Peter, rum has been my meat and drink before now, my mother and father, my mates and their sisters. If I canna got some rum into me, I'll get the cold horrors, so I will. I already seen K'zarr i' the corner there behind ye, wi' blood-boltered fur, matted fur, some of the blood his'n and some not. I've led a hard life, Peter, a turrible hard life, wi' hard kzin beyond anythin' ye could believe in. An' when I gets the horrors, why, I'll scream like a kitten or a kzinrett wi' the knife i' them, as they feels it turn inside 'em like." I shuddered and he saw it.

"Yes, there'll be screams as o' the dyin', Peter, dyin' in agony, dyin' o' the horrors, like a burnt-out telepath. So I begs you, as a gift to a dyin' old Hero, t' spare me o' the horrors, Peter. I'll gi' ye a gold star for your own, Peter, if ye'll just get me a noggin."

"I'll not take your money, but I'll get you one glass and one only," I told him. I went and got him one beer mug, half-full of rum, and gave it to him.

"Ah, thankee, Peter, yer a fine little *k'zeerkt*." He drank it slower than usual, but eventually it had all gone.

"Yes, that's a deal better, Peter. A deal better." He wiped his mouth and squinted at me.

"And Peter, when will I be able to get up and go accordin' t' that there human healer of yourn?" he wanted to know.

"Tomorrow, but the day after will be better."

He groaned. "By the Traveller's Moon, but it's all too late. Those *sthondats* will be after me afore then. I have to go, Peter, I have to go right now. Help me fool 'em, Peter, an' I'll see you right as a *driupthpn*. I'll fool them yet, can I but get away a while. Could I get astride a hoss wi'out crushing the thing, I'd be away where they'd never find me for many a year. But it has to be now, Peter, else they'll have the claw o' me, for sure."

Some hope, I thought. Only horses trained from birth will let kzin near them. He gripped my shoulder and made me cry out, and Marthar came in at a run.

"No, no lady, I didn't mean t' hurt the little *Kz'zee* . . . man," the Captain said frantically. "I jest need a little help t' get up. Maybe the two o' you could do it? I'm a big fellow t' be sure." He was far too big for me to lift, I knew. Yet somehow those words roused a queer little spark of empathy in me. Whatever his crimes, I felt sorry for him sitting there so helpless at that moment.

"Pass me that bindle there," he pointed at his great pack, and Marthar pushed it over to him. He felt in one of the pockets and produced a box. It was about seven inches long, two inches wide and over an inch deep, and black as midnight in a cave; he showed us how to press an invisible button at one end and the lid flipped back to reveal the interior.

"Here, take this, 'tes for you, Peter, a present. Certainly, 'tes no use t'me, for sure. Has come a long way, so it has, a long, long way."

The inside looked like ivory and was soft to the touch. There was one thing in the box, sitting in a triangular hole, an indentation in the ivory. I lifted it out. It was a gold color, but it was hard, and heavy, but not so heavy as gold, and it was a perfect tetrahedron. Four sides, all triangular, all exactly the same. It had each side just over an inch long and a little less from each vertex to the opposite face.

"What is it?" I asked.

"Now there you have me, little *kz'zeerkt.* But there was more, but 'tes lost, d'ye see."

And I did see. There were four other indentations in the box where other things had rested. The first one was a triangular space where the tetrahedron had sat; next to it was a square space; and in the middle the space was for a pyramid, point down. The next one had a pentagonal space and the last more sides than I could tell without counting them.

"It's obvious what they were," Marthar said. "Everyone should be able to work *that* out." She could be very irritating at times.

"Is that so?" the Captain asked with the beginnings of a growl.

"Yes. There are five of them, and only five. The first is a tetrahedron, the second a cube, the third an octahedron. Even Peter should be able to tell you the last two."

I ignored her; it's the only thing to do when she's like that. "Thank you, Captain, it is an interesting present. Perhaps we'll be able to make the other shapes to complete the set." I put the tetrahedron back in its place, closed the box and put it in my pocket. I was going to have to work out what the other shapes were, and I was definitely *not* going to ask Marthar, who was quite smug enough already. I had a faint glimmering already, but would need to do some searching.

"Well, if ye can do that, ye may have solved some sort of test, for that's what it seems to be. And not one I could pass, nor most of those I knew. Anyway, 'tes all useless now. Unless ye can get to K'zarr's treasure. Ah, I'll never get it now. No more will K'zarr himself." He sank back on the *footch* and a shadow passed over his face. He lifted himself a little and looked longingly at the empty jug.

"K'zarr's treasure," he went on. "I know where it's hid. Only I."

Even for us, K'zarr was a name of vague dread. There had been many kzin freebooters, outside the disciplined armed forces of the Patriarchy (who in all good faith had been more than bad enough!), but he had been the worst. Even kzin-occupied villages and asteroids had not been safe from him, and he had slain men and kzin who crossed him or stood in his way with impartial cruelty. He was one of the few beings who had had a reward placed on his head by kzin and humans both, a distinction in which, it was said, his crew took some pride. It had been the abbot at Circle Bay Monastery who had told me of him first—he had raided the place for the drugs in the infirmary, and carried them off with all the monastery's treasures, as well as human refugees the monastery had been sheltering from the slave markets in some God-forsaken back-blocks of the Kzin Empire. The abbot and a few monks had been attending a conference in Munchen at the time, or none would have survived. It was his horde who, during the initial landings, had cremated Neue Dresden when it had tried to surrender. After the human surrender to the Patriarch's regular forces he had destroyed what was left of the precious chain of meteor-warning satellites from sheer viciousness.

The Captain struggled and then gave up and fell back

as Marthar checked with me. I nodded. His grip had hurt, but he had not intended it to.

"Ah, Peter, and yer Ladyship, both o' ye, did ye see that Dog? *He* was a bad one, he was. Still is. But there's worse than him, Peter, yer ladyship. Far worse than him, them that set him upon me. There's the one wi' the red fur an' on'y one true leg, he's the one. He's a devil out o' the fanged demons' pit, that one. Last thing many a *Kz'zeerkt* and Hero saw was that one smiling at him, wi' his jaws like a man, and wi' his ears, like a kzin. And felt the blade o' the *wtsai* in his gut, reachin' for the heart at the same time, turnin' slowly, lovingly. An' when the poor scum saw the blood rush out over his belly, just as his eyes blacked out, he'd hear the devil whisper softly to him: *Gi' my regards to the Queen o' the fanged demons, an' tell her there's plenty more t'come*." That's what he'd say.

"An they get me here, Peter, 'tes the death claw for me. An' 'tes my gunnysack, m' bindle, they're after Peter, my lady. Now if ye could ride a hoss, Peter, like the wind, and if yer Ladyship could run wi' him, an' get that Doctor man t' bring the deputies an' the sheriff, why, they could find all of K'zarr's crew here, ready fer the plucking! But they'll need a mort o' Heroes an' some weaponry, for they is killers all. I was the first mate, I was, d'ye see, K'zarr's first mate, an' I'm the on'y one what knows where his treasure is. He gave it t'me, K'zarr did, when he lay dying, out there where the purple nebulae lit the sky, where ancient suns go to die, that's when K'zarr got his. The suns died and so did K'zarr. But not before he gave me the directions, so he did. An' the scum wants them, they wants them bad. An' it's the death claw fer me, 'tes so."

"What is this death claw, Captain?" I asked.

"Ah, 'tes the summons, the last one a freebooter iver gets. But keep yer eyes open, Peter, my lady, an' I'll share it all wi' ye both, in memory o' the last noggin. 'Tes on'y fair. You helped me face down the horrors, Peter."

He pronounced my name carefully, as he always did: Names are important to a kzin. But he was wandering, it was plain to see, and his voice trailed off and he lapsed back into sleep. When we heard him snoring, we tiptoed out.

"What was that about *where the purple nebulae lit the sky and ancient suns go to die*? It's where K'zarr died, of course, but where is it?" Marthar was as inquisitive as any monkey. She wanted to know everything. I had heard that Alpha Centauri B's lead Trojan position was a dust-collector, and in its neighborhood, space appeared purple. It was death for a ship to venture into it for any length of time without special shielding. Micro-meteorites got through the mass-detectors and eroded the hulls.

"I don't know. Sounds like a black hole, don't you reckon? And I also don't know what the directions that K'zarr gave him are for. This treasure he mentioned. What is it?"

"I think we can guess it's not milkweed and mushrooms, K'zarr's old crew want to get their hands on it."

"We can only hope he forgets he told us as much as he did, or we'll both be for the death claw or whatever it is they do to you before they kill you," I told her. I also thought that one thing about warfare had not changed through centuries and light-years: a real man still had a duty to protect the females. That thought gave me a sour little smile.

The next day the Captain got up painfully and, with much help from Marthar and me, he got downstairs. He lounged on the *footch* with his *wtsai* drawn and within easy reach, his other hand on the hilt of his cutlass. He got up only to help himself to rum, leaning against the walls as he did so, with a gray look about him. He ate nothing. Marthar and I had schoolwork to do, and did some of it in the room with the fire, after setting tables. Mother served behind the bar the few customers who came in. In the afternoon, the Captain looked a little better. I heard his crooning to himself in the patois, a strange song, quite different from anything else I had heard from him:

> *"There was a kzinrett in her kilt so green,*
> *Upon a morning on the mountain,*
> *Floating like the down o' spring*
> *O'er the scent o' dawn,*
> *O'er the scent o' dawn,*
> *Her fur was soft and fine*
> *And her body so warm on mine*
> *And I loved her well upon the mountain."*

It was something like that. It may not be a good translation. I suppose people tend to think of the kzin as just totally ferocious and can't imagine them having a culture. But you can't possibly maintain a star-spanning civilization on pure ferocity. Things are always more complicated than they seem at first sight.

🐾 🐾 🐾

I went outside into the chilly air. There was a kzin coming towards me, in a long black cloak. Kzin, except for ceremonies, seldom wore clothes like humans; they wore only webbing to hold pockets. They had plenty of fur. I had been surprised by the reference to a kilt in the song, although kzinretti wore them sometimes. But this was no kzinrett. The figure had no eyes and almost no nose. Where the eyes should have been, some horrible antennae quivered. Maybe they gave some sort of sight as well, but he looked like an insect, perhaps a cockroach from the Old Earth picture books. But a 'roach-two-and-a-half meters tall, maybe more, even with a stoop. The cloak had a cowl which hid much, but not the blank hairless face and the quivering antennae. It made me sick to look at him, but I couldn't let him know how horrible I found him.

"Ah, I sense somebody. Can you tell me where I am, kind being?" The voice was reedy and didn't fit the frame.

"This is the *Lord Templemount* Inn, sir," I told him with a quaver in my voice. He moved with shocking speed and gripped me, his claws surrounding my upper arm.

"And a young voice, a *kz'zeerkt*. Mayhap a servant? A juvenile?"

"Please let me go, sir, you are hurting me." I wished for Marthar, but she would be working through algebra problems. And perhaps it was unfair to wish this horror upon her. Mutilated as he was, to judge from the strength he had in him she'd have little more hope than I did.

"I shall release you when you have served your purpose, youngling. I want the captain. Skel, we called him. I know he is here. Take me to him, else lose your arm. For I could pinch it, like this, only clean through." He squeezed my arm and drew blood.

"I shall take you to him, sir, if you will release me," I told him.

"You will take me to him and *then* I will release you. For the young may be cunning, and a poor old blind Hero might be deceived. As happened once, long ago. But no more, youngling, never more. I found that one after a long hunt, and he goes more eyeless than I do. Now take me to Skel."

I didn't have a choice, so I guided him through the door, and he followed me in, still gripping my arm in his claws.

"Lead me straight up to him, and when I face him, call out *Here's a friend of yours, Skel*, and then I shall know if you lie." His voice was like a wind blowing from ice-capped mountains.

I led him into the room reluctantly. As I did, his robe came apart a little and showed me why he wore it. Underneath, his raw skin, like a plucked chicken, showed him hairless; his fur had nearly all fallen out, except for a few tufts, and his skin looked as though it had been burnt by flame or acid. It was horrible.

We walked slowly in front of the *footch* on which the Captain reclined, old and gray and unseeing. I spoke to him:

"Here is a f-friend of yours, Captain Skel," I said. He looked up and gasped as he saw the blind kzin.

The antennae quivered and seemed to focus on the Captain.

The Captain looked at death's door, but the rum had gone out of him.

"After so many years," the arctic voice came from the cowl. "Now don't trouble to move, Skel. I cannot see you, but I can tell any movement you make, be sure of it. Now boy, take his left hand and bring it to my right hand."

Both the Captain and I obeyed like robots. This was no telepath, but I think he had a related power, of which I had heard vague rumors, of compelling thoughts and actions in others. Something was passed from the blind kzin's hand into the Captain's.

"There, 'tis done now," the blind kzin said, and with that he released me and almost skipped in three quick steps to the door of the inn. He was out in an instant, and I saw him almost run up the hill, a strange insectoid scuttling. I noticed that, blind and noseless or not, he swerved to avoid obstacles.

I loosened my grip on the Captain's left hand. He looked into his palm.

He drew in a breath. "Midnight!" he said almost with exultation. "We'll do them yet, there is still time." Then he stood up, staggered and seemed to turn to stone. For a moment he swayed, then his eyes closed and he fell forward in a crash upon the floor, like a dislodged statue more than a living being. I jumped to him and touched his stiff body, with the fleeting thought that, however much the children of the two species might play together in Thoma'stown now, to touch an adult male kzin without leave on occupied Wunderland would have been courting death for the human. But he was gone. There was no more life in him than in the statue he resembled.

Strange to say, I wept. Marthar comforted me and I

hugged her. Why I cried, I do not know, for it could hardly be said that I cared for him. I had seen my father lie dead, he had been killed by lesslocks while out fishing, and his body had been bitten and disfigured until he had been hard to even recognize as human. At the time I had felt that I ought to have been more distressed than I was, but I was more angry than sad, angry at the waste, angry at the lesslocks. Well, we had seen almost the last of them now, there were few left in this part of the world. The men and kzin had gone out and hunted them down ruthlessly, the men on horses and the kzin either on foot or riding thoats, all accompanied by the sole aircar the town possessed. The thoats, some strange name from history I do not understand, were huge herbivores about the size and shape of the extinct triceratops of Old Earth, and had been well on the way to extinction themselves until one of the kzin, inspired by seeing men ride horses, had tried riding one, guiding it by the huge horns. Now they were never eaten by the kzin, but bred for riding. I had wished to go with them, on horseback or running, but was accounted too young.

Now I had seen a kzin die, presumably from another stroke. We had no ability to revive him in Thoma'stown. Few people died these days, for modern medical techniques, lost during the Occupation, were being restored, and actually seeing a death was rare. I knew that even if we somehow got him to Munchen and its hospital, central nervous tissue would by then have decayed beyond repair. I suppose I felt surprise, but also a sense of loss. He had certainly been large and imposing in life, even in his weakened state. In a funny way, I would miss him.

"Foolish Peter," Marthar whispered to me with a comforting purr. "He was a bad, evil creature, and the world is better without him."

I had wanted to look at the death claw, but Marthar stopped me. "I think it may have killed him, Peter. And whatever toxins are on it may still have the power to kill you too. And I feel nothing for losing him, but if I lost you I should be very sad."

I snuggled into the warmth of her fur. "You'd miss me, would you?" I asked.

"Ooh, yes. Really badly. For several weeks I expect. I would regret your dying. But those who caused it would regret it more." She bit me lightly on the neck. She thought me foolish and sentimental, and perhaps I was. My hand gripped the golden tetrahedron in my pocket. It was all I had left to remember the old pirate by.

CHAPTER FOUR

Marthar and I went to find my mother. I felt a little guilty that I had not told her all I knew before this, but confiding in her would have put more responsibility on her shoulders than I cared to see. I could say anything to Marthar, who was my confidante on everything, large or small, but Mother was, for me, too old, and had been sorely hurt by my father's death those two years before.

She was in her room, resting, and I stammered it out. She was very little distressed at first, then I told her of the manner of it, and Marthar told her she suspected poison, and I went on to tell of the blind kzin with the antennae for eyes, and his scorched, horrible body, and of Dog, which Marthar confirmed. "He was a telepath, not a proper kzin, and a coward. But he is evil, I can tell," she said vehemently.

"And it looks as though they will be coming at midnight. Which is six hours from now. And it is getting dark," I pointed out.

"Why, that wicked creature owes me, he has not paid his keep for five months now, and I too afeared to approach him," my mother said indignantly. "Where's the money to come from now, I want to know?"

"In his dillybag, his bindle, that pack he slung across his back, maybe," I suggested. "It is fair to take what he owed us."

"I have no spare room key, the monster had the only one," Mother said, more concerned with her loss of income than any fear of those who would be coming in a few hours. I felt very differently.

"He must have the key on him," Marthar pointed out practically. "Let's go and get it and take what is owing, for we'll never get it from those pirates, that's for sure."

So we trooped downstairs, and Mother shuddered as she saw the stark, cold body of the kzin. Marthar was unfazed, and with me squatting beside her, she searched through the pockets in the many wallets strung about his body. We found some small coins, his big phone, two knives but no key. Marthar tried the phone. "Dead. Keyed to his body. Pity, we could have called the cops."

"We haven't even a landline," I said ruefully. Only rich people had phones.

"We'll have to turn him over," Marthar announced, so we did, and a hard job it was, too. This revealed more wallets and the holstered gun. Marthar calmly took the needler from the holster on his thigh. It was big for her, but she slipped it into a waistband she wore. Then she pointed to a string about his neck with a key on it.

"Is that it?" Marthar asked calmly, and Mother, who had avoided watching us, looked at it quickly and nodded. We cut the cord with one of his knives and retrieved the key, then we went back upstairs and stood outside the door, but not until after I had bolted the doors of the inn, both front and back.

The three of us looked at the door of the Captain's room. It was strange how much fear it induced in me, and also in my mother, but Marthar quite prosaically put the key in the lock and turned it, pushing open the door without any concern for ghosts or hob-goblins.

The room was the awful mess it had been the last time we were inside it. The bindle, a huge backpack, lay upon the *footch*, open. Marthar started to spread it apart. It was divided into many compartments; one contained a framed picture of a kzinrett, almost a child. Another a wooden box of some size. Marthar looked inside, and passed it to my mother.

Mother looked inside too. "There are coins in here, gold ones," she said. "Funny foreign-looking things most of them, but enough to pay for his keep. The mean old thing could have paid with no trouble at all, he just preferred to frighten everyone." Marthar kept checking the pouches, and sighed with satisfaction as she found some ammunition for the needler. She took the whole pouch, and hung it around her neck.

There was one odd small pouch, and in it something like a phone, but smaller than the one the Captain had with him downstairs. It had a screen that was dark, and one button on the outside, which presumably switched it on, but although I held it in my hand, I didn't do more.

Mother started counting out coins and doing arithmetic in her head. "I won't be cheated," she explained, "but I will not take a penny more than is my due. Though it is hard to know what some of these are worth."

"Hurry, Mother," I said impatiently. "I want to get away from this place before we get K'zarr's crew about our ears." As I said it, the unpleasant double-meaning of the words struck me.

A faint whistling came from outside. I had heard it before when the blind kzin came. Then from below, I heard someone try the barred door. There was a curse. Then the faint whistling again, and the patter of feet, retreating this time.

"He will be back with the others before long, Mother," I begged her. "For heaven's sake, hurry!"

She was panicking, but stubborn. "I can recognize these, they are Munchen marks, and these are gold stars, there are crowns from old Neue Dresden, but he owes me at least ten and there aren't that many here, and I won't take these foreign things, for I know not their value."

There was a sound outside that might have been kzin marching, or maybe the wind, but it was enough.

"Well, this will cover much of it at least," Mother said, and put the coins in her purse. "Now let us be away, and get to the Doctor, or to the sheriff's offices."

I slipped the phone, or book, or whatever it was into my own pocket, thinking to make up the weight of missing gold. Marthar was by the window, peering out. "Now, out the back door, fast," she whispered. "There is a lantern out there, coming this way."

We ran down the stairs, my mother gripping her handbag, Marthar holding the gun in her right paw. We unbarred the back door, and looked out, cautiously. This part of the town had no electric lights still, and mist hung around the inn, although it had cleared further out. Alpha

B was still low on the horizon but lit the night like a great jewel. At midnight it would be at the zenith, and one could easily read by it, but now it was fainter, though a clear, small, bright disc. I closed the door behind us gently, letting the bar fall into place which would mean some skill in getting back in again once the coast was clear, and we ventured out. The Doctor's house was closer, and away from the inn in the opposite direction of the hill down which Dog and the blind creature had come. The north gate was a fair distance, and the sheriff's offices, with the protective deputies, was not far from that. So we made for the Doctor's, the three of us hurrying through the chill of winter.

We had got away just in time, for the sound of many foosteps came from the other side of the inn as we scurried away. The inn, at the bottom of the dell, was isolated, and the rest of the town at some distance. The town was almost a collection of villages, and the inn between three of them, so we made for the nearest as fast as we could go. Marthar could easily have outrun me in a minute, and I could have outrun Mother even faster, but with Marthar on one side of Mother and me on the other, supporting her, we made reasonable time.

We came to a group of four or five houses with lights showing, and I banged at the door of the closest. A stout lady opened it, her husband craned over her shoulder.

"Let us in and hide us," I begged them. "We are running from pirates. K'zarr's crew are after us, or will be soon."

I don't know if that was true or not, but I feared it might be.

"K'zarr!" the man exclaimed. "We'll have naught to do with those *teufeln*." And he slammed the door in our faces. The next two houses did much the same. Some of them wanted to be kind, but some of the men had been in the *Lord Templemount* and met the Captain, and although a little harmless terror in a few stories was agreeable, the reality of it, and perhaps reawakened memories of the Occupation, had them terrified. Marthar didn't help much by flexing her claws and telling them bluntly that they were gutless *sthondats* and bereft of honor. I asked if they would at least take my mother in, leaving Marthar and I to make a run for it, but they'd have none of it. The best we could get was a lad of about my age, who promised he would ride his pony to Doctor Lemoine's house and leave a message were he not at home, and from the Doctor's house summon the sheriff by using the Doctor's telephone, the landline.

"We must go on and hope for the best," Marthar said grimly. "If they try to capture us, some will die before I do, count on it." She touched the needler in her belt, and, fleetingly, her ear-tattoos.

We had slowed to a walk now, Mother puffing and finding it hard to go on.

"We must have some time, still," I argued. "They will have to break into the inn, and the doors are stout. Then they'll have to find the Captain's room, and decide some of the gold is missing. And they may decide it isn't important enough, for we took only what we were owed."

"A blaster will open the doors fast enough," Marthar pointed out. "If they find the map to the treasure world, that will keep them happy. We have to hope that Skel didn't hide it somewhere, as he might well have done. I would."

"You think they'll come after us if they can't find it? I didn't see anything that could have been it, so he must have hidden it." I wasn't too happy.

"Again, I would," Marthar told us in the same flat voice she had used on the telepath.

I had an inspiration. "Maybe this is it," I took out the book, phone or whatever it was that I had slipped into my pocket.

Marthar's eyes flashed green. "Oh, Peter, you are a rattle-brained *Kz'zeerkt*, and I says it as loves you. It's a memo pad. It might hold the key to a treasure world."

"Then I have to take it back and leave it with the body," I said, and I jumped up from where we had been resting. I started back the way we had come. I don't know what I planned, my non-verbal hemisphere hadn't bothered to tell me, but I knew that if I were to return to the inn, I had best do it fast before my courage gave out.

I had gone three paces before Marthar caught me and swept me up.

"No, Peter dear. I can hear them already at the inn. You can't, I know, being deaf as well as dumb as they come. But we don't have long before they start hunting us down. And there aren't too many hard choices for them, are there?"

I thought of handing it over to them, but one look at Marthar and the words died in my throat. Such tame surrender was not part of her mental universe.

We set off again, me carrying Mother's handbag with the gold in it. It was quite heavy. And Marthar carrying the memo pad, which she had confiscated. And both of us supporting Mother who was now very frightened and about to faint.

🐾 🐾 🐾

We turned at an angle to our original path, so we were heading east. The wall was quite close now, and cut off a chunk of the sky to the south. Generally speaking, the north of the town was where the shops and businesses were; the east was where the rich people lived, including the Doctor. Marthar's home was in that direction too; her parents lived in a big place that looked pretty palatial to my eyes. South and west were where the poor people lived, which meant me and my family. The school was in the center of the town, on which the phone tower rose—making it the tallest building in town. The town had grown bigger over the years, we could still see the post-holes of the original walls, which had been made of wood, as Marthar and I walked south after school. I wondered sometimes why her parents let her play with me, but Marthar seemed to be the apple of her father's eye, and if I was good enough for Marthar, I was good enough for anyone in his view. I had met him when he visited the school, when my father was alive, and man and kzin had talked politely, and he had looked down at me placidly. He could see I cared for his daughter, and he was so proud of her that, to his mind, that showed I was a person of sound judgment.

An explosion came from the direction of the inn, and a flare of light.

"They are in now, so we don't have long. I think we must find somewhere to hide, but we have to worry about the telepath. If he's with them, and I expect he is, he will be hard to evade," Marthar said quietly. Mother sobbed. She couldn't go much further.

CHAPTER FIVE

We three had to pause, my mother almost falling to the ground. She had all but fainted, and was certainly too exhausted to go on any further without a rest. We looked around. We were in a kind of square, with the houses on one side, the alley we had come through facing them, and narrower roads on the other two sides; there were some trees and bushes at the side of the roads. There was a stable between the houses, from which the boy had perhaps taken his pony and set off. It was small, so there must be room in it for Mother at least, certainly it could have no other horse in it. Marthar gently picked up my mother and carried her over and laid her down on clean straw. Then Marthar turned to me.

"Peter, the telepath, that Dog of theirs, he will hunt us down surely. There is little chance of standing them off. It will take a quarter of an hour for the lad to get to the Doctor's house and a quarter of an hour for the sheriff or the Doctor to get back; and that's the bare minimum."

"What can we do?"

"I must keep you and your mother safe, and that I can do. You are weaponless, but you can hide if I draw them away. And I will. I have something they want very badly."

I saw her plan, and I also saw the flaw in it, as I am sure she did too. My friend Marthar was going down in battle, with a song on her lips or perhaps a scream of delight as she took some of K'zarr's crew down with her. And I would have to tell her father, did I survive, and he would be proud but desolate. As would I.

We could hear the howls of the gang now, like tigripards hunting, getting closer. Marthar gave me a quick hug, and vanished. I covered Mother with straw., and hid myself as best I could, while keeping an eye through the open door on the street outside.

There was a sound of racing kzin and of howling as some nine or ten of them came into sight. The figure of the blind thing was in the middle; he was being led by some others, holding his paws, and the group was led by the telepath Dog. They paused after emerging from the alley, and waited for Dog, who looked around and seemed to sniff the air.

"Where are you, little lad?" he asked loudly. "Come, man-child, speak to me, tell me all. We are your friends, be sure of it." The others howled even louder at this, and their ears flickered in their laughter response. He held an old-fashioned syringe in his hand, and I guessed that he was about to inject himself with the telepath drug, the *sthondat*-lymph extract which raised a telepath's powers from the ability to make a good guess to a ruthless, deep-radar-like perception that nothing could hide from.

"Here is your death, Addict," Marthar stepped out from

a corner, close to the alley, speaking flatly. She had the needler drawn and held in two hands. The telepath turned and made a sound like a gasp. Then a hundred needles ripped his head off. It happened so fast there was no reaction from the others. The corpse crashed, the head rolling away from it, blood spattering. They gaped at the blood pumping out of the neck, and then looked back at Marthar. The naked skull, still warm, glared up at them.

"I think you are looking for this, scum. K'zarr's memo pad. Recognize it?" She tossed the thing in the air and caught it again. "Well, if you want it, you'll have to catch me." She got off another shot and slipped around the corner just as a blaster flash sizzled at the cobbles where she stood taunting them. I remembered how inhumanly quick the Captain had been in our own fight against the lesslocks, and in that moment the memory of that fight gave me another stabbing feeling of loss for him. Marthar must be right to call me a rattle-brain.

"No blasters, ye damned fools, and get after her," one of them, a huge kzin with orange fur, called out. The group surged after Marthar, howling as they went, save for the figure of the blind kzin and the two servants who were guiding him. They stayed, held back by the gaunt figure. His antennae quivered and his head turned until it seemed he looked straight at me.

"A diversion. We chase the kzinrett while she leads us towards the cops and away from the weaker partner. But we are not so easily fooled, are we, my Heroes, my kits? And when we have the boy, we have the kzinrett too, for she will not stand idly by while I take his eyes out. And once we have the kzinrett, then we shall have her eyes too. Oh yes, a feast we will have, a regular feast. So, my Heroes, search around and find the boy."

"Where does we look, Dominant One?" one of them asked.

"Use what little brain ye have," the blind kzin said and slashed at him savagely with the staff he carried. The servant cried out.

"Go on fools, search about, anywhere the *kz'zeerkt* and its mother would lurk. They are not far from here, I can sense them." He lifted his cowled head, and the antennae writhed. In the days of microsurgery, merely losing a biological eye was not a serious matter; it could be replaced with a natural one grown from your own body, or by a prosthetic one which would be superior. For some reason the kzin had not done this. What exactly he could sense was a mystery; maybe he thought the degradation in vision was compensated by the awe and fear he inspired, for he undoubtedly had something like vision, and perhaps something else as well.

"Mayhap they are inside one of the houses, and have been given shelter," one of the servants argued. The blind thing screamed and hit him again.

"Get to it, ye *sthondats*, knock them all up if ye must and then rout about every house until ye have them. Kill all who stand in the way, they are but apes. Ye call yourselves Heroes, so act like Heroes. I'll have that *kz'zeerkt* and I'll have his eyes; aye, ye'll see me swallow them whole before the night's out."

I was frozen with a suspicion that any motion on my part would draw the attention of either the blind thing or its servants. He was beating them now, and they were fighting back in a dispirited way, trying to take his staff from him, and whining. Then he drove them away. They turned and looked about to carry out his orders as the simplest way to avoid further beatings.

Mother, who had been unconscious or perhaps asleep, began to moan softly, and although the servants heard nothing, those antennae in the head of the blind thing began to roil and turn. Then there was another sound, the returning of the crew. There were but five of them now. "The cow took down three of us with needles, then we lost her," the big kzin with the orange fur proclaimed loudly.

"Small matter, lads, small matter. For you can be certain she is not far away, and once we have the *kz'zeerkt*, we have her too, be sure of it." It struck me later that, foul as it was, the blind thing still had a kzin's awareness of honor, though it might not share it. It knew Marthar would not leave me. "Search about, that way, and find him." He pointed with his staff, almost straight at where Mother and I hid in straw.

A whistling sound came. The orange-furred kzin took out a phone, very like the one the Captain had used. He glanced at it and listened to a message. "Ware, all o' ye. The deputies are coming this way, and fast. We must begone."

"No, the *kz'zeerkt*, ye fools, get the *kz'zeerkt*!" The blind one slashed about with his staff, and the others avoided him. This enraged him further. "Didn't I get the death claw to that damned Skel, when none of you liverless cowards had the nerve to face him? Ahh, I'll get him m'self, ye *sthondats!*" he shouted and started in my direction. There was another sound, a little like horses' hooves, but with more thud to it, a sound I recognized as running thoats.

They could run twice as fast as any horse over short distances, and carry an armed kzin on their backs, sometimes two.

The crew scattered, some back into the alley, which was too narrow for thoats, some towards each of the roads out of the square; those who had taken the north side suddenly turned and bolted back. The sound of the thoats was very loud now, and my spirits lifted, even as the blind thing made his way towards me. Then he recognized his danger. "Where are ye, help me, ye scum!" But the other kzin had left him, and he stood alone in his great cape, his head turning north, the staff waving wildly. He started back to the alley, but stumbled and went to one knee. That was when seven thoats surged into the square, bearing kzin upon their backs. They tried to avoid him; I saw one try to divert his steed, but those things had the momentum of a spacecraft and they went over him. Not one, but two. I heard the snap of his spine and the start of a scream cut off, and the hiss of air leaving his crumpled body. After the thoats had drawn up, there was a black, bloodstained cloak covering a flattened corpse. I had seen yet another death, and was heartily glad of it.

The sheriff got down, and a figure appeared from the corner.

"You got here just in time, Sheriff," Marthar spoke calmly. "How did you know to come?"

It turned out that the lad who had left on his pony had stopped at the first big house and borrowed their telephone to call the sheriff's office and warn him that K'zarr's crew were in town and bent on mayhem. There had been an alert posted that they were on Wunderland, so the sheriff had believed it, and had made for the *Lord Templemount* and then followed the noise.

I rose unsteadily and walked towards them. "They nearly had us," I said and half-fell, but Marthar was there to hold me.

"We must get Mother to the Doctor," I mumbled, but we didn't have to, for minutes later, the Doctor trotted his horse down the alley, leading some men. They had also heard the noise, and the lad on his pony had met them and directed them to us, and he was following at the best pace his tired pony could manage. Mother recovered under the sting of ammonia in her nostrils, and was greatly relieved to be in the hands of humans and the deputies. She was inclined to gabble, until the Doctor gave her a sedative.

"And why were they after you?" the sheriff wanted to know.

"The gold, but it was ours, and more of it should have been," Mother said shrilly.

"I think it was this," Marthar held up the memo pad. "We found it among the Captain's possessions. And if it's what I think it is, it's worth a lot more than any amount of gold."

"Then I should take it and hold it," the sheriff said firmly. "Give it to me, kzinrett child."

Marthar looked at him speculatively. "I think that I would rather give it to my Sire, Orion-Riit. Or the Doctor here. Or maybe Judge von Thoma."

The sheriff nodded in a very human gesture. Well, we had copied each other's mannerisms for generations now. Some of the humans who could do it would waggle their ears instead of laughing. But her use of the name "Riit" changed everything. I knew Lord Vaemar-Riit regarded her as one of the high nobility, but even I had not quite realized just how high until she said that word and I saw its effect. Had the villains injured or insulted her, I thought, the vengeance of her Sire and Grand-Sire would not have been quickly forgotten.

"Very well, but I want to see it handed over. Give it to Doctor Lemoine if you wish, and Doctor, I want the Judge to see it. The old Judge, the first one. Him I trust to do what is best. Far better him than the government, which is where it would have to go if I took it."

Marthar rather reluctantly handed the memo pad over to the Doctor, who looked at it thoughtfully.

"I shall take good care of it, and yes, Judge von Thoma needs to see it. And your father too, young Marthar. And I think it would be as well if we all met together and you can tell us everything you know."

A distant humming, and a light in the sky which rose and headed west interrupted us.

"That will be the rest of the crew making off, no doubt of it," the sheriff said. "You saw less than a dozen, you say. There would be three times that many in K'zarr's Horde. They must have collected the few you left alive and are escaping justice. Well, there's little can be done now. I'll send a message to Munchen and to the spaceports, but I doubt they landed at any regular place. They'll be back in space within an hour or two. At least, with luck we'll never see them again."

"But will not the sentry-satellites detect them?" I asked.

"They are keyed to detect objects approaching Wunderland, not leaving it," he replied. "And you know how many small moons we have. In any case, the surface of a whole planet is vast. We could not cover it all."

We went back to the *Lord Templemount*, me on the back of a horse behind one of the Doctor's men, my mother behind the Doctor, and Marthar behind the sheriff on his thoat, which she greatly enjoyed. The *Lord Templemount*, when we got back, was the most awful mess you can imagine, and Mother and I set about cleaning it up. The sheriff took possession of the corpse of the Captain, and of his belongings that were left.

"Come and see us in the morning, Peter, at my father's palace. We shall have a story to tell, and we must open the memo pad and find out what it has to tell us. And we'll have the Doctor and the Judge there too. It will be such fun!" Marthar had recovered from the events of the night on the ride back. If she ever felt bad about killing the telepath and several of the pirate band, she showed not the slightest sign of it, then or later.

How on earth humans managed to defeat the kzin I cannot imagine. We were lucky nearly all the kzinretti had such stunted intelligence. If many of them had been like Marthar, we wouldn't have had a chance.

CHAPTER SIX

We were gathered around a huge orangewood table in Orion-Riit's mansion. It wasn't really all that big, I suppose, not compared with the palace his father owned in the hills outside Munchen, but it was the biggest house in the town. Orion was the second son, so relatively free as to where he lived, and for some reason—probably because the hunting was good and there was plenty of elbow room—he'd chosen to live out with us in the sticks.

Not that our town wasn't quite famous in its way, we had some historic associations with the Riit family. I know the old Judge and Orion-Riit were friends, as well, of course, as Rarrgh, who ran Lord Vaemar's palace. Perhaps that was why he lived here. Marthar's uncle and aunt, Orlando and Tabitha, were frequent visitors; so was her other aunt, Arwen. But she had a whole host of uncles and aunts. I knew these things from odd scraps that I had picked up from Marthar, although she didn't talk about her family much. It was easy to forget she was a member of the most important kzin clan, and that meant the most important not just on Wunderland, but connected to the Patriarch himself. I wonder if that wasn't part of the reason Orion-Riit lived out here, too. I expect having everybody be respectful could be a bit of a drag at times.

There were five of us. The old Judge Jorg von Thoma sat at the top of the table in the place of honor, with Orion-Riit to his right, and Marthar to *his* right. The Doctor sat at the old Judge's left, and I sat next to him opposite Orion-Riit. There was a kzin butler, or something like, that who came in and out periodically to make sure we were well supplied with drinks, mostly lemonade, which isn't exactly exciting. The kzin drank something else.

The memo pad lay on the table. Marthar and I had told our stories, interrupting each other as we remembered bits of it, but at last we couldn't think of anything we had left out.

"Can't we just switch it on and find out what all the mystery is?" I asked.

Marthar looked at me pityingly. "Peter, for the millionth time, I says it as loves you, but you've got less imagination than a thoat. A thoat that has guzzled itself into a coma on wengle-weed. A thoat that wasn't all that bright to begin with. Or a particularly retarded *sthondat*." Her father looked at me and then at his daughter.

"Alright, explain, smarty-pants," I said, stung.

"Imagine you are a pirate. A truly evil pirate, a kzin pirate who is in the habit of plundering every ship he can find, who has raped whole planets, or at least a few good cities on them. And you keep some really important information on a little memo pad, which you give to your first mate when you are dying. Or which said first mate steals off your cold corpse, more likely. What would you do?"

"Uh, encrypt it? Maybe make sure there's a key, a password, and the stuff wipes if the user doesn't know it?"

She shook her head pityingly some more. "That too. Just in case they didn't trigger the booby trap to blow their paws off and maybe the rest of them, and anyone else in the same village."

She was right of course. All of a sudden, the pad looked much bigger and ready to explode and take us all out. Or maybe to spray acid or emit some poison gas.

"I think that opening it is a delicate job for a technician, young Miss smarty-pants. And I have already sent out for one," her father rumbled. He was big, even for a kzin. "In fact he is here now, and with your permission, I shall turn this over to him."

Everybody nodded, although Marthar was a bit put out that her father had anticipated her. The butler was given the memo pad and took it out, on a silver salver no less, to give to the technician, who was in another room. The butler was told to stay and monitor the technician. I suppose if the latter failed and it blew up, at least the rest of us would survive. Possibly. I thought this was hard on the butler, until I remembered that giving a kzin a dangerous job was a high compliment.

"There was no sign of a ship leaving since K'zarr's crew escaped. And no sign of one at any spaceport," the old Judge told us. "Didn't expect the last of course. But the failure to detect a ship leaving may not mean merely that it evaded our surveillance. It may mean that they are still here, waiting for another chance. You'd better be careful, kids." Things have changed since the old pre-invasion days when, I had been told, a certain amount of smuggling between Wunderland and the Serpent Swarm planetoids was tolerated and there were off-base landings and takeoffs, though, as I said, it was intruders that the watch was kept against. There were vast parks of derelict kzin and human pre-hyperdrive spaceships, obsolete now, and being slowly dismantled, and other war debris, as well as great cave systems, some far larger than Earth's thanks to Wunderland's lighter gravity. There were forests, too, and jungles further south. Old meteor craters had left swamps well overgrown with vegetation. Much could be hidden among them. After all, it had been Wunderland's plentiful natural cover which had allowed the resistance to survive all those years when the kzin were hunting its members with some very sophisticated equipment.

I shivered. The death of Dog and the blind thing had made me feel a lot better about the future, but now I saw that we also had to fear the others, who might be even worse. And I had to do all the being afraid for both of us; there was no way that Marthar would admit to it even if she was.

"Were you able to get the records for the phone that Skel had?" the Doctor asked. "They might tell us something."

"Yes," the Judge said. "But we didn't get a lot from them. Mostly he was checking on intrasystem and interstellar shipping, trying to make sure nobody found out where he was. I guess Wunderland looked a good place to hide, but when they came, they didn't register, and our defense coverage is weaker now that the truce with the Kzin

Empire seems to be holding, at least the part with Wunderland. I guess we can thank Lord Vaemar for that.

"Plus, now that they've got the hyperdrive too, it may even be that the Patriarchy are starting to realize that there are planets for all." Many humans had been terrified when it had been realized that the kzin had the hyperdrive too. So far it had not led to the Armageddon some had predicted, though what was happening on the other side of the vast Kzin Empire was anybody's guess. I thought again of the Captain's ramblings about the things he had seen and done, and suddenly I felt I understood my tears at his death. Whatever crimes he had committed, he had lived on a scale befitting a Hero.

The Doctor drummed his fingers on the tabletop. He wasn't good at waiting.

I remembered my tetrahedron and pulled it out of my pocket. I carried it with me everywhere now, although I had put the box down somewhere and couldn't find it.

"The old Captain, Skel, gave me this. It was in a box that had spaces for four other things like it. I don't know what it means, but it might be helpful."

"Yes, he thought it was a sort of intelligence test, one he and all his shipmates had failed. And I suppose it was," Marthar chimed in knowingly.

"Maybe it was. But I can't imagine how it worked," I told her and the others. "The next one was a cube, judging by the space, and the middle one an octahedron, two pyramids glued together at the base. So of course Marthar guessed they were the five platonic solids, which seems reasonable."

Marthar glared at me. I smiled sweetly.

The Doctor reached out to inspect the tetrahedron and

turned it in his hand. "As I recall there was a plan hundreds of years ago on Old Earth to signal Mars by having fires running in trenches in the Sahara; marking out the diagram for Pythagoras' theorem. The idea was to let the Martians know we human beings were intelligent," the Doctor said thoughtfully.

"It couldn't have done much good," I objected. "There weren't any intelligent Martians to see it."

"Yes, but that was long ago, before they found out. It might be that this represents something similar. A mark of intelligence. You have to be fairly smart to work out that there are exactly five regular solids, no more and no less."

The Doctor passed it around and everyone inspected it.

"Do you think it possible that some alien species made this and the other solids as a way of announcing they were intelligent, Doctor?" Orion asked politely. "Something like displaying what you call the Pythagorean Theorem?"

"It crossed my mind," the Doctor admitted. "But I daresay the notion is fanciful." I got it back again and returned it to my pocket. Well, that hadn't led to anything. But at least I'd let Marthar know she wasn't the only smarty-pants around.

It seemed an age, but eventually the butler came back. "The workman has successfully transferred the data on the pad, m'lord. And decrypted it. He seemed rather contemptuous of the encryption standard. And as you surmised, m'lord, the device was booby-trapped in several different ways. The information can be projected now, however. Shall I bring the new device in here?"

"Yes, and give the technician his money. Explain to him

that if he reveals anything about this transaction, he may pay for it with his life. The threat is not from me, but from others who have no scruples whatsoever. Take him out as you brought him in, I want no speculation about his visit here."

The butler nodded respectfully and departed. Within a minute he returned with a device smaller than the original memo pad, a module for a phone, I guessed, connected to an even smaller projector. "I shall see about returning the specialist to his home, sir. The new memo pad is the usual sort, but I would point out that its power and likely value is even greater than the original. The password is blank." He bowed again and withdrew.

Marthar grabbed the new pad and plugged in the projector, then switched them on. She looked around and selected the wall opposite the Judge as the best site, and pointed the projector at it. We settled down to watch.

The opening was just text, saying it was a record of some space-faring adventures and demanding a password. Marthar just tapped the return icon impatiently with a claw tip. The device obediently went to the next page which was a picture of a spaceship seen from space; it had a kzin skull and crossbones where the registry should have been, and the name of the ship in kzin symbols on the side.

"Ah, another instance of the kzin adopting human culture," said the doctor, indicating the skull.

"The Black, ah, Predatory Flying Creature—*Falcon*, perhaps, would be closest," Orion–Riit rumbled, translating the script. "That was K'zarr's ship indeed. The terror of the swirl-rift. A very newly settled region of space extending from the Montego system to the Quintana Row, and a natural route from the yonder worlds to beyond Sol and its neighbors." Sol was the brightest star in our skies, unless you counted Alpha B. brighter than Proxima. That was because Sol was close, at about 4.2 light-years, and bigger than Alpha A.

The next fifty pages were a list of settlements, ships and their cargoes that presumably had been seized by the pirates; the cargoes were priced, and the places they had sold them were listed. Kzin worlds, many of them unknown to us. Well, we had always known the Kzin Empire was big and disunited. It was because of that disunity that we humans were still free.

"ARM should have this information," the Doctor said in anger.

"ARM might just use it for selling their own illicit stuff," the Judge remarked drily. "Put not your faith in princes. Or governments. And that goes double for largely secret instrumentalities. ARM nearly destroyed us all, with their perverted principles. God save us from the high-minded. They do far more damage than the evil malicious bastards; us evil malicious bastards just don't have the numbers."

Marthar scrolled through them quickly after the first few pages. "These evil psychopathic bastards certainly did plenty of damage," she pointed out.

"They wouldn't have got more than a fraction of a percent of the wealth transferred through the rift. Enough to pay for their fuel and the occasional bender on kzin-settled worlds that were too poor to have much anyway. Places like *Tortuga*, where there's less than a million beings on the whole planet," the Judge told her.

"Why would anyone live there?" I asked.

"Because nowhere else would want them. Scum who were failed pirates don't make good citizens," the Doctor explained. "With the hyperdrive, there are lots of worlds like that now, particularly in the vicinity of the rift. Barely in the Goldilocks Zone, half of them. Nobody counts them as part of the Kzin Empire or the Human Diaspora, mainly because they are barely habitable. With the hyperdrive, we can barely afford to leave habitable worlds alone now, and new colonies are cheap to start, compared to what they were. Oh, eventually we'll take them over when the various species start growing their populations enough, if the kzin ever cut down on their internecine dueling and the humans recover from their war losses. Even with immortality drugs, our populations aren't big enough for our people to want to take over somewhere like *Tortuga* or *Royale*."

"Piracy doesn't look like a good way of making money," I said. "Not if what you say is right."

"They were making hundreds of millions a year," Marthar objected.

"And they had almost equal expenses in fuel and arms bills, not to mention buying up medical materials to replace bits of busted pirate by autodoc," the Judge told her with a laugh. "The main attraction of piracy is that you think you're going to be free of the constraints of society. But you exchange having to be civil to your neighbors for living in fear of your captain and his officers. Living with government is bad enough, but living without any government at all becomes very . . . wearing . . . after a time. And I suppose pillaging and rapine look more fun than holding down a steady job. Raping females looks good to the very unattractive."

"People with a low threshold for boredom wind up in that sort of state," the Doctor stated.

"Well that's me and Peter for starters," Marthar pointed out.

"Yes, but you two can find excitement in ideas," her father rumbled. "At least I hope you can. That isn't an option for the stupid."

If Marthar's father thought she could get excited about homework, I rather thought he was wrong. She was thorough, she was honest, but I wouldn't say she got excited by it very often. And I never had.

Marthar had come to some pictures. One showed a planet like Saturn, but with many more rings, and another a purple nebula with a swirl at its core. "*Where the purple nebulae lit the sky, where ancient suns go to die*," she quoted. "That must surely be a black hole at the center of that one."

I felt pleased that my guess had been correct, or at least likely. Marthar swept the picture and it showed some more purple nebulae, or bits of the other one which had become disconnected from it. She zoomed in, and what was purple became a range of colors and textures, from rose-pink to lilac and even green. They were lit by hot young stars and there were older ones, more likely to have planets than the babies, which would still be accreting them from junk worldlets. Marthar tapped on the picture and enlarged it to show more details. There were other things disturbing the nebulae, more black holes or neutron stars. She swept down and the picture was framed by snow-capped mountains with a spaceship, possibly a tender, in the foreground. It had the same kzin script anyway. The sky was black between a million stars, telling us that there was next to no atmosphere.

"Where are we?" muttered Marthar. She tapped at various places until she got the data file which told where and when the image had been captured.

"Ten years old. About the time we stopped hearing tales of K'zarr. This must be where he died. And we've got galactic coordinates, so we could find it," the Judge said thoughtfully.

"Why bother?" the Doctor shrugged. "There's no shortage of planets or stars. That's a pretty view, 'tis true, but we can see that without stirring. And at least as well as if we saw it through the helmet of a spacesuit."

"We haven't found out anything about the treasure yet," Marthar said. "There must be some. Nobody would go to any trouble to get accounting records and some pretty pictures." She scrolled through some more pictures and then paused. "Now that's interesting."

She had found a sequence of pictures of a world with a thin but definite atmosphere. The sky was a kind of indigo and the sun lime green, casting violet shadows on red soil. There was little life; mostly it looked as dead as Mars had in the early days, but with some lichens and stunted bushes that trembled in a faint wind. There were signs of a long-departed civilization. There was a canal which was too straight to be natural, and as she swept the image it showed broken towers in the distance. She went up over the canal, and it still had some dark liquid at the bottom, with growths of plants sticking up through it. Then she zoomed in to one of the towers. There was a doorway at the base, open. There was no sense of scale, so she fiddled with the data file until she found where the images had been collected and eventually discovered how far away from the doorway we were. She did some arithmetic in her head.

"Wow, those doors are three times as big as daddy. You could ride a thoat in there."

"Go inside, and see if there's anything for the thoat to eat," suggested her father.

Marthar went back to the image and zoomed in through the door. The inside was dark at first, then it automatically went into low-light mode and brightened.

"It looks like a huge storeroom for metal bars," the Judge said. There were boxes with bars inside them, each as long as my arm and with funny-looking dents on the ends, millions of them. There was a central column in the tower with a sort of ramp winding around it and disappearing up into the gloom. I hoped the bars were gold, but they didn't look like it. Platinum perhaps. Or uranium. I didn't know what uranium looked like.

"Nothing for thoats," Orion said. "But something for human and kzin, perhaps. Pan around, small fry. Look at the floor."

Marthar obediently checked the view up closer. There was dust on the floor, and the prints of kzin made a clear impression, although there were so many that it was impossible to count the number of beings who had made them. Could it be the work of the ancient slavers? Who knew? But the doors looked too big for slavers or their Tnuctipun techno-slaves. And ancient as it all was, I doubted it was *that* ancient. Perhaps it was something to do with the strange creatures who had saved humanity in the last stages of the war by selling a human colony the secret of the FTL drive, which Dimity Carmody had translated with several miracles of intellect and intuition. Who knew how many civilizations might have risen and fallen in the galaxy's history?

"There's a video sequence embedded here. Let's see . . ." Marthar clicked away rapidly. The viewpoint climbed jerkily up the ramp into another room, this one containing tables jutting out of the wall, with a rod like a broomstick sticking out below. Each rod had a sort of saddle on it. The room held about a dozen kzin, some of them pirates; I recognized the big one with orange fur. They were hiss-spitting to each other in the Heroes' tongue, sounding like the power cables of a battery of launching lasers dropped into acid. One of the pirates sat down in a saddle, his tail hanging over the end. In front of him were two antennae, like dead serpiforms from Grossgeister Swamp. He picked them up idly, one in each paw. As if drawn by instinct, he held them up to his head, as though to show his comrades what it would be like if he had horns. Like lightning the antennae came alive and the base of each attached itself to the kzin's head. He jumped and then screamed. He tried feebly to pull them off, but they seemed to be growing into the skull. One of the other pirates drew a *wtsai* and slashed at the twin snakes as they writhed and cut halfway through the skull instead. The kzin with the new antennae screamed, his brain splattered and we could see something white wriggling in it. Then he died.

It must have been K'zarr himself taking the video. We heard his cold, gray voice giving orders. He was obeyed instantly. Three kzin seized a figure in his cowled cloak and threw the cowl back. A fourth held the cowled one's head firmly; though he was hairless and burnt, he wasn't blind. His eyes were glazed and staring; his muzzle was scarred and burnt and bald but his nose was still there. A fifth kzin picked up two more antennae from another table and held them out towards him. The antennae stirred as they were held closer to his face. The sharper ends started to grow little roots and almost jumped out of the paws of the kzin holding them; instead they thrust themselves deep into his eyes. He shook and fainted. His holders put him in the saddle of the table from where the antennae had been taken. He slumped and had to be held up. Another order from K'zarr, and one of the bars was placed on the table in a slight indentation which fit it exactly. The antennae strained. Another order. The head of the blinded one was moved forward, and the blunt ends of the antennae found the indentations on the end of the bar and fixed themselves to it greedily, as though sucking from it.

"Dear God," exclaimed the Doctor. "That K'zarr was a monster!"

"A clever monster," the Judge pointed out. "He had noticed the indentation on the table that fitted the bars, and he noticed the blunt end of the antennae fitted the indentations on the bars. He worked out that this is some sort of link from brain to bar. It's an alien book reader."

"He was prepared to expend his crew to explore it," the Doctor pointed out hotly.

"Pah! He makes me ashamed for my species! Still, we know that the experience didn't kill him," Orion observed in a low growl. "Of course, K'zarr didn't know that beforehand. Life is cheap in a pirate world. And now we have an idea what the bars are. They are books. This is a library."

"We don't know what was in the book, or even if it made any sense to him," Marthar argued.

"Likely it didn't. If you took a book from the university library at random and read it, it could be anything from a treatise on hyperdrive physics to *Pride and Prejudice*. And an alien version of *Pride and Prejudice* would be hard to follow," the Judge pointed out.

"Here's another video sequence." Marthar announced and started it. We were in another room, this one was bare except for some discs that seemed to be painted on the floor in a hexagonal pattern, each disc about a single pace in diameter. The discs each had something like a speech waveform on it that might have been writing. Two of the pirates wandered in through a doorway about three times their height and wide enough indeed to allow a thoat through. In response to an order from the camera-holder, they stalked in front of the camera. They looked around, saw nothing and turned to the camera. When they started to go back, one of them stepped onto a disc and vanished instantly. A breath was drawn in, then another order. The remaining kzin looked rebellious, but gave in, and deliberately stepped onto a different disc. Nothing happened for a moment, and he started to move off, then he vanished too.

"That could have been some sort of camera trick. It would be easy to fake," the Doctor said doubtfully.

"Why bother?" the Judge asked. "I think we are seeing some kind of technology, nothing we are likely to understand. The universe is big, and we know there are intelligent species that are way ahead of us. Some of them lived on or visited that world. Remember, Earth was starting to experiment along those lines until the war made such experiments too expensive."

Marthar looked through the rest of K'zarr's memo pad. The last image was of an elderly kzinrett. She looked tough and mean. Who she was I could only speculate about. Would an utterly ruthless kzin pirate keep a picture of his mother? A mate? It didn't seem likely. We never found out who she was.

"That seems to be it. Where's the treasure?" I asked.

Marthar did her pitying look again. "Oh, Peter, wake up, my darling human. You haven't got the sense of a wabbitoh. We spent an hour looking at it. You've got the records of an entire world, a civilization that was technologically well in advance of ours and died. And it left us its records. That's treasure beyond belief. Even K'zarr could see that."

"You are a revolting little smarty-pants, to borrow Peter's term, but you are right, my daughter," Orion nodded. "And I think we need to mount an expedition to find it. I suggest we look around for a spacecraft and crew, and that you, Doctor Lemoine, come with me, and you my old friend, who saved my sister's life so long ago, yes, and Peter here too, as a cabin boy. It would be inadvisable to leave him here, far too dangerous. Anyway, for the sake of interspecies trust and cooperation, we should have a few humans come with us. I know my Sire would think so."

My heart swelled with pride and excitement. I saw it now, yes, we had unimaginable wealth to find.

"Is Marthar coming too?" I asked. "She deserves to, after all."

I got the pitying look again. "Of course I'm coming. Daddy wouldn't dare leave me alone here; this place would have burnt down before he'd been gone a day and I'd think of much more frightful things to do the day after."

Orion's ears flicked, but he didn't attempt to argue the point.

"That's the way to do things," the Doctor said with approval. "Had something like this discovery of a treasure world been made on Old Earth, nobody would have thought of setting out to look for and explore it, not for most of a thousand years, while we got permits and it worked its way through one interfering government department after another. For over three hundred years, anyone who came by it would have passed it over to the government like the obedient slaves they turned into. Well, we've got out of that mindset and learned the cost of slavery. You kzin taught us that, and most of the natural slaves among mankind died. Many of the rebellious too, of course, but you had to catch them."

"Obviously we did not catch all of them," Orion said with his deep rumble. Then he flicked his ears again. "And I am heartily glad of it, for slaves are damnably dull company."

PART TWO
THE SPACE-TUTOR

CHAPTER SEVEN

For an agonizingly long time, nothing much happened, or so it seemed to Marthar and me. We were left in Orion's house and grounds, where we ran riot. We were in the charge of the butler, or whatever he was, who was called Redroar. Orion was away, as were the Judge and the Doctor. We got messages from them, mostly from Orion. The Doctor had gone to Munchen to see about finding a replacement for himself, a locum tenens; the Judge was setting up some sort of financial arrangements with the von Hohenheim bank, which he partly owned. He cancelled Mother's mortgage, which meant that she could run the inn as a sort of hobby activity and to keep herself in food. The boy who had brought help was appointed to replace me.

Marthar and I played a lot. We had the GALACTIC WEB to surf, which meant we could go on with our schoolwork. Teachers can be very irritating, and they tend to disapprove of playing games unless they are horribly complicated. I think the idea is to get you ready for the algebra needed for understanding the difficult stuff, what was called *Soft*.

I don't know why. Marthar was good at *Hard*, which was about physics and astronomy and stuff. I suppose it is called *Hard* because it is about hard things, like raw matter. *Soft* is about social science and living organisms, which I suppose explains the name a bit, but is a whole lot more difficult than the *Hard* stuff. The easy bits are interesting, but when it gets complicated, I scream for Marthar to help me. Of course, we aren't really ready for doing it sequentially, neither of us, but then, that's why it counts as play. When it stops being play you know the teacher has lost track of how smart you are. Or maybe they are programmed to pretend you are smarter than you are so you have to fight back. It can get exhausting.

Redroar wasn't exactly sympathetic either, but the grounds were big enough to hide from him, and we did. Although when he really wanted us, we both had phones he could use to summon us, which he did when we had messages from Orion that weren't just text. And, of course, there were plenty of animals to hunt, large and small. Marthar made me improve my killing techniques, and even to develop a taste for raw meat, which turned out later to be more useful than I would have imagined.

Since the fauna of three systems were present, we referred to a guidebook on our phones that listed edible and inedible for both of us, as well as good- and foul-tasting. Some of the most innocent-looking animals on Wunderland, like the Beam's Beasts, are the most dangerous. Then there are the advokats and their foul relatives, the zeitungers. That's a beginning. Professor Rykerman once told me we have hardly begun to classify Wunderland's fauna yet. Even I, when out camping, have seen what I'm sure are unknown species, and there are times I've been thankful my tent has been made of strong modern materials.

Orion had gone to the spaceport, which was south of Munchen and had been a kzin spaceport in the old days, and his first message had explained that he had appointed a human called Blandly to set about the ship purchase. He thought it important that every message should be encrypted and that there should be as few as possible, for security. Blandly didn't seem to be very bright, and sent long messages to all of us, trying to prove he was working hard, I suppose.

We saw pictures of some possible ships, some too small, some too big, some monsters which were horribly expensive, some too new and costly and some too old with hyperdrives retrofitted. We eventually got one of the last sort. It was of the same class as the old *Valiant*, the last ship to get to Wunderland before the Liberation, now sunk in the Southern Ocean, and a popular site for diving. It was certainly big enough and had carried a crew of fifty once, with room for freezers and supplies to last for years and years. Orion insisted that our ship be renamed the *Valiant*, in honor of the ship that had been shot down by renegade humans long before I was born. The new *Valiant* was built in Sol System, and I think Orion spent as much to update it as he did to get the ship itself. All this on the advice of Blandly, Orion having to do some sort of politics like his father. Anyway, eventually it arrived, and even later it got through the yards that were doing the upgrading. At no point were Marthar or I allowed to go there and see it, which was very annoying.

Most of the business of flying a spaceship is automated, though it is practice to keep a skeleton crew of living watchkeepers, and our new ship-computer was a good one. She could design and build repair robots for anything that needed fixing, there were already repair robots for the usual things that could go wrong, and she could mine asteroids for minerals and water. It was like an animal's body with an immune system and an ability to heal. Marthar and I found this cheering, because we thought it would be a sort of bridge between *Hard* and *Soft*, and if we could figure out enough about how the computer worked, we could be really ready for more school when we got back.

Of course, the ship still needed a crew. A modern ship would hardly have needed any organic life on board, at least as far as the flying was concerned, but the older models were designed to have a lot of human interfaces, for all sorts of strange reasons. When she was first built, human beings hadn't wanted their computers to be very bright, and in battle humans could show more initiative than any computer or robot. I knew battles had been won in the Great War because humans had switched off computers which told them everything was lost. Now they would be a mixture of human and kzin interfaces. Beings who were equally at home handling both systems, and both interfaces, were rare. And getting a human or kzin crew proved difficult.

Blandly to Lord Orion Riit,
Judge Jorg von Thoma,
Doctor Thaddeus Lemoine,
Verderer Redroar:
Subsequent to your instructions, the Hispaniola *has been*

renamed and refitted as the Valiant. *The on-board computer insists on a crew of at least forty, and it has been difficult to find them. I found seven humans and five kzin who were willing to crew her but their specialities have not always been acceptable to the computer (who is also called* Valiant, *of course.) Some, I think, were running from the law and I have been at my wit's end until recently. A kzin called Silver turned up one day; he was a spaceman many years ago, an auto-chef programmer apparently, and when I told him the ship would have two young people on board, he agreed with some persuading to travel as their tutor. The* Valiant *wanted one, so I appointed him there and then. Since then, some of his old companions have come to join up, and they seem to make a whole crew. No doubt they have sailed in similar ships before, although all but three are kzin. Silver was good enough to suggest that of the twelve I had already appointed, all were unsuitable for one reason or another, and his arguments were convincing in two cases. But I am sure he will get on with the kzin I found, and he will surely tolerate the other two humans who are husband and wife.*

"A tutor!" I exclaimed. "A living breathing one we can argue back with properly. We've never had a human or kzin tutor, only a few human teaching assistants who were hopeless. That will open lots of possibilities, don't you think?"

Marthar considered. "I suppose a kzin tutor would be better than the humans we had as teaching assistants. They were afraid of you even, because of the questions you had. And they were terrified of me eating them. As long as he's not too old we should be alright. Oldies are mainly ever so dull. Their brains calcify or something."

"The Doctor and the Judge are alright," I pointed out.

"True. And Daddy isn't too awful. Some people don't calcify as readily as others. And there are those who are on the geriatric drugs and stopped themselves aging before calcification set in. But nearly all wrinklies are as dull as thoat poo. Well-known fact number three million and seven."

"What's well-known fact three million and eight?" I asked.

"That's the one about females being smarter and better at algebra than males," she told me sweetly. I can't win many against Marthar, but it's fun trying. And sometimes, not often, I ask a question or make a remark that stops her in her tracks and she looks at me with something approaching respect.

I used to think it was funny that you could love someone of a different species, but actually human beings have done it for thousands of years. We can love pet dogs and cats with no trouble at all. I sometimes think that's how Marthar feels about me.

"When are we going to go and see this ship, the *Valiant*?" I asked.

"How would I know, doofus?" she answered.

"What's a doofus?" I asked.

"Dunno. Found it in an old book. Sounds a bit Latin, doesn't it? I don't think it's exactly flattering."

"That makes you a doofa," I pointed out. That started a fight, which I rapidly lost. Hardly surprising when you're fighting a being that would consider dismantling a Bengal tiger no big deal. With a young male kzin I would never have dared risk even a play-fight. She sat on me after a certain amount of rolling around and wrestling, keeping her claws sheathed. She's a lot stronger than I am, it isn't fair. One of the first things you learn about life, I guess. I saw the effort she made to prevent tearing my throat out with her fangs, and thought the fight had gone far enough. It would have been unfair to test her self-control too far. Kzin instincts are strong.

We spent a lot of time looking at the memo pad, the safe version. We found the galactic coordinates of the planet with the towers and the lime-green sun, and copied them to our own phones. We searched through the galactic atlas, the source of which was in the spaceport's main maproom, to locate it and its neighbors. It was not too far from the great swirl-rift, but out in a strange direction, well to the Galactic North. My Trojan theory had been wrong. Of course, there are millions of stars in the region, some lost in clouds of gas, some in the hyperbaryon clouds, some in highly unstable orbits of clusters, and a few single and binary systems.

We also speculated on the treasure planet. Perhaps it had some old remnants of the race that had built the towers, now reduced to savagery and cannibalism. Or there could be aliens, like some of those that the Captain had talked of, those with two heads, or the ones who could appear to be beautiful females and seduce space-farers. Or others, even stranger. Most of our discussions involved finding books which had scientific miracles we could bring back to a grateful Wunderland, although how we were to read them without attaching those horrible antennae we never quite worked out. "If we could interface them to a computer, it would be alright," Marthar said optimistically.

"I should think they only sense organic brains," I argued, and shuddered at the recollection of those things seeking out eyes.

"You don't know that," Marthar announced. "Or perhaps we'll find some aliens who don't mind having antennae and we can get them to do the reading for us. Or perhaps *Valiant* will figure out some alternative way of doing it, build our own book readers, I mean. Or maybe we'll find working models of the technology. We could look at those transit discs and dig them up and figure out how they work."

"I have a strong suspicion that reverse engineering alien technology could be a long job," I said. "How long would it have taken Isaac Newton to build a mobile phone if he'd seen one working on a video? He'd have had to invent electricity first. And you're just guessing that they are transit discs, maybe they just dropped the pirates down a big well to be fed to carnivores and then closed again quickly."

This led to us watching the video sequences again, and to lots of endless but happy bickering as we tried to justify our positions by digging up supporting evidence from the web and then changing our positions. Marthar was really good at that.

Eventually we got the letter from Blandly that led us to travelling to the Spaceport:

Blandly to Lord Orion Riit,
Judge Jorg von Thoma,
Doctor Thaddeus Lemoine,
Verderer Redroar:

My lord, the ship is finally ready. I have appointed a ship's mate, a kzin named Arrow, a somewhat stiff fellow, but admirably competent, and he has supervised the loading to the satisfaction of the Valiant *herself. I have also set about the last task you gave me of finding a second ship which will set off after you within a matter of months if we do not hear from you in that time. I have a suitable candidate, and will set about crewing her and provisioning her the moment you leave for the rift, or for the treasure planet. All here are most excited at such a destination, I might say!*

"Orion-Riit won't like that," I muttered. "The idea was to keep it secret, and this man Blandly is an idiot who seems to have no discretion at all."

"Talking of treasure!" said Orion-Riit when he saw it. "As if treasure and murder were not the oldest of old friends! And what is this so-called Name, 'Arrow'?" Kzin Names are given to a minority as signs of high distinction and, to a Noble like Orion-Riit, conveyed information about the bearer that could be read like a book. Rarrgh's name, for example, conveyed the tightly-coded description, "Slayer of Morlocks in the great caves when fighting against heavy odds and without prospect of relief." There were also nursery names given to young kits of high birth, which at the end of the war had not been replaced by proper

Heroes' Names. Vaemar-Riit himself bore such a Name and had decided to keep it, since under that Name he had fought his first battles. Since the end of the war, too, a few Kzin had taken to appropriating Names for themselves, or even, especially in the case of some of the telepaths, taking up human names. Of course, there were also descriptive nicknames, like "One-Eye" or "Brown-Fur," but, as far as I understood kzin society, these were used only by the lower classes. None confused them with real Names. Anyway, Orion-Riit (his own Name conferred by his Sire as being easy for humans to pronounce but very uncommon among them) certainly looked askance at this one. The letter finished:

I suggest the juveniles should come to the ship within two days, and that the adults should come within three. If the adults are delayed for any reason it will not greatly matter, as Silver will surely take good care of the juveniles. Your obedient servant, Sven Blandly.

"Another reason for thinking he's an idiot," Marthar pointed out. "He calls us *juveniles*. It sounds calculated to irritate us. And irritating me is a really bad idea, as he is shortly going to discover."

"Oh, what does it matter?" I asked. I jumped to my feet and danced. "We're off to join the *Valiant*! Tomorrow! No more hanging around. We'll be able to move into our cabins. We'll be able to run around the ship and explore. It's going to be more fun than either of us have ever had before."

"And then off to the treasure planet. Which might be fun and could be dangerous," Marthar agreed.

Of course, for her, the dangerous bit made it even more attractive..

Packing took us the afternoon, and Redroar agreed to take us to the spaceport the following day. We were going in one of Orion's aircars, a big one with plenty of space for our luggage. I had few possessions anyway, but packed my best clothes. I made sure that the tetrahedron was in my pocket at all times: I thought it just possible that it had come originally from the treasure planet, and that I might find the other solids; the cube, the octahedron, the dodecahedron and the icosahedron, and maybe a neat box in which to keep them all. There was something attractive about the idea that the tetrahedron was going home again, although it might have come from some other world altogether, of course. Marthar had a huge amount of luggage, at least ten times as much as I did, including food for the journey for both of us. That was thoughtful of her, because my feeling for fish-flavoured ice cream was not altogether kindly. She somehow got away from the house early in the morning and did some last-minute shopping in the town, making Redroar furious when he caught her coming back over the wall; he swore horribly in the Heroes' tongue and she answered him pertly. She was covered by parcels strung around her, and he wanted to check that nothing explosive or toxic was among them.

After some serious thought, Redroar passed the swords. A kzinrett isn't supposed to carry a *wtsai* of course, and this sword was about the same size, though used for slashing rather than mainly thrusting like the *wtsai*. Now I knew why she had been practising with sticks during our picnics in the grounds. I got one too, a sword, I mean, although mine was much smaller and had a grip and balance for a man rather than a kzin. I hoped I never had to use it. In fact, we left them behind after deciding they would be pretty useless against anything except each other.

Then we had to transfer the new luggage to the aircar and, with Redroar sitting opposite us, we set off.

It was only a bit over a hundred kilometers, which had been a lot when it was all done by walking or on horseback, but we passed over the abbey and the town that had grown up on the flank of the old volcano next to it within minutes. And about as many minutes later we were close to the spaceport and were craning to see the *Valiant*. We didn't get nearly close enough to be sure which was ours; there were dozens of ships in the various bays, all of different sizes and styles, not to mention a park, like the one at Munchen only smaller, of old Kzin pre-hyperdrive dreadnaughts, being nibbled away for scrap. Then we moved over the little town, and eventually landed on the roof of a hotel, were whisked down in the lift as our bags were unloaded into another, and descended to floor level.

Orion met us and licked his daughter briefly, while a stout man next to him beamed at us all. "Ah, the juveniles!" he said, but Marthar merely looked at him and drew her lips back only a little, saying nothing but exposing a respectable amount of fang. I suppose having her father there inhibited her a bit, which saved Blandly a nasty bite, or the verbal equivalent.

"Where are the Doctor and the Judge?" I asked.

"They are on board already, and we join them almost immediately. There is nothing to keep us here," Orion answered. "Come, the baggage is being transferred to the landcar already. Blandly, settle the hotel bills and any others. Take the payment from the running account."

We got into the landcar while our baggage was being loaded, and after a few minutes we were off to the port proper. I gawped out of one window while Marthar gawped equally out of the other. We saw spacefarers, Kzin with their loping prowl and humans with their conditioned glide that had to keep the feet in contact with the ground at all times lest they lose their grip in space, some of the first free adult Jotok with their five legs and curious whirling motion. It made me feel keenly how provincial my life had been, and I resolved to see more of the universe.

Then we drew up at the spaceport, and, carrying only hand luggage, we followed flickering arrows onto walkways which carried us and needed care when hopping off, although they slowed down a lot before we had to change. And then up a tower in a lift, and a short walk across a bridge. And we were inside the *Valiant*, without ever having seen her from the outside.

Redroar stopped. "I'll be getting back, my lord. Any instructions?"

"Just keep everything neat and tidy until we get back, and make sure that man Blandly does what he has contracted," Orion told him. "I've little faith in his judgment, but he was wished on me by a political colleague. And if anything goes wrong, I'll expect to see you on the replacement ship with a squad of Father's guard. And I'll hope you have more luck keeping the destination secret than we've had."

"Very good, my lord. Since I am not so obligated, I'll

replace Blandly just as soon as he completes the existing contract. In my judgement he is a fool. Best to stay away from fools, folly is contagious."

Orion grunted. "We shall at least be off before he can spread it around that we are due to leave. We go in ten minutes, just enough time to get the kits strapped down and the baggage stowed. Take care, Redroar."

And ten minutes later, as an honorary kit, I felt myself drawn back into my acceleration couch and we were off into space. I could guess how my friends would envy me, if they knew.

CHAPTER EIGHT

The acceleration couch was a sort of narrow bed that turned into a coffin. Sides went up and a top slid over it, lights came on inside and there was a hiss of air, and then I floated. I didn't understand it, because I expected to be pressed down by the acceleration. I had forgotten about the kzin gravity-planer, which all ships, human and kzin, now carried. I counted two minutes by pulse beat until a bell rang, a green light flashed and the top and walls slid down again. I looked around, thought, got up and ran to the door. I opened it, and there was Marthar, just about to knock on it.

"We're in space!" I told her.

"Really? I thought we were underwater. Golly, aren't you a clever little doofus?" she said, flippantly. "Are we going to explore?"

We walked down the corridor that held our cabins into a great space with a ramp in the middle of it leading up. The floor was soft but smooth, a bit like a dojo. Marthar's claws would have torn shreds out of the one at school, she had to wear funny shoes that covered them up when she went into the dojo, but here her claws had no effect. It meant that we walked very quietly.

"Just over a standard gravity," she remarked.

"Oh, that's it. I felt sort of heavy, as if I'd eaten too much. I suppose that explains why the floors are soft and spongy; it's in case we fall down. I guess the gravity is because the ship's accelerating. It's the right direction. How long before we get to use the hyperdrive?"

"Think, doofus. What's the acceleration of gravity on Wunderland?"

"Almost eight meters per second per second," I replied promptly. "Everyone knows that."

"Then we are accelerating at about ten meters per second per second, a tad over a standard gravity."

"I guess so."

"And how far do we have to go before space is flat enough to use the hyperspace thingy?"

"Um, I dunno. About a thousand light-minutes at a guess. Call it sixteen thousand million kilometers roughly."

"And how long would it take us to cover that distance?"

"You've screwed up all the units," I complained. "It's a distance of sixteen times ten to the twelve meters. And at a constant acceleration of ten meters per second per second we'll be there in, um, the square root of thirty-two times ten to the sixth seconds. Which is nearly six million seconds. Or something under two thousand hours, which is over two months. It seems a long time."

"Well, there's your answer. But what assumptions have you made?"

"You're not my teacher, you pest. That's what the teacher

always says. *What assumptions are made in that analysis*? and usually it thinks of twice as many as I do." I complained.

"Well, now you can see why it matters."

"Alright, the big one is that we assume we are accelerating at ten meters per second per second just because it feels as if we are. Given the technology we got from the kzin gravity-planer, we might be going ten or a hundred times that and never notice. That's why I was floating in the acceleration coffin, I suppose."

"Good, doofus. In fact, not a doofus at all. I'm proud of you."

She jolly well should have been, I thought. This subject was definitely *Hard*, and I was better at *Soft*. So far.

"We need a map of the ship. How do we attract the ship's attention, I wonder?" Marthar looked around for a way of talking to the ship. Her phone dinged. She looked at it.

"Gosh, it heard me. That's the *Valiant* calling. Hang on, I'll put it on loud so you can hear her too."

"Hello, Marthar, this is *Valiant* here. I put my name in your phone, and in Peter's also. Just click on zero at any time if you are not in a public area or your own cabin. I can always hear you there unless you ask me to close down. You want a map? You have that on your phone too. Try the *ship* application. Goodbye."

"When did she mess about with our phones? No, never mind, *Valiant*, I wasn't talking to you. Gosh, it's worse than being at home and having Redroar or one of the other servants always hanging around. You've no idea how good it was working at your place, Peter; at mine I had the sensation of being followed around every minute."

I suppose being sort of royalty must have problems. You don't think of the drawbacks, only the advantages, but I hadn't thought of Marthar as being special. You don't wrestle with people if you think of them as royalty, even when it takes them only a second to throw you. I suppose once in a while I realized how important her family was, but I soon forgot. She was just my best friend, Marthar, who argued and fought with me and treated me as a sort of pet rabbit.

"*Valiant*, how long before we go to hyperdrive?" I asked.

"Two hours, forty-three minutes and ten seconds, mark." *Valiant* had a woman's voice, not old exactly but not young either.

"Alright, we can go and find a few places," Marthar said. "The map is cool. We can go up to the next deck and see the view from the ship."

Marthar ran up the ramp to prove she could handle higher gravity, and I walked more sedately after her. The next deck was full of screens, but nobody was there. One screen showed our trajectory in the Alpha Centauri system; we were headed north of the ecliptic at an angle of about thirty degrees, and we were not far from Alpha B already. We were somewhere over the asteroids of the Serpent Swarm. From here it looked rather like the rings of Saturn, only orbiting Alpha A instead of a planet, and fainter, and more a crescent than rings, for it was denser on one side. And sort of skewed because we were not heading directly north. North, if you are a landlubber, is the direction from which the planets of a star look as if they are going in the positive direction, that is, counter-clockwise.

There was a back view which showed Wunderland, but

it was only a point of light. We found out how to magnify the image until it filled the screen, and looked down at home. Well, sort of. Munchen and Thoma'stown were the other side of the world, so it was not terribly interesting, really. I thought I might have felt sentimental about leaving our world, but discovered I didn't. Marthar is as sentimental as an old boot, so it would be deeply suspicious if she expressed any sentiment, but she didn't either. I just felt excited to be in space for the first time in my life.

We looked ahead in the direction the ship was travelling, hoping to see the swirl-rift, but it was much too far away, or maybe hidden behind some dust clouds. There are more of those than you'd think if you didn't know some modern astronomy, and didn't understand why the galaxy rotated a fair bit faster than it ought to if you count only the stars you can see.

"*Valiant*, where is our tutor?" Marthar asked.

"In crew territory, at the sign of the Spy-Glass," *Valiant* replied promptly. "Eight decks down. You can get there by elevator." This time she just talked to us directly, not by the phone.

"I was planning to avoid him, not go looking for him," Marthar whispered at me.

I doubted if whispering would fool *Valiant*; the voice didn't seem to come from any particular place, it was vaguely like what you'd think ghosts would sound like, female ghosts.

"*Valiant*, is there anywhere we can try out what zero gravity feels like?" I asked. I mean, we were in space. If you can't practice floating and being weightless in space, where can you do it? And I'd already had a small amount of it in the acceleration coffin, so it didn't sound like an unreasonable request.

Valiant told us to go to the recreation room two decks up, which she said could be made weightless if we wanted since there were no other occupants yet. So we did, and it was absolutely glorious. It was a huge room. There was equipment for playing games of all sorts, but it was all safely stowed away and we certainly didn't need it. The walls and the floors were padded and soft here too, which was just as well because we did a lot of bouncing off them. We yelled and shrieked like small children as we zoomed around until we were out of breath and energy, and just floated companiably. You might think it is hard to just float, and it takes a bit of careful estimation: you have to bounce off opposite walls with the same but opposite momentum, bump into each other and then hang on. The same momentum meant that Marthar had to be going a lot slower than I did, because she has twice my mass. Getting back is easy, even if you drift apart, because you can swim. Not very fast, it is true, but you can swim together in a reasonable time. And if there's two of you, each of you jumps off the other. You sure get to believe in Newton's laws this way.

"What's next, chimpy?" Marthar asked. Note that I am the one asked to provide new ideas and things to do when she gets bored. I suppose she's better at the critical thinking, that is, pulling apart all my brilliant ideas and giving clear incisive explanations of why they won't work, right up to the point where they do.

"It's coming up to the flip trick, the transition to

hyperdrive," I pointed out. "Less than half an hour. I dunno where we should be for that, probably back in our cabins."

"Correct, Peter," *Valiant* broke in. "The likelihood of anything going wrong is infinitesimal, but I don't like the thought of broken, mangled bodies about the place in the event that I have to perform an emergency maneuver. It's so untidy."

Maybe *Valiant* is smart enough to have a sense of humor, and maybe she isn't. We went back to our cabins just in case she wasn't. Maybe that was the idea. There was something of the schoolteacher about *Valiant*, though that's a terrible thing to say, even of another computer program.

I was a bit muzzy after we changed to hyperdrive, so I was late to join the others. I found Marthar along the end of the hall, sitting at a table with the Judge and the Doctor. Tables and chairs just appeared when you asked *Valiant* for them. Of course, they were made of hyperbaric matter—the fuzz, and it could be summoned up at will and shaped into anything you were prepared to program. I haven't decided what to do with my life yet, but fuzz metaprogramming is definitely a possibility. Another is designing proper teacher programs that tell you a bit about why they say some of the weird things they do.

"Hello, Peter," the Doctor greeted me. "We've been trying to talk Marthar into going to find your new tutor and starting schoolwork, and your absence was her best excuse for deferring it. So now she hasn't got one."

"You just want to go on wrangling, and you think I'll

listen to you and store the awful things you say and bring them up later," Marthar retorted.

"True," the Doctor admitted, blowing smoke at her from his pipe. "And you'd learn a deal of disgusting bad language from the Judge if you stayed. So better you go off and talk to your tutor instead."

Marthar looked thoughtful. "He used to be a spacer, as I recall. So maybe he'll know some bad language himself. Although, I've never really grasped the concept myself. What's the point of having words too awful to say?"

"Oh, there are no words too awful to say, just words you mustn't use too often, in case you wear them out," the Doctor laughed. "Now get along with you, we're going to sample the ship's beer."

So we went looking for our tutor. *Valiant* told us he was still at the sign of the Spy-Glass, so it sounded as if he spent a lot of time there. We went down eight levels to find him, and also to find why spy glasses had to have signs.

To my surprise, the Spy-Glass was an inn, and its sign was an old-fashioned telescope stuck up outside it. Inside, kzin crew were sitting around tables, drinking rum. I suppose it was some sort of space-farer subculture thing. We wandered in, and collected some odd glances, but nothing else happened.

There was a sort of mine-host, a big kzin with fur that was a sort of golden chestnut, neatly trimmed; he looked like a giant teddy bear more than a kzin warrior. His right leg was prosthetic, a metallic and ceramic thing, and it didn't match his natural leg very well, so he sort of hopped a bit as he moved around spryly enough. For one moment,

I wondered if he was the one that the Captain had feared so much, but it was impossible to believe that, because he radiated good nature and affability, joking with some of the customers, and warning them when he thought they were in danger of becoming intoxicated. A very different character from the ghastly crew I had seen. Also he didn't have the silver blaze on his chest that the Captain had warned me of, and it would have been a bit of a stretch to call his fur red. He saw us and came over to us with the ear flick of humor.

"Good day t' ye, young kits, and what brings you to crew country? For ye're plainly officer types, I'll lay to that."

I was quite pleased to be thought to be an officer type, although he probably meant that to Marthar, who was certainly poised and confident, but then, she always was. And he could see her ear-tattoos.

"Sir, we are looking for a Mister Silver, for he is our tutor, and we thought we would find him here," I said.

"Well, ye've found him at one stroke, young master Peter Cartwright, Lady Marthar Riit. For I'm Silver himself, at your service, and pleased to make your acquaintance. It's a fine time we'll be havin' the three o' us, I'm thinkin'."

He offered his paw for me to shake, or at least a small part of it, for of course it was far too big for me to hold it all. Then he shook hands with Marthar, bowing low. She looked up at him steadily. He opened his eyes wide and put his head on one side as he returned her gaze with a twinkle in his eye. This was a mannerism which we later found he had frequent recourse to, the head tilt and the wide open eyes. They were tawny and black, and only a little bloodshot, but enough to make it clear he was an old space-farer.

"Sit ye down, sit ye down, and I'll find some juice for ye, a broth for the lady and a lemonade for the gentleman, if that should suit ye?"

We sat down and he brought us some drinks, and then, with a big sigh, reclined on a *footch*. He looked from one to the other of us.

"And when d'ye want t' start the tutorin'?" he asked. "To my mind, d'ye see, there's more t' be gained by your findin' out about the ship an' the crew than on learnin' regular algebra an' sichlike. Ye can do that anywhere. An' anyway, book learnin' has some limitations. It's a preparation for life that I think ye should be after, not a preparation for bein' a learned academic, which is a very different thing, I'm thinkin', bein' closer to a preparation for death."

I was most heartily in favor of this approach.

"We planned to figure out how the *Valiant* works, because it looks like a bridge between *Hard* and *Soft*," Marthar told him.

"Arrgh, that's close thinkin', m'dear, and I approve. Mind you, the same might be said o' studyin' the crew."

He said this without a flicker of his ears, so I wasn't sure what he meant, but just then my eye was caught by a movement from the back of the room. One of the kzin had risen stealthily and was gliding towards the door, and I recognized him. It was the orange-furred kzin who had been with the pirates back in Thoma'stown! I gasped and the other two turned to me. I pointed.

"It's him. It's one of the pirates. I know it."

The figure had slipped out as I said it, but Silver's

response was like lightning. "I know not who he is, but he hasn't paid his score. Claws, be after the *sthondat*, find him and test him. Ef he's one o' K'zarr's crew, I want his pelt, see to it. And either way I want his score settled."

Claws was a kzin who obeyed Silver instantly and was out of the door with his *wtsai* out within seconds.

"Are you sure, Peter? I didn't see him, but it doesn't seem very likely," Marthar objected.

"Best be safe rather than sorry," Silver said firmly, and I was comforted to think our tutor had our interests to heart. He might look like a gigantic teddy bear, but there was nothing slow or uncertain about him. "Claws will check him thoroughly. Ef he's a regular Hero, he'll come to no harm, but were he ever with K'zarr, why, Claws will find out and will take care of him, I'll lay to that."

We took Silver's picture on our phones, so we would be able to see instantly if he called us, and he took ours. He seemed unenthusiastic about having his picture taken, but stood up for it so we would have the top half of him. He explained that he was shy about having his prosthetic leg in the picture, and he moved as Marthar took the picture, so he came out a bit blurred, but mine was fine. This seemed a bit strange to me, for I had never known a kzin to be shy about anything. Then he took our pictures for his phone, which was four times the size of ours. So we parted on good terms, with instructions to set about finding out as much as we could about the *Valiant* and reporting back to him within two days. He told us where to get a copy of the ship's plans, and that the first thing we should do was familiarize ourselves with the fire-fighting equipment (all dread fire in a spaceship) and next the location of the gun-mountings, their local control and the central control on the bridge. He suggested that after that, we talk to Arrow. Marthar asked if he'd like to come with us, but he demurred, explaining that a humble tutor would hardly be allowed in with the officer types, but that if we just asked out of curiosity, we would probably get access.

"No need to mention me at all, at all," Silver explained. "Just say you have a taste for finding out all about spaceships, and one day you'd like to fly one, and who knows? One day indeed, Peter, ye might."

"We'd better report this to my father," Marthar said slowly. "Peter's seeing one of the pirates, I mean."

"Indeed we must," Silver said approvingly. "And we shall do it now while the story is still fresh in our minds."

So we went up eight levels, with Silver amazed that he could lose the score for three glasses of rum and not know the kzin. "For I can vouch for the most o' the crew, and ye may lay t' that. They are a fine set of kzin, and the men are as good, or very near. Why, I wouldn't be here to tell ye were it not for that Claws, who saved m' life on Karador once, or was it Damask? Or maybe Venth. Anyway, one o' the places where there's many a bad creature, and me a poor innocent space-farer wi' no idea o' the wickedness of some o' the legal entities about." I'd heard none of those names before, but as I said, the kzin Empire was big, and no human approached knowing all about it.

We found Orion, the Judge and the Doctor, still arguing and drinking, although Orion had only a sort of brown soup in his glass. He was a kzin who, like his daughter, would insist on staying in control, and alcohol was not for him. And we told the story of my seeing the pirate, with Silver expostulating and asking for confirmation of everything he said. At length he took his leave, with a bow to each of us, and an affable twitch of his ears. He gave the kzin equivalent of a beam, and we waved him goodbye as we left.

"A good choice of a tutor," the Doctor said mildly. "I think Blandly did well." The Judge said nothing, nor did Orion-Riit, but both looked thoughtfully after the retreating kzin.

CHAPTER NINE

The next day was the same length as an ordinary day on Wunderland, and started about the same time we decided to go to the bridge and look about. We all had breakfast together, and Orion said we could go up in a group, for he needed to meet the captain of the *Valiant*, who was a kzin called S'maak. Whether it was a true Name or a nickname or a ship name I don't know, but on a human-registered ship, everyone has a name, so the ship can keep track of them all. But the way it was spoken, it sounded to me like a true Name, so I looked him up on my phone and found out about him. He was a famous warrior.

When we got to the bridge, there was a lot of activity among the kzin and humans there. They were poring over computers and running simulations. S'maak-Captain turned and looked at us bleakly for a moment and then came over. He had fought in one of the battles for Ceres in the Great War, and he looked as if he could have won it single-handed. He would have been a bad enemy. At least, I thought to myself, stern and stiff as he was, he would be respectful of the Lord Vaemar's family and associates.

"I've a number of things to say to you, m'lord, and you are not going to like them," he growled to Orion. He was tall enough to look Orion directly in the eyes, and he did.

"Say on, Captain," Orion said mildly.

"I don't like the crew, Dominant One. I don't like the cruise, and I don't like my first officer. And that's the long and the short of it."

"Perhaps you don't like the ship either?" the Doctor answered sarcastically.

"The *Valiant* is old, but for a mon . . . a human ship she's trim, sir, and well set up," S'maak-Captain said just as coldly. "I'll know more of how she handles in a few more days."

"And do you disapprove of your employer, perhaps?" the Doctor challenged.

"Steady, Doctor. Let's not provoke bad feelings. S'maak-Captain, it seems to me you have said either too much or too little." The Judge was patient and calm. But I sensed his hidden alarm. It was very foolish indeed to provoke a kzin.

"As it's been said, mayhap I must say more, sir," the Captain allowed. "As to the crew, I find they have set up an inn down in crew territory and they serve rum. Now alcohol fuels discord in man and kzin alike, and kzin are less used to it. It impairs the efficiency of all who partake of it, and I'll have none of that on my ship, sir, save by way of reward and by my leave. And I have found that with the connivance of my first officer, whom I do not trust, they have loaded the personal arms down at crew level. I am ordering them all to be transferred up to officer levels immediately. I'll not have weapons at the disposal of the crew. And I have no faith in an officer who would."

"Do you anticipate a mutiny, perhaps, S'maak-Captain?"

the Doctor asked, with biting charm. "Is that your objection to the cruise?" I gave silent thanks he had not said "*fear* a mutiny." I knew enough of kzin to know that that would be an insult beyond any possibility of repair. I noticed S'maak-Captain's heavily-loaded ear-ring. Yes, it seemed what I had read about his wartime exploits was true.

"Sir, had I reason to suspect a mutiny I would turn back to Wunderland immediately," the Captain answered. "Whatever my own inclinations, I would have no right to carry on in such circumstances, with the Blood of the Riit aboard. But as to the cruise, I signed up to sail under sealed orders, to receive my directions today. All I knew was that we should head north of the ecliptic, and that I have done. I had no other notion of our destination than that. But what do I find, sir? That every member of the crew is better informed than I am. That it is known that we head for the swirl-rift, and in search of treasure. I do not care for searching for treasure at any time, sir. And the rift is exceeding dangerous territory, being infested by pirates. Having accepted the commission, I should have carried it out. But now I discover that every man and kzin on board knew the destination before I did. They have the full coordinates of this star, which is orbited by what they are calling the *treasure planet*. Now I ask you, is that right, Dominant One, sir? Is it proper?" He appealed to Orion and the Judge, having given up on the doctor.

"No, S'maak-Captain," Orion rumbled. "It is neither right nor proper. And I am at fault for having used a factor with neither sense nor discretion. I beg you to forgive me."

We are making progress, I thought. *From what I have read, a generation or so ago, those words would never have passed the mouth of any kzin. But perhaps Orion-Riit found it easier to apologize because of rather than in spite of being a high Noble. In the old days, again from what I had read, kzin discipline had been largely a matter of swinging claws and hot needles.*

"And the crew, Dominant One. I should have had the signing of them, and if I had, I'd not have taken many of those we have, I assure you. It was taken from my hands, Dominant One, which again is most improper."

"So it is, S'maak-Captain," Orion agreed. "And all I can do is to ask you to tolerate a discourtesy which I never intended and which came about because I was not diligent enough to oversee things better. Part of that is inexperience; I suppose I had assumed that everything was being done in a standard and orthodox manner."

"Well, Dominant One, it's as far from being ship-shape and Bristol fashion as could be. It is far from satisfactory, far indeed."

"Would you think it best to turn back and start again?" Orion asked. It struck me then what a great kzin Orion-Riit was. He, who if he wished could speak in the Ultimate Imperative tense reserved for Royalty, could put to another kzin, without giving offense, a question the substance of which, in the mouth of a less-skilled leader, 'Riit' suffix to his name or not, might have provoked a death-duel. And it was as well they had not learned such skills and restraint when they were our enemies, I thought also.

"The Fanged God knows I am sorely tempted, Dominant One. But none shall have reason to call me a coward. I am willing to complete the bargain so long as I have no further interference."

"You may be sure of that, S'maak-Captain," Orion rumbled. "I understand that you are wholly in command and that we are all of us within the grasp of your claws."

"Then why are you here, Dominant One, with all these supernumeraries? You have made me responsible for the safety of yourself and your female kit, both members of the Riit Clan. I do not fear responsibility, but that is a heavy burden. And that young man is not even that." He glared at me as if I was to be his next meal, and pronounced the word 'man' in, well, in a marked manner. "He is entered up as a ship's boy, a servant. What in the thrice damnation of V'irrt is he doing on my bridge?"

"He's my friend," Marthar shouted at him. "And you can be as peppery as you like, and good luck to you, but you'll not stop me from being with my friend."

The Captain scowled at her with distaste, then looked hard at Orion-Riit. "I'm little disposed for parleying, to fit the wit of a chit of a kit, Dominant One, and no ship can function without respect for authority."

I hated the Captain at that, and so did Marthar. And it was a fearful situation, to be standing there with these monstrous kzin quarrelling. Again, I saw them not as intelligent beings with whom we shared a world, but as terrifying aliens who would have reduced us to slaves and prey-animals if they had been able. Most, at one time or another, would have eaten human flesh.

Orion-Riit nodded. "You have a point, S'maak-Captain, and if there is nothing more we shall leave. I have entered up the coordinates of our destination into the *Valiant* just before we came, so I have fulfilled my obligations, I believe."

"I shall confirm that the crew got it right, then, Dominant One," he said with extreme distaste. "And I note that your kit has a tutor who is one of the crew, and presumably has the run of most of the ship in consequence. I'll not have it, lord. Apart from that, there is nothing more. I should be obliged were you all to withdraw." And with that he turned back to his computer, and according to species we all slunk or strode away.

"Well, there's a fine tyrannical oaf, and what do we do about *him*?" the Doctor asked as we returned to our table in the eating area reserved for humans. He started to fire up his pipe. Orion-Riit and Marthar also joined us. I saw the Judge unobtrusively program the robot waiter: while the kzin were present it would bring no offensive monkey food. But perhaps the ship had guessed that anyway.

"He's an honest kzin, I reckon," the Judge said calmly. "I've dealt with many. And his complaints were entirely reasonable."

"What about being rude to Peter?" Marthar demanded.

"Oh, S'maak-Captain's a trifle authoritarian, no doubt, he wants to follow the rules," the Judge said as he lit a cigar. "He is in a difficult position: Captain, but with, as he says, the Blood of the Riit in his charge. From his point of view, Peter should be below with the crew. Them's the rules. The trouble is, you and Peter are bright enough to see that some rules are not appropriate to the situation and should be ignored. You look at the *reasons* for the rules and ask if they make sense in the here and now. But it does cause trouble if you do that, you know. Before you know where you are, stupid people who really ought to follow the rules decide they can break them too. You need to think of precedent, of the danger of setting what might be a dreadful example."

"But we're setting a good example in asking what the point of the rules is, and doing some thinking about them," Marthar argued.

"It's not so easy to follow an example of someone thinking, because most folk don't see the process, only the outcomes," the Judge said drily. "And for you troublemakers, the outcome is frequently chaos."

"It might be simplest if we promote Peter to being a supernumary," Orion-Riit said thoughfully. "I think that in the circumstances it had better be approved by S'maak-Captain. I shall ask *Valiant* to seek his approval immediately." Orion had his phone built into his skull instead of having a thing you had to carry about with you. Marthar was too young to have that, and I could never afford even the oldest and most obsolete; mine was a present from the Riit family. So when Orion went silent you never knew what he was doing; it might be having an argument with the *Valiant* or surfing the web. I was inclined to rule out playing games, except possibly Chess or Go.

"And his intention of banning Silver from venturing out of crew territory?" the Doctor demanded.

"It means that the kits will have to go to him, I suppose," Orion-Riit said. "I don't suppose they'll object to that."

We didn't, of course, although it didn't seem fair that we could go where we liked but Silver could not. Of course, the rotten captain had put a stop to the whole business of studying the ship.

"We'll never be let near the bridge again, that's for sure," I said, with intense gloom. "How are we going to do our assignment for Silver?"

"I don't think it's quite that bad," Orion told us. "You can be given permission to study the general structure of the ship and find out how she works as an organism, all the many feedback loops. There's nothing secret or confidential about that; it's all publicly available knowledge. You can't go near the real bridge, but you can simulate one in the rec-room and test your understanding by working out what you expect to happen when various things go wrong, then try them out to see if you are right. *Valiant* can easily let you have enough computer power for that."

"What I don't understand," the Doctor said, "is how the old bugger could be so rude. I mean, you're Royalty. Shouldn't he show some sort of respect himself?"

"It's because Orion-Riit *is* Royalty, and so is Marthar, that he can't," the Judge explained. "He's in charge of the ship, and he doesn't feel any too secure with his officer, so the last thing he can afford to do is to show any weakness."

"You are right, Judge," Orion-Riit rumbled. "And tolerating lip from a kzinrett kit doesn't go with maintaining his authority either. You got off lightly, child. I think he wanted me to beat you there and then."

"You wouldn't do that, Daddy, would you?" Marthar crept up to her father in mock trepidation. At least, I suppose it was mock. kzin are known to be stern with their offspring by our standards, and even Wunderkzin of Vaemar-Riit's clan are still coming to terms, sometimes painfully, with the whole new factor of intelligent females. It has meant a huge upheaval of ways of thinking.

"Holding you up by your tail and smacking your stern, you mean? Teaching you respect for force and for authority? I suspect it's too late for that. Anyway, I want you to question authority, and I expect others to question yours in due course. Obedience is something I value less than the captain does, I daresay, but you need to understand why he needs it. We travel into danger, and if he insists on running a tight ship, I'll not question him. Nor should you. Your life may depend on obedience one day."

We went to the rec-room later, where we had enjoyed weightlessness so much, and explained to *Valiant* that we wanted to study the ship and please could we have a mock bridge to play with. She was quite happy to do this, and made us one within seconds. It was all fuzz of course, programmable pseudomatter. Not the sort of thing poor people like me had much direct experience with, but basically it's a huge collection of communicating viruses made of non-standard matter. There's lots of it about, and in the natural form it doesn't have mass or interact with normal matter much, but it can be made to simulate mass and you can program it. Well, I can't, but I shall someday. The viruses replicate under command and communicate with each other, so it's a bit like tigripards' spots, once you start, they sort of replicate themselves and fall into a pattern.

So Marthar sat at one computer console and I at another, and we brought up the design of the *Valiant*.

The difference between *Hard* and *Soft* can be summarized in one word: feedback. *Hard* doesn't have any, or hardly any, and *Soft* does. The more complicated the organism, the more feedback. A spaceship is loaded with feedback loops, squillions of them. Plants have about a squillion times as many, and animals a squillion times more than plants. Socioeconomic systems are a squillion squillion times worse than animals of course, because animals, men and kzin among them, are part of these systems. Anyway, there's positive feedback which can be as bad as a snowball sliding down a mountain, getting bigger until its an avalanche; and there's negative feedback, which usually makes things oscillate, like your heart, or a spring bouncing, or the business cycle in economics.

"I hate all these feedback loops, nested six million deep, and half of them positive and half negative so you can never tell what's going to happen when you poke something. It's all so . . . *unhygienic*," Marthar complained. But she started to get the hang of it after a while, although she never admitted to actually enjoying it. Marthar and I make a good team: I provide the intuitions and she explains what is wrong with them, and sometimes she's right.

CHAPTER TEN

We spent the next day working with a simulated *Valiant* and the time just seemed to shoot past. It was interesting, for me at least. We certainly learned a lot. Then we broke for lunch, and shortly after that, Marthar got bored.

"Come on, we've done enough to get the outline. What's the point of being on a real spaceship if you spend all your time playing with a pretend one? Let's go check out the launch bay for the landers. I want to see something real."

We had found the launch bay on the schematics, and knew to go down twenty-two levels. The bay was big; each of the three ships in it was capable of doing exploration of a planetary surface. Of course the entire *Valiant* could be landed, too, but more exploration could be done with the three babies. They were pretty big babies, each capable of holding a crew of twenty kzin or a lot more human beings. And they could be launched from deep space, not just in atmosphere, so they were spaceships in their own right.

The bay was occupied by a dozen kzin doing things to great tubes of wiring which linked the landers to the mother craft. Each of the landers was embraced by a huge mechanical thing that held it upright and fed it through yet more tubes, some as thin as my body and others ten times the size. Occasional vents of something that looked like steam, but was more likely to be liquid nitrogen, squirted into the air. The whole place was huge and noisy.

We wandered around, ignored by everyone else, with the clatter of moving robots, shaped like aircars mostly, but with wheels and tractor treads at the base, and metal arms coming out of the tops. I had never seen the crew at work before, but then, I'd never been anywhere where they might be working so perhaps it wasn't surprising. Long cylinders, bundled onto trucks, were being moved towards the landers. I had no idea what was in them. All this industry was impressive, and made me feel even more ignorant than usual.

"Do you think they'll let us see inside a lander?" Marthar asked optimistically.

"I'd rather we stayed out of the way, or we'll probably get thrown out for being nuisances," I told her. I dodged a small vehicle carting boxes. There was no driver, it was all robotic. Or perhaps *Valiant* herself was driving with a fraction of her brain power.

The huge doors to the vacuum of space were each much bigger than the ships; we could see the seams where they were sealed. Launching one of the landers would mean evacuating the entire room first, pumping the present atmosphere into pressure containers in the walls, and then when the vacuum inside was comparable with that outside, the great doors would slide away, and the small residue of air would fluff out into space. Then the landers would be carted towards the door and pushed outside. You'd never see this part, of course, unless you stayed inside wearing a pressure suit, and you'd have to hang onto something to make sure you didn't get blown outside with the last bit of air. The air was helping to seal the doors, one atmosphere of air over things that size would amount to hundreds of thousands of tons. It would be easy to calculate it; there is a pressure of about a ton on every square meter on anything down on planet. When you find this out, you wonder why we aren't all squashed flat, but the air is inside us as well.

We went over to one of the landers, which was a scarlet color and very shiny. The three landers were different colors, red, blue and green, so they could be individually recognized from a great distance. You might have to watch them from a telescope.

Then from behind a column strode a figure I recognized. The orange-furred kzin who I had seen in the Spy-Glass and who Silver had sent Claws to chase. He recognized me at the same time. There was absolutely no doubt; I'd seen him at the sign of the Spy-Glass, and I'd seen him in Thoma'stown with the rest of K'zarr's men. I froze as he came loping towards us. Marthar looked at me then she looked where I was staring and saw the great kzin. She recognized him too.

Neither of us had any weapons beyond Marthar's *wtsai*, and they wouldn't have been any use if we had. I looked around, hoping that someone was watching, but we were alone at that moment, just us and the mountain of orange fur and fangs coming towards us. There was no doubt in my mind that we would be killed within a minute.

"Help!" I yelled at the top of my voice. I pulled my hand out of my pocket where I'd been fingering my tetrahedron, and I threw it with all my strength, right in the face of the kzin. He fielded it by reflex, and looked at it in puzzlement. For a moment, he stopped.

"It won't do you any good to kill us, the ship knows where we are, and will catch you," I shouted at him. "*Valiant*, we are being attacked!" There was no answer from the ship. I felt for my phone. Zero would get her, surely, even here.

He had a cutlass over his shoulder and pulled it out with a snarl of pleasure. Seven or eight feet of gleaming steel glittered in the glare of lights high overhead. Marthar hadn't moved, she was as helpless as I, but her eyes flickered over the scene. She was planning something, but there was no time.

Then help arrived. It arrived behind the kzin. The first we knew of it was when the kzin dropped his cutlass, then a yard of steel errupted from his chest along with a gout of blood. It squirted all over the floor and spattered us. Killing a kzin warrior takes a bit of doing, but a sword thrust straight through the heart from behind will do it. The orange-furred mountain sagged and fell. Behind him, Silver withdrew his bloody cutlass, carefully wiping it clean on the orange fur.

"Seems t'me ye're really good at findin' trouble, young kits. Now isn't it a good thing ye have a wakeful tutor around ye?"

"Silver, thank you, you saved our lives," I told him. A silly thing to say, given the cooling body with its drawn sword, but I was gabbling.

"Aah, well, glad I am t'be of assistance; this 'ere be that one what Claws chased after but could never find. Well, he's paid for his score now, to be sure. But what be this?"

His eyes were sharp enough, and he bent over and picked up my tetrahedron which his victim had dropped. His speed in bending over made up for any myth that he was old and stiff.

"It's my tetrahedron. It's part of a set."

"Is that so?" Silver looked at it curiously.

"Just a toy Peter plays with. At least it slowed down this orange fur for a moment. Peter threw it at him," Marthar explained.

"Then mayhap it be a lucky tetrahedron," Silver said whimsically, and handed it back to me. I was curiously reluctant to talk about it. It would be hard to explain where I'd got it from without going into details of the whole trip to the treasure planet, and Marthar changed the subject too, as though she felt the same way.

"The robots will clean up the mess," Silver said, giving the corpse a gentle prod with his cutlass. He finished cleaning the weapon on the corpse and slipped it back into its sheath over his shoulder. "Now I think after all that excitement, ye'd do well to take the rest of the day off, get back forrard to office country, and maybe get a bit of studyin' in tomorrow."

Marthar and I went back into the elevator and emerged at our regular meeting place. The others were sitting and talking as if they'd not moved all day. I told them what had happened, and the Judge and Orion-Riit looked at each other. Then I excused myself and went off to bed. It was only mid-afternoon ship's time but I felt drained. I was still spattered with purple blood and needed to wash it off and change my clothes; Marthar had just licked the blood off her fur quite casually. Sometimes the gulf between us seems very wide.

I thought I would toss and turn, but fell asleep within a minute and slept for twelve hours, though I had some awful dreams.

The following morning at breakfast we learned that Arrow had disappeared. It's hard to disappear on a spaceship and so it was all a bit mysterious. Arrow had been every bit as bad as S'maak-Captain had said, being anxious to be liked by the crew, which, I have learned, is bad enough in someone who is supposed to be a leader and an officer, but it was much worse than that. He'd been found drunk on several occasions, staggering as he arrived at the bridge, and the Captain had sent him to his quarters. Had it been a kzin ship of the Patriarch's Navy, the discipline, I guess, would have been considerably more than that (there are still a few old kzin on Wunderland who had been disciplined during the occupation. They walk oddly and painfully, and other kzin try not to notice them). He had spent a lot of time in crew territory, and I suspected that the crew had got him drunk, possibly because they despised him. It's easy to despise someone who courts your favor, and the kzin hated that sort of thing.

But being drunk and disappearing are different matters. Had it happened on an old-fashioned sailing ship, one that sailed on open waters, I mean, it would have come as no surprise. Of course we talk about *sailing* in space because of our history, and the kzin also had sea-faring terms taken from the Jotok, whose technology they had seized long ago (their own culture was too barbaric for them to have got into space on their own). Anyway, how did someone disappear on a spacecraft?

"We all got RFIDs when we stepped on board," the Judge said. "So *Valiant* should be able to locate every one of us at all times. She's programmed to do crowd-control even."

"Have I got an RFID?" I asked.

"On your shoulder. It's sprayed into you along with a few other things to check your medical condition and report it to *Valiant*. I thought you'd been finding out all about her," the Doctor teased.

"Not all, not yet," Marthar said thoughtfully. "When did the RFID on Arrow stop transmitting, and where was he when it happened? And," she added thoughtfully, "in what part of his body was the RFID located?"

"*Valiant* isn't saying, but she asked for anybody who has any information to contact her. And nobody has said anything, which itself is a bit of a worry," the Judge answered. "*Valiant* thinks he must be dead."

"Well, he's no loss," Marthar replied.

"A blaster bolt could have taken kzin and RFID out simultaneously," the Doctor mused. "But if it were that simple, *Valiant* would know where it happened and who else was there at the time, even if it didn't damage the ship. The same applies to all the other ways of disposing of a body. Plenty of devices on the ship which could get rid of both a body and its implants in one hit; you could chop it into bits and feed it into the food system and it would be recycled within minutes, but as soon as the thing stops transmitting, *Valiant* would know when and where. Presumably she does know when it stopped, and where, but I suppose she has some reason for not saying."

"Yeuk. You mean this sausage could have bits of Arrow in it?" I asked, indignant.

"That may be why *Valiant* is being coy," laughed the Judge. I saw from their ears that Marthar and Orion were amused too.

"Doesn't matter to me if he is," Marthar said cheerfully. "Turning him into sausage meat would be an improvement. Although it would probably come out rum-flavored, and this isn't. Nice flavor of *zinyah*, actually." She took another mouthful. I could only hope that if Arrow was food, he was kzin food and not human food.

After breakfast, we worked some more in the rec-room at a simulated *Valiant*. We had lunch after making some painfully slow progress, and then went down to the Spy-Glass, but it was closed; that would be S'maak-Captain's work. But when we knocked, Silver opened the door and squinted down at us. He led us into a small room he called the snug, which seemed to be his, because it had an amazing collection of things in it.

There were a dozen weapons of various sorts: things that looked like *wtsais* but couldn't quite have been, because those were only worn and used by their owners; there were kzin-sized cutlasses in a rack, there were needlers and sabers and a katana, strange-looking knives with big leaf-shaped blades; and what looked like a suit of armor for a kzin, which is to say it looked like space-warrior armor but much older. There was a waste bucket made out of the monstrous foot of some animal that still had the claws on it, and an umbrella stand with an enormous umbrella, or probably a sun-shade, in it. There was a computer with a huge screen and an old-fashioned kzin keyboard with hard metal keys which were horribly scratched. There was what must have been a refrigerator in one corner, and bits of machinery laid out on a table with a pseudomatter programmer next to it. There were chess boards set up, with kzin and human pieces, and a life-sized statue of a human reaching for a banana—at least, I *thought* and *hoped* it was a statue. Marthar and I looked around with interest. We had never seen the like of many of these things before.

"Sit ye down, sit ye down," Silver said, clearing some sort of mechanical device off an old kzin *footch*. Marthar and I sat down on it next to each other, there being plenty of room.

"Now have ye been good an' vartuous an' worked hard for your old tutor? Ha' ye found out much about the *Valiant* an' how she works?"

"We got banned from the bridge proper, and the whole command deck," Marthar told him. "But we got a reasonable simulation going in the rec-room, and we spend hours playing with it. Here's our report, where do you want it?"

"This old computer here will do fine, as I don't like those itsy-bitsy liddle screens you childer use, not havin' young vision like."

I knew perfectly well that Silver's vision was superior to my own, but it seemed to amuse him to play the old dodderer. Marthar pointed her phone at the machine and clicked a claw tip to transmit the file. Silver sat at the console and looked at our report.

"So ye had to start a long way back then, if ye were using complex functions to understand the thing," he said. "There's much more modern ways, but I suppose ye're not ready fer them yet. Still, complex functions are worth knowin' for other reasons, they be wild an' beautiful things, nary a doubt of it. An' can ye explain t' me why that should be the case?"

"Because there's just enough of them," Marthar answered promptly while I was still trying to make sense of the question which was totally unexpected.

"Expound, young kit," Silver squinted at her with his head on one side.

"Well, the fewer functions there are, the more constraints they must satisfy. I mean there's more real functions than the cardinality of the continuum, so we constrain them to be continuous. That reduces the number of them, so what's left must have more power. And every complex function has a power series. So there's even fewer of them." I had tried to read the life of Dimity Carmody once. There had been pages in it like that.

"Well, the fact that it's a proper subset don't mean it has a smaller cardinality, do it now? So I think yer blethering, young miss. An' even if you was right about the number, why should that make them more beautiful? An' what if we was to reduce the set o' them to say the quaternionic functions, or even down to just a single one o' them, would it be even more beautiful still?"

Marthar tried to defend her ideas and got minced. It was fun to watch, but after mincing Marthar, Silver started on me, while Marthar watched and gloated. It was obvious that, despite his manner and his position on the ship, Silver was in his way highly educated. In those great heads, kzin have brains bigger than those of humans.

After a while, Silver started asking more about the *Valiant*. He seemed very interested in her, although he must surely have been able to get the design off the ship herself. I wondered why he hadn't.

"Now I wonders whether we could do all that stuff down here?" Silver mused. "Setting up a mock bridge room, I means, same as ye did in the rec-room. Then ye could play wi' it an' I could watch ye, an' question ye' in real time, d'ye see?"

Marthar considered the matter. "If you've a pseudomatter programmer here, and I see you have, I don't see why not. Why don't you ask *Valiant*?"

"Better if ye do it, I'm thinkin'. Why don't you ask ask her yerself, young missy," Silver answered smoothly, so Marthar did. For some reason *Valiant* wasn't having it.

"But why not?" Marthar protested.

"Captain's policy," *Valiant* answered.

"That creature is a total pest," Marthar said, although if it was said to *Valiant* it didn't get an answer.

"No, no," Silver told her. "No doubt the good Captain 'as his reasons, an' is followin' 'is dooty as a good captain should. Ye'll just have to go back to the rec-room. An' what's the harm in that, I asks ye? 'Twill slow us down a little, but 'tes no great matter."

"Do you have any ideas about what happened to Arrow?" I asked him. "He's disappeared and his RFID isn't responding, which it surely ought to even if he's dead."

"Aargh, that be a great mystery, that be. But there's many mysteries in space, an' recall that we're under hyperdrive, an' who knows, maybe the god's o' hyperspace reached in and took him, an' he's now the other side o' the galaxy." His eyes twinkled, and it was obvious he wasn't serious about mysteries of that order. I told him.

"Now that's where ye're wrong, Peter, lad. Oh, I misdoubt there's any gods o' hyperspace or any others fer that matter. But mysteries there be aplenty. 'Tes far from the first o' impossible things ha' happened in deep space, ye know. Some I've seen wi' these own lamps, I tell ye, an' there's plenty passed on in bars where us spacers gather 'twixt voyages."

And he proceeded to tell us some of them, most of which neither Marthar nor I believed.

That was our first tutorial, and in the weeks that followed, they all went like that, which is to say he made us feel stupid and ignorant half the time and told us tall tales the rest of the time. He gave me a *wtsai* of my own, too, a beautiful thing, much smaller than those carried by the full-grown kzin warriors, but beautifully worked and made, I would guess from the precious stones that adorned it, for some high-ranking kitten. I wondered how he had acquired it.

Sometimes he would lecture us on military psychology, a matter in which he seemed to have some experience.

"'Twas the Third Battle for Ceres," he told us one day. "I'll never forget it. A line of cruisers was coming in, line ahead, in the old style. Looks impressive, but actually tends to reduce the number of weapons you can bring to bear.

The leading ship had expended all her decoys and taken several direct hits aft—she had been venting a cloud of that terrible blood-colored fog into the vacuum. Compartments in that part of the ship were open to space, and everyone aboard in that part was dead unless they had a suit on. But she was keeping her station in the line, and her forrad rail-guns and laser-mountings were still firing as regularly as if she was on an exercise. That's training and discipline for you! I reckon that demoralized the enemy more than if she'd been undamaged."

"What was her name?" Marthar asked.

"I can't pronounce it in Wunderlander," he said, "but I could see her through the range-finder, and I'll not forget the sight."

If it had been a descriptive name, and most on both sides were, he could have found a Wunderlander equivalent easily enough. Wunderlander is very close to the scrambled Earth dialect called Angdeutsch. But he had avoided saying whether the cruiser has been a human or a kzin ship. "Cruiser" was a class designation used by both sides, but more commonly by humans. To have seen the ship by visual sight when the ships were in line ahead strongly suggested that he had been aboard a ship of the opposing fleet, not another in the line behind it, though of course he had perhaps watched it from a slaved drone-camera. Silver was always discreet about what he'd done in the war, but that was understandable, when there were ferocious representatives of both species on board, and when, towards the end, there had been a few telepaths, at least—not that he was anything like a telepath—fighting on the human side. Strange, anyway, to think of him in the uniform of any Navy (Kzin had found uniforms useful and copied them, like talcum powder, blow dryers and toilet paper). We laughed at some of his stories, such as the tale of one old villain of a kzin who, learning long after the war that the monkeys were giving out medals to those who had fought in the siege of Proxima Base, also applied for one, on the grounds that he had also been there, and without him and his pride there would have been no siege and no medals for anyone.

Marthar and I had a row. It started over whether I had said anything sensible to Silver about functions of several complex variables, which is about a million times worse than functions of just one. I said that although I didn't claim to understand it at all really, I thought that there was something in my ideas, I just needed to work out the details.

"No chance of that, usually that's my job."

"Well, that's because you never have ideas of your own," I retorted, and we were off. We finished up shouting at each other. I gather that females have these times when they are totally irrational. My father used to complain about it in my mother, and maybe it happens whatever the species; so I suppose I should have just put up with it nobly, but I didn't feel very noble just then.

Marthar flounced off and left me, probably to have a good sulk, something females of all species do, I expect. So I went back down to the Spy-Glass to talk to Silver, which I thought could be useful. He must know more about kzinretts than I did. Maybe he knew how to manage them when they got mad for no good reason.

When I got there, I knocked on the door and nobody came. Silver must have been out, so I wandered around looking for him. I saw some of the crew loping about on some business of their own, but there was no sign of Silver. I found an empty room with screens and computers; some of the screens showed the other parts of crew territory, but none looked outside the ship, because there was nothing to see. You don't want too look into hyperspace—you don't just go instantly (though temporarily) blind; for a long time you forget how to see. And I'm told that for most kzin it's worse—one reason there hasn't been another war so far, I guess. We were in deep space and under hyperdrive, and hadn't actually got any location in the galaxy. I found a heavy metal door and tried to open it. The handle was meant for kzin, so it was a struggle, but eventually I managed to swing the door open and looked through. A blast of cold air greeted me, and I took a step through.

It was a storage room, if pretty big, bigger than Silver's snug, and there were racks. In fact, I bumped into the first one because it was right next to the door, and as I recovered, the door swung shut behind me. The lights went out, so I fished out my phone and switched the thing on so the screen was bright enough to show me where I was. On the rack were fillets of meat. I realized that I had first got into something like the crew's rec-room, and then into the place where they kept their snacks. For a moment I panicked at the thought that I would freeze to death, locked in to a freezer, but I realized that *Valiant* must know where I was. Even if the metal shielding around me prevented her from receiving my RFID transmissions, she would notice that they had suddenly stopped and where, and could easily figure out where I must be, so I shouldn't have to wait too long. Still, I was glad modern clothes were good insulators, and with the ones we were wearing there were membranes that could be extended to cover hands and head. They could even, in emergencies, be used for a short term as spacesuits. And anyway, one of the crew must be here soon, looking for a snack, and as soon as he opened the door, I would surprise him by popping out. So I stood by the door, waiting to be released. Then I saw, on another rack, a little behind the first one, there was an arm, with dried blood on the floor below it. It was a kzin arm, and furry, although it carried some of the dyed markings that the kzin space-farers used as decoration. And the last time I had seen that arm it had been on first officer Arrow while he was alive. It seemed unlikely that he was alive now.

My brain was working fast and I realized that I was in big trouble. Any crewman finding me here would assume I had seen the body, and the conclusion that the crew had murdered him was forced on me at once. And it had to be a lot of the crew in on the murder, or else they'd have hidden it with some care. And letting me report it would not look like a good idea to the murderers. As these thoughts rushed through my mind, the door opened, the lights came on, and the sound of kzin voices growling at each other came loud and clear. One of them was Silver's.

CHAPTER ELEVEN

A kzin arm came around the side of the door and a huge claw reached just above me. I ducked and the claw stabbed at the rack next to me, missed, tried again and snagged a lump of raw meat and then withdrew. The door started to close, but I stopped it just before it slammed shut. I sure didn't want anybody outside to know I was here, but I didn't want to be left locked in either, so I put a foot in the way just as short of closing as could be. The voices were still audible, but the speech was in the Heroes' tongue, and my understanding was not too good. I fished out my phone, set it to translate into text, and with mounting horror, read what came out.

"No, no, not I," said Silver. "K'zarr was cap'n then, I was quarter-master. Metal leg and all. Not a very modern job, is it? Went in a broadside at Ceres Castle. Missile came through the wall like a *wtsai* through a man-child, and battle armor meant nothing; slivers o' silicon everywhere. I was lucky to keep my head; 'twere shielded by a gantry and a counter-missile. That was Raarkar's Heroes, that was, and served us right for changin' the ship's name—*Spear in the Gut* should ha' stayed, and K'zarr's old ship *Warrior Beast* should never ha' been changed to *Black Flying Predator*. 'Twas ill luck came o' it then and more later. I seen the old *Warrior Beast* amuck wi' the blood o' Heroes from stem t' stern, mind you, but never so many died as arterwards,"

"Ah," another voice growled in admiration. "He were the greatest of them all, were K'zarr. No Hero to match him, not from the Patriarch on down."

"D'vor Argh were a true Hero too, so 'tis said, though I ne'er sailed with him," Silver said. "First wi' Raarkar kzin, then wi' K'zarr, that's my story; and here now on my own account, in a manner o' speakin'. An' it comes from bein' a savin' kind o' kzin, for I laid a million stars by from Raarkar an' twice as many from K'zarr. All safe in a few banks, an' earnin' money from the humans. Not like most o' Raarkar's Heroes. Where are they now? And where's K'zarr's? Most o' them on board here and glad to get a berth, that's the truth of it. An' look at how they lived! They was like old Gra-Prompyh, who lived like a lord for years wi' no trace o' sense, even wi'out his eyes what he left behind on this here treasure planet so-called; until 'e got broke an' had to go back to beggin'. Well, 'e's dead now, and wi' the Fanged God or the Mist Demons, but not long before 'e was starving, so he was, an' cuttin' throats o' human outlaws for a livin'."

"It ain't much use then, unless you're in it for the glory and the danger," another voice broke in.

"'Tain't no use if yer a fool, and you may lay to that," Silver growled. "But yer young, and yer smart, so iff ye'll listen t' those who done well, ye'll do well too, see if it ain't so. There are plenty of fools, 'tes true.

"I was at the Third Battle of Ceres, you know, what we call G'rnazzh-Ra, aboard Kzarr's ship. *At* it, I say, not *in* it. We left the war to fools. We hung around in deep space, watching the *Vengeful Slashers* go in against the *Darts,* and when it was over helping ourselves to pickings among the wreckage. Heroes and monkeys had left salvageable loot—monopoles and such—in a spiral stretching out past the cold gas-planet the humans call Neptune, and that little rock-ball they call Pluto. Ho, those were sweet times!

"I remember we boarded the human hospital ship—it was damaged and couldn't flee. Loaded with medical radioactives. That's where I got these—the monkey admiral's and the Chief Medical manrett's ears! I don't show 'em to everyone, of course. No sense in risking them being analyzed and recognized. And then there are these . . ."

"But those are . . . Heroes' ears! With admiral's tattoos!"

"Aye, and quite a fight he put up to keep them! But his ship was a wreck, and we cut the air supply lines to the last compartments where the survivors of the crew were holed up. We caught a telepath, and made him scramble their brains with his screaming. See! I have the Captain's ears as well! The Captain would have served us as we served him—as our precious Captain here would serve us now if he knew what was what!

"How we laughed when we heard the monkeys and the Heroes had both put prices on our heads, in between killing each other!

"There was another thing, too. The humans had adapted

some of their geriatric drugs to work on kzin and keep them young—to use on telepath traitors, I guess, since they were rare and valuable. We captured a slashing great load of them from the hospital ship. They've kept me and a few of the other free-booters young—for I'm older than I look.

"But K'zarr, his liver was a cool one! He had us search the wreckage and all the dead ships for computer parts, especially memory-storage bricks. Some of them were worthless, but some contained battle codes and such like. Do ye know what he did? When we had taken a few things away from certain prisoners to leave them harmless but leaving enough so that they were still alive, he dispatched them with messages to both high commands, offering to sell the codes and everything else to the highest bidder! No narrow-mindedness about old K'zarr, no species prejudice when there were monopoles and crystals to be had—not to mention geriatric drugs and kzinretti and telepaths—they were all included in the price we charged the Patriarch's armed forces."

"And they paid?"

"Aye, they paid. What choice did they have? Chuut-Riit, now, when he heard about it, swore vengeance to the death and to the generations. But he paid. He had to kill a couple of so-called Nobles who said *No dealing with pirates*, and I gather some humans felt likewise. Well. Chuut-Riit's gone to the Fanged God now, and his grandson is aboard this ship, suspecting nothing, because his Sire is a monkey-pet . . . Aye, I remember after Ceres how the crippled human ships limped back towards *Earth*, crying for help. 'Lame ducks' the humans called them, and sent out ships to assist them. But often enough we had heard their squawking and got there first . . . They didn't like dealing with us to buy the codes we had captured, none of them did, but what could they do? Both sides had to keep it secret that they were dealing with us. And we had mounted a fine array of battle-lasers and rail-guns by then. Chuut-Riit wouldn't have lasted so long in his high and mighty palace if the word got about that he, the Patriarch's nephew his own self, couldn't even catch a horde of free-booting Heroes. The monkeys, too, were having trouble enough maintaining morale. They were losing the war before they got the hyperdrive.

"Never forget the free-booter's great ally—the fact that space is *big*. And the hyperdrive has made it bigger yet. Oh, some called it a disaster for us when man got the hyperdrive. But some of us knew it for an opportunity. We knew then that we'd get it too, sooner or later. One reason we had never researched beyond the gravity-planer was because our theories said nothing could break the light barrier. But once it had been proved others had different theories . . . Now there are plenty of worlds on which to hide. Plenty of bored, landless Heroes we can use to carry out our commissions, and launder our money, as the humans say, when we have the wealth to pay. A fine game it can be. Could be a great start for a smart young Hero like you. End up with your own Name that none dare challenge, some planet far away from the monkeys and the Patriarchy both, with your own harem of kzinretti and hunting preserves, and a couple of ear-rings full of ears . . ."

I felt sick at heart to hear Silver use almost the same sort of flattery on a piratical thug as he had used on me. I think

I'd have killed him if I could. Not knowing he was overheard he ran on:

"Skel showed a bit o' sense, though not enough, an' he's gone to where they don't come back. Now, here it is about kzin warriors o' fortune: we lives rough, and we risk death and worse, but we eats and drinks like lords, we face danger like Heroes and defy it, and when a cruise is done, why, we ha' hundreds o' thousands o' stars in our pouches instead of a weekly wage of tens if we're lucky. Now the most goes on rum and a few kzinretti, and then it's back into space. But that's not my course. I puts it away, some here an' some there and none too much anywheres, by reason of suspicion. And once I get back from this cruise I'll set up as a lordling in earnest."

There was a silence broken only by the sound of eating.

"Let me tell you how I became a free-booter," said Silver. "My Sire's Sire was a junior officer of the Patriarch's Navy. The very first reports of contacts with humans were starting to come in. My Grand-Sire was in a cruiser, the *Hunter's Moon* (the really good names were reserved for capital ships, of course). They were quite near the *Ka'ashi* system. There was the asteroid belt—what the humans call the Serpent Swarm.

"They detected a human mining operation of one of the bigger asteroids. The telepath reported an intelligent, cooperative, space-faring race, devoted wholly to peace—not a weapon among them apart from kitchen knives. All the promise of a prize to set up every member of the crew for life, plus Names from the Patriarch hisself. Nothing remarkable about that, we had detected and conquered such races in space before.

"Indeed, except for us, and the Jotok so foolishly recruiting and training us, it seemed a necessary condition for achieving spaceflight. To make it even better, the telepath reported they had mined large stockpiles of ores, and also monopoles. Saved the Heroes the trouble.

"The *Hunter's Moon* carried two frigates. They landed, with the usual infantry contingents aboard. The human mines and living quarters were under bubble domes. One of the frigates had damaged its take-off and landing gear, and my Grand-Sire was ordered to remain with it and commence repairs if he could, him being a good engineer. The rest attacked the humans.

"Grand-Sire heard what happened over the comlink. Most of the humans were killed, those who had got into spacesuits ran screaming out onto the surface. They had never even seen kzin before—thought they were the only species travelling in space. The Heroes let them go. There was nowhere for them to run. They had a ship, of course, but judging from its size it was only a small shuttle used to communicate periodically with a bigger carrier. They would die on the surface when their oxygen gave out.

"Suddenly, the radio went mad, and died. Grand-Sire saw the human ship taking off, burning a drive like a torch. Then it passed over the second frigate and destroyed it with its exhaust flame. It headed straight for the *Hunter's Moon*, that was all unsuspecting, and rammed it! Ever seen two spaceships collide? I have. It's something to see. Lit up the whole sky like a supernova for a moment.

"Grand-Sire's frigate was still immobile. He got suited up and ran to the bubble dome. Dead monkeys and dead Heroes everywhere. He found the Captain, still just alive.

He had his spacesuit on and that had saved him when the dome opened to vacuum. Before he died, he told Grand-Sire what had happened.

"After the weed-eaters had fled, the Heroes had been making an inventory of the loot. They had not bothered to set a guard against the weed-eaters. What was the need?

"Then the humans had counter-attacked. They had cutting torches, signal lasers dialed up, mining tools, *everything* they had they used as weapons. They were already beaten and they *counterattacked*—the captain kept saying that, over and over as he died, as if he couldn't believe it. Then the surviving humans took their ship, destroyed one frigate and then the *Hunter's Moon*. I guess they reckoned they had no time to get the other frigate before the *Hunter's Moon* deployed its weapons. They only achieved what they did there because most of the crew had been landed, and because of surprise . . . utter surprise.

"Grand-Sire was alone on that asteroid for several weeks, with just the corpses of monkeys and Heroes for company and food, repairing the frigate for takeoff. Then he flew it single-handed to where the fleet was gathering. And the first chance he got, he deserted.

"He had had plenty of time to think. Why had the telepath reported a weaponless, pacifist race? And he hit on the right answer, though others would not believe him and nearly dueled him over it: the monkeys had suppressed their warlike nature deliberately because, freed of inhibitions, they were *too* savage and warlike. He had found a religious shrine where they had worshipped on the asteroid, and it was dominated by what looked like a stylized sword. Later he found he was wrong, it wasn't a sword but an instrument of torture, a *crucifix*, but he'd been following the right spoor. Anyway, he alone guessed that the kzin species was going to be in for the fight of its life, and it would be better to be a live free-booter than a dead Hero. He joined Gutfoot's Horde, lurking beyond the outliers of the fleet, and started a family tradition.

"And what's the lesson of this: leave nothing to chance, never underestimate your enemy. If they had posted sentries at the bubble-domes, the humans would never have lived to bring their weapons to bear. Never stop thinking."

"Thinkin' is all very well, but how are ye to get yer claws in your money again?" another voice growled. "Ye'll never dare visit *Ka'ashi* ever more, I'm sure of it. An' what if ye run into some old comrades what didn't do so well?"

"Ha," said Silver, "we shall move in different worlds in more senses than one, though to be sure *Ka'ashi* is a whole planet. Who knew we had landed there, until we chose to show ourselves? But we don't need it. Like I said, thanks to the hyperdrive there are plenty of worlds—kzin worlds—that we can set ourselves up on.

"An' there's another thing. There was those as feared Gra-Prompyh, and those who feared Skel, and more who feared K'zarr. But K'zarr hisself was feared of me, an' good sense he showed there, ye may lay to it. And K'zarr's crew was the roughest crew in space, be sure of it, and the demons in hell would ha' feared to sail wi' K'zarr. But when I was quartermaster, they was *lambs*, they was. No, ye be safe in any ship I run, be sure of it. Ye see I've done well. So can you."

"Well, Master Silver, I had me doubts about this venture

when ye first broached it, but now I'll take yer arm in my claws and you do the same to me, and we'll seal it with the drop o' blood."

"And a brave, smart kzin ye be, and a finer figure for a warrior o' fortune I never did see."

I realized I had been overhearing the corruption of one of the few loyal kzin on board, maybe the last of them. But another kzin came in to the room.

"Vaarth is square," Silver said to the newcomer.

"Ah, I knowed Vaarth was square," came the voice of Claws. "Vaarth is no fool. But lookee here, Silver, what I want to know is how long afore we take the ship? I've had it to here wi' S'maak-Captain. I want to feel my *wtsai* turn in his belly and see his eyes go glazed over an' that black tongue of his coming out."

"Claws, ye've a deal o' courage, but yer head is of no account whatever, and never was. Now hear what I say. Any time ye can report to the Captain's bridge, ye take it, and ye keep a weather eye out for all ye can see. I needs t' know all I can 'bout the *Valiant*. So ye'll stay sober and respectful fer as long as I tell ye, d'ye hear?"

"Well I don't say no, do I? What I say is: when?"

"The last possible minute I can manage it, that's when," Silver told him. "We got a first-rate spacer takin' us where we want t'go, and if 'twere up to me, I'd have him bring us halfway back too. No, when we make planetfall is the right time. That's when we take out the first-class passengers. Those cursed kits ha' the run o' the ship, they's even got K'zarr's memo pad data in they's phones, demons take them. When we are neatly parked next t' the treasure, when the Doctor and the Lord Orion and the Judge have made their choices of the most valuable bits, that's when we strike, d'ye hear me?"

"Allright, Silver, I know's ye got a good head on yer. But how are we gunna take over the ship? And how d'ye know for sure she's not listenin' to us this very minute?"

"Oh she is, she is, but she's hearing something different from what we're saying, Claws, and ye may lay to that. Disgustin' breach o' regulations it is too, there's privacy laws on *Earth* that ban placin' microphones in secret, but *Valiant* had them installed under directions from the captain. Shockin' lack o' trust, and illegal too on *Earth*, but *Ka'ashi* is where she's registered, and *Ka'ashi* don't ha' so many human laws yet."

"Well, ye're the Hero wi' a head on yer, nary a doubt," Claws growled. "But how are we to take a ship? She'll ha' many defenses, no doubt."

"Ye don't doubt I ha' a plan for that too, d'ye?"

"No, Silver, but I'm impatient, d'ye see."

"So ye are, like all fools at all times!" Silver's voice rose in a snarl. "Ye'd be drunk even now were it to you. I don't know why I'm fool enough to sail wi' ye and the other *sthondats*."

"Easy all, Silver, who's a crossin' ye?" Claws sounded fearful.

"An' how many great ships have I seen taken? An' how many brisk Heroes drying in the sun, and spoutin' blood into hard vacuum, watching it freeze into scarlet icicles as it went? And all for this same hurry, when a little patience would ha' saved them. Too much rum, when a little o' water and blood would ha' done better."

"Aah, ye've the manner of a priest on ye, Silver, what's

wrong wi' a little relaxation betimes? There's others could hack a program as well as ye who had the time for some diversions."

"And where are they now, Claws? Tell me that. Gra-Prompyh could do that, and Skel. But where are they? Gone to the Death Demons, that's where. And K'zarr, he were a Hero of Heroes. But where's K'zarr now?"

The younger kzin's voice, Vaarth, broke in: "When we do lay them athwart, those passengers, what d'we do wi' them?"

"Ah, there's the kzin wi' a sharp mind to cut to the bone o' things!" Silver said admiringly. "What would ye think then? Do we leave them alive on the planet maybe wi' a little food and drink? That would ha' been the way of it under Raarkar kzin. Or do we cut them down? That would ha' been what K'zarr did, or Skel."

"Skel was the hero fer that," said Claws. "If ever a sharp set o' fangs came to port, 'twere old Skel."

"Right you are," said Silver. "Sharp and ready. But I'm a lordling, so what say I? Well, says I, dooty is dooty, mates. I give my vote: death. When I'm a lordling for real, I don't want some lawyer t' come calling, no, nor the human ARM, nor the Patriarch's forces neither, nor that *kz'zeerkt*-loving Vaemar that calls himself Riit and the little army the monkeys allow him. 'Wait' is what I says, but when we've done waiting, why, let the flesh rip!"

"Ye're a true warrior, Silver," Claws rumbled.

"Ye will say so when the time comes. But I make one claim, that is to the Lord Orion. I wants t' take him apart meself. Ye can ha' the Captain an' Vaarth can ha' the Doctor and the Judge and the kits for his pleasure, but I wants the Lord Orion fer meself," Silver purred at the thought, as did Vaarth. I trembled in horror.

"Ye're sure that we can take over the ship, Silver?" Claws asked.

"Wi' a little help from those kits, indeed I can. And no trouble they'll be, I promise ye."

"But ye're banned from the bridge, Captain's orders."

"What will his orders be worth when he's dead?" Silver asked. "To be sure, it's an inconvenience. But I ha' me own little sensors installed on the bridge, thanks to Arrow, before he became a risk in consequence. Well, he's gone. Most of him. Still a wee bit left in the meat-locker, I believe, ha! An' the door's not fully closed, push it to, or he'll rot afore we gets to finish him."

The door was pushed against me and locked me in again. I could hear nothing. I tried to phone Marthar, but nothing worked inside the locker, it was all metal and shielded. And the lights were out.

I was frantic that a crew-kzin would come in and find me before *Valiant* noticed I had gone missing. So when the door started to open, I hid behind a meat-rack, although the intruder would almost certainly have caught my scent. If nothing else, I probably stank of cigar-smoke from the Judge or pipe-smoke from the Doctor. A familiar face peered in.

"Peter, come out. We've only got a few minutes before *Valiant* will have to release them. They're on a practice drill of some sort." Marthar was friendly again, which meant more to me than the actual words for a moment. I stumbled out into her arms. She picked me up, threw me over a shoulder and ran from the empty room, pushing the door of the meat-locker closed behind her. We shot out, far faster than I could go on my own, and didn't stop until we were in the elevator heading up. Then she put me down and I turned to face her. I hugged her around her middle.

"Thanks, Marthar. I'm sorry we quarreled." I looked up at her.

"Silly, you can't think I'd worry about what a monkey says, can you? Anyway, it's *Valiant* you should thank. She keeps us all covered, full time after Arrow disappeared, and when you vanished suddenly she started me off to let you out. She guessed what had happened from what she knew of where you were and where the meat-locker is, and sent me off. Then she stopped me. I was going down in the lift and she stopped it, and then explained why by showing me the translation she was picking up from your phone. She decided that it would be better to collect as much data as possible. So now everyone knows all about it. Except the crew, I hope."

I sighed with relief. "Well I'm glad I don't have to remember it all and tell people, they'd never believe me. Are we going to keep it a secret from the crew? I don't think I could ever look at Silver the same way again, and I expect he'd notice."

"I'm sure he would. The likes of Silver live by noticing how beings look at them. But we'll be making planetfall soon, and I guess lessons are suspended until after we're down. And then at least we're forewarned about what to expect."

"But how are we going to manage? We can't lock them

all up, there isn't room, and anyway, how would we run the ship?"

"I don't know. But Daddy and the Judge will figure out something. I don't know about the Doctor, I think he's still in shock. He liked Silver."

"So did I. Or at least, I liked the Hero I thought he was."

"He makes me ashamed of my kind."

When Rarrgh-Hero and the Judge had been talking together, I had heard the Judge address him as "You old villain" or "You old *teufel*." That had plainly been said with affection, as Marthar sometimes called me "chimpy." But there was no trace of affection in my feelings for Silver now.

Marthar ran her claws through my hair very gently as if she was combing it. "I suppose he's a mixture like all of us. He's learned how to *look* civilized, but doesn't want to *be* civilized. I can relate to that."

I didn't understand what she meant at the time, but later I did.

CHAPTER TWELVE

When we got out of the elevator we found everyone waiting for us at the usual table. Everyone means the Judge, Doctor Lemoine, Orion-Riit and S'maak-Captain, who was sitting stiffly at the end of the table, unsure of the social niceties of sharing a table with Orion and the humans. It also turned out that there was an invisible being present, *Valiant*, herself.

"Over here, kits," Orion commanded, and pushed out seats for us, a small one for me and a bigger one for Marthar.

We sat down and I opened my mouth to speak until the Judge stopped me.

"*Valiant*, can we be sure we are competely isolated here? It occurs to me that we may be bugged."

"No information released in this meeting will travel beyond those present," *Valiant* answered. The voice sounded as if she were somewhere on the table. "Peter is carrying a recording device which would have revealed the events following his entering the meat-locker when it was quizzed. I shall delete the relevant passages now. The device is presently inoperative."

So that unspeakable swine had taken advantage of me to listen in on everything I discussed with Marthar. I hated the wicked devil. That was private, he had no right to do anything so slimy.

"Can you destroy the thing now, *Valiant*?" Marthar asked the ship. She was clearly every bit as angry as I was.

"Not so fast, we may be able to use it for misinformation," her father stopped her. "Think, child, don't just react." She growled, but accepted the idea. Her eyes gleamed as she started thinking about how to get her own revenge on Silver by deceiving him. This was now warfare, and deception was a part of warfare that kzin could be very good at. They learned it from us.

"You have all seen the transcript of what I overheard when I was in the meat-locker?" I asked.

"And heard the original," Orion said. "The translation got the rough ideas right. There were nuances concerning you two which I'll not expand upon. Just kill the turncoat Vaarth as soon as you get a chance, so you do so undetected."

"Well, S'maak-Captain, you were right and I was wrong, and I apologize to you for it," Doctor Lemoine said. "It looks as if we're in a pretty pickle, which would have been even worse but for your relocating the weapons. The question is, what do we do? Since you have been right so far, you should give us your orders, sir."

S'maak looked at Orion, who nodded. "My lord, men, we have but one advantage, perhaps two. The obvious one is that we know their plans and they don't know we know.

The only other advantage we have is the ship, *Valiant*, which is now in a position to defend herself better against whatever hell those pirates plan. Tactically, the sooner we take out Silver, the better. He is clearly the only one of them with brains, and I would advise assassinating him immediately. With those brains blown over the floor, the rest will fold."

"That's making us as bad as them," Doctor Lemoine protested. S'maak just looked at him and said nothing. I was of two minds. Just killing Silver seemed cowardly. It would presumably be done by *Valiant*, remotely, using one of the myriad of ship weapons I knew she had. She could send out a flying dart, hunt down Silver and get it into his head before exploding the thing. There were other, even more horrible things she could do. A cloud of pirana-nanobots could hit him in mid-stride and leave his pink bones tumbling to the deck. He could be spaced, he could wind up in the food supply, or he could be used to provide raw material for the kzin autodocs. It made me sick to think of it.

"No, it isn't, Doctor," Marthar objected. "I don't know how you can say that. I know you humans are prone to sqeamishness, but saying there's a moral equivalence between taking out a murderous menace to decent creatures and taking out the creatures themselves is really, really stupid. There's no such equivalence. It's like saying that cutting out a cancer is every bit as bad as the cancer growing and killing off healthy cells. Speaking as a healthy cell and a decent legal entity, I say wipe him out. And take Vaarth and Claws out at the same time. Show them who's in charge. Sometimes"—she turned to the humans—"our kzin honor is mistaken for mercy. Let there be no opportunity for such a mistake now."

"I must say, the logic of the situation seems unassailable. Also, I own to a feeling that it is cowardly to kill him so," Orion said in his deep voice. "I would prefer to kill him myself. Also, he is the one at present holding the others back."

"Killing him would alert the crew to the fact that we know their plans, Dominant One," S'maak objected. "Of course it would be out of the question for you to fight him. It would do him far too much honor to die under your *wtsai*. I should face him myself if I thought him worthy of my own *wtsai*, but I do not. My opinion is that he and most of the crew are scum and do not deserve even the combat pits. I would put them down as animals not worthy of the hunt. I would grant them no Fighters' Privileges."

Doctor Lemoine set his face obstinately. He didn't like being outargued by a kzinrett child, and he had seen the flicker of approval on S'maak-Captain's face when Marthar had spoken. The Captain might have been rearranging his opinions about the wit of a chit of a kit.

"You are in command, S'maak-Captain," the Judge put in. "Even the good Doctor acknowledges that, and if you decide to simply destroy Silver, I doubt anyone here would dispute your right to do so. Yet it is a dreadful waste; I hate to see an intelligent being destroyed so cavalierly. Time was when I myself might have been judged guilty and disposed of in just such a manner, but for fortune and Rarrgh-Hero, who had a sense of honor as deep as a well."

"Suppose we destroy Silver," the Doctor argued. "Are we then to trust the rest of the scum to take us home? Who will arise as leader in his place? We do not know, and better the *teufel* you know than one you do not," he pointed out. "I daresay we shall be running without a full complement whatever happens. We can't just destroy the lot, we need them."

There was a silence while everyone chewed on this.

"Well, Sire, I need orders," S'maak-Captain said eventually, turning to Orion. "Do we put down on this planet? Do we kill Silver and others before or afterwards? If necessary, we could return home with a skeleton crew, providing we do not land. If we land we shall need the crew to cooperate, and also when we lift. If we could be sure they would not strike before we are ready, we could get back into space first and then take out the half of them. *Valiant* could get us back to Alpha Centauri under those conditions, is that not so?"

"True, S'maak-Captain," *Valiant* answered smoothly. "We would need assistance at the end of the journey, but a parking orbit would present no great problems. The bigger problem is what plans Silver has for corrupting my programming. There must be some such plan, and it is imperative to stop him before he implements it. If I monitor him carefully, I should be able to identify the precise threat before it can be put into effect. It would be harder if he were to be disposed of, some of his lieutenants might be willing to proceed with the plan, and I might not identify the threat until it is too late."

"Have you any ideas of what such a plan might be?" the Judge asked.

"It must involve replacing a substantial part of the command chips. They are not easy to get to, and I have strengthened my defenses in all the ways I could devise. But organic life makes for some creative solutions which do not yield to easy analysis," *Valiant* admitted.

"It seems clear that if Silver must be murdered, then it should not be until we have landed, or until we have decided to return home without landing," the Doctor said.

"Not *murdered,* Doctor. The word you want is *executed,*" Marthar corrected him sweetly. "But we mustn't just give up now we're practically within sight of the treasure. Of course we land. Then we take out Silver and a few others. Then we explain what is going to happen to any of the rest of them if they misbehave." She turned to S'maak. "S'maak-Captain, I apologize for being rude to you the last time we met. You have more sense than anyone else here, including Daddy. You see things straight and you see them clear."

S'maak-Captain looked at her, and there might have been a faint flicker of amusement in one of his ears.

"I do not like giving up before we land, any more than my impulsive daughter," Orion growled. "I agree that we should land. And that we should strike the pirates before they can strike us. Enough to cow them, though Kzin are not easily cowed. *Valiant*, I would think it a prudent move to have some sort of back-up made of your present identity, and give copies to us and instructions for restoring you, should you be subverted."

Valiant answered. "Done, my lord. The ship application on your phones now contains the present state of my linguistic knowledge together with instructions for restoring me should I fall to the enemy. I have also set up some subsidiary identities with which you may communicate to assist you."

"Then I have your orders to land on the planet, my lord? And then to take such action with Silver as I deem appropriate after we have landed?"

"Yes, S'maak-Captain. And I thank you for your devotion to duty. My Sire shall get my recommendation of your ability and character when we return. As we shall, one way or another!" Orion-Riit turned to me. "Peter, what you did in the meat-locker was also most commendable. You showed courage and resource. I see why my daughter counts you as a friend."

I blushed. I didn't think I had done anything brave or clever, in fact I had been competely deceived by Silver, which was foolish. Still, even Marthar had been fooled by him, so maybe I was not an utter idiot.

We came out of hyperdrive and, after a relatively short (but for me, and I am sure for the other human leaders, dreadfully tense) passage through the system, prepared to land on the planet. The landing site was to be close to the tower that had been featured in K'zarr's notebook which we had got from Skel. We had its precise coordinates relative to the planet as well as the galactic coordinates of the lime-green sun, so it was fairly straightforward to identify the place. There was only a handful of planets of any size, although there were several rings of asteroids right out to something like Sol's Kuiper belt. I wish we had seen more of the system when we had emerged from hyperspace, but we had been too busy, with Marthar and *Valiant*. Fortunately, Silver had been kept busy and we hadn't seen him.

I talked to Marthar about what it would be like when we

landed. We, or at least I, would need some sort of protection from the world, which had a rather thin atmosphere, although the pirates of K'zarr's band had survived well enough, it seemed. Marthar explained to me that they might well have been wearing some sort of protection, it was very light and skin-tight and unobtrusive these days, and we would have to get them constructed for us, but *Valiant* could do that. First *Valiant* would have to analyze the environment by sending out probes to measure everything from radiation levels to oxygen pressure, along with every other gas and particle in the vicinity, in case there were poisonous gases or phages. This was standard operating procedure when making planetfall, not to mention measuring things from space to make sure the surface actually had the structural strength to support the ship. Although the gravity-planer technology helped there: The *Valiant* could be pretty close to weightless if she chose.

When we broke up, Marthar and I went off together with the same objective. We wanted to look at the information in the updated ship app; we wanted to know how to restore *Valiant* if she got corrupted. It was as well we did.

PART THREE
THE PLANET-FALL ADVENTURE

CHAPTER THIRTEEN

The planet was named *Garth* in the human astronomical catalogues, and the green sun was called *Vanity*. Garth was quasi-sun-locked, evidence of an old solar system, first generation. The planet took about two-thirds of a year to rotate, so the same side was shown to the sun for much of the time. Mercury and Venus do something similar around Sol. The tower we wanted was not directly under the sun, but in the daylight side, about a quarter of the way around the planet from the sub-solar point, and from orbit it flashed away pretty quickly. S'maak-Captain ordered us into L1, the first Lagrange point. This was between the sun and the planet, and of course as it is only stable in the plane perpendicular to the line joining planet to sun, it is not really stable, unlike L4 and L5, two of the other five Lagrange points, but it would do for the short time *Valiant* would be there. It is relatively close to the planet, so it was possible to see the place close up, at least through telescopes, including the lines of canals and the many, mostly heavily-eroded meteor craters.

A first-generation sun has no heavy metals in it, so the planet Garth, although a fair size—bigger than Earth—had less gravity than Wunderland, and had lost some of its atmosphere over time in consequence. It could not have developed intelligent life, I thought; certainly not space-travelling life, because you can't even have an iron age without iron, and there wouldn't be any, but hundreds of millions of years ago it might have had oceans and been warm enough to have evolved some lifeforms. And it might have looked like a dream planet to another species. The sun wasn't very bright, and Garth was fairly close to it; the year was about half as long as Wunderland's. All my knowledge of other worlds up to now was based on reading about them and watching documentaries at school, which I'd always loved, but of course it isn't at all the same as being there. There were the new game rooms in Munchen, where you could play in a simulator, but my family was too poor to go there often. Anyway, you'd be bound to know it wasn't real.

The crew were in a very bad mood as we moved slowly into L1. *Valiant* showed us some of them, and there were growls aplenty. Even the crew we thought still loyal were less than anxious to respond to S'maak-Captain's orders. In fact, the best and most agreeable of them was Silver, who, when he got an order relayed by *Valiant*, would salute the invisible voice and call "Aye, aye ma'am" and set about the task with energy. The general air of tension was palpable. I suppose that most of the bad ones were like Claws: wondering why they hadn't had a mutiny yet, and impatient for it. The bad feeling seemed to spread to the whole crew.

"This doesn't look good, S'maak-Captain," the Doctor observed. "They are almost ready to blow."

"I observe that, sir," S'maak-Captain said stiffly. He was never comfortable talking to the humans. "And I also observe that Silver is our ally just at present; he too is trying to keep them under control and would do so better had he the opportunity. I propose to give it to him."

S'maak-Captain ordered over the public address system that some of the crew would go down to the surface in landing craft to take some more measurements of the stability of the ground near the site. I have a suspicion that he had actually decided not to put the *Valiant* down at all, but to handle everything with the small landing craft. That would stop us loading any very big treasure but allow an easier job of leaving with a reduced crew.

The announcement cheered the crew, many of whom seemed to be under the impression that the surface was full of treasure and they'd find handfuls of valuables as soon as they stepped out. There were to be two landing craft: the scarlet one led by Silver and a green one led by the human couple, Sam Anderson and his wife, Ursula. It looked as though there would be about twelve beings in each boat, which would leave something like the same number of crew back on *Valiant*, and of course us as well. In fact, it rather looked as though the strategy was to keep us all on board *Valiant* until the strike against the crew was made, and Silver was safely dead. When we worked this out, Marthar and I looked at each other. We were in the rec-room watching everything happen on screens, and trying out our surface gear in a simulated planet landing. The air in the rec-room was a good indication of what it was like on the surface; the temperature was pretty much the same as at the contact point, and we had no trouble breathing or staying warm with the micro-packs we wore. Drones had already gone down and relayed information back, and Marthar and I had realized at the same time that there was some sort of segregation going on and we were on the losing end.

"Come on, Peter. I refuse to stay here when man and kzin are going down to the surface. I want to go too. Let's stow away. There's plenty of space. And we've got all the landing gear, we can go out on the real surface instead of this pretend one."

I looked around. The rec-room was doing a pretty good simulation and the view stretched into the distance, even if it was all faked. We could clearly see the broken tower we had visited on the memo pad, and the sun high in the fake sky. There was more vegetation around than I had remembered; maybe it was a different season, although what seasons were like here didn't bear thinking about. When the landers returned images from the surface, the rec-room simulation could be made practically identical to the actual surface, but it was a sight safer here since we could switch off the simulation any time we wanted. However, there was no point in even trying this argument on Marthar.

"*Valiant* will know, she knows everything," I pointed out.

"Unless it's going to cause damage, she can't stop us," Marthar said optimistically.

"I want to go in with the Andersons' lander," I told her. "I can't stand the thought of being anywhere near Silver."

"No, it might not be altogether advisable," Marthar said

thoughtfully. I don't know if she'd guessed S'maak-Captain's plan, but it wouldn't surprise me; they had similar minds. I found out just how similar later. Considering Marthar's subconscious, or wherever the ideas came from, it's amazing how nice and kind her conscious can be. Sometimes.

"Come on, then, I have the map to get us to the lander bay, and if we're quick we can sneak in before the rest get there. Bring your *wtsai*, the one Silver gave you; we may have to hunt." Strange, I had got so used to thinking of Marthar simply as a friend. I had almost forgotten she was a kzin until I heard her pronounce the word correctly.

We managed it rather well, we thought at the time, and without a murmur from *Valiant*. This was because Silver had the same sort of mind as Marthar and S'maak-Captain and had also worked out the likely consequences of going down to the surface. So Silver struck first, and we never knew until later.

We thought we'd hidden very cleverly, but the Andersons found us. They just smiled at us, as if they rather admired our enterprise, so we wound up in regular coffins along with everybody else. There was the usual weightlessness as we moved away from the *Valiant* and fired our engines to start the fall down to the surface. I could see the graphics on the inside lid of my coffin, so I was ready to jump out as soon as we were down and then it opened. We were on the surface of another planet, the treasure planet!

Marthar was there even before me. Everybody else was still emerging. The lander was running standard checks on the atmosphere, and our external packs were charged and ready. The crew were busy checking the readouts on each others' packs. Marthar and I had already checked each others', but we were double-checked by Ursula Anderson. The exit light flashed green, telling us it was safe (orange is the kzin color for safety, which can be confusing), and it opened to the inside of an airlock. Pressure was lower outside, and we didn't want to waste our internal air by flushing it out, which in any case was forbidden because it would have contaminated the treasure planet with our own phages. We were immune to them, of course, by millennia of coevolution, but they might be deadly to any indigenous life forms. Six of us got into the airlock, the inner door closed and the air cycled out, leaving us in vacuum for a fraction of a second, which made my eyes water a bit even though I followed instructions and closed them, then the alien atmosphere was let in. It stunk a bit at first. There was a faint tang of ammonia and a smell of acetone, but it was okay to breathe it in, and we did, in my case with excitement at the thought that I was breathing the air of another world. I knew the oxygen levels were lower than on Wunderland, but the pack was feeding oxygen straight into my blood stream, so I didn't feel as if I were choking. I grinned at Marthar, who flipped an ear at me casually.

Then the outer door opened and I had my first glimpse of the world. It was silent, the sky was a light orange color on the horizon and a brilliant indigo at the zenith, with faint clouds. The ground was ochre, like Mars, and there was a lot more vegetation than I had expected. There were no trees, but lots of scrubby-looking bushes, the leaves the green of chlorophyll. It was mostly perhaps a darker green, like holly, possibly for the same reason holly is so dark.

There was quite a lot of variation though, including orange leaves, like vegetation on Kzin. I didn't see any animals; if there were any they were small and hiding. I suppose the lander might have frightened them away. Then I saw some birds; more like winged lizards than the birds of Old Earth or the various flying things of Wunderland, flying in groups. They didn't make any sound. The banks of a canal were visible in the distance, with some stringy-looking bushes standing up from the middle of it, a long streak of dark green cutting across the red of the landscape. It was warmer than I thought it would be, and also more humid than one would expect.

The steps unfolded from underneath the door, and the Andersons led the way down, Marthar and I following. Then we saw the other lander descending about quarter of a mile away, much nearer to the tower which spiked in the distance. That was Silver's lander, and Marthar and I glanced at each other and made a run for the bushes.

"Hey, kids, come back," Ursula yelled at us, but we didn't. We wanted to be out of sight of Silver, so we hared into the wild. It wasn't difficult to run and be out of sight of the rest of the crew within minutes. We stopped running and walked a while. I took sightings of the sun, to make sure we could find our way back, although the phones should guide us. There was no GPS on this world, of course. But there was a perfectly good tracker which homed in on a signal from the lander, but who knew what was about to happen?

Marthar pulled out her phone. We had the lander as a local station, of course, and she dialed zero to talk to *Valiant*.

There was no answer.

"Uh-oh. I have a nasty feeling. I'd say S'maak-Captain's plan was to send down two landing craft to the surface; I'd guess he had decided to put Silver and the obvious baddies in one of them, while the other would take some of those we thought were still loyal, those who Blandly had hung onto. Then I reckon he was going to get *Valiant* to destroy the bad guys' ship in such a way as to make it look like an accident to the pirates still on *Valiant*. It's what I'd have done, and I am pretty sure it was what S'maak-Captain was going to do, and I would guess Silver thought so too. So Silver struck first. He disarmed *Valiant* somehow; I think she's probably dead. It would account for her not answering the phone. I'll try calling Daddy and see what he says."

She dialed another single-digit number and waited. She listened for half a minute before giving up. "There's a dial tone, but that's just local and doesn't mean we're getting through. Somehow the whole communication system is shot."

So we were alone and isolated on a strange planet.

The sun didn't move in the sky, at least not noticeably. We walked steadily.

"Marthar, where are we going?"

"I'm heading towards the tower, and incidentally, Silver's lander. I'm going in a curve so it won't be obvious to anyone tracking us."

"Can they do that?"

"I don't know. Our packs may have some sort of RFID transmitter buried in them, and we've both got our own

RFIDs buried in our skin. I don't know how far away they can be to be quizzed, but the only answer is to be far away from any possible quizzer."

"We can't stay away indefinitely, we need to eat," I pointed out.

"That's why I told you to bring your *wtsai*. We may need to live off the land," she said happily. Marthar was really enjoying herself. She didn't actually claim the planet for the Riit Clan, probably because she felt that she owned it personally.

"But what makes you think we can eat the local protein?" I objected. "It will be totally different from what either of us have evolved with. Probably toxic and with no nutrition in it at all."

"Oh, pooh. Humans and kzin can eat each other for quite a long time and have, often enough, in the past. You can eat lobsters, squid and even insects at a pinch, which are pretty remote from you genetically. Proteins that are toxic are pretty rare, animals secrete them by way of defense. I don't say that everything is edible, but I loaded my phone with pictures of the native species we can't eat. Everything else we can."

"They might be a bit nippy. And also small. I haven't seen anything bigger than a bird so far, I haven't seen any insects, and the birds look pretty reptilian."

Marthar looked pityingly at me. "You humans have been happy to eat crocodiles, you'd have eaten tyrannosaurus rex if you'd been around at the same time. Oh, he'd have eaten you if he could catch you, but humans are ingenious. You'd have come out from behind a boulder and waved at him, after digging a nice big pit between you and covering it with sticks and straw. Then he'd have fallen in and you'd have dropped rocks on his head, then skinned him and eaten him. Brains wins every time. If you can predict your enemy better than he can predict you, you eat him. That's the evolutionary pressure to develop intelligence. The more of it, and the more you embrace it, the higher the intelligence. That's why I'm smarter than you."

"So you reckon intelligence is just about being able to predict others?" I asked.

"Yes. It's what it's for. Although I suppose if you are smart, you can also use your smarts for deceiving others into being food. But that involves a bit of prediction, so you can figure out what might work. We can regard this little excursion as a sort of intelligence test. Are you going to eat the local lifeforms, or are they going to eat you? It's the ultimate test of competence."

"So not much of a place for music or painting or poetry," I said lightly.

"Music and painting and poetry are magic," Mathar claimed loftily. "And magic is just another way to influence the environment. It only works on intelligent beings, but it works quite well on them, even kzin. You'd think it wouldn't, but a speech to encourage soldiers before a battle can help them win. So there's some sort of effect of word magic. And marching to rhythmic music works well in building *esprit de corps*, and Scots' bagpipes must have terrified the enemy. They frighten me. I'm afraid I'll go mad."

"Getting back to the food question, I still haven't seen anything to eat, except some of the bushes have rather small, nasty-looking lumps on them which might be fruit.

And I suppose we could dig for tubers and roots. But how are you going to get one of those lizard-birds with only a *wtsai*?"

Marthar sighed theatrically. "You'd die without me, no question. See, your strategy of being a cute little pet is going to pay off. I'll keep you alive. First off, I've seen lots of tracks of some things that might be flightless birds. At least they move on two legs. And they are about as big as a turkey, which would make us a good meal. I could make a bow with the *wtsai* and some local wood, also arrows, and cord for it from vines until we kill something with sinews to plait and braid into a better one. It would be a pretty awful bow and arrows, but it would only have to be good enough to kill a turkey thingy. Anyway, none of that will be necessary. I bought my needler. The one I took from Skel."

I wasn't the least bit surprised to find she carried a gun. Marthar had the self-reliant gene in spades, and would have taken it for granted that her job was to look after herself. It was why she had been looking for animal tracks, too. I hadn't seen any tracks, but then, I hadn't been looking for them. I suppose she had worked out the mass of the animal and its size by the depth and spacing of the footprints. I guess that evolution would invent legs and feet on any world that had animals of any size, and they would come if there was enough vegetation. Or enough other animals. "Do you think we might meet anything that could eat us?" I asked.

Marthar laughed. "Let's hope we find something dumb enough to try," she told me.

"Where are these turkey things? I haven't seen one."

"Neither have I, but I've heard them, whuffling away

quietly in the bushes. They go quiet when we pass, which is a way of saying they are more afraid of us than we are of them. A good sign."

"The kzin is a mighty hunter." I said. It was one of those sayings humans had been conditioned to use when dealing with kzin duing the occupation. "I don't feel hungry yet. Would that be the packs, do you think?"

"Yes, we're being drip-fed glucose as well as oxygen. But I'm always hungry. And we should save the packs, we may need them for a long time."

I didn't like the sound of that. "You think we could be here for long?" I asked her.

"We could be here for life," she told me briskly. "I don't know how long that will be. As long as possible if I have anything to do with it. We know that *Valiant* is dead, it's possible that the Judge, the Doctor, Daddy and S'maak-Captain are too. Unlikely, but possible. Killing S'maak and Daddy would take a bit of doing. If the rest of the crew managed it, there won't be many of them left by now, that's for sure. The Riit Clan didn't become what it is by being soft and easy, trust me."

I did. It wasn't difficult.

CHAPTER FOURTEEN

We were curving in towards the tower now. It must have been enormous when it was complete, it still dominated the landscape. It loomed against the sky, the broken spikes of different heights at the top showing black against the faintly pink skyline. I suppose we had been walking for two or three hours; I could have checked with my phone, which was still on ship-time, local time not passing very fast. There were still enough shrubs and bushes to shelter us from Silver's lander, although we could see the red spire of the nose sticking up.

"Where are we going?" I asked Marthar in what was almost a whisper. Somehow, the knowledge that Silver was in the vicinity made me uneasy and disposed to hide.

"I want to get in the tower. And to size up the situation with the pirates. If we can disable their lander that would give us an edge; difficult, but not out of the question. Even better if we could steal it."

I shrugged. I was more inclined to stay as far away from the pirates as possible, and little inclined to explore until we had worked out what to do about them. My heart was in my boots when I thought of the ominous silence from *Valiant*. We both knew in principle how to restore her from her corrupted form, but that required us to be on the ship. Maybe we shouldn't have run from the first lander. If we went back, maybe we could persuade Sam and Ursula to take us back to the *Valiant*. And stealing the pirate lander looked a crazy idea. Anything that got us closer to Silver seemed like a crazy idea to me.

"Alright, stay here and wait for me," Marthar said. "I'll make much less noise than you. The whole animal population of the planet could hear you coming a mile off."

"What if you get caught? What will I do on my own?"

"I won't get caught. And if I do, find your way back to the Andersons and try to get them to take you back to the *Valiant* and get *Valiant* back online. But beware of saying that you know how to do it in front of any possible pirates. They'd kill you instantly."

She disappeared with a casual wave of her left paw. The other held the needler. I watched her go and my heart sank even lower.

I waited in a little glade that was carpeted by something like grass, but also like moss, because the leaves were very tiny and tight together. The glade was about twenty paces long and seven or eight wide, and I sat down on a small boulder near one end of it. I had absolutely no idea how long Marthar would be, I couldn't phone her and ask her because she might be hiding from danger and wouldn't be pleased if anyone heard her alarm ringing. More likely, she'd thought of that and switched it off anyway. Of course, we didn't even know if we could phone each other; we hadn't tried, which was thoughtless of us. Maybe we couldn't even get through to the lander.

Altogether it wasn't a very pleasant wait. I tried to make up my mind when to go back to the lander and the Andersons, and checked the time on my phone rather a lot. About an hour had passed since Marthar had disappeared when I head voices. I jumped up, looking forward to company, then thought again and scurried to hide. Fortunately, the vegetation was thick enough to hide me. I lay prone and waited to see who it was.

I heard Silver's voice. They came into view, Silver and a kzin, and I froze.

"Mate, it's because I thinks gold dust of you—gold dust, and you may lay to that! If I hadn't took to you like pitch, do you think I'd ha' been here a-warning of yer? All's up, yer can't make nor mend, it's to save yer neck that I'm a-speaking, and if one o' the wild ones knew it, where'd I be, T'orr—now, tell me, where'd I be?"

"Silver," said the other Kzin, and his voice was hoarse, and quavered like a taut rope. "Silver," he said, "you're old and you're honest or has the name for it; and you've money too, which lots of poor spacers hasn't; and you're brave or I'm mistook. And will you tell me you'll let yourself be led away wi' that kind o' mess of *sthondat* droppings? Not you! And as sure as the Fanged God sees me, I'd sooner lose my ears. If I turn against my dooty—"

And then he was interrupted by a noise. Here was one of the honest kzin, and at that moment came the sound of another. Far away, out near the lander, came a shout of anger, then another on the back of it, and then a horrible, long, drawn-out scream. The rocks re-echoed it a score of times, and the lizard-birds rose into the sky, darkening the heavens with a simultaneous whirr; and long after that death yell was still ringing in my brain, silence had reestablished its empire and only the rustle of the redescending flying things disturbed the languor of the permanent afternoon.

T'orr had leapt at the sound, like a horse at the spur, but Silver had not winked an eye. He stood where he was, leaning on the seven-foot-long cutlass he had taken from his back, watching his companion like a snake.

"Silver!" said the spacer, stretching out his arm.

T'orr's voice was shaking, for this was surely the first and only time in his humble life he had spoken out in the Ultimate Imperative tense, which a kzin not of royal blood may use only when the honor of the kzin species is at stake. "Silver!" he cried. "In the Name of the Patriarch and by the honor of the Heroes' Race, I command you to return to your dooty!"

"Away!" Silver exclaimed, springing back two yards with the speed and assurance of a gymnast.

"Away if you like, Silver," said the other kzin. "It's a black conscience that can make you feared o' me. But in the Name of the God, what was that?"

"That?" returned Silver, his head on one side, his eyes black and gleaming. "That? Oh, I reckon that'll be Araarr."

"Araarr! Then may he go to the Fanged God's home for a true Hero! And as for you, Silver, you're a companion of mine no more, must I die like a Dog. You've killed Araarr, have ye? Then kill me too if ye can, but I defies you!" And with that, the kzin turned his back directly on Silver and set off walking away from him, towards the first lander. But he was not to get far. With a cry, Silver lifted the huge cutlass and sent it hurtling through the air. It struck T'orr point foremost and with stunning violence, right between the shoulders in the middle of his back. It takes a lot to knock a kzin down—no human could do it—but that blow must have broken T'orr's spine. His arms flew up; he gave a muffled cry and fell.

He was not dead. I heard him gasping and trying to cry out—a dreadful, pitiful sound from that great bulky creature. But his limbs were not moving. Even if he were not paralyzed, Silver gave him no time to recover. Silver was as agile as a monkey, and was on him and had twice buried his *wtsai* up to the hilt in that defenseless body. I could hear him grunt aloud as he struck the blows. He was snarling like . . . well, like a kzin.

For a time the world swam in front of my eyes and the sound of chanting crowds and bells rang in my ears. When my head cleared, Silver was still there, minding the corpse not a whit, but cleaning his *wtsai* on the other's fur, then licking the last of the blood from the blade. I could even hear him purring. Everything else was unchanged, the sun still shone down and the bushes glistened dark green, and I could scarcely persuade myself that I had seen murder done.

Silver sprayed a little urine over the corpse and cut off its ears. Then he reached into a pouch and pulled out a phone and clawed a digit into it, held it up to his face and spoke a word. Then he put it away and waited. When he turned away from me, I very slowly backed up and then turned and crawled. The other pirates would be coming this way soon, and what chance would I have if I were found? When I was far enough away from Silver, I stood and ran away. I didn't stop to think where I was going so long as I was as far from the horror of that scene as I could get. I ran and I ran, over small hills and through valleys with bushes that were almost trees, and when I came to something like a dried river bed, I went down the bank, tripped, stumbled, fell and hit my head hard enough to send me out like a light.

I awoke to feel myself lifted up and was taken by panic until I recognized the soft fur and smell of Marthar. She raised me to a sitting position, and I opened my eyes to look into those big green and yellow eyes of my friend.

"You banged your head, little Peter," she crooned at me. "I don't suppose it did much damage, it isn't as if there's much inside it. But it's good to see you alive again."

"Marthar, I saw the most dreadful thing," I told her. "Silver killed one of the crew. I just ran. It was horrible." I shuddered. She hugged me.

"Not the first creature he's killed, nor the last. Silver is quite the most lethal Kzin around." She sounded as if she rather admired him for it.

"How did you find me?"

"You leave the sort of trail a Gagrumpher or a male *sthondat* would make when mad and in a hurry. It wasn't hard, I just had to cast around a bit. Not many of the native species would leave a Gram and Henry shoe print in your size. We'll have to get you some sensible foot coverings that don't leave big fat tracks everywhere you go. Being with you is going to be too dangerous if you stomp around like that."

"Do our phones work here?" I asked her.

"Yes, but I switched mine off in case you were silly enough to call me when I was concentrating on other things. Such as not getting seen. We can switch them on, but make sure it does a vibrate only with no tone, or one of us will call the other and tell everyone for quarter of a mile around. Here, let me fix yours." She took my phone and set it so it would be silent, then did the same with hers. "And don't call unless you have something important to say. We aren't going to be in the social chat business for a long time, I can tell you."

"What happened? Did you get to the tower?"

"Yes, but there was nothing new inside. Silver hasn't been there yet, well, he hadn't as of a few hours ago. Maybe he's started collecting the books by now. Although I suspect he's going to be doing some experiments to work out which are likely to be valuable, and how to handle them safely—he'll use others for that. Now he's killed *Valiant*, he has lots of time, I guess. Though eventually he'll have to repair her if he's going to get home. He's going to be picking off the Andersons and any residual loyal crew, like the one you saw him kill. But he'll have trouble keeping enough to crew the *Valiant* back if he's is too murderous. It's his main problem. There is another thing, too. You heard him swear to kill my Sire"—there was a ring in her voice when she said that, something I had never heard before, and for a moment I felt more terrified of her than of Silver—"He can't do that or even attempt it from the ground."

"What about the lander? Did you get near it?"

"Enough to see it was guarded rather closely. Claws was

there. Silver thinks he is particularly loyal to him. So because the lander is his link with the *Valiant* and he must have it, he covers it carefully. Very sensible of him. And why we win hands down if we can steal it. Though it may be damaged—there were signs of it. Maybe it could be fixed. You heard him say in the meat-locker that Great-Grandsire Chuut-Riit had sworn vengeance to the death and the generations."

"Yes."

"That means that if Silver is alive after this coup, he had better start running. Either his kits, if he has any, may survive, or some members of the Riit Clan, but not both. He will be pursued. And Grand-Sire Vaemar has a hyperdrive ship. Not to mention that the Patriarch now has some also."

"That makes me feel better," I said, thinking of the murder of the honest kzin in the glade. I had grown up with kzin like that . . .

"We'll make a Hero of you yet! But it will be difficult."

Difficult! I thought she was drunk with enthusiasm and the prospect of revenge, hunting and killing to even contemplate the idea. But being with Marthar was intoxicating; she radiated competence and confidence. She would have made an excellent leader in almost any military role. One just soaked up her own boundless zest and certainty.

"You know, I'm starting to get hungry," I told her.

"That's because I turned down your glucose drip a bit. It had increased itself when you were unconscious, and if it had stayed at that level you'd have gone into shock when it was all used up. So we have to hunt. And I'm not going to light a fire, so you'll eat it raw. Just as well you tried it back home, so you should be able to handle it."

"Why no fire?" I protested. I had eaten raw kill, but I can't say I liked it much.

"You want to make finding us so easy we might just as well go and hand ourselves in to Silver so as to save him the trouble? Fire gives off smoke and heat, both of which can be seen. We must assume that the now-corrupted *Valiant* can see us and is going to tell Silver where we are. I suspect he already knows, I would guess he could smell you watching him. And he could follow your trail as well as I could. I think he's saving you."

"Saving me? What for?"

Marthar looked at me. I couldn't read her gaze at all. "If I were him, I'd be thinking of getting someone to read some of those books for me. Telling me which ones had details of the transfer discs and how they worked and which ones were just knitting patterns."

The recollection of the burnt thing being blinded by those groping snakes hit me, and the prospect of having them thrust into my eyes in order to read the mysterious metal bars gave me the cold horrors. I would sooner be dead. I asked Marthar to kill me before that happened and she agreed in a disturbingly matter-of-fact way. Plainly she has considered no other possible courses of action available, she simply said that it was a pity I had no kits to carry on my line. I keep forgetting that despite human speech, a kzin is still a kzin.

Marthar had no difficulty locating prey. She twitched her ears, then lunged into a bush, snarling with the pleasure of it, and dragged out a thing about as big as a turkey that looked a little like a kangaroo but had a beak. It tried to peck Marthar, who screwed its neck in one movement. She hadn't needed to use the needler or to make a bow and arrows. She just ripped it apart, drank some of its blood and handed me one of its legs. I ate it gloomily. At least it didn't poison me. No worse than steak tartare, I suppose. Marthar ate with pleasure, licking her lips and getting through the rest of the carcase. She was bigger than me and had a faster metabolism, so I guess she needed it. Anyway, kzin always eat raw meat. Cooked food actually makes them sick. Then she told me to wait for her and went out to do some more hunting; she was still really hungry. I found out later that she had turned her glucose drip off altogether, partly to save it for emergencies, partly because she was happier doing things 'naturally,' which meant killing her own food. I suppose eating steak tartare after someone else has killed the cow and yet another person has minced the meat is rather good at hiding the reality from us. We kill for our food too, we just like to pretend otherwise. We may be fooling ourselves, but I prefer to do my hunter-gathering at the markets.

I looked around. There were something very like small green oranges on some of the bushes. I pulled one off and tried eating it. It was possible, for me at least; I knew Marthar would eat such things only when faced with starvation. I chewed thoughtfully. I guess getting used to this was a good idea. All the same, it didn't taste good. It didn't taste much of anything, just sort of faintly squishy.

By the time Marthar got back, I had eaten three of them. Some things are acquired tastes, and a taste for these things most definitely took a lot of acquiring. I had heard that there were plants on kzin that, if you tried to eat them, ate you right back, but these did not seem to be related to them.

"What do we do now?" I asked her. "Do you think it's time to sleep yet? It won't be easy in a place where it's going to be mid-afternoon for another couple of months."

"Sleep? Not for another four or five hours. I think we should try to raise the Andersons. If we can't steal Silver's lander, we shall just have to steal theirs, or at least borrow it. I figure getting *Valiant* back up is our top priority, and next is staying away from Silver. And finding out what has happened to Sire and the others."

"Sire," not "Daddy" now. Not the kzin battle-tongue yet, but moving that way.

I shivered. Staying away from Silver was my first priority. It was also my second, third and fourth.

Marthar had no luck with trying to raise the Andersons by phone. "I'm sure it's the right number. Almost sure. I saw a list of people's numbers, early on the voyage. But I might have transposed a few digits. I suppose we'd better walk back there."

I pulled out my phone and checked the tracker. "Okay. The phone says it's that way."

"Of course, it is," Marthar was exasperated. "Don't you have any idea where you are? It's not as if the sun moves much in the sky, you just use it to orient."

"When I ran away from Silver, I didn't bother to check which way I was going," I confessed. "I just ran. As fast as

I could, and I only had eyes for any sort of path through the bushes."

"You should have at least noticed which way the shadows fell," she scolded me. "What a poor sad, terrified little monkey you are sometimes. You're lucky you've got me."

"I know," I told her. She was a bit taken aback. I think she cared for me, even if I was mostly a pet monkey, but she was surprised when I cared for her.

We set off, well away from the direct line indicated by my phone, in a direction we'd never been before. I pointed this out and she looked at me.

"I want to give Silver's lander as big a miss as possible. Horizons are a long way off on this world, even with the hills in the way. And I want to make sure they can't see us. I said that if they want us they will be able to get the *Valiant* to see us easily enough, or maybe they don't have much control of whatever they have left of *Valiant*'s capabilities. Not the sort of thing you'd take a gamble on in my book. So we'll go by the scenic route."

This struck me as a good argument. So we walked off briskly towards a hill. In fact it was practically a mountain by local standards.

"Why is the soil red?" I asked idly. "It would be easy to understand it looking like Mars or the Australian outback if this were a second-generation planet, but those places are red because of haematite and iron-based minerals. And this planet shouldn't have any iron."

"I think the system acquired a second-generation planet, and it seems to have collided with this world a long time ago. Second-generation planets are all over the galaxy. They get detached from binary systems pretty easily, and sometimes they get captured by another system. So there's a certain amount of iron and other metals around on the surface, but the core isn't iron. One of the reasons there's no magnetic field to speak of. And one of the reasons eating the local food isn't a waste of time. If it were all first-generation life it wouldn't be very nutritious. In fact, you should have been able to taste the iron in the meat you ate."

"I think the fruit I had was first generation. It was pretty bland. Still, there was water in it."

Marthar looked at me amiably. "You monkeys have disgusting habits. Still, I've got used to them. Mostly."

We bickered in friendly fashion as we walked towards the mountain. I'll call it that, even though it was a pretty sad sort of mountain in comparison with the ranges of Wunderland.

"So this world is pretty old. Much older than Wunderland or Old Earth?"

"Three times as old. So some of the early lifeforms ought to have done some serious evolution; but if it was hit by an asteroid big enough to spread iron and nickel around the surface, it might have had all life wiped out and had to start again. Earth nearly had that happen. But life is pretty tenacious. I don't know how deep the oceans are, or how deep they were five billion years ago, but if they weren't very deep we might be looking at a place that's quite young as far as the life on it is concerned. And we don't know where the things that left the towers came from. They might have put the iron here deliberately. In which case it would have been the first thing they did, I suppose."

"You mean they might have deliberately crashed a big

asteroid here? And wiped out most if not all of the lifeforms? They must have been pretty murderous, don't you think?"

Marthar yawned, an impressive sight. "You know why you're so squeamish, you humans? It's because you are afraid of yourselves; you know that there is something truly black and horrible inside you, something utterly murderous and evil, and you think if you can hide from it, it will go away. So for most of you, it only comes out at time of serious need. But no lifeform dominates its planet unless it's murderous. Evolution takes care of the nice guys. And you beat the might of all Kzin in a war by being more murderous than we are. It's why I'm nice to you, Chimpy. I don't want you mad at me."

She was joking of course. At least I thought so.

CHAPTER FIFTEEN

We were halfway up the mountain and walking around it in a curve when Marthar stopped. She sniffed the air.

"Don't look now, but there's some sort of animal following us, a big one."

I froze but didn't turn around. "How big?"

"About my size, more or less. May even be a bit bigger. Might be wounded, it's got a funny way of moving. Or maybe it's got its legs on backwards or something silly. I mean, evolution produces some very odd stuff, and things that look as if they'd never survive for a day manage to keep themselves going for mega-years."

"Usually by being unpleasant to eat," I said. I knew a bit about evolution too.

"When we get to that boulder just ahead, carry on as if I'm still with you, and talk to me normally. I'll wait and catch it. I don't like being followed."

"Alright. Be careful. And don't eat it if it looks really clumsy."

"Right. Or if it has poisonous quills."

"Hey, be careful," I told her, suddenly worried. Of course it was a stupid thing to say, but Marthar was used to me. I don't know if she thought the only reason I was concerned for her was because I knew I couldn't survive without her, or if she knew I cared for her. I'd told her I did, lots of times, but she wouldn't just believe me. Not Marthar, I thought ruefully. She'd think I might be deceiving myself the better to deceive her.

She didn't even bother looking pityingly at me, she just stepped back behind the boulder and I carried on.

"I know you don't trust anyone, not even me," I told her in my normal voice, even though she wasn't there. "I suppose you don't do empathy with anything except prey." This was unfair and untrue. Sometimes she could read my mind. Well, not my mind, my feelings. Just as some animals can read your fear and respond to it, so kzin and kzinretti could read a whole range of feelings with uncanny accuracy. In a few it can be made into the telepath's power, but all have it to some degree. It was just that they didn't react the way a human being would. It all got taken into account, even when the reaction was an impulsive one, and Marthar was certainly impulsive. It was why I had some hope that she did understand my feeling for her, she must have been able to read it. I was an open book to Marthar. I wondered if the creature that followed us was the same. If she didn't like the look of whatever it was, it could be dead very quickly.

"I do wonder a bit how far I have to go like this," I continued in a conversational tone. Wouldn't the creature work out that this was a rather one-sided discussion? Then there was a squawk and shriek from behind me. Neither sound came from Marthar, although there was a low growling. I turned and ran back.

Marthar had the creature on its back. It was a kzin, though hardly a warrior or Hero. It was gaunt and starved-looking. It had few of the fabric pouches of an ordinary kzin, and these were held by vines rather than leather bands, but it had no weapons that I could see. Marthar had her *wtsai* at its throat and was interrogating it.

"Are you one of the pirates?" she hissed at it.

"No, kzinrett-that-speaks, please spare my life. I will be your servant, I will help you!"

"How did you come to this world?"

"I was marooned. Marooned! I was abandoned here. I was press-ganged by that devil K'zarr; from Argent, a poor enough world in truth, and brought to this world, I was, by that master of evil. Made to step on a black disc, I was, which moved me a thousand miles away in the blink of an eye."

"I think we saw it in the memo pad," I told Marthar. "I think this is indeed one of K'zarr's crew who was left behind. Do you remember seeing two of them step on one of those transfer discs and vanish?"

Marthar released the poor devil, who was no match for her at all. He struggled to his feet.

"Thank-ee, kzinrett."

"My *Name* is Marthar. Marthar-*Riit* . . . Get up!" She commanded, as he went down in the full prostration at the Name. Some of the kzin at home called her "My Lady" on formal occasions, but that was a term used by some Wunderland kzin only, taken from human speech. I realized he had almost certainly never met an intelligent kzinrett before, or at least not one that did not hide her intelligence. He had almost certainly never met a member of the Riit Clan, either. I realized later that, quite apart from her ear-tattoos, the possibility she was an imposter never occurred to him. Falsely pretending to be Riit was something no kzin would, literally, ever dream of doing.

"And how did you get here?" he asked. "Don't say you're with K'zarr, I beg of ye!"

"K'zarr is dead," Marthar told him. "But some of his crew are here, and they are our enemies. They are led by a kzin called Silver."

"Silver! He were as bad as K'zarr. Worse, he were, if 'twere possible. Years and years since they left me here to die. Hah, but I didn't die, did I? Old Bengar is still here, still alive, though I had to eat scuttling vermin and worse." So he called himself *Bengar*. It sounded like a nursery name, and I doubted this creature could ever have acquired a real Name of his own.

"And me the child of brave and honorable kzin," he went on, almost babbling, "though poor, 'tis true. An' I tried to be as bad as they pirates, so I did, for a kzin has to be loyal, but loyalty cuts both ways, don't it? Pray ter the Fanged God now, is what I do. Pray for another meal, an' sometimes I gets it and sometimes I doesn't. But I'm still here. And what I begs yer is take me away from this world, for 'tes not natural that it be always daytime. For when the sun goes down, it grows dreadful chill, and I walked ter keep it higher in the sky, so I did. I walked all around this cursed world, more than once. An' a day that lasts forever is part o' the curse, I should say, for a poor tired old kzin, trudging his way about ter keep the sun where it belongs, overhead. Ah, there be daymares, d'ye see, nightmares bein' nothin on daymares, where there be no easy dusk, on'y the threat of endless night. So ye walks, d'ye see? Ye walks."

The picture of an endless trudge to outwalk the sun was as horrible as anything else I had seen. I felt sorry for the poor creature. But I wasn't sure I could believe it. I suppose it might just be possible in high enough latitudes.

"Where did you come out when you stepped on the transfer disc?" I asked Bengar.

"Why, in another tower, on another disc. Thought it were the same tower at first, and everyone gone and me alone in it. I were alone, o'course, but when I got out, there were differences outside. I were near some water and the sun were lower in the sky. And the tower were in even worse shape than this one. Some of they discs lead to stranger places. Some must lead off this world, and I was tempted, but no, there be places worse than this, I seen some o' them wi' K'zarr. Places where the air is green and burns. Places where there's beasts can tear yer heart out o' yer chest before yer can draw a *wtsai*. Once, I saw a beast with three legs and two heads, if you'll believe me, but it were dead and where it came from I don't know. No, I found out some things, I can tell yer about them. Yes, I can help yer, Marthar-Riit, young man-kit, I can tell yer things that there K'zarr never knew, may his soul burn for ever wi' the Demon Goddess' fangs in his throat."

Marthar looked at me. "Please let him live, Marthar," I said. "I believe he is an honest kzin, and he may be able to help us defeat the mutineers."

"You are a softie, Peter, though I love you for it. But

sometimes your human methods seem to work. I don't say I understand it, but you don't have to understand facts, just to face them." She turned to Bengar. "Very well, in the hope that you are honest and will keep your word and in the hope that you can see that I am a deal more dangerous than K'zarr and Silver combined if I am your enemy, I will spare you in exchange for your help. You have a family somewhere?"

"Yes, Marthar-Riit.'"

"Then, if you swear loyalty to me, you swear loyalty to the generations. I bind you in the name of the Riit Clan and give my Name as my word!"

Bengar flinched a little at what must have been for him a dreadful oath. Then he knelt clumsily before her. "I pledge my fealty. For ye be a warrior-lady come again out of the ancient legends, those stories what was told i' the old days afore the Fanged God punished all kzinretti. Ye can be sure o' me, to the death. For yer gives me something to die for if I must, something wi' some point and meaning to it."

"You must know that this man-kit here, my friend Peter, begged for your life. And that you owe him fealty too."

Bengar looked at me vacantly. I don't suppose owing fealty to any other than a kzin made any real sense to him. An intelligent kzinrett must have been strange enough. To my surprise he nodded to me. "Protect you I will, wi' me life if need be," he promised me. Or perhaps he promised Marthar. It wasn't easy to tell. Anyway, he promised.

"Is kzin fealty like human fealty?" I asked Marthar as we went on.

Marthar considered. "I suppose so," she said. "I think it varies from world to world. Some of the earlier worlds settled are more, well, feudal, I suppose. Fealty is about duty, and I guess it's a sort of trade between kzin rather than just obeying all orders. I don't suppose that any kzin could even think of turning into an obedient slave, but an oath of fealty gives those who swear it more freedom. I guess it sort of regulates things so it isn't necessary to threaten force all the time. But the thing is that force and power are all things that ensure the race won't degenerate. That's something we have that human beings don't: a sense of duty to the species."

"We do," I protested. "We look after each other. If one of the tribe is threatened, the others try to help."

"There you are. If a human is weak and falls into a trap, the other humans help it escape. That's not thinking of the species at all, that's thinking of the tribe. It has a good effect on the tribe, but a bad effect on the species, because it keeps alive a weak creature with the lousy judgment to fall into a trap. If a group of kzin found one of its members had fallen into a pit, they'd just look hard at the pit to make sure they never got caught the same way. Then they'd move on and leave the inept kzin there. That way, the group survives, the group learns, the same as your system. But we don't dilute the gene pool with incompetents."

"It might not have been incompetence, just bad luck," I pointed out.

"We believe in weeding out the unlucky. You keep them. Eventually you'll all be unlucky. Or incompetent. Same thing. It's strange how lucky you've been so far."

In school, I'd been told that Napoleon asked people if

they were lucky, wanting to appoint only generals who were lucky. It had seemed strange at the time and still did.

"Why do you think being lucky is the same as being competent? Luck just happens."

"No it doesn't. Anytime some idiot has a disaster, he blames it on bad luck. He can't or won't see it was always just a consequence of a bad decision. When things go wrong, you have to figure out what you did to screw up and make sure you don't do it again."

"And if it leads to you getting trapped in a pit, you don't get the chance to change or learn, not under your system," I retorted. "The rest of the gang just look down at you in the pit and wave goodbye. That's an awful waste, don't you think?"

Marthar shrugged. "Saves the gene pool. Maybe there's a middle way. We could hoick them out of the pit but the price is sterilizing them so they don't pass their stupidity onto the next generation. If they find some way to get out themselves, good for them!"

I decided that kzin and man were very different in some ways. "I'm not ashamed that we humans are more compassionate than you kzin," I told her.

"You aren't. You just save your compassion for losers, we save ours for the species. It's called evolution in action when some idiot gets himself killed. It's the way the Fanged God does things. We accept that and go along with it; you try to fight it. As if you think your god got it wrong, and you're going to improve on creation. Doesn't look to be a good strategy in the long run. We've never exterminated a species in all our conquests, by the way."

No, I thought, *just reduced them to slaves and prey-*

animals, like the wretched Jotok, who once had a great trading empire that lifted races out of barbarism, and the God alone knows how many other peaceful societies. But this was hardly the time to be picking a fight.

"What if I got hurt, or fell into a pit, would you help me?"

"Of course. You're my friend, and more to the point, you aren't my species. I don't mind if your species fills up with more incompetents. But I won't have it happen to mine."

I don't think she meant to be hurtful, but I also don't think she cared much whether she hurt my feelings or not. kzin don't put much store in feelings about other kzin, much less humans. I think she was just giving a truthful answer, but it was a bit chilling. You can get along with kzin and feel that they aren't all that different from human beings on the inside, and then they say something which just shows you that you were wrong all along. There are similarities, but deep down, kzin are different from us, or at least from me. When she said she was more dangerous than K'zarr or Silver, she meant it.

We continued walking towards the Andersons' lander in silence, Bengar trudging after us.

Bengar came up to us. Kzin are less gregarious than humans, but I think he was hungry for company, as who wouldn't be after years of solitude?

"Ye'll take me back off this world, will ye not?" he asked, with almost a whine in his voice. "And ye'll not gi' me up to Silver, will ye? Else I'm prey. And you treat poor Bengar right and there's much he can tell ye. The treasure, ye know. I can lead ye to the treasure, so I can."

"We know where the treasure is, it's in the tower," Marthar told him.

"Ahh, that's what K'zarr thought, and he left me to it, so he did. I reckon he knew that if either of those of us that he abandoned by those discs came back, 'twould do us no good. For we'd have had to fix those dreadful snakes to our eyes and be blinded like Gra-Prompyh. So though he didn't know what was on those bars, he thought they was treasure. But I knows different. I knows which of they is valuable and which is dross, so I do. And dross there be a-plenty, unless ye be awful interested in stories o' aliens and their follies, and lore of other worlds, long since passed away, I should think."

"What do you mean?" Marthar asked.

"What I means is, I found meself in another tower, far from here. And when I was shivering in the long night, I braved one o' they discs on my own, I did, and gradually I learned a few things. Like I made some sense o' the writin' they aliens put on the discs. An' not just the discs, and there was other ways o' reading them silver bars, there was. 'Cos there was more kinds o' aliens than those what they were aiming at in the first tower. There be ways o' getting information about what's in the bars, an' they don't need to put yer eyes out to get it. So if there's treasure in the knowledge o' how the discs work, for instance, and how other things work, engineering sort o' stuff, mathematical sort o' stuff, not just stories for kits and kzinretti, beggin' your pardon, warrior-lady, for I sees you aren't just an ordinary kzinrett, indeed I do."

"Gosh, that sounds just the thing!" I said enthusiastically to Marthar. "We were worried about making sense of those bars, now it sounds as though we can bypass the snake things."

"'Tes so, young monk—. . . master, indeed, 'tes so. And be sure that poor Bengar will show ye both exactly how 'tes done. Safe will ye both be with me, so long as ye treats me right, which I've no doubt ye will. I can tell ye that there is such matter there will be very excitin' for the scientists and the engineers, though 'twas no use to poor Bengar, who knows nothing o' such matters. Being but a poor lad from the country when I was took by the press gangs of K'zarr, may he live wi' the mist demons in hell, and havin' no education to speak of. But K'zarr knew nothin' of it, d'ye see? Oh, given time, I daresay he'd have found the true treasure, but it took me a year or so, and I was lucky to find the right tower."

This sounded pretty good, if we could trust Bengar. I had no idea whether we could or not, but no doubt Marthar could think of some way of keeping control of him. We kept walking in silence for another hour, broken only by the panting of Bengar. He must have used up his implanted oxygen a long time ago, and was struggling to find enough in the local atmosphere.

We could see the spire of the Andersons' lander, and almost broke into a run. Then a kzin stepped out from behind a bush and halted us with a gesture.

"My lady, go no further," he said with some formality to Marthar. "Wait while I get Ursula. The renegades have taken the lander. We can't get in, and they seem to be unable to take off. It's a stalemate." He looked thoughtfully at Bengar for a moment. Then he stalked off, and a moment later Ursula bustled into view. "Marthar, Peter, thank God you're safe! Terrible things have happened." Ursula hugged me and beamed at Marthar. She gave Bengar a bewildered look.

"What happened?" I asked.

"There were some mutineers on board the lander, taking orders from Silver. They pulled back inside and sealed the doors. The last one in shouted something at us, something to the effect that they were going to join Silver at the tower. We ran for it so as not to get scorched by the rockets when they lifted, but they never did. They never came out, either. We tried to raise them by phone, to ask what was going on, but they cut the phones. Now nobody knows what is going on."

"How many of them went back inside?" Marthar wanted to know.

"Seven. That left three loyal kzin and Sam and me."

"*Hmmm. Now who stopped them taking off, and how*?" Marthar asked herself. Then she brightened. "It must have been Sire and S'maak-Captain. They must have managed something with even the corpse of *Valiant*. Now we have to get in touch with them."

That was the moment when we heard a humming sound, and the third lander came into view. For an awful moment I thought it was Silver's lander, but the colors were different. The Andersons' was green, Silver's was red, and the one coming down close to the green one was a beautiful silvery blue. My spirits soared. Soon we would be back on the *Valiant* and we could take Bengar and get *Valiant* back into life again, or at least give it a jolly good shot.

It didn't work out like that.

PART FOUR
A DEFENSIVE POSITION

CHAPTER SIXTEEN

The lander settled on its four spindly legs and the hatch opened, and Orion-Riit stood at the top of the steps within minutes of the flames closing down.

"Daddy!" Martha shrieked and ran towards him. He looked astonished to see her running across the field, but he went down quickly to hold her as she threw herself at him. Where he had stood, S'maak-Captain took up nearly as much space, and behind him, the Judge and the Doctor looked out more cautiously.

"What happened?" Orion demanded. His daughter explained it all at speed, the mutineers held the other two landers, and the loyal crew were there in the clearing, coming in despite the possibility that the mutineers were armed and would shoot them down. It was true that there were no known weapons on the lander, but it certainly didn't seem safe to assume they hadn't brought some with them.

S'maak-Captain looked up at the other lander with some satisfaction, I thought. "Get everyone aboard! We must get back to the *Valiant* before Silver and his cutthroats arrive," he ordered. "We saw them heading this way as we came into last descent. I want us away, and we have only minutes!"

I was calling out to Ursula and Sam to come quickly. Not knowing who was in the lander until they saw S'maak, and not having the best reflexes, it took them an agonizingly long time to explain.

"Sam is some miles off, he went to spy out the land," Ursula explained, worried. "And the other two of the loyal kzin went off in the opposite direction for the same purpose. There's only me and Ruarrgh here."

"Damn," muttered the Judge. "Nothing goes according to plan. We hoped to come on down, pick up the good guys and leave the bad guys to stew. Now it turns out that the bad guys are much easier to pick up."

"And here they come, I think," Orion said drily. The hatch of the green lander was opening and one of the mutineers peered out. S'maak-Captain shot him with a needler. He yelled and the hatch door slammed shut behind him.

"Phone your mate and the other one, and tell them to rendezvous with us, say ten miles away, north of here. We can lure Silver away in the opposite direction, then double back and pick them up," Orion ordered.

"But the phones stopped working. Oh, I suppose now you're here they'll work again, right?" Ursula was rattled.

"Get in the lander first!" S'maak-Captain ordered.

Flustered, Ursula, followed by the loyal kzin, moved towards the lander. I started off to go with them, as did the other humans.

"Too late for that, me little friends," said Silver, coming out from some bushes. He pointed a gun at S'maak-Captain. Not a needler—a blaster. S'maak dived and rolled and shot at him with his needler, but Silver roared and fired. The needler must have hit the weapon, for it flamed out, a brilliant white fire that missed S'maak but hit one of the legs of the blue lander. The spindly thing evaporated, the lander tilted and then very slowly fell over, its gyros whirring futilely. We all looked at it in horror as it canted, seemed to settle then came down like a great tree. The sound of fracturing metal and plastic seemed to go on for ever. Silver disappeared. S'maak-Captain leapt up after him, but stopped to pick up the blaster where Silver had dropped it. Then he threw it away contemptuously.

The lander lay on its side, the door gaping open and half off.

"Inside. It will still give us some protection!" S'maak bellowed. We all sprang for it. Getting in was only a bit awkward. Although the door was sideways, the kzin had to twist to get in. The inner door was open, so the air inside was still that of the treasure planet. We got inside just before the rest of the pirates turned up. All the rooms were sideways too, so it felt very strange as if we were standing on the walls. We couldn't close the door, but we could try to block the entrance and hold it by firepower. S'maak wasn't the only one with a needler. And if they blasted us, well, at least the hull would hold off the ravening fury of the blaster bolt for a while.

There were eight of us, looking at each other. Bengar had vanished as soon as Silver had appeared. Outside, there were nine of Silver's men, standing there with no sign of Silver himself, and another seven in the green lander. And no way of escape for any of us. Nothing we had would get the blue lander back into the air, let alone into space.

S'maak ordered one of the crew to look to see if we had any communications capacity, then went to guard the door. The rest of us looked at each other.

"I suppose this gives us time to catch up," Marthar remarked philosophically. "We seem to be stalemated. I always hate that."

Orion looked at her fondly. "You begin. Tell us what happened after you silly kits eloped."

Marthar told the whole story, and how we'd caught Bengar, and what he had told us about the treasure, then finishing up with us seeing the blue lander come down. I added what I might, including the story of the murder of the faithful crewman.

"What was his name?" he asked me.

"I think he had no official Name, sir, but he was called T'orr."

Orion-Riit made a strange, clearly ceremonial, gesture. "He will not be forgotten," he said.

"The rest you know because you were here," Marthar finished. "Bengar seems to have vanished. Now it's your turn. And why didn't you restore *Valiant*? No, tell us everything in order."

So Orion settled down to tell what had happened in the *Valiant*, and here is the tale.

The four of them, S'maak, Orion, the Judge and the

Doctor were in the eating area, sitting around a table. S'maak had the closed look of someone who was communing with the ship and studying readouts in his head.

Orion asked *Valiant*, "Where are the kits?"

"Inside the first lander," Valiant answered.

"Dear God, not with Silver?" the Doctor exclaimed.

"No, in the lander commanded by Samuel Anderson," *Valiant* told them.

"Well, that's something to be grateful about, I suppose," the Doctor said. "Why the devil did they have to do it?"

"High spirits," Orion answered comfortably. He seemed more pleased with their enterprise than annoyed.

"*Valiant*, Silver's lander has just left. I want you to ensure that neither lander can lift again without a direct order from me. Can you do that?"

"Certainly, S'maak-Captain," *Valiant* replied.

"Now I want you to destroy Silver's lander while not damaging the Andersons.' Can you do that? I would prefer it to happen on planetfall and to look like an accident."

There was no answer.

"*Valiant*, that was an order." S'maak-Captain said with a trace of anger.

There was no response.

"Why is *Valiant* not acknowledging your order?" the Doctor wondered.

"Uh-oh," the Judge said thoughtfully. "I rather think that Silver has anticipated that."

"*Valiant*, acknowledge," S'maak-Captain said coldly. There was no response.

"I think we had best get to the control room," Orion

suggested. "We may have to put into action the emergency measures."

They all went up in the lift, looking at each other. When they got to the control room, the door was closed; this was normal, but when S'maak ordered it to open it did nothing.

"There is a subsidiary intelligence node called *Vorchar* which is supposed to respond in an emergency," S'maak said. "*Vorchar*, acknowledge."

Nothing happened.

"Mine was called *Vi'irth*," Orion told them. "*Vi'irth*, please reply." Nothing happened.

"Mine was called *Victor*. *Victor*, please acknowledge," said the Judge. There was only the hum of the engines and the faint hiss of atmosphere controls. They turned to the Doctor.

"Mine was called *Victor* too. I guess we shared one," the doctor admitted.

"I should say that Silver anticipated this too," the Judge sighed. "Anybody else got any bright ideas?"

The elevator sighed and went down.

"The armaments. Quickly, one deck down, before the crew get to them!" S'maak called over his shoulder as he moved to the stairs, Orion after him instantly. The humans rattled after the two kzin, making a deal more noise as they clattered down. One deck down and the small room where the hand weapons were stored was close. S'maak-Captain wrenched it open and took out some human needlers, which he gave to the men. He also took some kzin-sized needlers, sticking three in his belt and giving three more to Orion. There was a blaster, which he also stuck in a belt, and some rifles, which he looked at for a moment. He gave three to each of the humans and broke the others like dry sticks. The ammunition boxes for the rifles he handed out to the Doctor and the Judge, and spare magazines for the kzin needlers went into his pouch and Orion's. They heard the lift coming back. There were many weapons left, including some huge kzin cutlasses, which he ignored, but Orion took one.

The lift opened on three kzin who saw them and in the same moment screamed and charged, *wtsais* drawn instantly. S'maak-Captain shot them with a needler. Their bodies came apart under the hail, but the corpses wouldn't admit they were dead until Orion sliced their heads off with the cutlass. He swung the great blade casually as though it weighed nothing, and the Doctor winced as it went through tissue, bone and cartilage like butter.

"Your ears, I think, Lord," S'maak-Captain said politely.

"Not my custom," Orion said, equally politely.

"There are more where they came from," the Judge warned. "By my count there were thirteen kzin still on board when the landers left. That leaves ten of them."

"Leave the lift, with those bodies there so the door won't close, which cuts off access to the mutinous scum. We take the stairs down. You humans, stay behind us. And keep those needlers on safety. I don't want to be shot in the back."

The two kzin prowled down the stairs like ghosts in a hurry, the two humans following them with less speed but more noise.

"Do you think we can take out ten kzin?" the Doctor whispered.

"You and I can't, not even with a blaster apiece. They

move too damned fast," the Judge answered with an air of regret. "But S'maak doesn't seem to have any problem with needling them. Orion would probably want to do it the old-fashioned way in single combat. But I'd back him to win that too. S'maak would think it a waste of time. He's a realist. Like young Marthar. If she were here, those mutinous scum would already be dead I suspect, probably vaporized. The female of the species is more deadly than the male."

There were seven kzin in the eating area, looking around aimlessly. S'maak-Captain got two before the others worked out what was happening, then they all drew *wtsais* and attacked. S'maak-Captain took down another one, and Orion took down another three with his cutlass. The Judge and the Doctor killed one between them, though S'maak-Captain had to finish him with a *wtsai*.

"Not our custom either," the Judge thanked him. "Help yourself if you collect ears, though; you did a good job of finishing this one off."

"I already have plenty of ears, ears of genuine warriors, not scum like these," S'maak said briskly, cleaning his *wtsai* fastidiously on the mutineers' fur.

"Waiters, can you clean up the mess, please?" the Doctor asked the mechanical trolleys with arms which brought the food. The trolleys had a little trouble, but they started cleaning up the corpses between them. Somehow the machines managed to give the impression they both enjoyed cleaning and disapproved of the mess. What happened to the meat after that was something the *Valiant* party never found out.

"How do we find the others?" Orion asked.

"We try crew territory. I rather think the Spy-Glass Inn has been reopened for business," S'maak-Captain answered. He was right. They found the remaining three kzin largely drunk, but still capable of putting up a fight, though not very effectively. S'maak-Captain shot them before they could get their coordination back. It was rather noisy for the human beings, with the screams of outraged tigers and the hiss of the needlers in counterpoint. Orion and S'maak hefted the corpses to an airlock and spaced them. Both kzin treated it as a day's work. The Doctor was almost in shock by the time it was over. He'd seen plenty of death before, but retail rather than wholesale. And usually with a lot less blood.

The kzin had cleaned themselves before they all met again in the eating area, which was now clear of bodies and indeed any sign that there had ever been any. The kzin drank a warm broth, while the Doctor looked on in fascination.

"You think it might contain bits of mutineer, Doctor?" Orion asked with a flick of his ears. "Very likely some will at some point. Were *Valiant* still operating, she would disapprove of our spacing the last three. A waste of good organics."

"I think I'll have a whisky and soda, waiter," the Judge announced as he lit a cigar.

"And I think a medicinal brandy for me," the Doctor added. This was a very unusual request for the Doctor, who would seldom drink, even wine and never spirits. He took the glass, sniffed at it, sipped it, made a face and started to fill his pipe.

"Speaking of the *Valiant*, what do we do now?" the Judge asked. "We've no control over anything more central than the waiters and lifts. I suppose that Silver controls everything else, unless *Valiant* managed to get him before he got her."

"I hardly think he had time to install his substitute for *Valiant*. It is possible, the swab is clever. But my guess is that he has fallen back onto direct command from the console. And he can't get to it, he's grounded. And his men can't get to it, for they are dead."

"And we can't get to it, because the residual control won't let us in," Orion pointed out. "We're here for a long time by the look of things."

There was a long, gloomy silence.

"There is one faint possibility," Orion growled thoughtfully. "It depends on Silver having made a slight miscalculation, and whether we can get down on planet and back."

"What is your idea, Dominant One?" asked S'maak-Captain. Now they'd got over the excitement and the killing, S'maak was back on formal terms.

"The kits. *Valiant* gave them access to some portion of her. They might not have been stopped, Silver may not have thought *Valiant* could do such a thing. But she did, or at least I hope so. I'm sure my daughter would have checked and complained vociferously had she not been given access. So there's a good chance Marthar or Peter could get us into the command center, but we would need to be able to get down there, find them, pick them up and bring them back. Is that possible, S'maak-Captain?"

S'maak considered. "We can get down, and maybe we

can get back. There is one lander left, and it can be controlled manually in an emergency. I can fly it by claw. It's hardly a difficult orbit to compute since we are in Lagrange One, as you humans call it, directly between the planet and the sun. Getting down requires little power and no great skill. Getting back is harder, requiring a careful rendezvous with the *Valiant*, but I could do it. Finding the kits might be more of a problem. We don't know what has happened down there. Silver may have got them and killed them."

There was even more gloom at this.

"Killing Marthar would take a bit of doing," Orion said. "She has the training of the Riit. I am thankful now that my Sire Lord Vaemar insisted on it. And she has the temperament, too. I think it more than likely that she is alive and causing trouble for someone."

"Finding her might not be easy," said S'maak-Captain. "The fact that she is of the Royal Bloodline and trained does not counter the fact that she is young, impulsive and a little inclined to disobedience. I would not expect her to obey the Andersons, in particular. Still, since it appears to be the only course of action open to us, we must take the last lander and set down close to the Andersons' craft and hope she and the man-kit are still there."

"Then let us do it soon, S'maak-Captain, before Silver can get to them and make more trouble for us!" Orion growled. "Do these landers have any weaponry? I should like to destroy Silver's lander and any of his crew of mutineers from the air if that is possible."

"I fear not, Dominant One. The landers are hardly military-style machines. They have no weapons at all. The tail jet might serve, though not very effectively. And the hulls are thin, a blaster would rip a hole in one and render it unspaceworthy. We do not know that Silver has any blasters, but it would be foolish to take the chance if we are to return to the mother ship."

Orion growled. "Pity. I'd have taken some pleasure in using their lander for target practice. And now I think we had better move. It would be prudent to take with us as many small arms and as much ammunition as we can easily carry. So back up those stairs."

Getting to the third lander required climbing down more stairs to crew levels. There was a big hangar with bays for three craft, two of which were empty. The third held the blue lander. It was locked in the embrace of something that looked to the humans like a crane crossed with an octopus, with cables and hoses joining them. S'maak-Captain stalked purposefully toward the lander and pulled out his phone. The others followed hopefully. He seemed to know what he was doing, which gave them some badly-needed comfort. He inserted the phone into a socket in the octopus part and started pressing keys. He had soon established some kind of communication with the lander, or rather with its computer, which seemed to be a primitive one. More like the brainstem of a reptile than the mind of a ship like *Valiant*. And reachable by unsophisticated methods that didn't require the mother ship to supervise, they thought with some gratitude.

"The problem with high-level automation is that once it breaks down, you're totally stuffed," the Judge remarked as he watched S'maak clicking on buttons with his claw tips.

"A point which has been rediscovered many times by the military," Orion remarked drily. "Subverting other ships' computers is an art form and one of very considerable use to pirates, I should imagine. Which is, no doubt, why Silver is so expert at it. If I recall correctly, he presented himself to Blandly as someone who had programmed autochefs. I think he rather undervalued himself."

The lander started to light up and the door swung open.

"It is going to be necessary to program the boat from inside. I have only established the most simple communication at present," S'maak-Captain cautioned them. He withdrew his phone and climbed up the stairs to a gantry which gave access to the now-open door. Lights gleamed inside. They followed him into the door, which was big enough for them to pass through, though only just. S'maak gave a single-button press, the outer door closed and the inner opened. They went into the empty vessel. There was room for about a dozen kzin and maybe as many humans in the acceleration couches.

"I suggest you all get into the couches. They are much like those on the *Valiant*, though with less monitoring," S'maak told them. "I shall have to remain at the console. I cannot program the whole maneuver, and I shall need to make course corrections."

"If there is room, I should prefer to watch with you, S'maak-Captain," Orion told him.

"Very well, Dominant One. There is a pilot's couch and a co-pilot's also. The acceleration should not be too great. But it might harm you humans. Also there is no room for you."

The Judge and the Doctor accepted the advice and lay

down on the acceleration couches. The walls raised themselves to turn into coffins. Not for too long, they hoped, as the lids slid down.

"Are there going to be any problems I need to know about in advance, S'maak-Captain?" Orion rumbled.

"I think our problems will start when we have landed, Dominant One," S'maak told him.

And, of course, they did.

CHAPTER SEVENTEEN

"They will try to spray needles in here and rely on ricochets to kill us," S'maak-Captain said mildly. "To stop that we have to narrow the doorspace as much as possible and put some of the acceleration couches in the way of any direct line of fire. They will absorb the needles reasonably well if we arrange them correctly. They may have another blaster, in which case we are finished. But the one Silver used was destroyed by my shot."

"Good shooting, Captain," the Doctor said.

"No such thing," S'maak-Captain told him circumspectly. "I didn't aim at the gun, but I was in a hurry."

Ursula and one of the kzin went back and began demolishing some of the larger acceleration couches, handing back bits to us. Marthar and I busied ourselves. She swung the broken door as close to closed as possible, then we started stacking material in front of the small slit that was left.

"They'll probably sneak up from the side and try to open

the door, so let's make it as hard as possible," Marthar said. To someone who didn't know her well, Martha was shockingly good at anticipating the reactions of someone murderously evil. To someone who did know her well, as I did, it didn't shock, it impressed. She jammed shards of metal into where the hinge would have been if it hadn't been broken.

"If they can't see us, we can't see them," the Judge pointed out as we blocked up the entrance. "I'd like to take a crack at them."

"What I would like to do," said S'maak, "is to keep those kzin in the green lander there. Or better yet, entice them out and kill them. The question is, how long do we have before Silver and his gang attack?"

His question was answered immediately. With a mixture of screams and roars, the pirates attacked. Marthar threw herself behind the door and hoiked me close to her with a quick grab of my belt. She had her needler in her right paw, pointing up. Needles sprayed around the outside, screeching as they hit mostly metal, but a few made it through the slit and buried themselves in the wadding we had made. There were a few tiny gaps at the side, and Marthar waited patiently until an enormous violet eye peered in at us and then put half a dozen needles through it. It fell back without a sound. Those needles could cut through almost any tissue, but they would ricochet inside the skull, cutting the brain to shreds and killing instantly. Someone put a needler through a gap, and we ducked. Marthar shot the gun from underneath and as it recoiled up she shot through where the paw holding the gun had to be and got a satisfying scream of pain.

Only one or two of them at a time could get close enough to get a shot in, and we hastily put more wadding from the couches just about everywhere a shot could go.

"Is there any other way they can get inside, S'maak-Captain?" Orion asked.

"Not without a blaster, Dominant One. And while they cannot get in, we cannot get out, not while they are still there. And then only with difficulty, as your most competent young daughter has jammed the door."

Marthar studied him, unsure whether some irony had been thrown in, but seemed satisfied that it had not. Kzin had always had trouble with irony. Marthar had mastered it to perfection, but she'd had me to practice on.

"We need something like a periscope. I don't suppose the control console has anything left that functions to give an outside view," Orion said.

"Let us see," S'maak-Captain said. "I gave orders to see if any communication gear was operational or could be repaired. I think we can rely on your daughter to keep out the renegades while we check. Come with me, Dominant One."

They went off together without a backward glance. "Golly, that was a vote of confidence," I said, amazed. "I think he's come to like you."

"Respect, not like. But that's just as good, indeed much better." Marthar was offhand in tone, but I think she was pleased. S'maak was one tough cookie. I suppose it was tough calling to tough.

Another eye looked in briefly and Marthar put only four needles in it this time. There was a brief cough and a thud, then a long silence. I wondered what on Earth they were up to. What would I have done in their place, I pondered? I'd have got something like one of those endoscope thingys that the Doctor has; you poke it down throats or up the other end, and you can see through a fish-eye lens by fiber-optics with a tiny light. It didn't seem like the sort of thing the average pirate would carry about with him, but I suppose they could have got their lander to make one. Without that there didn't seem to be a lot they could do.

S'maak-Captain came back. "Quick, get the door open, we have to get out of here. They've gone back to their lander. Why they didn't use the green lander I don't know, but if they have in mind what I suspect they do, this place could be a death trap."

Marthar and I began obediently pulling out the wedges she had put in. I soon discovered they were in far too hard for me to budge, but I took them from Marthar as she extracted them.

"I want one of you Heroes to remain. It is almost certain death, but an honorable one," S'maak-Captain said to the loyal crew. They all volunteered immediately. S'maak made his choice and instructed him in some low growls and spitting sounds.

I began to think about all the things that could go wrong. All the things that Silver would *make* go wrong if he could. Might he be the one planning the ambush? Had his gang not so much gone as hidden so we would think what S'maak had thought and come running out? Were they waiting in the bushes until we were out of the lander and then gunning us down? I didn't know, but a feeling of dread came over me.

I was shy about talking to S'maak-Captain, but it was important so I forced myself.

"Please sir, what if the pirates are waiting in ambush for us? You can't be sure they went back to their lander. Maybe they are hiding in the bushes for us to come out."

He looked at me out of big violet eyes that would have terrified a tiger. "Well-thought of, man-kit. The possibility had occurred to me, and for that reason I shall go out alone first while you stand ready to reseal the door." Marthar gave me a look of approval. It was worth being brave sometimes, although I wasn't as brave as S'maak-Captain.

We watched as he ran to the bushes, dodging as he went in case there was any shooting, either from the bushes or the green lander, but nothing untoward happened. He checked up thoroughly any possible places of concealment. Then he called us out and made his disposition.

The rest of us shot out, everyone carrying weapons, and following S'maak as he ran for the woods.

"What makes you leave, S'maak-Captain?" Ursula asked. "I thought we were reasonably safe in there."

"If I were Silver, I should take out some of the fuel in gaseous form and pipe it into our lander. It would be highly flammable, but it would poison us long before they needed to set it alight. They have the makings of a flame-thrower and also a way of driving us out. I think they have gone back to their lander to get it, because they plan to use the green lander to escape if they can jimmy the software that stops them from leaving. I should have thought of the possibility before. Through scanning, we found that everyone had left. Hardly any of the equipment is functional, but some of the external monitors could be made to work after a fashion.

And we need to capture the green lander. It is fully functional except for the software lock that stops them from taking off. And you, young kit, may be able to get around that. I hope so, or we are due to stay here for a long time."

"Ah, *Valeria*. Our code-word name for the fraction of *Valiant* allocated to Peter and me," said Marthar with satisfaction. "Yes, I'm looking forward to trying that."

"I want to ambush them. I want them to think we're still inside, which is why I left a Hero. When they are all busy trying to poke a hose in, then we gun them down.

"You will hold fire until I shoot first. Then open up and try to get every one of them. Fire at the enemy directly in front of you until they scatter. We have to even the numbers. Peter, you are the smallest, so you take the place of honor: I want you in that dip, but keep your head down. Here is a human needler for you, and one of the rifles. I wish you to be reserve, and to shoot only if it seems that our ammunition is exhausted or if you are directly threatened."

That didn't much sound like the place of honor to me, although it was closer to the lander than any of the others would be. I sure hoped that I wouldn't be directly threatened; taking out a kzin with only a needler looked pretty difficult. They have big eyes, but not so big given that a needler tends to spray a lot. You'd have to be awfully close to one of them for that to work, and if you were that close you probably wouldn't live long enough to get off a shot. I had the *wtsai* that Silver had given me, but it would be useless against a kzin.

S'maak positioned us and gave low-voiced orders to all.

He signaled the Hero left in the lander to close the door, and came to me.

"You will have to remain motionless for a long time. And you must not use your phone. I want them to cluster around the lander and be committed to getting gas into it before we strike. Do you understand?"

"Yes, S'maak-Captain," I told him. Then he vanished behind me. The ambush was ready. I hoped we didn't have to wait too long. We monkeys aren't very good at waiting.

They came. They made a lot of noise, and they were dragging an enormous cylinder with ropes. They also brandished hoses: it looked as though their plan was to force us out of the now nearly empty lander, just as S'maak-Captain had guessed. I held the rifle: it shot a tiny rocket-propelled grenade. It was too big for me, but it had a very considerable impact without too much recoil. I kept my head down and could see little. Anyway, I was not to fire until everybody else was slowing down, which meant I might not get to fire at all. It wasn't what I thought of as a position of honor; I felt that S'maak was trying to flatter me. It didn't seem much like his manner, though. Maybe things would go differently from the way I imagined, which was that we'd cut them all down in the first few seconds.

The pirates gathered around the lander, and I thought it must surely be time for S'maak to start the shooting, but nothing happened. I took a quick glance to see what was going on near the lander. Silver was among them, wearing a headband of green silk, and directing them. Then he looked around as if puzzled and slowly fell back. He returned to directing affairs, and they were trying to connect a long tube to the tank they had brought back, while others were holding the nozzle. Silver was a little way from the door of the lander, watching the activity. He had his back to me, and I brought my rifle to bear on him. I was tempted to shoot him.

Then when I had more or less given up hope of our side doing anything, we launched a burst of fire from the bushes. There were screams and roars of shock and pain but mainly rage. I took aim at Silver, who had whirled and was looking above me at the bushes. For a moment I had a clear shot, but somehow I couldn't bring myself to fire. I hated the evil monster, but I couldn't shoot him. Then he threw himself on the ground and rolled, calling to the others to do the same, and my chance was gone.

How many of those down were dead and how many were still a threat was impossible to say. I learned later that we had killed or disabled five out of the fifteen on the first wave of shooting, which meant that they still outnumbered us. And our human beings were almost useless against kzin, so the inequality was still much in their favor. I held my fire as instructed, feeling that I should have shot Silver.

I risked another glance over the edge of the dip and saw that the pirates were crawling towards our position and reflected that perhaps I was in a position of honor after all. They would get to me first. Perhaps I was expendable.

One of the pirates stood up. I guessed our side had run out of needles. A rifle went off and the grenade shot across, but the kzin moved away like lightning and it missed. Other pirates stood too, waved their *wtsais*, and started towards us. There was a roar from our side and our people also stood and advanced in a row. I put my head up and looked out, and there was Claws, a few paces away, looking at me with a horrible grin. He had a *wtsai* in his left paw and a huge cutlass in his right. I pointed the rifle at him. It was all right to fire now, I had every justification. My rifle wobbled. I was just so frightened I couldn't think. Then Claws stood up and looked down at me.

"Hello, little *Kz'zeerkt*," he said. "You will taste good. It's too long since I had monkey-meat."

He raised the cutlass, and I knew I should fire, but I was paralyzed with fear. Then a scream of rage came from behind me and Marthar was there. She carried only her *wtsai* and held it as if she meant business, but Claws was twice as big as she was. Still, she went for him. He deflected her thrust easily with his own *wtsai* and then swung the cutlass at her. She tried to parry with her own *wtsai*, bringing the blade across her body and she almost succeded in stopping the huge blade, but it bit into her left arm. Then Claws moved in for the kill, about to bring his *wtsai* up under Marthar's ribcage. I put the barrel of my rifle nearly against his head and pulled the trigger. The explosion was almost quiet. His head vanished, the fragments of bone and brain spattered over Marthar and me, and the body went boneless and collapsed at Marthar's feet. Marthar slipped down into the hollow.

"I need you to help me bind this wound, Peter," she whispered. "It's urgent. And look to see if you can find the implant in there, I'm frightened."

Marthar *frightened*? It wasn't possible, but I tore off my shirt, ripped it into strips and went to her left arm. The fur had been driven into the flesh and the flesh hung in gobbets, blood streaming out from the slash. I sobbed with relief. It was bad, but to a kzin or even a kzinrett, it would be accounted a minor scratch. I didn't know what the implant looked like, but there was no sign of it. Marthar looked around frantically. Then she saw something on the ground, a chunk of bloody flesh, and in it something blue and broken. Marthar gave a howl that raised the hackles.

"I'm done, Peter," she said looking at me with horror in her eyes. "It's broken and has leaked out. I don't have my implant anymore."

"What will happen?" I asked.

"I will turn into an animal, Peter. I will be dead. The friend you had will be gone forever. And my body will house nothing but a mewling beast. I can't bear it, Peter, I'd rather be dead. Much rather."

I had tied the bands around her arm, and the bleeding had slowed if not stopped, the bands already sodden with her blood. I knew she would already be healing. At least her body would. Marthar stood.

"I will take a few more before I go, Peter. I want you to remember me as I was. And I want you to know I cared for you, little friend. And I admired you for your strength." Then she was gone, howling up over the crest of the hollow like an unstoppable wave. Marthar was going out and was going to take as many of the pirates with her as she could.

I took my rifle and stood too. Our people had risen and advanced against the pirates. Orion stood with two rifles held under his arms, his claws on the triggers, and he scored some hits, but mostly misses. The rifles were too small for him to use them properly. Then he threw them down and drew the huge cutlass and his *wtsai*, and went forward faster than I thought possible. He was ahead of Marthar, and S'maak was by his side. The two of them alone were unstoppable, and the pirates fled. Marthar was disconsolate. Kzin can't weep or she would have wept. Dying gloriously in a screaming charge is impractical if the enemy has already fled.

We all looked around the field of battle. We had not a single casualty except Marthar, and she was being held firmly by her father. He had inspected the wound and then laughed at it, whereupon Marthar explained to him. I was too far away to hear the words, but I could see the look on his face. He saw me and beckoned me over.

"Peter, you must somehow get Marthar back to the *Valiant*, and get her into a kzin autodoc. I do not know how any of this is to be done, but it is vital to my daughter's safety. I think you know why."

"Yes, sir, if it can be done I shall do it, I promise. But I have no idea how we can get there."

"Nor I," he said grimly. "All three landers are down, and none of them is able to lift off, the other two because *Valiant* grounded them, and ours because it is smashed beyond repair. We must see if S'maak-Captain has any ideas."

He didn't, but he took us all back to the lander. "I want the tanks disabled so they can't try to poison us. It should be enough to confiscate the hoses, but the devils might find an alternative. I still don't know why they had to go back to the red lander to get this; the green lander would have done."

"I think that the red lander was damaged on planetfall," Marthar told him. "I think they have some hope of using the green lander to get off, but the red lander looked as if it had been shot at and taken a laser-beam through the nose. I didn't get close enough to see much, but it looks as if they will not be able to use it for return to space even if it was not grounded."

S'maak looked approvingly at her. He bowed. "Most important intelligence, My Lady," he said. Marthar had moved up several notches since their first meeting. She'd been a bad-mannered kit then; now she was his Lady.

"What I don't understand is, where is Bengar? He seems to have vanished," Marthar remarked. I had almost forgotten the marooned pirate.

The tanks were opened and the escaping gas soon burst into flame spontaneously. It seemed a waste, but I don't suppose fuel was the problem.

"Into the wreck, we are all due for a rest. Tomorrow, ship's time, we shall have to hunt some food. We are better provided with weapons than with food, though we have little ammunition left. But I think the pirates are less of a threat now. Let us see what tomorrow may bring."

S'maak set a series of sentries, all kzin. I don't think he trusted Ursula, the Judge or me, still less the Doctor. He knew that human beings slept for long periods, while kzin could nap with one eye open and one ear ready for anything. Sneaking up on a sleeping Kzin was a waste of time; you might as well come with a big brass band playing.

I lay down to sleep, my mind a blur. Obviously there was nothing wrong with Marthar's brain yet. How long did we have? I wondered. Then I fell asleep.

CHAPTER EIGHTEEN

When I awoke, I discovered I'd slept for ten hours. Everybody else was up and some had gone out hunting. Marthar, the Judge and the Doctor were still there, and the Doctor was talking to Marthar. She looked sunken and there was clearly something wrong. The vitality just wasn't there.

I had slept in my clothes and felt disgusting. There was some water in small containers, but this was precious,. There was some which had been taken from the canal; it had been purified by filters and still smelled funny, but I used some for washing and felt almost human again. Then I joined Marthar and the Doctor.

"It's reversible, my dear, it's reversible," the Doctor was saying. "If all else fails, we wait until the next ship comes. It will be some time, but we can all survive, including you. And then we can get you back to your usual bubbling, lively self, I promise. The worst thing is that you'll have no memories of most of the period. But we shall look after you, won't we, Peter?"

"With my life, Marthar, I promise."

She just looked at me, and there was something ancient and indifferent looking out of her eyes, but she said nothing. Whether the mental degeneration she feared so much had already started or whether she was only badly frightened by the prospect I could not tell; but she had declared her fear, which was not a bit like her. She does not have the sense of fear that I have, to her, fear is a stimulant. I suppose the difference was that if a physical threat came, she would rise to the occasion and fight back, but this was something she couldn't fight, or so she thought. Maybe she was wrong.

"Doctor, is there any way Marthar can fight this thing?" I asked. "What if she were to do calculations or something, or maybe practice talking?"

Doctor Lemoine looked uncomfortable, but he tried gamely to put the best face on it. "There are bound to be some parts she can do little about, the neurotransmitters will dwindle gradually. But yes, doing some reasoning will perhaps help. Anything that exercises the brain will be good."

"No, it will just use up the neuro things faster," Marthar spoke slowly as if it took concentration to put the sentences together. The Doctor looked embarrassed.

"Well, perhaps, but there is still a pool of them in your brain, in your blood supply. That will last for a while. And it will be gradual at first. But we will look after you. Your father is deeply concerned for you, you know."

"I know daddy cares. But there is nothing he can do."

"You will only make matters worse if you get downhearted, you know," the Doctor said earnestly. "I shall look to see if there is any alternative, perhaps some local plant life which can help."

"Chewing plants?" Marthar asked solemnly, as if the prospect was terrible.

"Perhaps an infusion. I must look up my biochemistry and see what I can find," he told her soothingly, and he got up and left us.

"Marthar, you know I would do anything for you, don't you?" I asked. I was so angry that she could sense it.

She looked at me again out of those ancient eyes, like a tiger that has seen everything in the universe and found it too little to be of interest.

"Thank you, Peter. But what I fear most is the shame. I don't want anyone I know to see me as I am going to be."

"There is no shame, you idiot," I told her hotly. She almost looked angry for a moment. I began to see that it was not just fear, she had already lost the ability to sense nuance. She thought I had insulted her. Then she relaxed.

"You do not see it at all, Peter, my friend. If I were to come back from being a . . . a sort of pet, I should know what others have seen. Nobody could forget what I had been, if only for a time. Nobody could look at me without remembering a mindless beast. That I could not bear."

"Marthar, you are more than just a smart kzinrett, you have so much more than that. I will love you when you are what you call a mindless beast, and I will love you when you return. I know I will."

"I want more than love, Peter, much more. I want respect. I want my own respect much more than the respect of others, but when this happens I shall have neither. And without that thing which lies underneath honor, I am nothing."

There didn't seem to be anything much to say. I burst into tears and she stroked me and licked me. She'd never done that before. It was wet and raspy, and I can't say I enjoyed it, but it was meant as affection, so I treasured it anyway.

Sam, Ursula's husband, and one of the loyal kzin that had been on their lander, had come back. Bringing them up to date on the battle we had survived took only a little time I gather. I didn't spend any with them. I wanted to be with Marthar. I feared what she would do. She had intended to die in battle, and that didn't seem to be an option anymore, but I feared that she had some sort of plan to do away with herself before the degeneration got too far advanced, and I was determined to thwart her. If the only thing I could do for her was to keep her alive until the relief ship came, I would do it or die trying.

Others brought back food from the hunt. The humans cooked their share over an open fire outside. There was not much in the lander: a small amount of provisions, some frozen, and a microwave oven. The landers weren't expected to be used for much more than some exploration of the environment and to check the suitability of landing sites for the mother ship. They had tried to revive our communications but so far there was nothing. The only idea that had been presented was to try and take over the green lander, but no one knew how to do this. There were still a half a dozen kzin inside, as far as we knew. Some had come out to join the other pirates in the attack on us, but they had retreated when the others fled back to the red lander. If we'd been able to get into the green lander, or the red one for that matter, then Marthar or I could try to get in touch with the fraction of the *Valiant* called *Valeria*, and maybe call for help. If we could get Marthar back to the *Valiant*, she would be all right: an hour in the kzin autodoc would see her restored. It was well within its capacity to fill her up with green pills, and perhaps even to construct another implant. Somehow I had to get her back to the *Valiant*, but how was totally beyond me. I thought of one impractical plan after another. I am sure Orion was doing the same, trying to find a way into the green lander. But they were sealed in and, although we might have damaged the lander enough itself to make her unspaceworthy, that would have done us no good.

I was outside, sitting on the stony ground, when I overheard a conversation between the Doctor and the Judge that I'd have much rather missed.

"Doctor, is there really any chance of keeping Marthar alive without the implant?" the Judge asked him.

"Alive, yes. After a fashion. But there are worse things than death, though I'm not supposed to believe that."

"What were you thinking of?" the Judge asked slowly. He was smoking a cigar, which was why he had come outside. Ursula wouldn't let him smoke in the lander.

"The poor female is in adolescence, Judge. Think about it."

"You mean she'll go into heat at some point, and if it happens when her mind is gone, she'll be signaling that she is available and receptive to any male kzin around the place."

"And it's against all reason that one or more won't avail himself of the offer. Kzin are not much given to reflection about consequences."

"Neither are human beings, doctor. But I take your point. But hell, it's natural enough, I guess."

"And when she discovers, when her mind returns, that she is pregnant by one of the pirates or has had offspring and doesn't even know the father? I think she might take it rather hard. Intelligent kzinretti don't so much look down on the unintelligent ones, they don't despise them; rather, their feelings are something between pity, horror and loathing. To carry forever the mark of having been one is something it would be impossible to live with. So if Marthar is to survive this, she needs to be kept in a cage, or all the male kzin on the planet except Orion need to be. It's hardly practical, is it?"

I crept away feeling sick. I simply hadn't thought about it, but Marthar would be coming up to an age when intelligent kzinretti thought about marriage. In the old days they'd be bought into a harem and that would be that. I tried not to think about it.

Nothing had been seen of Bengar. I suppose the sight of the kzin around us made him wish to keep well clear of the wreck that we inhabited. He seemed to be good at not being seen. I wondered what he was doing, and if there was any way he could help us. It didn't seem likely. He hadn't been able to help himself much.

I think we were all a little frustrated. Orion had said nothing to me, although his eyes flickered over to where I was sitting with Marthar, sometimes stroking her fur in an attempt to comfort her, sometimes having her lick me and run her claws through my hair with great gentleness in an attempt to comfort me. She could feel my feelings with all the acuteness she ever had, and she still cared enough to want to make me happy, although being happy wasn't something that was going to happen until I had my old Marthar back. I went back to trying to devise a plan.

One of the sentries called out, and S'maak-Captain and Orion went to see what it was. They were careful not to expose themselves, because they half-expected another attack by the pirates. But it was only two kzin. One of them was waving a white flag, and a dirty grey thing it was. The other was Silver. I left Marthar to go and see what he wanted, feeling hatred in my heart. I hated all the pirates, the dead Claws most of all, but Silver next. Between them, they had hurt my Marthar and for that, I would destroy them given even half a chance. I'd never hated anyone or anything before; I thought I had hated S'maak at one point, but found I hadn't. What I felt as I looked at Silver was building up from underneath into something that might drive me to a suicidal attack, like a kzin in battle fever. I contained it, though; I was going to use it to destroy Silver someday. I didn't know how, but he was going to die at my hand if I could devise a way.

He looked as amiable and sociable as ever. He wore the green headband which seemed to be some sign of rank among the pirates, while his lieutenant waved the flag.

"Hoy, S'maak-Captain, we come under a flag of truce, will ye respect it?" the one with the flag called out. Flags of truce had been used in the wars, according to my teachers. An idea which the kzin had copied from us though only on rare occasions.

"What do you want?" S'maak-Captain asked, his voice expressionless.

"For Silver-Captain to join ye, to make terms," the lieutenant replied.

"Silver-Captain? There is no such person," S'maak answered with only a brief rictus of anger.

Silver answered, almost apologetically. " 'Tes me, sir, only Silver, these poor spacers have chosen me captain after your desertion, sir.

"We're willing to submit, if we can come to terms, and no bones about it," Silver called. "All I ask, S'maak-Captain, is that ye give your word that I can come up and leave me safe and sound to go back afterwards. One minute to leave before ye shoot, and no attack on me person, or the poor spacer here wi' me."

"I've no desire to talk to you. If you wish to talk to me you may come, and I'll respect your truce until a minute after I have thrown you out. If there's to be treachery, it will be from your side, and then may the Fanged God help you."

"That's enough for me, S'maak-Captain," Silver cried out cheerfully. "The word of a Named Hero is more than enough for me, and ye may lay to that."

We could see the flag-waver trying to stop Silver coming closer and, given the coldness of S'maak's reply, that was not too surprising, but Silver clapped him on the back as if the idea of alarm was absurd. Then he advanced, climbing slowly up the small hill where the lander had fallen over, making heavy weather of it with his limp most pronounced, until he came right up to the half-open door and peered in, past S'maak and Orion. His eye caught mine for a moment and his ears flickered in greeting, but he said nothing. For me, the image of the murder of T'orr was back in my mind. Silver was tricked up in his best, his fur was combed and his belts were clean and neat in their different colors. The Judge held his needler in both hands, pointing it in the air but ready to swing down at a moment's notice. Orion likewise held his cutlass loosely, playing idly with it and resting it on one broad shoulder.

"Here you are, Hero," said S'maak, with a slight sneer in the *Hero*. "You may sit down if you wish."

"You ain't going to keep me outside, S'maak-Captain?" He complained. "'Tes not so civil as I would ha' thought ye'd be."

"Why, Silver, had you pleased to be an honest kzin, ye'd be tutoring still and have your own tavern to lord it over, so long as ye didn't make the crew drunk with alcohol. Your situation is your own doing. You're either tutor to the kits and programmer of the galley, when you were treated handsomely, or ye're Silver-Captain, a mutineer and a pirate, when you can go to the hot needles."

Silver seated himself on the ground with some difficulty. He didn't have his cutlass with him, and his *wtsai* was not in evidence. "Well, well, a sweet pretty gig ye've got yerselves here, ain't it? And there's Lord Orion himself, me respects to you Milord. And to you, Judge, and the Doctor too. And there's Peter, I see. Top of the mornin' to ye, Peter, so to speak, though 'twill be mornin' for quite some time yet, I'm thinking. Why, there ye all are, all together, like a happy family as it might be!"

"If you have anything to say, then say it!" S'maak said.

"Aye aye, right you are, S'maak-Captain. Dooty is dooty,

to be sure. Well now, you look here, that were a good lay of yours that ye did when we was sleeping. I don't know how ye managed it, silent as the grave ye were. Some of ye is pretty handy wi' a *wtsai*, and 'tis not easy to kill one of us wi'out waking any. And more than one, ye got, I allow. And I don't deny there was some of us shook by it. Maybe all was shook. Maybe I was shook meself. Maybe that's why I'm here for terms. But mark me, S'maak-Captain, it won't do twice, by thunder! We'll have to do sentry-go and ease off a point on the rum. Maybe you'll be thinking we was all of us a sheet in the wind's eye, but I wasn't; I was sober as . . . as the Doctor there. I was tired, that I'll grant ye, and if I'd woke a second sooner, I'd ha' caught ye in the act, so I would."

"And so?" asked S'maak-Captain, as cool as a cucumber. He might not have worked Silver's intentions out yet, but you could never have said so from his manner. I slowly realized that Bengar had been at work in their sleeping period. And he must have moved among them like an avenging ghost not to be detected. Of course they would have been drunk; Silver had ensured that there was rum on their lander. At least two had gone down by the sound of it. The odds were improving.

"Well, here it is," said Silver, with his head to one side and his eyes opened wide. "We wants that treasure, and we shall have it. You, I would say, wants your lives, and ye may have them. But we cannot get back to the *Valiant* and no more can you. But if we was to cooperate, then maybe we could get around the little difficulty. I'd be willing to let ye have *Valiant* back if ye'll take it that we will be with ye and watching ye closely. Oh, briefly, briefly, there's limits to how trusting the lads would be, d'ye see? But if I can get through to what remains of the computer in the other lander, and that would be easy enough since my men have her, and if I restore the ship to the *Valiant* as was, and if ye let her free the lander, why then we could all get back into space again. And us with the treasure or enough of it. Now I've never wished any of ye harm meself. Just the treasure it is, and always was."

"That won't do, get of a *sthondat*," S'maak told him contemptuously, an insult I knew to be one of the most mortal and unforgivable in all the kzin's rich vocabulary. "We know exactly what you planned. And we came within an ace of destroying your lander before you subverted *Valiant*."

"Ah, well, you will be glad to know that your precious *Valiant* got off a shot and damned near destroyed us before my hack took effect," Silver replied, still politely.

"Pity we didn't have another second or two, for it's deep in hell with the mist demons where you belong, every damned mutinous one of you," S'maak said. "There'll be a second ship along to pick us up before long, and then we'll be only too happy to leave you here, if I don't command your execution by destroying you from space."

I worried that S'maak was being too intransigent. If we went with Silver's idea, we might get Marthar back to the *Valiant* much sooner. I knew she was listening to all this behind the door, and I could imagine her feelings. But could we trust Silver? I had heard him while I was in the meat-locker, and I would never trust him again. Was there some way to bind him, to cheat *him*? I'd have broken my word to Silver without a moment's hesitation if it would save Marthar. Of course, Silver didn't know how desperate we were to get Marthar back to the *Valiant*, and he must not know. Which explained S'maak's manner. He wasn't going to give an inch until he had worked out how to spoil Silver's plan.

This whiff of temper seemed to calm Silver. He had been growing nettled before, but now he pulled himself together.

"Like enough, like enough," he said. "I'd set no limits on what a lord might consider shipshape or not, as the case were. I don't suppose ye'd have a drop o' rum wi' ye? Ah well, I think not; not your style, is it now?"

He and S'maak looked at each other for a long moment.

"Now, here it is. You agree to let us get the treasure into the green lander, ye agree to cooperate with us and stop shooting poor spacers, you help us restore *Valiant* to some semblance of her old intelligence for a while, and we'll offer ye all a choice. Either ye can come aboard when we ha' the treasure shipped and then I'll gi' ye all me word to drop ye off somewhere not too far away, some world that ye can use to get back t' *Ka'ashi*, d'ye see? Or if that ain't yer fancy, seein' as how some o' the lads are a bit rough and ha' some scores to settle, then ye can stay here and wait on your fine new ship coming in due course. We'll divide stores and leave ye enough to live like princes, and I'll even signal any nearby world that ye are here and waiting. Me word on it. Now you'll own that's handsome talking. Handsomer ye couldn't look to get. And I hope," he continued, raising his voice, "that all here have got that clear, for what is spoke to one is spoke to all."

S'maak-Captain was immovable. "Is that all?" he asked.

"My last word, by thunder!" Silver roared. "Refuse that and ye've seen the last o' me 'til ye ha' my *wtsai* in yer entrails, and ye may lay to that."

"Very well," S'maak said. "Now you hear me. My name is S'maak-Captain. I have sworn allegiance to Vaemar-Riit because I believe peace between kzin and man is the only hope for both species. If you will come up one by one, unarmed, I'll undertake to clap you all in irons and take you all back to Wunderland for a trial. I think, seeing *Valiant* is a human ship, that it would be before a combined human-Wunderkzin court. If you won't, then as I am S'maak-Captain, I shall see you all on ship to hell. You can't get your treasure back even if you could identify it; you can't sail the *Valiant*, you don't know enough; you can't fight us. You're in hyperspace with no way home, Silver, and those are the last good words you'll get from me, for by the Fanged God, the next time I see you I'll have your heart's blood. Now get away while you can."

Silver's face was a picture, his eyes started in his head with wrath. He put one paw on the ground. "Give me a paw up," he cried.

"Not I," said S'maak.

"Who'll help me to my feet?" Silver roared. Nobody moved. Growling curses, Silver crawled until he got to the hull, whereupon he hauled himself upright.

"We shall see whose heart's blood spills first," he swore with a murderous look at S'maak and Orion. Then he stumbled off, returned to his lieutenant, tore the flag off him and threw it far away.

An instant later they had vanished in the bushes.

CHAPTER NINETEEN

I slept wrapped around Marthar that night. Not that it was night outside, of course, but we had shuttered the windows and were running ship's time still, so it was dark and all the humans were asleep, and the kzin were resting. Marthar very gently picked me up, and I felt her rough tongue rasp my forehead briefly. Then she put me down and waited. I kept my eyes closed and pretended to sleep; it was easier because I almost was. I had to take care that my breath was steady; fooling someone with that level of sensory perception was hard. At length she decided I must be asleep and rose. I waited until she had slipped aft into the airlock, slipped my shoes back on and followed her.

When I came to the outer door, which she had opened a bit to get through it, I heard her say something to the guard and waited. Then I went out too. I waved a cheerful greeting at the kzin as he looked at me, poker-faced. He nodded briefly. Marthar was loping away into the distance and I ran after her, as silently as I could. She could move much faster than I if she wanted to, but she seemed half-drugged now and empty of energy. My blood sugar pack cut in, and I turned up the rate a bit. Running after Marthar was going to be a difficult business even when she was going so slowly, as if every pace was pain.

She went straight to the bushes where we had ambushed the pirates, then she looked up at the lime-green sun and walked on. I went after her with determination. I had an idea of where she was headed, but she didn't go in a straight line. She didn't try to conceal her path, she left tracks that I could easily follow, which was as well, because she was still moving faster than I was. Sometimes I would glimpse her fur through the bushes. Kzin were less well-camouflaged here than in the vegetation of their homeworld. I turned the oxygen feed up too, which could be dangerous if I kept it high for too long. But this was an emergency; my friend was going to need me.

We went on for some miles, and as I had expected the path curved. Marthar was headed for the tower but intended to come upon it from the opposite side to Silver's red lander.

It seemed hours, and I ran and panted in the thin air, despite the oxygen pack. I had lost her, but her track was clear enough in the bright sunlight, the violet shadows thrown by boulders and bushes showing the way. I nearly stumbled several times in my hurry. I was getting desperate that I should be too late when I ran into the ambush.

It was Marthar. She rose out of the bushes and grabbed me. "Noisy, noisy," she growled.

"Marthar, you can't leave me," I said and hugged her. She responded in a half-hearted way.

"Peter," she said. "Peter." It sounded odd, as though she

were savoring my name. "Peter. I must go. There is no choice. I have to leave everything."

"What do you mean?" I asked, my heart still pounding from the running.

"I must leave this world. I cannot stay and shame myself before all who know me. And there is only one way. The discs. The gateways to elsewhere. They are my only road, Peter. I must walk them wherever they lead."

I clutched her and sobbed. "Marthar, there will be death that way. Most worlds will be impossible to live on."

"That is but a small thing, Peter. We all die in the end. One must decide whether to go with honor or without, and to be without honor is to be without any reason to live. Perhaps for us kzinretti who have been given intelligence equal to males, our honor is even more precious than for others. For us to live dishonored would be even worse than for a male kzin, and for most of them dishonor is worse than death. So there is no choice, don't you see that?"

I thought of appealing to her as a dutiful daughter, of the disastrous effect her death would have upon her Sire and on the great Vaemar-Riit, but I knew I did not understand kzin psychology and value systems enough to be sure it would help. It might make things worse.

"Then let me go with you, Marthar. If you go without me, then it will be *me* having to live without my honor. And without my friend." I looked up into her great golden-green eyes.

She considered. She knew it meant death for both of us, and she knew I knew. But Marthar didn't fear death, she feared dishonor, and she could see that even for a human this might be taken as a reasonable way of seeing the world.

"You would prefer to die with me than live without me?" she asked, her brow furrowed in concentration. I had seen her working on algebra problems with much the same look.

"Yes," I told her unflinchingly. I meant it too. If I couldn't persuade her to come back with me, then I couldn't leave her. I would go with my friend wherever it led. If we were to die on some alien world with unbreathable air, in the swirling snows and ice of one world or the fire pits and roiling lava of another, better that than spending a lifetime wondering what would have happened, feeling myself a traitor for leaving her.

She saw that I meant it, and for a moment she was shaken. She shook her head slowly, as though to clear it.

"I think I understand you sometimes, little Peter, and then I find I do not. Well, I would welcome the company, though it may not be for long, little monkey. Come then, we go to the dark tower and the discs, and we take what the Fanged God sends us."

We walked on together after that, side by side. She slowed her pace to mine, and I went forward with a spring in my step. This was as it should be, I felt. I was quite serene about it. I knew that in a way I was being rather cowardly. I couldn't face going back and telling Orion and the others what Marthar was going to do, nor could I face living with myself after she went, never knowing what she had come up against. Far better to do it with her. We all die, as Marthar said, and she was going to do it with style. And so was I.

We were getting close to the tower when Silver and his men struck. Three of them launched themselves at

Marthar, and she didn't even have time to reach for the *wtsai* at her belt. She had left her needler behind; I don't know why. Perhaps beause it was out of ammunition, perhaps because she felt it wouldn't be much use where she was going and it would be better if the others had it to use against the pirates. She went down with a squeal. When it was over, both of us were tied up, our arms behind our backs, our feet tied together. We both had our *wtsais*, but we couldn't reach them and they would have been useless if we could. A big brown-striped pirate who I had seen on the *Valiant* carried Marthar casually over his shoulder, and Silver carried me even more casually over his. It was humiliating. I just hung there with my head down, looking at his belts and his naked rat-like tail with my face banging against his back as he walked. I could sometimes see Marthar's legs and tail hanging down over the red-striped pirate, who was, I think, making jokes about what he planned to do to her later. I felt sick.

They didn't take long to get us back to the red lander. They threw us down and broke out the rum and sat in a circle and set about getting drunk. One tied us up, sealing the bindings with a smart electronic lock—a kzin version of the type that only opens when it recognizes the palm-print of its master.

"When do we share the kzinrett around, Silver?" the brown-striped one asked.

"Soon, me brave Heroes, soon, ye ha' me word on it. But we have something better, we have a bargaining counter, we does. For she be by way of bein' a princess, so she is, and princessies are worth more than their bodies, indeed. So nobody is to approach her until I have used her meself,"

Silver finished. "And not for what ye might think, ha!" There were growls and calls at this, but they were more interested in the rum at this point. They sat in the sunlight, but had thrown Marthar and me contemptuously in the shadow of the lander. I looked up at her and saw her muscles were bunched up as she struggled against the ropes. I struggled myself. Modern "ropes," though still called by the old name for spun fiber, are considerably stronger than steel. She had a rope around her muzzle so she could not even speak. Male kzin, I knew, were sexually aroused almost entirely by the odor of a female in cycle. Until that happened, they would be almost indifferent in that direction, apart from bawdy jokes.

This was close to the endgame. I knew that Silver would threaten to kill us and worse than kill us if Orion and S'maak did not negotiate. And I don't believe either would have given anything for either of us. The war had shown that on the rare occasions kzin had been taken hostage by humans, it had almost always been a waste of time. They would reason that we would not want them to, and the humiliation of living knowing that your life had been bought at cost to another would be intolerable to us. As indeed it would for Marthar, and probably for me too. If Silver lived because I lived, I would be angry beyond the point of sanity. Better by far had we got to the tower and stepped together on one of those mysterious transit discs to go who knew where.

It was while I was thinking such thoughts and trying to wriggle free with not the smallest prospect of success that a huge paw came from behind and practically stifled me. I assumed that one of the pirates had slipped away and was going to dispose of me in a light meal. But then the bonds behind me loosened and my arms came free. Marthar was staring behind me and nodding. Then I was picked up as though I weighed nothing and turned to face Bengar. He put his claw across his mouth to bid me to silence, and I nodded comprehension. He released my face and I drew breath to relieve my lungs. The oxygen feed meant that I wasn't too badly out of breath.

Bengar pointed to the tower. It was the other side of the lander from the pirates, so it would be possible to get to it unobserved if I were lucky. Then Bengar moved slowly towards Marthar. He was dragging behind him the body of one of the pirates, a guard who had been on some sort of sentry, I presumed. He slowly pushed the body forward between Marthar and the pirates and then pulled Marthar back, where he loosed her bonds using, I noticed, the detached hand of the kzin who had bound us. Then he turned to me and gestured: he wanted me off to the tower. I bent down and ran as quietly as I could.

Behind me there were only the roars and spitting sounds of the pirates as they got drunk, then Marthar sprinted past me towards the tower. I was picked up and thrown over Bengar's shoulder and had to endure the view of *his* tail and pumping legs. He couldn't run as fast as Marthar, but he could certainly go a lot faster than I could, even on two legs with me over a shoulder. We got two-thirds of the way before there was a cry from behind us.

Then screams of rage came as they discovered the bodies of the sentry and the one whose hand Bengar had availed himself of, which from a distance had looked like Marthar and me, until one of them had gone to check on the prisoners. I could hear them pounding towards us, then we were through the doorway, which towered above us as we shot through. Marthar was already out of sight up the ramp. I could hear her, then we were following her. We came onto a landing but Marthar was still ahead, so we went up again. Bengar was wheezing now. The air was too thin for this sort of exercise for someone without an oxygen pack. Then we were on a second landing, with a corridor leading off, and huge open doorways with no sign that there had ever been a door. Marthar was waiting for us.

"Which one?" she asked. Bengar pointed.

"Do not step on a disc, My Lady. Follow me carefully, and when I point to the one we want, follow me instantly."

I could hear the pirates at the open doorway below. Then they started up the ramp.

Bengar strode into one of the rooms. The floor was covered by hundreds of black discs, with only room for one to walk between them. He made his way about three-quarters of the way down the room, then to one side.

"This one, My Lady, quickly, lest they see which one we choose." Then he took a firm pace onto it, and the room vanished. He stepped away. We were in a very similar room, but I knew it was different; the sound was different, the smell was different, and the light was different. Suddenly Marthar was there on the disc, and Bengar motioned her to join him.

"Now we has to get out. Did they see you coming, My Lady?"

"No, but they were almost at the door when I came. They weren't sure which room to try."

Bengar gave an almost human sigh of relief. "Then we

has a little time, My Lady; follow me out of this room, and do not step on a disc. Even a little touch of one of them 'twould be the end of ye, d'ye see."

He led the way out of the room, turned down a corridor and then into another room which looked almost the same as the one we'd come from. This also had hundreds of black discs on the floor, and Marthar followed him carefully. He went almost to the far corner before pointing to another disc.

"This be the last one, lady, then we be safe, for even K'zarr hisself would not use up all his crew on trying the combinations, d'ye see?" I could see Marthar upside down, and she looked exhausted. Bengar stepped on the disc, and again the room vanished, to be replaced by another one. This one had fewer discs on the floor, with more space between them, so we had no trouble moving well away until Marthar came through. I'd had a terror that she wouldn't follow us, but she seemed content to let Bengar lead.

We went out of the room through another huge arch, and Bengar put me down as if he forgot he had me. It was nice to be the right way up again. I ran to Marthar and hugged her. She patted me absently and looked around.

"We be safe now, My Lady, young manling; they'll ne'er find old Bengar here, no they won't. We can rest and go into the sunshine, which is bright still, for a few months, so we don't have to leave for a while."

We followed Bengar as he led the way down the ramp, passing another floor on the way, until we walked into bright sunshine.

🐾 🐾 🐾

We sat on mossy ground that was soft and quite comfortable. The sun was lower in the sky here, and to the southwest, assuming that the gates all faced north as the first one had. We must have come thousands of miles in seconds. The tower here was recognizably similar to the one where we had left the pirates, but looked subtly different, perhaps being less eroded. Still, it bore the marks of many centuries, perhaps millennia.

"Thank you for rescuing us, Bengar," Marthar said in a hopeless sort of way. I could see that she had still decided to take her road to infinity in short order.

"Ye will be wanting some food, I daresay, warrior-lady; well, that is something will be easy enough, for I have a stock of it just around the corner. Let me be showing ye both."

He stood and walked with his strange shuffling gait, and we followed him. We found he had a sort of farm, with wires strung up on posts to form small enclosures, and in them a variety of small animals.

"'Tes not the sort o' food for ye, my lady, not at all what ye'd be used to," he said apologetically. "There be no hunting, but ye can help yourself to anything when ye feel the hunger." He reached over and grabbed one of the things like kangaroos or big rabbits, and, as it screamed, he bit its head off, spat it out and then proceeded to munch on the warm corpse.

"Thank you, Bengar, but I'm not hungry," Marthar said. She sounded apathetic. And I recalled having heard it said, more than once, that a kzin was never *quite* full.

"Perhaps you can help us, Bengar," I said. "You see, we have somehow to get to the ship, the *Valiant*. It's up there in L1, and we need to get the Lady Marthar there urgently, she has a sickness, and it will kill her if we delay."

Bengar looked puzzled. "Ye have a spaceship in orbit?"

"Not in orbit," I explained. "At least, not in orbit about this world; in orbit around the sun, but keeping close to the planet. It's in the direction of the sun. You can't see it, of course, but a big telescope pointed at the sun would show a small black dot. That's the *Valiant*."

Bengar seemed to want to think about this. "You are sure 'tes not a ship of K'zarr, nor full o' pirates?" he asked timidly.

"No, there's nobody alive on it at present. And it was never a pirate ship, though we accidentally brought a load of pirates with us. But they are now down on planet. You rescued us from some of them," I explained slowly. I had the feeling he was a few asteroids short of a solar system.

"Why can't ye call her down here?" Bengar wanted to know. I don't think he was suspicious; I think he trusted us, but he wasn't able to make sense of it all. He had been alone a long time, and I suppose he'd got used to taking his being stranded on this world rather for granted. Also, I realized, he was perhaps smarter than I had thought a moment before.

"We have no way of getting in touch with her, and anyway, she would need a crew to get her down here and also to get us back up, and there isn't one. A crew, I mean. She is an old human ship, retrofitted for hyperdrive, and she needs a big crew. We could maybe get back home from orbit, but we could never get her down on planet."

"Then how did ye get here? Ye must have a pinnace of

sorts, but a big one if all o' K'zarr's crew got here in it." He waved an ear, as if this was a joke.

"We carried three landing craft, and they are all down here on planet. You rescued us from just underneath one of them. Two are badly damaged, including the one where we were tied up, and the third had its drive locked from the ship. It's a long story," I told him. It was frustrating explaining things to him. He seemed to want everything reduced to terms he could understand before he would commit himself to anything. Not that I had much hope of getting anything useful out of him; but I'd try anything to get Marthar back on the *Valiant* for an hour. Who knew? Maybe one of those transit discs could be programmed to get us inside the *Valiant*. It didn't seem very likely since transport seemed to be from disc to disc.

"So your ship is empty?" Bengar was amazed.

"Yes, I told you. And Silver killed the ship's mind, so it can only be controlled from the console on the bridge, and we can't get to the bridge because we have nothing that can fly us there."

Bengar considered this carefully.

"I don't suppose we could get there using your magic discs, or something like that?" I asked him.

"No, no, they discs are stations; ye cannot take them anywhere."

My shoulders fell in dejection. "Then we are finished, because Marthar is desperately sick and she needs an autodoc urgently," I said hopelessly.

"Ah, I thought there was something wrong wi' the little lady," Bengar said with satisfaction, as though he was pleased to have his perceptions confirmed. "She is so quiet and sad seeming. What is it ails her? Mayhap I might help. I know a little doctoring, I does."

"No, you cannot help. She needs an autodoc, a kzin autodoc, and even then it will have to be programmed. I think I can do it, if there's a sensible interface. But the nearest one is on the ship."

"And this ship is straight up towards the sun, ye say? And not too far away?"

"Little more than a few hundred planetary radii, but going straight up is a little hard," I said. It all seemed hopeless.

"Not too far, I should say, not too far for a pinnace." Bengar said compacently.

"But we haven't got a pinnace," I shouted at him in anger. Why couldn't he understand?

"Ah, but we does. K'zarr left one behind when he went, so he did. I ha' flown it meself, though not for a year or more. 'Tes not so difficult, a kit could do it. And if it is only a matter of a few hundred thousand miles, why then, I can have ye both there in jist a few hours."

PART FIVE

THE RETURN TO THE VALIANT

CHAPTER TWENTY

"Ah, did I not tell ye? Old Bengar he knows a thing or two, yes he does, and he knows where the treasure is too, so he does. And if ye will promise to take me with ye, I can help ye and show ye how the truth may be read from them there bars; so ye keep that Silver away from me." He shuddered at the name of his enemy. "Ah, everyone was afeared o' K'zarr, save Silver, and K'zarr was afraid o' *him*, him being so genteel, d'ye see. K'zarr he were fierce, an' he were cold, so he were, an' he reckoned a life as nothing at all, but Silver, he could seem to be anything he wanted, so he could. He could be your friend or teacher one moment and bite your throat out the next; not angry like, not in a rage, cool as liquid air he were, wi' a friendly flick o' the ears before he drank o' a kzin's heart's blood. Oh, the on'y ones did not fear Silver was those what didn't know him. And K'zarr knew him, so K'zarr feared him. There was talk among some of the crew, beggin' yer pardon, Lady, that he was full of rage, because his Sires had fallen in the world, fallen far." He touched the fur on the center of his chest.

We were following him to the so-called pinnace, although I had doubts as to whether it existed outside his imagination. My heart sank when we got there, for there was what at first looked like nothing but a very large bush or broad tree. Then I began to hope, for it was clear that Bengar had carefully concealed the machine beneath vegetation, no doubt to hide it from pirates. Fortunately he had more than a touch of paranoia about K'zarr, not truly able to believe the old monster dead. Between us, he and I cleared the vegetation away from the machine while Marthar watched. I felt something of dread when I looked at her. I could almost see her mind failing. I returned to clearing the vegetation away from the small lander. Another nasty thought: let her mind fail enough, and she might see *me* as prey.

The pinnace was small; there was room in it for only two full-sized kzin, but since I was small, I could fit on Marthar's lap. Bengar was jumping up and down in excitement.

"Best we get away as soon as may be; are ye sure there be none o' the pirates still on this here ship o' yourn?"

"The Captain and Orion, Marthar's father, said they had cleaned them all out," I told him.

"Arrr, but they be cunnin,' they pirates, so they be, yes they does." He looked at me with some cunning himself, I thought.

"I'm sure that the only thing on board will be us, if we can get there," I told him. I still had limited faith in his ability to fly the thing; was there even enough fuel to get us up to the ship? If there wasn't, we presumably would fall back and crash on the planet. That would be quick, anyway.

And if we could not rendezvous with the ship, maybe we would fall into the sun. But anything was better than watching Marthar lose her mind.

We helped Marthar into her seat, and Bengar climbed into the main pilot's place beside her. I sat on Marthar's lap and struggled to put our belts and webbing around us both. Bengar closed the door and sealed it. Then he went through some sort of checklist, muttering to himself. Little lights came on and illuminated the panel in front of him. The computer came up and checked the functioning of the ship and seemed happy. I breathed a sigh of relief. If the computer thought we were in reasonable shape then perhaps we were.

"I cannot program the pinnace, d'ye see, on account o' we doesn't know whereabouts the destination is, save in a general way, no we doesn't. We could tell her to head for L1, o'course, but she would not know where that is exactly, on account o' she doesn't know the mass o' the planet, her bein' only a poor little bit of a pinnace what doesn't need to know sich things. But I can tell her to head up into the sun, straight up, an' she can do that; then when we're close enough we shall find that there ship on the radar no doubt."

I hoped it was going to be that easy. And when we got there, would the ship let us in? I hadn't thought of that problem.

There was a humming sound that climbed into a scream and then we lifted. I looked out of the window to see where we were. We shot up very fast, but I had no sense of being pressed into Marthar; the gravity-planer technology was operating. Outside, the tower was well below us. I made a mental note of the surrounds. Three canals crossed in a junction, not far away, and some craters made a unique pattern. I pulled out my phone and took a shot of it so we could find our way back. From space, one tower would look much like another, and there seemed to be scores of them, dotted around in no obvious pattern.

The sky changed: the horizon was now a pink ribbon around a curving planet, and the sky was indigo only a few degrees above it, then above the indigo ribbon it was black. The sun dominated above us, but out to the side I could see stars, or maybe other planets of the system. And as we climbed higher, there were more and more stars, and then the nebulae shone faintly, purple mostly, but green and gold with streaks of rose pink and flecked by stars. It was very beautiful and I pointed it out to Marthar, but she was listless and uninterested. I felt panic again. She was going from me, faster and faster. We had to get her into the autodoc soon.

"We be about twenty thousand miles up now, and we should be a tenth o' the way there, if I'm any judge," Bengar announced. I had no idea if he was any judge or not, I am ashamed to say. Marthar had probably calculated how far L1 was from the planet but I had been too lazy. If I knew both masses, the sun and the planet, I could do it in my head, but I didn't have the data, and neither did my phone. It was laziness and sloppiness that got you killed in space, and I was painfully conscious of it for the first time in my life.

"Do you know who built the towers, Bengar?" I asked him, as much to take my mind off Marthar as for any other reason.

"No, young monkey, I do not. Maybe one of the ancient races—the slavers or the Tnuctipun . . ."

Though I had already decided the buildings were too recent as well as too big for that, they were words to send a shiver down any spine. From what our archaeologists had pieced together, when the war of the Slavers and the Tnuctipun ended, there has not been a sentient mind left in the Galaxy, save the Bandersnatchi found on Jinx and a few other worlds created by the Tnuctipun to be immune to the Slaver power. By the time the Slavers had blanketed the Galaxy with a telepathic suicide command, both sides had begun using anti-matter. The war of men and kzin had been a chivalrous, genteel affair by comparison.

It was another hour before Bengar gave a grunt, and pointed to a green speck on a screen. "That be your ship, that be. A bit further out than I thought, but we shall be there within the hour or thenabouts. We be goin' quite fast now."

It was less than an hour before we heard from the ship. It spoke in kzin, the harsh roars and spittings, and my blood ran cold. I looked at Bengar. He had started when he first heard the voice of the ship. It was a voice I recognized too, cold as ice.

"'Tes the very voice o' K'zarr that it be usin'," he said quietly. "Though 'tes but a machine, when all's said an' done, and I ain't afeared of no machine, be sure of it."

Now he was calm. Marthar was taking an interest too.

"'Tes the ship, enquiring who we are and warnin' us to hove to before we hit her amidships, which be fair enough. She told me that she'd destroy us if we don't slow down or change course."

"Can you ask her if we can board her with an injured kzin for autodoc treatment?"

Bengar looked doubtful. "I can, but the ship has been programmed by pirates, d'ye see. They doesn't care much about showin' "—he groped for a word of which there was no concept in the Heroes' Tongue—"*mercy* to strangers. And she wants some sort of identification. And this be a ship o' K'zarr we be in. Which may be a good thing, if ye think about it, for if Silver had the doing, he may have used the standard hack. In which case, the ship will be on'y too happy to welcome us. It might have fired upon the landers ye used from the *Valiant*, for 'tes not *Valiant* that ye have to reckon with now, d'ye see, but something closer to the old *Warrior Beast*. Though it speaks wi' the voice o' K'zarr hisself, so it does. Let me see now, I shall find if the ship knows us."

I thought of talking to a *Warrior Beast* instead of *Valiant*. I supposed it could speak other languages, but my heart sank to my boots again. I hadn't anticipated these problems. I'd just assumed we could talk directly to at least a portion of the old *Valiant*. But the thought also came to me, and it was a comforting one, that Bengar, at least sometimes, was not as stupid as he appeared.

"Aargh, she knows enough to recognize us. Which means she won't just turn us into starlight as long as we doesn't threaten her. So I shall need to turn the ship around so as to slow down, so we will be coming to her slowly. And not in a straight line, for we doesn't want to make her even a bit nervous, no we doesn't."

Bengar seemed to know what he was doing. I remembered he was an old spacer, and I watched as he deftly tapped panels and gestured to control sensors to swing the universe around us. Marthar seemed to have lapsed back into apathy. Now the sun was underneath us, and the glory of the nebulae burned bright. It looked as if swathes of silk had been swirled about and then frozen in motion. Of course the swathes were in fact moving, and doing so quicker by far than silk fabric, but no trace of that showed because of the sheer size of the thing. I suppose if you could watch for millennia, you would see it swoop and turn and spin, like ladies dancing in long dresses. But for now it was a fixed image. I took some pictures of it on my phone. If I ever got back to Thoma'stown, I would show them off to my friends and my mother.

And then I saw the massive bulk of the *Valiant* swing slowly past the window. We had arrived. Now we had to get in.

It was suprisingly easy. The monstrous gate opened onto the lander port, and Bengar slipped us slowly inside. We waited while the gate closed and the air was cycled back in. Long cables and hoses slithered towards the pinnace; presumably we were going to be refueled, which was a relief, since sometime we would want to get back to the planet. Something on wheels came towards us, and we opened the door and climbed down. Marthar ripped off her main belt and dropped to all fours, prowling, her tail long behind her, as we went towards the robotic thing that was inspecting us from a camera and also looking at Bengar. It seemed puzzled by Marthar and me. It spoke to Bengar in Kzin.

"Welcome, Hero, your RFID shows you to be one of K'zarr's older crew, but I do not have your individual identification. But who are the others?"

"Captives from the planet," Bengar told him. I hoped he was lying.

"Pass, Hero." The machine turned to supervise the hoses and cables.

Marthar and I left the hangar and went towards the lift. I was taller than she was now. I fished out my phone and ran the ship app to find out where the autodocs were. There were lots of them, mainly in crew territory, but a few in officer territory. I turned to look for Bengar, who was out of sight, presumably also confirming that the refueling was taking place, and heard Marthar give a sudden hiss. The door to the elevator opened and someone came out.

Vaarth. Silver must have ordered him to remain on the ship, and he must have hidden when Orion and S'maak had been destroying the rest of them. He stepped forward with a cruel rictus on his face.

"Ssso, the kits have returned," he said. He looked at Marthar hungrily. She looked back at him, and purred. There seemed to be nothing left of my friend, she seemed not to recognize Vaarth at all. I recalled Orion saying we should kill him if we could, and felt hopeless. Marthar didn't seem to want to, and I had only the *wtsai* that Silver had given me; it was but a toy as far as Vaarth was concerned. Marthar was still on all fours, all feline, and she seemed excited by the kzin, who was dropping his cutlass and *wtsai* and taking off his belt.

"You are mine, kzinrett. I was promised you, and now I will have you." He came proud and erect and advanced with gleaming eyes on Marthar, who purred some more and sniffed at him. He sniffed back and his ears flicked.

Marthar sidled towards him to meet him and I looked on in horror. Both of them ignored me.

Marthar put up her head to be caressed, but Vaarth was impatient. He put his paw on Marthar's shoulder, bending slightly; he was preparing to turn her around, and Marthar seemed quite agreeable, but she twisted slightly to face him and made her deep rumbling purr again.

Then she struck at his groin, her fangs meeting in his body between his legs. She pulled her head back, and ripped, and Vaarth screamed and doubled up. Marthar hit him with more power than I could believe. She had three clawed paws on the floor and caught him on the side of his lowered head with a fourth; she struck with enormous force and I heard something snap. He went down, and I hurled myself at him. I knelt next to Marthar, and saw his eyes turn to me, and a snarl started to erupt. It takes a lot to kill a kzin. There was still intelligence in his eyes, though he seemed to have little control of his body, and I thrust my *wtsai* in his left eye as deep as it would go. The blade was only a little longer than a carving knife, and I screamed with anger as I twisted it about in his brain, hacking it, stirring it like porridge. The light in his other eye dimmed and he gave a great convulsion and died.

Marthar and I moved back and looked at each other. There was something oddly dreamy about the way she looked back as she swallowed, blood dripping from her jaws.

"Peter," she said slowly. She flicked an ear at me, and growled. "Peter." She licked the blood off her face. She was always fastidious. "Enough . . . of . . . me . . . left. Just . . . enough."

"You said there was no pirates on board," an accusing

whine from Bengar, who was looking at the two of us and the body of Vaarth.

"I didn't know about this one," I said thickly. "I hope there are no more. Silver must have left him behind."

Bengar shuddered. He wasn't much of a warrior. I suppose not all the kzin were, or they couldn't have run any sort of civilization.

"Bengar, we must get Marthar to an autodoc, the closest is in officer territory. I shall need your help to get her in, I expect. She's in a bad way."

"Not so bad if she could kill a pirate, I think, with a little help from you, to be sure. And I hopes there's no more about, for if there are we are surely finished," Bengar said. We went into the lift, Marthar still prowling on all fours. She was silent, but there might have been some hope in her eyes. We went up and I prayed that there were no other pirates on the ship.

If there were, we didn't see them. We found the autodoc where the ship app had said it would be, and I looked at it. Opening it was easy. Getting Marthar in was harder, but there was still enough of her functioning to help us.

"Enough of me . . . left," she said to me as she slipped down. She slid in and we closed the sliding panel on top. It was transparent, and I could see her big golden-green eyes looking at me, then the lights came on and the panel misted up. A bank of control lights flashed and a touch screen opened up. The symbols were all in kzin script, and I could only understand a few of them.

"Bengar, I need to tell it that we need to inject some new neurotransmitters; how do I do it?" I implored him. He looked at the symbols, and pressed one with a claw tip.

"Aarr, that one tells it that you think there is a brain malfunction, though the machine will mainly make up its own mind as to what's wrong. There has to be a dialogue, but ye can choose the language. There, make a choice."

I chose Wunderland language, and it was much easier after that. I told the machine that Marthar was an intelligent kzinrett who has lost her implant, and got a confirmation that it understood the problem. It asked if there was any further information we could give it. I couldn't think of anything, so tapped *No*, whereupon it told me it would take an hour. I stood and looked at it as it hummed away.

An hour. "I guess we wait, Bengar," I told him.

"Mayhap we can look at the control console in the command center," he suggested. I brightened. It would be wonderful if, when Marthar came back, restored to life, I could tell her that we had control of the ship. If I could restore *Valiant*, then we had won, we would have defeated Silver and his gang. If I could get the *Valiant* to destroy them from here, I would do it gladly.

Bengar and I went up to the command deck. Cleaning robots could take care of the dead pirate. I didn't like to leave Marthar, but if there were more pirates about we would imperil her more by remaining with her, I reasoned. The ship would know where she was, but it would have no reason to tell anyone, and I doubt it was anything like as intelligent as *Valiant* had been. And would be again, I hoped.

We stood outside the command room. The door was closed, and I wondered if we could get in. Bengar was crew, and probably didn't have access, and I certainly didn't. My heart sank again.

"Bengar, can we get in? Surely it won't let an ordinary crew member into the control system of the entire ship?"

"Aarr, there be ways, there be ways, manling, and though I be an honest kzin, in a general manner o' speaking, I don't mind deceiving a dastardly contrivance put there by Silver, no, I doesn't mind a bit."

He squinted at the door. "I did not tell you all the truth, when we first met," he said. "Before I joined K'zarr's crew, I was a thief on Homeworld. A perfessional, and good at it, for you see I bear none of the punishments of a failed thief." I did not know what these punishments were, but could hazard a guess that they would be highly visible. Among the concepts kzin seemed to lack was therapeutic jurisprudence. Bengar seemed to possess a full ration of fingers, toes and other parts. "There's not many a lock, electronic or mechanical, that can get the better of old Bengar, given time."

There were touch icons on it, and he inspected them carefully. Then he pressed one.

The voice of K'zarr came out of the door, roaring a question. Bengar answered. Another question from the door, and Bengar answered it; it was a bit too quick, but I worked out that the ship had asked him to justify his request, and where was Silver-Captain, and Bengar had said he was dead, and that he, Bengar, was the highest ranking crew member left on board.

The ship considered this for several seconds, which is a very long time for a computer program. I crossed my fingers and prayed.

The voice of K'zarr asked what I was doing there, and Bengar explained that I was food, and he was keeping me fresh. Bengar flicked an ear at me as he said it, and winked one eye. There was a short delay, then the door opened and we went in to the command center.

There was a kzin standing by the control computers. I had never seen him before. He was dressed as S'maak had been, and had the most evil expression I had ever seen. He looked at Bengar, ignoring me completely, and asked something in the voice I had just heard. There was only one voice like that in the universe, the voice of K'zarr. Bengar clutched his heart and tried to speak, but couldn't; then he fainted away, collapsing on the soft floor.

CHAPTER TWENTY-ONE

I just gaped. K'zarr didn't seem to know I was there. I wondered what on Earth I could do. The door had slid shut behind me, and I was there alone with the scourge of the swirl-rift himself. But K'zarr was dead. Everyone knew it. Skel had said it. Silver had said it.

Then it clicked. Silver had a sense of humor. It would be just the sort of thing he'd do.

I drew my *wtsai* and threw it over arm. It went blade first, as it was supposed to, and passed right through K'zarr. I had expected that. K'zarr was indeed dead, and this was his ghost. The *wtsai* clanged against a bulkhead and fell to the floor. I breathed again. Looking hard at K'zarr, I could see through him. He was an artifact, made of fuzz, hypermatter. He was barely in this universe, and his interactions with it would be faint and programmed. You *can* make fuzz solid and interact with normal matter, but it's an art that requires a lot of computer power to keep it that way. I had nothing to fear from the thing; I couldn't touch him and he couldn't touch me, or not directly. He was the ship, however, a kind of symbolic form of it, and the ship could certainly destroy me. But he knew no more than the ship knew. I ran over to Bengar. His heart was still beating and he groaned.

"Bengar, K'zarr isn't real, he's just fuzz. He's not here, he's just an illusion," I shouted at him. "Look!" His eyes opened in horror as he caught sight of K'zarr's ghost. I ran to the ghost and walked through it to show Bengar that he had nothing to fear. Slowly, he pulled himself to his feet.

"By all the demons of every one of the nine hells," he swore. "Stopped me heart it did, for half a minute. But yes, I see what he is now. And I ain't afeared of ghosts, not that sort anyway. But what a horror he be to look at, I says, and I would be shot of the ghost if I could."

"That's easy enough if we can get at the control console," I told him briskly. I marched over and looked at it. It was exactly like the one Marthar and I had used in the rec-room, the symbols in Anglic. That was close enough to what we used on Wunderland to be readable without difficulty. There were some stickers on top of some of them with kzin script, but I knew what was underneath. I banged the heel of my fist down on a big red button. Under the kzin script I knew it said *Manual Control*. The ghost of K'zarr had opened its mouth to speak but then it evaporated into mist.

"I've switched off all the higher functions," I explained to Bengar, although I suppose he must have known that. "The ship is back to autonomic functions only. Now I have to try to get *Valiant* back."

Bengar found a kzin chair and sat down. "To be sure, and I hope you know how to do it. And the first thing we need to know is: are there any other pirates on the ship? Don't forget, it could be the end of us, indeed it could."

Yes, it could. But we were safe in here for the time being. I started to access the computer. I typed on an old-fashioned keypad: I want to communicate with *Valeria*.

The screen showed text demanding an address. I couldn't remember it. It was a twelve-digit number. I pulled out my phone and looked it up, copying it carefully.

Hello, who is that, please? the screen printed out.

This is Peter Cartwright. Your main personality has been compromised and I wish to restart Valiant, I typed in.

There was no sense of the thing thinking, but I felt a faint tingle in my arm as she read my RFID.

Very well. Authenticated. You have reduced the computer to manual only, I see. That is the first step. Now you must delete the resident personality. I knew that. I also remembered how, and it took only a few key strokes to do it.

Now you have to reinstall Valiant. *I need only the address.* I typed in another twelve-digit code from the phone and pressed RETURN with relish.

Almost immediately, there was a response.

Verifying integrity . . . Verifying stability . . . Updating recent memories from subpersonality . . . Verifying compliance with fixes . . . Verification complete. You may return from manual mode.

I toggled the manual control and held my breath. There was a full two-second delay.

Something materialized out of thin air and held Bengar in a grip of steel. The fuzz could indeed be made to interact with matter. It had Bengar in chains.

"Hello, Peter," *Valiant* said. She had the same soft female voice I remembered. "I have immobilized an unknown kzin. He bears the RFID I associate with pirates. Please explain his status."

"Bengar is one of us, release him immediately," I shouted. I was almost angry with *Valiant*, although I realized as soon as I said it that what she had done was quite sensible seen from her point of view.

"Very well, pending further explanation I shall release him under sanction. He is free to move so long as he does not make overt threats against another authorized crew member."

"More than half the crew are pirates," I said bitterly. "You are a bit behind."

"I know that S'maak-Captain ordered me to destroy one of the landers but I was unable to do so. I presume he believed that the crew inside it were mutineers, and some of the memories I have extracted from the K'zarr personality confirm a mutiny. But I do not have any information about the happenings on the planet. Perhaps you would tell me now."

"Before that, I must know if there is any live being on this ship, because there may be pirates aboard," I told her.

"Organic life comprises you, the kzin here, and the kzinrett Marthar in the autodoc on level five," *Valiant* replied.

"No other crew members?"

"No."

"How is Marthar? Her implant was destroyed and we are hoping the autodoc is replacing it," I asked anxiously.

"Marthar is in good condition and will be waking within

thirty minutes. The autodoc is working normally. It is doing a little more than you suggested; there is a certain hormone modification which is being corrected. Lack of the appropriate neurotransmitters triggered an early hormonal development, which is premature for an intelligent kzinrett. She is in need of some minor changes. She should be the Marthar you knew in a very short time." *Valiant* was soothing. I think she was discreetly checking up on my health and decided I was on edge, and she was dead right. She could monitor my pulse rate and the stress patterns in my voice, and probably pick out any number of odd chemicals the body emits.

"Perhaps now you can give me a status report on the affairs on the surface of the planet, Peter," *Valiant* said patiently. "You should perhaps know that I have been checking to see how I was hacked. It was ingenious and quite unexpected. It would seem that the pirates have some very clever software, and they installed it some time ago. It is now disabled; the same trick will never work again. And I shall ensure that the trick becomes widely known. That will protect other ships."

I sat back with a sigh of relief. If *Valiant* was back and she couldn't be hacked again, or at least not by the same methods, we were likely on the home stretch. But there was still Silver. He was awfully clever. I wouldn't feel safe until he was dead. I started to tell *Valiant* all that had happened. It took a long time.

Bengar and I were waiting patiently for the autodoc to finish with Marthar. At last it did, and the panel slipped back and Marthar sat up.

"Marthar!" I cried. "How are you? Are you back to normal? Can you talk and think?"

"Peter, now I know what it feels like to be even dumber than you, and it's truly terrible," Marthar said with a yawn and a flick of the ear. "Sorry. I want to thank you. I remember what you did, every bit of it, and I owe you. Oh! I am as deep in your debt as anyone could be. And you are my Hero! You are braver than I am, much. Whenever I tease you, remember that. Now, how do I get out of this wretched box?"

It didn't seem to be much of a problem. She sprang out and marched up to Bengar.

"Bengar, if you are willing, I would have you be my personal guard and also my friend. And if not, when I tell my Sire, Orion Ritt, he will reward you so you need never labor again."

Bengar stood silent for a moment, struggling to take in something too big to understand. Then he made a claw-across-the-face military salute, went down before her in the Full Prostration, clutching her ankles. "My Lady, I have no combat skills such as your guard will surely need, but I will gladly be your servant, as I am anyway. For I swore fealty to you, and that can never be undone save by death."

Marthar did something I have never seen any kzin or kzinrett do before: she motioned him to his feet, then held out her arm horizontally with the fist clenched and the palm down. Bengar bent and licked her paw. They looked at one another, both showing pleasure. I didn't know what it meant exactly, but I thought it meant that they had some relationship that went beyond fealty and acceptance. One of those feudal things that some of the more backward kzin worlds still followed, I daresay.

"I took my belt off down in the lander hangar, and I want it back," Marthar announced positively. She was back in her body alright, as full of bounce and certainty as ever. So we went down in the elevator until we got to the hangar and went in. The body of Vaarth had been removed; Marthar was slightly disappointed. "I would have liked his ears. Well, one of them for you, Peter, and one for me, I guess. Joint effort. Or at least a photograph." She hoped the body was in a bin somewhere, but it was already in recycling. The belt with its *wtsai* had been removed too, but it had only been moved to storage, and she took it with pleasure. "I shall have to get it mended; I seem to have clawed right through it."

"I could do with a proper belt again, indeed four of them," Bengar said ruefully. "I have made do with vegetable belts, and a terrible thing that is, to be sure. And now I am ready to rejoin civilization. Perhaps I can get something a little more in keeping for My Lady's servant, don't you think?"

"See to it, *Valiant*," Marthar told the ship. "I want to see the full equipment for a senior servant of my house as soon as possible. Oh, and a new belt for me too. Just don't lose the old one. I shall keep it as a memento." Bengar would do all right, I thought. There were several old and war-battered kzin on Wunderland to whom the Riit Clan felt it owed a debt. Under Vaemar and his sons, it paid its debts.

"I'm surprised you want to be reminded of the whole ghastly business," I said. Marthar looked at me thoughtfully.

"I shall explain it to you someday, Peter, my Hero. You

are a fine and noble being, but not overbright. And you don't understand me a bit. But then," she relented, "I keep thinking I understand you and discovering I don't. Maybe we are just not mutually intelligible in the end. Still, we get along, don't we?"

I grinned at her. Once upon a time, a human couldn't grin at a kzin without risking his life, but those days are long gone back on Wunderland. Well, the bits I know about anyway.

"Yes, we get along pretty well," I told her and gave her a hug, which she returned, along with a brief lick of the forehead. I still don't know exactly what it means, but I think there's something like affection in there somewhere.

"*Valiant*, can you make us some more landers? And how long would it take?" Marthar asked.

"Yes, I can have another lander operational in about a week," *Valiant* spoke in her warm, feminine voice.

"Well get started, because we've lost two. But we want one quickly. We could ferry people up here one at a time in the pinnace, but it would be a problem as the numbers down planetside get too small to hold off the pirates. The best bet is to take everyone off at once."

I had a question. Meeting K'zarr's ghost had given me an idea. "*Valiant*, if we made a ghost, could it be maintained on the planet? A solid one, not one you could walk through."

Valiant thought about it. "It would need more computer power than you have down there at present. A dedicated machine could be built in twenty-four hours and sent down in the pinnace. It would not be big, nor would it take up much space."

"What's in your mind, Peter?" Marthar asked.

"I was thinking of ghosting Silver. It might be useful to have a Silver that could be mistaken for the real one but was under our control. And ours could be even faster than the real one; move faster, I mean. Maybe we could get them to fight it out down there, or give orders contradicting the real one. Lead the pirates around in circles."

Marthar looked at me. "I'll say this for you, Peter, you do a fair amount of lateral thinking. Some of your ideas are really weird. Do we have enough information to make a good one that would fool people?"

"Silver must have got at the records to make the ghost K'zarr. And he fooled Bengar for a bit. And he terrified me. I guess *Valiant* would know if we have enough data on Silver."

Valiant spoke. "I could produce something that looked like him and moved like him and sounded like him. There would be the things he knows that I don't, which would allow those who know him well to tell the difference in any sort of interrogation," she told us. Marthar and I looked at each other.

"You know, it's so utterly silly, nobody would even think of it. Of course, it would mean holding us up for a day. I really want to let Daddy know I'm safe. He'll be worrying. He won't show it, of course, but that sort of thing eats you up and deforms your judgment. So it's important to get back soon, and also to have some regular communication with *Valiant* from planetside."

"*Valiant*, is there any way of getting those pirates out of the green lander?" I asked her. "From here, I mean. They seem to be pretty much impossible to shift from down there."

"I have no real control from this location. But if a Silver were to be manufactured, he could be programmed to order them out. That would give you a fully functioning lander once I released the lock. And you could kill the pirates in her at present, which would improve the odds."

Valiant was cold and heartless and very, very practical. Well, she was a computer program.

"I like it," Marthar said enthusiastically. I didn't think I could kill anyone who was helpless, even a pirate. Except Silver, I'd kill him the first chance I got.

"*Valiant*, I need to let Sire and S'maak-Captain know I'm back in play. We have no communications to them. Is there anything we can do?" Marthar wanted to know.

Valiant considered a few squillion possibilities, most of them ridiculous. "I could send a message by laser. I managed to hit the red lander in the last few microseconds before I was disabled. So I could put a laser beam with enough power to fuse rock in the vicinity of the blue lander. You could send a handwritten message. Of course, it would not be exactly private, nor would it be temporary. It would last tens of thousands of years, perhaps longer."

The thought of handwriting a message on the desert that would last a million years was bound to appeal to Marthar.

"Won't it be too big to read?" she asked, obviously thinking about what to write.

"Make it a short message; the very fact that it is being written from the ship will say quite a lot, I should think," *Valiant* said.

"I think I have just the thing," Marthar said with a wolfish look.

🐾 🐾 🐾

And that's why there's a smiley, a hundred yards across, made of melted rock, not far from one of the Garthian canals, and visible from L1 in a reasonably good telescope. It was written quite slowly so anybody there had a good time to get out of the way of the beam. I gather it made enough noise to get even the pirates in the green lander outside for a look. I have no idea what they made of it, but the Judge laughed every day for a week.

Marthar decided that we would wait for the computer on which we would run a fake Silver, so we had a day to kill. I wanted some sleep, so we agreed that I would go into a human autodoc for a few hours to repair the small amount of damage to me and also to get me out of the way and cleaned out of toxins. Our oxygen packs and glucose feeds were replenished and Bengar fitted with his own, which heartened him even more. He was also cleaned of some small parasites. Bengar obviously felt trusted and that his life had improved rather a lot in taking an oath of fealty. He worshipped Marthar, and he had seen her at her best and her worst, which in turn comforted Marthar.

Before I went into the autodoc, I talked quietly with Marthar.

"Peter," she said. Then she stopped.

"Yes, what is it?" I asked, puzzled.

"Peter, I don't know if I do remember everything. Maybe the autodoc told me to think I did. Maybe I'm benefitting from a well-meant post-hypnotic suggestion. It's not the sort of thing you can ever be sure about, is it?"

"So what do I do?" I asked.

She took a deep breath and looked directly at me.

"Peter, on your word of honor, did I ever do anything to shame myself while I was under the influence? Or not under the right influence?"

I could see that she was genuinely concerned and worried that she might be fooling herself, with a little help from the autodoc.

"Marthar, you did one thing that horrified me at the time: you pretended to be attracted to Vaarth. But I can see that it was a desperate move to get close enough to him to use the only weapons you had, those you were born with."

Her eyes went out of focus. "Hmm. The thing is, Peter, I *was* attracted to him, in a way. I felt a strange . . . excitement. But yes, I used it to deceive him. There was still enough of me left to do that."

"It's over now, Marthar, my darling. I know it was horrible having your mind go on you, but it will never happen again."

"No, it will never happen again," she whispered, more to herself than to me. "But you don't understand, Peter. It wasn't horrible at all. I was losing all the things that make me an individual, and I was going back to being pure animal. And I loved it. No worrying about consequences, no inhibitions, no thought at all; only sensual pleasures heightened by the total switching off of consciousness. It was so good, Peter. That was what was horrible. I enjoyed it."

I didn't understand it then, but later I came to see the same temptation in human beings. Some of them love to surrender their individuality to a giant collective, or to submit their own judgments to a religion, or a political belief. I suppose it has the same appeal. You never have to think. You never have to worry about consequences. Perhaps it is the doom of all sentient species.

CHAPTER TWENTY-TWO

We went back the next day. We took the computer that *Valiant* had made; it sat in a pack on my back. We also took two com-systems so we could stay in touch with *Valiant* and pile of weapons, mostly needlers but also some blasters. Bengar was resplendent in some new belts and pouches. I sat on Marthar's lap again. It was a bit of a squash, with two of the blasters at our feet.

There had been some debate about where we were going. Bengar assumed we were going to take the pinnace back to where he had hidden it, but Marthar wanted to return directly to the wreck of the blue lander. Bengar was worried about the safety of the pinnace, but Marthar persuaded him.

"The safest place for it is with the *Valiant*, so here's what we do: we land and go out with the blasters ready in case Silver is anywhere near. We get the rest of them, including Daddy and S'maak-Captain, armed and dangerous; then we get the Andersons to return to the *Valiant* with you. You wait there until the new lander is ready. Then you fly the lander back here, pick us all up, and we go to your hidey-hole and collect the treasure. When we have a good share of it, we all go back to the *Valiant* and blast the red and green landers and anything that moves on planet before sailing for home. How does that sound?"

"But, Ladyship. that means I shall be away from you for a whole week. My place is by your side, so it is," Bengar fretted.

"We can manage a week without you, Bengar," Marthar said firmly. Bengar could see there was no point in arguing, so in a resigned way he said, "Yes, Ladyship, 'twill be as you command." He was going to have to get used to giving in, I decided. I already felt sorry for Mathar's mate when she chose him. If he had old-fashioned ideas about kzinretti, he was going to have to change them, fast.

We squashed into the pinnace. Bengar went through the checks and we drifted up. There was a hum from outside which faded as the air was pumped out, and then the great door opened and we slid sideways until we were out in space. We were in the shadow, with the sun on the other side of the *Valiant*, so we could see the planet, ochre and green, below us, a disc, with only traces of clouds. There were dark blue patches which must have been lakes or small, shallow seas, and we could even see some of the craters and canals. The disc was set in the swirl-rift, the gorgeous swathes of diaphanous fabric, billions of miles wide and lit by stars like gems on a dress and with dark clouds interwoven with it all. It was beautiful in a cold, mind-numbing way. It made the planet look friendly by comparison, though it was more Martian than it was like Wunderland or Earth. The only sound was our breathing as

Bengar let us drift further away from the *Valiant*. I don't think he saw anything beautiful in the sight; I don't think he even bothered to look at it. Then a hum, as he rotated the pinnace.

In L1, your orbital speed around the sun is greater than that of the planet you are close to. If you want to get to the planet, you don't just point the ship at it and fire your rockets. You fire sideways so as to slow your speed relative to the primary when you drift out from the primary. Orbital mechanics are easy enough once you understand that you are actually moving in a gravitational field even though you don't feel it, but I have seen old movies about space travel that make everyone laugh now because they show spacecraft maneuvering like aircraft, which is ridiculous. The reason that L1 even exists is that although anything in it is moving faster than the planet, which would tend to move it away; the planet pulls it back. There are nice pictures which illustrate this. Marthar showed me some of them when S'maak-Captain said we would be taking up L1 position. If the planet had a sensible rotation period, we'd have gone into the orbit that matched it in order to stay fixed over the equator, but Garth was so slow that there was practically no sensible place to go.

Gradually at first, we drifted away from L1 and the *Valiant*, and fell towards the treasure planet.

We landed halfway between the edge of the picture of the smiley face and the wreck of the blue lander. There was no airlock on the pinnace—it was too small; you just opened a valve and the pressures equalized, which meant swallowing fast and hearing your ears pop. When this had happened, I opened the seatbelts, then the door, and sprang out.

"It's good to have that damned backpack off of me; it was getting painful," Marthar said. "Here, take a needler."

I did and stuck it in my belt, and grinned at Marthar. I took off the offending backpack and dropped it at her feet. I also took a blaster, a kzin one, which required both hands to hold it. I was going to present it to S'maak-Captain.

I ran towards the hole that was more or less the door in the wrecked lander, carrying the blaster. There was nobody on guard, which was a puzzle, but I could hear voices coming from inside. Kzin voices. I slowed down as some instinct told me that something was wrong.

Then one of the snarling, hissing voices became louder and a kzin came out sideways and stood up. I didn't recognize him, and realize this as he moved in a blur and took the blaster from me. I just stood and gaped. Then another figure came out, who I did recognize. It was Silver.

He took in the pinnace, me and the blaster that the other kzin was holding. That was when the pinnace shot into the sky, soundlessly, faster than you could believe. Silver grabbed the blaster and raised it towards the pinnace, but he didn't fire. He watched it streak up until it had vanished, to my eyes at least.

Silver turned to me, sticking the blaster in his belt. "Well, well, 'tis young Peter back again, after all this time. And wi' some interestin' stories to tell us, I'll lay to that. And what looked rather like one o' K'zarr's boats, I'd say." He turned his head on one side and opened his eyes wide as he looked at me. "Interestin' indeed, an' I'll be sittin, an' listenin, wi' my full attention while ye tells me what's been happenin' to ye. And I thank 'ee kindly for this present, what you made me." He tapped the blaster with a claw tip. He was as jocular and friendly as he had been when we first met him.

The other kzin snarled something and made a move towards me. I thought my last moment had come.

"Belay that, this man-kit is my friend, I tells ye," said Silver, pushing him away amiably. The other kzin looked at him resentfully, but didn't try to dispute the matter. He glared at me, and at Silver's back, then went back into the wrecked lander, where we could hear him roaring at the others.

"Let's you an' me walk a little way to get out o' the noise and babble o' the rabble, shall we? But not too far, for as ye know, when I set down, 'tes hard for me to get up again." He walked further down to the nose of the crashed lander, broken and cracked, took off the great cutlass on his back, stuck it in the rocky soil, then lowered himself down next to it, sitting not on the ground but on a broken shard of the lander, and motioned me to join him. I didn't have much choice, so I sat down on the ground facing him. A kzin can usually crouch quite easily, but I suppose his artificial leg was stiff. It must have been an emergency repair rather than a proper prosthesis, perhaps done on a backward world, far inferior to those fitted to kzin war veterans on Wunderland. But he was poised to rise again quickly.

Silver looked at me quizzically, his gaze flicking over my belt and the needler before returning to my face. He made no move to confiscate the needler. I don't suppose I could have killed him with it before he killed me anyway.

"I suggests we has a little trade, Peter Cartwright, yes, a

little trade o' information: you tells me o' the explanation for ye vanishing, an' who was the other kzin wi' ye when ye vanished. And how ye came by the pinnace, and how ye got back to the *Warrior Beast*, which must be dead now and restored to the old *Valiant*, if the thing over there is to be used in evidence," he indicated the smiley face carved in molten stone. "Then I'll explain to ye how it comes that we're here and your friends are not. So fire away, me little friend, blast me wi' surprises, and then I'll answer any questions ye may have o' me, and we'll both be up to date."

I thought about it. I wanted desperately to know if Orion, the Judge, the Doctor and the others were still alive. But could I believe Silver would tell me the truth? Kzin almost always do; their pride would make them disdain to tell a lie except as an occasional tactic with an enemy. But I thought Silver regarded everyone as an enemy and would lie and tell anyone what he thought they wanted to hear.

I didn't have much choice. "All right, one question each alternately. And I go first. Are the captain and Orion and the others still alive?"

"Well, well, 'twas my idea to trade, so by rights I think I should go first, but I'll waive all that." He waved an arm to indicate his generosity. "Yes, so far as I know they are all alive, save the three kzin who was here. Now, my question is, who was the kzin who untied ye two kits and ran off to the tower wi'ye?"

Would it be a betrayal of Bengar to tell of him? I suppose that the question was a probe of my reliability, and he already had an idea of the answer. It might be worth getting Silver's trust. If I was going to lie to him it would be on something important. The noise from inside had died down, and two of the crew had come out and were standing nearby, listening to the exchange between Silver and me.

"It was a former member of K'zarr's crew who was marooned here many years ago by you." I decided to give the very minimum information.

"Well, well, well. Must be that Bengar survived, which is a great credit to him, so it be, a great credit. And how is me old shipmate? And 'twas not me marooned him, never agreed wi' maroonin' kzin or man."

"No, you'd rather just kill them," I said hotly. I felt like telling him that I'd heard him from the meat-locker, but if we were trading information, I'd be a fool to give him any for nothing. I should have kept that back, but I was angry.

"The dead 'uns don't bite, 'tes true," Silver agreed easily. He didn't seem to feel any shame at this, but then, he wouldn't.

"Where are my friends?" I demanded.

"Well as to that, I has to say I doesn't know exactly, but I rather suspicions they be occupying that there tower," Silver answered promptly enough, with a gesture in the direction of the tower.

"Why are they there?" I demanded.

"Ah, I think it be my turn, ain't it? Fair's fair, dooty's dooty, as I'm sure ye will agree. And my question is: has me old friend Bengar found out how to use those there discs to get from one place to another, because ye vanished, and I knows that's what they does, because K'zarr hisself said that any living thing placed on them went away. And I'm thinking they must be some sort o' transport system like, an' old Bengar must ha' found out how to use them. Would I ha' the rights of it?"

"Yes," I answered shortly. I felt an inclination to amplify the answer as if I were talking to Marthar, but I bit it back. The less the old villain knew the better. "How did my friends come to be in the tower or wherever they are?"

"Well, as to that, 'twas their work, and their error. For they set out to attack us where we was, near to the red lander, d'ye see. And damned near did for us, so they did, comin' when half the scum was drunk, which was my fault for letting them have the rum, d'ye see. But then, if I'd had no rum for them, they'd ha' mutinied for sure. I'd ha' had to kill half o' them meself. Well, S'maak-Captain, he saved me the trouble, so he did. But those of us what got away reasoned that there'd be few left in this here wreckage, d'ye see, an' maybe we could get our revenge on the smaller group. And the swabs what lived in the green lander, they comes out to help us when they saw it were easy enough and that S'maak-Captain weren't there to defend it. For they're nearly as frightened o' that S'maak as they are o' me, ye may lay to that. Anyway, we sort of swapped places as a result o' ye marauding kzin, and they humans too. Near nobody left here, there was. Three kzin, all gone now. But then your party took down five of us, five damned drunkards. Happened the day after ye drew that there smiling face in the sand. Or night, if we be keepin' ship's time."

I began to have hopes. If Bengar landed at his old place, and he and Marthar went by the discs to the tower, they would meet up with the others. At least there was a good chance of it going that way. And with the weapons, our side would outgun the pirates. There was not much chance for me, of course, although Marthar would rescue me if she could, I had no doubt of it.

"Ask your next question," I said grimly. Some more of the crew had come out and were studying both Silver and me.

Silver looked at me thoughtfully. I had no idea what was going on in that great head, but there was no doubt he was a very clever creature. He must have reasoned as I did, that my party now had the upper hand. We had taken the *Valiant* from him, we could get there and back and he couldn't. But it wasn't an occasion to boast about it.

"Ah, Peter, Peter, ye've bested old Silver, nary a doubt of it. Bested by a couple o' kits, I've been. Never hear the end of it, I won't. Ivery bar in the swirl-rift, they'll be laughin' at old Silver, so they will. And that Marthar, she be a kit-and-a-half, so she be. Well, we be distant relatives, her an' me, in a manner o' speakin,' so 'tis not so surprisin'."

"And now I suppose you're going to kill me," I said, standing up with what courage I could muster.

"Why should I do that?" he asked with apparent surprise. "No, I admires ye. Ye seized the opportunities as they came, so ye did, the pair o' ye. 'Twould be a shameful thing to harm ye now, a stain on old Silver's honor. No, ye be safe wi' me, I promise ye."

There was a growl from some of the crew.

"Your honor didn't stop you bugging me, didn't stop you trying to kill us all," I told him with contempt.

He looked at me. "Sit down again, Peter," he gestured. "You're young, and you're proud, and I respects ye for it, d'ye see? But a kzin can take his pride in things ye'd not yet know about, and a man likewise, I've no doubt. There's them as takes their pride in bein' an obedient servant, no question, an' then there's others what doesn't. I takes me pride in other things than obedience, so I does. 'Tes a harsh, cold universe, and there be many ways o' livin' in it. Ye'd do well not to judge until ye've tried more an' learned more."

I sat down, my mind in a whirl. Silver was a monster, I had no doubt at all. But I felt my hatred for him weaken; I was no longer able to despise him quite so much. But I didn't imagine for a moment that I could trust him, either.

One of the crew men broke in. "The man-kit has bested ye right enough, Silver, wi' yon kzinrett. And ye might ha' destroyed the boat wi' her in it, but ye didn't. And why not, we asks us? Maybe 'tis that she is a distant relative, maybe? Just who's side are ye on now, Silver?"

Silver looked at him. He was the big brown-striped one Marthar had been carried by when they caught us.

"Ah, Rraangar, ye ha' no sort o' brain, ha ye? Destroy the on'y link wi the mother ship? Not I, not so stupid. Better to capture it in due time, and have it for ourselves. I'd ha' no trouble takin' down an enemy, as many know, as ye should know yourself. Many a good Hero's gone before now, some to the battle pits, some by the board to black space, and some wi' my *wtsai* in their bellies."

"Then take down the man-kit, Silver, or gi' him to us for a snack. It's long since I had monkey-meat. Prove you're not lyin'." The brown-furred kzin was obstinate.

Another broke in. "Do it, Silver, for this is one o' the pair took down Gra-Prompyh, the pair what got the pad from Skel, the pair what ha' done much o' the harm we suffers from. First and last, we've split upon those two, an' ef ye hands him over then maybe we'll say no more on it."

I stood again. "Kill me as you please, I don't fear you!" I

cried. "But one thing I'll say and no more: if you spare me, bygones are bygones and when you are in the dock for piracy, I'll speak for you and save you all I can. Kill another and do yourselves no good, or spare me and keep a witness who might save you all from death."

I stopped, for I was out of breath, and to my wonder, not one of them moved, but all stood staring at me like as many sheep. And while they were still staring, I broke out again. "And now, Silver, I believe you more than any other here, and if things go to the worst for me, I'll take it kindly if you will tell Marthar the way I took it."

The only kzin I knew were those at home, who were used to living with humans, and who to some extent we had come to understand. I realized I knew very little of the psychology of these savage and predatory pirates.

"I'll bear it in mind," said Silver with an accent so curious I could not decide if he was laughing at me or had been affected by my courage.

"I'll put one to that," Rraangar cried out. "It were this one what knew the Dog and t'other what took him down. So here goes!" And with that he drew his *wtsai* and his jaws opened in a roar to the killing gape.

"Avast there!" cried Silver. "Who are you, Rraangar? Maybe ye thought ye was Captain here, perhaps? By the powers, but I'll teach ye better! Cross me and you'll go where many has gone before." He stood and took up his huge cutlass. "There's never a Hero nor human looked me in the eyes and seen a good day afterwards, and ye may lay to that."

Rraangar paused, but a hoarse murmur rose from the others.

"Rraangar's right," said one.

"I bin fooled before by you, Silver, and by a few more, but I'll not be fooled again, so I won't," said another.

"Did any o' ye want to have it out wi' *me*," roared Silver, leaning forward. "Him that wants shall get it. Ha' I lived these years and a son of a *sthondat* speak t' me o' folly? Ye know the way, ye're all Heroes o' fortune, by your account. Well, I'm ready. Take *wtsai* or cutlass, him that dares, and I'll see the color of yer liver, aye, and so will all t'others here."

Not one of them moved.

"Ahh, that's your sort, is it?" Silver sneered at them. "Well, all so brave when there's a gang o' ye and not so much alone. Not much worth to fight, you ain't. I'm Captain here by election. I'm Cap'n here because I'm the best here by a couple o' parsecs. Ye won't fight as a Hero o' fortune, then, by thunder, you will obey, and ye may lay to that! I like this man-kit, he be more of a Hero that any pair o' *sthondats* here, and what I say is this: let me see him will lay a paw to 'im, that's what I says."

There was a long pause after this. I stood up with my heart hammering away, but with a little hope in it. Silver leaned back against the hull, his eyes on the crew, full of contempt, as calm as ever. Yet his eyes kept wandering over them, and he kept half an eye on the tail of the crew. They on their part drew gradually away together, towards the door into the wreck and the low hiss of their whispering was like a stream. One by one they would look up, but it was upon Silver that their glances fell briefly.

"Ye seem to have a lot to say," Silver called out to them. "Pipe up, and let me hear it too, or lay to."

"By your leave, Cap'n, you bin free wi' the rules; maybe you'll kindly keep an eye on the rest. This crew is dissatisfied, so it is, an' it has its rights, like other crews. I grants that ye be the Cap'n at present, but I claim my rights, and steps away for a council." And with a salute, the kzin stepped into the door to the wrecked lander. One after another, the rest followed his example, saluting and making some sort of apology. "Accordin' to rules," one said. "Crew council, sir," said another. And they left Silver and me outside in the sunshine.

"By your leave, Cap'n, you bin free wi' the rules; maybe you'll kindly keep an eye on the rest. This crew is dissatisfied, so it is, an' it has its rights, like other crews. I grants that ye be the Cap'n at present, but I claim my rights, and steps away for a council." And with a salute, the kzin stepped into the door to the wrecked lander. One after another, the rest followed his example, saluting and making some sort of apology. "Accordin' to rules," one said. "Crew council, sir," said another. And they left Silver and me outside in the sunshine.

CHAPTER TWENTY-THREE

"Now lookee here, Peter Cartwright," Silver said in what was a barely audible whisper. "You're within half a step of death, and what's a long sight worse, of torture. They're going to throw me off. But, mark you, I stand by ye through thick and thin. I didn't mean to, no, not 'til you spoke up. I wouldn't ha' given ye over to them, not to be played with, but I wouldn't have kept you alive either. I were not too happy wi' being bested, I tell you; but I see you are the right sort. I said to meself, you stand by Peter and Peter will stand by you, Silver, so I said. You're his last card, and by the living thunder, Silver, he is yours! Back to back, says I. You save your witness, Silver, and he will save your ears."

I began to understand. "You mean all is lost?"

"Aye, indeed I do. Ship gone, treasure gone, ears gone, and that's the size of it. And as for that council, well, they're fools, mark me, outright fools and cowards. I'll save your life from them, if so be as I can, but tit for tat, you save Silver."

"What I can do, that I'll do," I said.

"It's a bargain!" he cried. "You speak up plucky, and by thunder I've a chance."

He stood up and stretched.

"I've one last question for ye, though I doubts I shall get an answer. 'Tes this: That Orion, he gave me this, when we was pulling back from the tower. Why did he do that, d'ye think?" He held up Skel's memo pad.

I looked at it in puzzlement. "I've no idea," I said truthfully. He tossed it thoughtfully and caught it again.

"Hmm. Well, maybe I have my own ideas on that. Understand me, Peter," he said. "I've a head on my shoulders, I has, and a good 'un. I'm on Orion's side now. I know you has a way of getting to the ship. How you managed it all, I don't know, because Vaarth was there and he should ha' taken you all down, easy as winking, but he didn't. Well, I never believed much in *him*, for sure. No, mark me, I know when a game's lost, so I do, and I know one who's staunch and true. Ah, you and young Marthar and me, why, we might have done a power of good together!" He reached into a pouch and pulled out a bottle of cognac.

"Will ye taste, messmate?" he asked, and when I had refused: "Well, I'll take a dram meself, Peter. I need a caulker, for there's trouble on hand, to be sure." And he took another swallow of the brandy, shaking his great red-golden head as someone looking forward to the worst.

The council of pirates had lasted some time when one of them came out, looked at us briefly and then returned.

"There's a cold wind coming," Silver said, and his fur fluffed up.

They came out of the door, one by one, sideways, then coming upright, gathering. I saw the sunlight gleam of a bare blade. The others were watching him as he held a bottle in one hand and the *wtsai* in the other, kneeling down as he did something. Then he rose to his feet and the whole party came towards us.

"Here they come," said I and turned away, for I did not want them to think I was spying on them.

"Well, let 'em come, Peter, let 'em come," Silver said cheerfully. "I've still a shot in my locker."

The group came up slowly, seven of them, and all the others pushed one member forward. In any other circumstances it would have been comical to see his slow advance, hesitating as he set one foot in front of the other, but holding a clenched paw in front of him.

"Step up, Hero," Silver called to him. "I won't eat you. Hand it over. I knows the rules, I do. I won't hurt a depytation."

Thus encouraged, the pirate stepped up more briskly and passed something to Silver, trying to drop it into his paw, but Silver carefully taking it in his claws. Silver looked at what had been given to him.

"Ah, the death claw. I thought so. And whose claw was this, afore it got dipped, that's what I'd like to know. Were it one of those poor kzin what we killed here? Ah, I sees it were. Not a pirate claw then. Not one of the fraternity. Ah, but you didn't ought to take a claw off someone who died for loyalty, d'ye see, 'cos if ye does that, then the one what takes it is the one what dies. And I thought you said you knows the rules as I does, d'ye see. And the rules is that I'm still yer Cap'n until I hears yer grievances, an' this here death claw ain't worth a biscuit. So yer grievances please, an' after that we'll see."

"Oh, don't you be under any misapprehension, *we're* all square, we are," answered a pirate. "First, you've made a hash of this cruise—you'll be a bold kzin to say no to that. Second, you let the enemy come and get us and now they hold the tower where the treasure is. And third, you lost us the ship, which is the end of things, or so it seems to the council. And then fourth, you didn't shoot the pinnace when you had the chance. And fifth, there's this here man-kit."

"Is that all?" asked Silver quietly.

"Enough," growled the kzin. "We'll all die for this an' all your bungling. Whether it be the ARM, or the Patriarch, or Lord Vaemar-Riit, they're all after us now."

"Well now, lookee here, I'll answer these p'ints one by one, one after another. So I made a hash of the cruise, did I? Ye all know what I wanted. I wanted no reason for S'maak-Captain and the others to have a single suspicion of us until we took them by surprise. But who was it looked mutinous afore we even landed? Though I did everything to be helpful and to keep them happy, who was it wanted to get their claws on the treasure as soon as we were in orbit? Not me, as I recall. But you, Rraangar, and you, Sraurr, ye announced yer intentions by the way ye cursed every order ye got, and snarled at any who looked to obey them. And so S'maak struck first, or leastaways he would ha' done, had I not turned the ship against him. Oh, he knew, he did. And I fathomed he did, else the red lander would ha' been destroyed and everyone aboard it. An' if we'd done it my way, why we'd be aboard and countin' the treasure by now, so we would have been. But no, and who crossed me? Who gave S'maak the idea that we was a risk? I think it was you, Rraangar, Sraurr and pretty much every damned one of ye. And ye have the insolence to stand for Cap'n over me, you that sank the lot of us! By the powers, this tops the stiffest yarn to nothing."

Silver paused, and I could see by the faces that the words had much effect.

"That's for number one," Silver remarked, snarling; his vehemence had loosened his temper. "Why, I give ye my word I'm sick to speak with ye for ye've neither sense nor memory, and I leave it to fancy to speculate where yer mothers and Sires were that let ye come into space. Heroes of fortune? I reckon vegetable growers is more your trade."

Rraangar snarled. "Go on to the others, Silver,"

"Oh, the others. Well, I let the enemy take us down, did I? And who was it ordered a watch, and who was on watch when they came? Someone drunk, I'll be bound. Ye can't hold yer liquor, not one of ye, and ye can't think of the morrow, misty hells, ye can't think o' ten minutes hence, not one of ye. And ye can't obey orders from them as can think ahead, ye useless swabs. And ye think 'twas me lost you the ship? Well 'twas me got it for ye in the first place, so I did, else ye'd ha' been crisped meat while still in the lander, so ye would. And I'm the on'y one could get it back, I'll ask ye to remember. Oh, and ye'd ha' me destroy the pinnace, which is the on'y way back to the ship, ye half-witted swabs. Aye, the enemy has it an' we don't, which is bad, but nowhere near as bad as neither of us havin' it. And for why? Because there's a consort coming, so there be, a sister ship to the *Valiant*; and that brings us to the last point, the man-kit here. Where will we be, think ye, if the consort arrives, or if they choose to get the new *Valiant* to make a few more landers? Why, they takes the treasure, and they leaves, but not afore they take us all out from space. And what's to stop them doing that? Why, think you little Marthar would let them destroy her pet here? I'm after thinkin' that she would not. But if they thought we had ate him, then she'd be egging them on for vengeance, as though our race—as though the Riit Clan—ever needed any egging. Ha' ye never heard of a hostage? No, 'tis too hard and complicated an idea for ye to get your heads around, I daresay. Waste of time with Heroes, but not with humans." He spat on the ground before them with contempt. "And lost ye the ship, have I? Well, maybe I have an idea of how to get it back, and maybe I haven't, but I reckon my chances a little better than yours, Rraangar, just a little better. For ye can't program worth a damn, can ye? And then there's this." He threw Skel's memo pad, or more accurately, K'zarr's memo pad, on the ground before them. They gaped at it. Then they started to talk excitedly.

Why Orion had given it to Silver I had no idea, but its effect on the crew was extraordinary. They leapt upon it and passed it from one to the other with excitement. You would have thought they imagined they had the key to the universe and were home and dry with the treasure. "Yes, that be K'zarr's pad, I seen it before."

"Very pretty," said Rraangar sourly. "But what use be it wi' no ship?"

Silver motioned me and we walked away. I remembered that the thing had been booby-trapped, and thought that maybe it was still lethal, so I caught up with Silver quickly.

"Cap'n, where be you goin'?" one of the crew whined.

"Oh, I knows where I'm not wanted. I resigns, I does. Ye've got another Cap'n now, Rraangar wants the job, I'm thinkin'. Well, ye're welcome to him is all I says. But I wouldn't want him for *my* leader. He ain't safe is what I be thinkin', 'cos he got no gumption, and has no ideas worth half a damp fart in a thunderstorm, he don't. He's got the invention of a *sthondat*, so he do. So I be leavin' ye all, an' I wishes ye well, but I doesn't expect ye to have much luck, no, I doesn't. Still, we goes our separate ways wi' no ill feelin', I hopes."

"No, Cap'n, don't leave us. You is our Cap'n, be sure of it," one of them cried, and the murmurs from the others supported him. Only Rraangar seemed uncertain. I think he liked the thought of being in charge, but he didn't care at all for the responsibility. Pirate captains who can't show success have a short lifespan.

"So that's the toon, is it?" cried Silver. "Rraangar, I reckons you'll have to wait your turn, friend, and lucky for you I'm not revengeful, but 'twas never my way. And now this here death claw, what does we do with it? 'Tain't much use now, is it? And never was a lot, what with it comin' from a trusty. Ye've crossed your luck there, I'm thinkin'." Silver threw it derisively on the ground, and I was tempted to pick it up, but I remembered what one had done to Skel, and I had noted the care with which Silver had handled it, using only his claw tips, which he then wiped surreptitiously on a bit of fabric from a pouch.

That was the end of the business, and the crew took a drink all round, and retreated to the wreck. Silver's only revenge was to appoint Rraangar as sentry, and threaten him with death if he should prove unfaithful. Silver and I stayed outside, while he cat-napped and I eventually fell asleep in the broad daylight, huddling under a part of the wreck so as to keep the sun out of my eyes. It took some time to get to sleep. I had matter enough for thought in my perilous position, and above all in the remarkable game that I saw Silver engaged upon—keeping the mutineers together with one hand, and grasping with the other every means possible and impossible to make his peace and save his miserable life. He sat there, as relaxed and peaceful as if he had no care in the world, one eye closed, and a soft droning sound coming from his throat—he was actually purring. Yet my heart was sore for him, wicked as he was, to think on the dark perils that awaited him, and the shameful death he faced and no doubt deserved.

I was awakened by a hail; the voice was human and one I recognized. I stood up yawning and rubbing the sleep from my eyes. I have to say, nearly perpetual daylight is very wearing. With the sun always high in the sky, you feel as though you have been very late to awake and faintly guilty in consequence. The sun may have moved perceptibly during our time here, but it was by very little.

The hail came again: "Ho there, mutineers and pirates, it is your friendly neighborhood doctor come to visit!"

And indeed it was. Doctor Lemoine stood there, where Silver had stood under flag of truce. The Doctor carried no flag, but he waved his little black bag in token of coming in peace. He looked his usual fresh self, in dark suit and white linen, with his long pipe in his hand.

Silver stretched and made himself agreeable.

"Welcome, doctor, and top o' the mornin' to ye, and how be yourself this live-long day?" He was cheery and welcoming, as he could be when he set his mind to it. "Your patients spent a quiet night, I'm glad to tell ye. Leastaways, they didn't make no noise to speak of."

That was the first time I realized that there were wounded kzin in the wreck of the lander and the Doctor had been giving them medicines to keep them alive. It says much about the man that he took it for granted that his duty was to help all who were sick, without reference to their species or their allegiance. And that he put his own life at hazard to do so, for a wounded kzin might not be entirely rational.

I was confused as to how to treat him, for our insubordinate conduct had caused a deal of trouble. I saw what it had brought me, among what companions and surrounded by what dangers, and I felt unable to look him in the face.

"Rraangar, help the good Doctor up the hill, blast ye for a lazy oaf." Silver was quite the old agreeable tutor, in voice, manner and expression.

"We've a surprise for ye, Doctor, and a pleasant one, to be sure. We've a little stranger come among us, a new boarder and lodger, sir, and looking taut and fit as a fiddle. Slep' like a supercargo he did, right alongside o' Silver, for the whole night, so we be talkin' ship's time, o'course."

By this time, Doctor Lemoine was close to the wreck, and I could hear the change in his voice as he said: "Not Peter?" He saw me at the same moment, and his eyes widened. He stopped and looked at me strangely.

"Well, well," he said at last. "Duty first and then pleasure as you might have said yourself, Silver. Let us overhaul our patients."

A moment later he had followed Silver into the wreck, with one grim look at me before he did so. He was as cool as always, though he must have known that his life among these treacherous demons depended on a hair. I followed him in, getting a black look from Rraangar, though he said nothing.

The Doctor rattled on to his patients as though they were ordinary Thoma'stowners and he paying an everyday professional call; his manner reacted on the kzin, who treated him as if he were the ship's Doctor and they faithful hands, and as though nothing uneventful had occurred. "You're doing well my friend," he told one with a bandaged head. "You must have a skull of stainless steel, for it was close to finishing you, that cutlass blow. Did you take your medicine?" The kzin said little. "Well men, did he take his medicine?" the Doctor asked in good humor, and they rumbled that he had indeed done so.

"And did you pass up on the rum, as I told you?" There was less agreement on this, some of them looking almost shamefaced. "Well, it is important that I keep you all in good condition, for I want every last one of you to come to trial for mutiny and piracy in deep space, I'd not lose one of you. The Lord Vaemar would never forgive me. And as you may be aware, on Wunderland he has co-jurisdiction in criminal cases involving kzin. The kidnapping, risk and insult to his son and grand-daughter will doubtless interest him. Perhaps you know that he was kidnapped himself when not much more than a kit—by crazed humans who had risen under Chuut-Riit during the

Occupation and wanted him to lead them again. Poor creatures! Or perhaps, now that the peace treaty is holding, you'll be handed over to the Patriarchy—though I'm an honorary magistrate, I'm afraid interspecies law is not my specialty."

They looked at each other, but swallowed the thrust in silence. ARM would perhaps not wish to get involved, but remembering what I had heard of Silver's boasting of their exploits during the war, and of Chuut-Riit's vow of vengeance to the death and the generations, it seemed to me that neither Vaemar nor the Patriarchy could be expected to err on the side of leniency. He carried on binding their wounds.

"There, that's done, and I should warn you not to displace those bandages, for there are bacteria here which can get into an open wound, not to mention some nasty fungal things that would take your insides out and turn your guts into green rot. And you'd be better using that rum for antiseptic than for drinking, for it affects your livers, and under these conditions you need all the liver function you can get. But then, when did anyone take medical advice, eh? All right, and now I shall go and talk to Master Peter Cartwright, if you please."

"No!" cried Rraangar, and drew his *wtsai*. Silver knocked it aside and roared like a lion, shaking his mane about as he looked around.

"Doctor," he went on in his usual tones, "I was a-thinking of that, knowing as how ye had a liking for the man-kit. We're all humbly grateful for your kindness, and as ye see we puts faith in ye, and we takes our medicines down like so much grog, so we does. And I take it I've found a way as'll suit all of us. Peter, young monkey, will ye gi' us your word as a Hero, for though ye be but a monkey and by no means rich, I can see ye ha' the sperrit o' one o' the nobility, would ye give us yer word of honor not to slip your cable?"

I readily gave the pledge required. A human could not outrun a kzin anyway.

"Then Doctor," said Silver, "ye may step down the hill a little way, and when ye're there, why, I'll bring the man-kit down to ye, so I will, within an easy talkin' distance. Good day to ye, sir, and all our dooties to Lord Orion-Riit and S'maak-Captain."

The Doctor looked at him, then at me, with no expression on his face, then nodded and left the wreck. As he did, the explosion of disapproval which nothing but Silver's black looks had contained erupted in roars and hisses. Silver was roundly accused of playing double—of trying to make a separate peace for himself, of sacrificing the interests of his accomplices and victims, and in short, of exactly the thing he was indeed doing. I found it impossible to imagine how he could conceal it from them, but he was twice the kzin any of the rest were, and his victory of the previous day had given him an enormous preponderance on their minds. He called them all the fools and dolts you can imagine, as well as other of the Heroes' Tongue's remarkable range of suggestive insults and said it was necessary I should talk to the Doctor. He waved K'zarr's memo pad in their faces, and asked them if they could afford to break the treaty the very day they could hope to take the ship back.

"No, by thunder," he cried, "it's us must break the treaty

when the time is ripe; 'til then, I'll gammon that Doctor if I have to polish his boots wi' brandy."

Then he admonished them to contain themselves, threw them the memo pad, which one of them caught, and stalked out, his paw upon my shoulder, using his great cutlass as a support. He left them in disarray, silenced by his volubility rather than convinced.

"Slow, Peter, slow," he said quietly. "They might round upon us in the twinkle of an eye if we was seen to hurry."

CHAPTER TWENTY-FOUR

We walked slowly towards the Doctor, who stood at some distance, waiting patiently. When we were within talking range Silver called out: "You'll make a note of this here also, Doctor, and the man-kit will confirm it; I saved his life at risk to me own, and was deposed for it, too, and ye may lay to that. Doctor, when a Hero is steerin' as close to the wind as what I am, ye wouldn't think it too much, mayhap, to give him one good word? You'll please bear in mind, 'tis not only my life now, 'tis the kit's as well. And you'll give me a bit o' hope to go on, for the sake o' *mercy*." At the back of my mind I noted that expression 'close to the wind'. The kzin had picked up many nautical terms from their former employers, the Jotok.

Silver was desperately earnest, his voice trembled. It was the third time I had heard a kzin use the word "mercy." Trust Silver to know it.

"Why Silver, were you not a kzin Hero, I might think you afraid," Doctor Lemoine said quizzically. This was a risky thing to say to any kzin.

"Doctor, I will willingly die for somethin' worth dyin' for, d'ye see? Even for the chance to make a healthy profit. But I face torture and for what? For nothin'. For standing up for the young man-kit here in the face of ignorance and stupidity, maybe. For nothin' a kzin can take pride in, save that. Now ye are a good man, and true; one o' the best o' humankind to be sure. And you'll not forget what I done that's good, no more than you'll forget what's bad, I know. So I steps aside, see? And I leaves Peter and you alone, and you will put that down for me too, I hope, for it's a long stretch, is that!"

So saying, he stepped back a little way until he was out of earshot, and leaned against his great cutlass with the hilt under his arm, waiting. He would turn away to look at the ruffians in the wreck, and back again to regard the Doctor and me.

"So, Peter," the Doctor said sadly. "Here you are. And yet you have done much good; Marthar has returned with this old kzin Bengar, and has shown us hope to get off this accursed planet. And yet here you are, a hostage in the hands of the enemy. A sad lack of judgment, you have to admit."

I was greatly cheered to hear that Marthar and the others had met up and that, whatever my follies, they would be safe. But I was mortified that I had been captured through lack of thought and admitted as much.

"Doctor," I told him, my lip quivering, "I have paid the price. My life is forfeit, I know it, and I should have been dead by now had not Silver stood by me. And Doctor, believe this, I can die—and I daresay I deserve it—but what I fear is torture. If they come to torture me—"

"Peter," the Doctor interrupted, and his voice was quite changed. "Peter, I can't have this. Whip over here and we'll run for it."

"Doctor," I said, "I gave my word."

"I know, I know," he cried. "We can't help that, Peter. I'll take the whole thing on my shoulders, blame and shame, my boy; but I cannot let you stay here. Jump, and we'll run like antelopes."

"No," I replied. "You know right well you would never do the same thing yourself and no more will I. Silver trusted me; I gave my word and back I go. But, Doctor, you did not let me finish. What I fear is that under torture I might lead them through the discs to where the pinnace is. Or was, at least. So I beg you to move it somewhere safe, somewhere I don't know about, else all is lost."

The Doctor looked at me for a few seconds. "Peter," he said at length, "you have saved our lives and above all you have saved Marthar; she told us the details. It would be a poor return were we to let you lose yours. You found old Bengar, the two of you, the best deed you'll ever do; but that reminds me, talking of Bengar. Silver!" he cried out. "Silver, I'll give you a piece of advice," he continued as the kzin drew near. "Don't you be in any great hurry to take the treasure."

"Why, sir, I do my possible, which that ain't. I can only save my life and the boy's by leading my Heroes to that treasure, and ye may lay to that."

"Well, Silver," replied the Doctor, "if that be so, I'll go one step further: look out for squalls when you take it."

"Sir, as between legal entities, that's too much and too little. What you're after, why you took up in the tower, why ye gave me Kzarr's pad, that I don't know now, do I? But no, this here's too much; if you'll not tell me what you mean, just say so and I'll quit the helm."

"No," said the Doctor musingly. "I've no right to say more, it's not my secret, you see, Silver, or I give you my word I'd tell you. But this I will say, if we all get out of this tigripard-trap alive, if you save the boy, I'll do my best to save you, short of perjury."

Silver's face lit up. "You couldn't say more, sir, I'm sure, and my grateful thanks for it."

"Well, that's my first concession. My second is a bit of advice: keep the boy close beside you and when you need help, call for it. I'm off now to seek it for you both. Farewell, Peter."

And Doctor Lemoine shook hands with me, nodded to Silver and strode off at a brisk pace into the bushes.

The Doctor was gone for a few minutes when Silver looked at me. "If I saved your life, Peter, then you saved mine, and I'll not forget it. I seen you out of the tail of me eye when the Doctor begged ye to run for it, so I did; and I seen ye say no, as plain as hearing it. That's one to you, that is, and the first glimmer o' hope I had since the attack failed, and I owe it to you. And now, we have to go on this treasure hunt, with sealed orders too, and I don't like it. You and me we must stay close, back to back like, and mayhap we'll save our necks in spite o' fate and fortune."

Just then one of the crew tumbled out of the wrecked lander and hailed us. "Silver-Captain, what was the password that K'zarr had on his pad?" he called.

"Bloody fools ha' tried to open it," muttered Silver

savagely. "What sort o' eedjut would not know better than that? Old K'zarr were not the one to leave a memo pad open for anyone to read."

"I don't have any idea," he called back. "K'zarr kept his council, so he did. But ye may trace a triangle, so ye may; 'tis a faint possibility."

The kzin was holding what must have been the memo pad, and he put a claw tip to it and began to trace something when it exploded in green fire. It wasn't loud, but the fire ran up the kzin's arm onto his face, and he screamed horribly as it consumed him. He twisted and fell, with the pad underneath him. Then there was a *whump!* and his body jerked once. One more of the crew tumbled out, looked at the body and roared to the inside of the wreck, then jumped back and fanned the air, roaring a warning to the others. A faint green mist hovered over the corpse. Kzin came rushing out, their paws over their faces as they saw the green mist, until the whole of them, even the wounded, were outside standing well away from the lander, looking with horrid fascination at the corpse and the slowly dissipating mist.

Then they turned back to Silver. "Silver-Captain, what do we do now, we ain't got the memo pad?" one of them wailed. They came staggering towards us, coughing, eyes streaming. They had not been very close to the green mist, but it had affected all of them nonetheless.

Silver looked wrathfully at his crew as they stood there looking lost.

"And what fool tried to wrest K'zarr's secrets from him?" Silver asked. "What fools among ye thought that K'zarr was to be easy? Ye're lucky that it happened outside; had ye tried in in the lander ye'd all be deader'n cow guts by now, so ye would and deserve to be too."

Some of them looked furtively at the others. "But Cap'n, we done lost it. How are we to know what the treasure is and where, izackly?" Rraangar was the spokesman.

"The damned thing was useless; I already ha' the information on it," Silver growled. "And so does the man-kit here, on his phone. And K'zarr hisself knew little. I was there when he found it, so I was, all I needed to know was the coordinates of the planet and the place on the planet where the tower be. And ye can almost see it from here. So there is but small loss in the contrivance, else why would Orion ha' given it to us?"

This gave them pause for thought, and they gradually brightened. "Well, we shall have *him* for a feast when we get there," one of them said with a snarl. "One last attack in the tower and we shall see to that."

Silver said nothing. He knew about the discs. He knew that there were ways in and out of the tower that the pirates did not. Their position was weak indeed, but only Silver would accept that. The crew seemed to believe that a brutal assault would get them what they wanted, prisoners perhaps to extort details of where the pinnace was. Men who served in the war had told me that the kzin's addiction to head-on attack had been what had saved the humans time and again. But I knew and Silver must suspect that the others were now better armed. All the crew had were *wtsais* and cutlasses, with the needlers out of ammunition. They wouldn't do much against the blasters which Marthar would have gotten to Orion and S'maak-Captain by now. The crew had no idea of the perils of their position, and I surely wasn't going to tell them. And neither was Silver. Which carried its own perils for him.

"Right then, let's to work!" roared Silver. He clapped Rraangar on the shoulder, and gestured to the others. "Once we get the treasure we can cast about for the pinnace; we need to take prisoners who can give us a little help on that!"

They cheered him at the prospect, snarling in anticipation. He was lifting their spirits, and, I rather more than suspected, his own at the same time.

"As for our hostage," he continued, "that's his last talk, I guess, with those he loves so dear. I've got my piece o' news, and thankee to him for that; but it's over and done. I'll take him in line when we goes treasure hunting, for we'll keep him like gold in case of accidents, you mark, and in the meantime. Once we get the pinnace and treasure both, and back into space like jolly companions, why then we'll talk to Peter Cartwright again, so we will, and we'll give him his due share to thank him for all his kindness. Meanwhile we'll take good care of him, so we will." Saying which, he took a metal rope and tied a noose around my neck and took the other end in his paw.

The crew were in good humor now and for my part, I was most horibly cast down. Should the scheme he had sketched prove feasible, Silver, already doubly a traitor, would not hesitate to adopt it. He still had a foot in either camp, and while the pirates offered him wealth and freedom, our side offered him, at best, a bare escape from death.

Indeed, while the humans might bargain with him for his life, I was certain the kzin would not do so. Apart from anything else, there was the matter of which I had overheard him boasting: Chuut-Riit's vow of vengeance 'to the generations.' Kzin were not disposed to overlook such vows once made, though centuries passed, the Riit Clan probably least of all, and I did not see how we could make them do so. At best we might be able to offer him escape to one of the remote new colony worlds, but how would we find a ship to get him there? I was sure Silver had thought of all this as well.

Even if things fell out so that he was forced to keep his faith with the Doctor, even then what danger lay before us! What a moment that would be when the suspicions of his followers turned to certainty and he and I—a cripple and a boy—should have to fight for life against seven armed kzin!

Add to this double apprehension the doubt as to where my friends now were and the Doctor's last warning to Silver about the treasure: *Look out for squalls when you find it.*

Silver ordered them to work: "We can be there in the hour, be we brisk and business-like, so form a file and we go that way yonder. And be silent, for we want to gi' them no warning."

The pirates obediently set off after Silver and me in a single file. There were seven of them, two wounded, but it takes a lot to stop or even slow down a kzin. Silver and I were in the lead at first, but with his artificial leg and his limp, and with me being little over half their height, the crew gradually moved in front of us, until we were at the tail of a procession of dangerous monsters descending on my friends. I hoped they were keeping good lookout. Or better, had vacated the first tower for the one to which Bengar had taken us. Or better yet, some other I knew nothing of, for although I had no absolute certainty, I felt that I could recall the discs we had stepped on to get there. And under torture, I might betray my friends. I hoped I would die first. I had taken on some of Marthar's kzin ideas in the years of being friends with her. "Everyone has to die, even with the so-called immortality drugs," she had said with a shrug. "There were nearly fourteen billion years before the brief time now when I exist, and no doubt there will be many trillions of years after. I don't worry about the second period any more than I do about the first. So long as I make the best use of this brief window and live life with courage and honor. DNA and self-respect. That's what makes us the Kzin. And it should make for you too, little Chimpy, although it's not the same DNA."

DNA and self-respect. I had no pride of ancestry as Marthar did, but I had nothing to be ashamed of either. I was a human being, and we had made a difference to the Universe. And I understood how she felt about self-respect. I'd seen the sad people who had lost it or maybe never had any, and I pitied them. There's an old Earth saying that the coward dies a thousand deaths, the hero dies but once. It's not true. The coward never really lives. Once you see that, and resolve to live without fear, you don't fear death or anything else much, save losing your self-respect. In my case death might well come as a friend.

I thought, for some reason, of the nameless, almost certainly long-dead kzin Hero who, when Wunderland was falling to the victorious human forces, had found a terrified kitten in the ruins of the governor's palace and handed it to

Jorg, and he to Rarrgh-Sergeant, commanding the last kzin garrison, a handful of cripples beseiged in Circle Bay Monastery. That kitten had grown into the mighty Vaemar-Riit, who had played a great role in bringing peace between man and kzin on Wunderland. We cannot even try to see where things will lead.

The way led through scrub and past the occasional taller bushes over hard-packed ground that had never seen anything like cultivation, with its red dirt and rocks and flints. The kzin wore nothing to protect their feet but seemed oblivious to the grit and stones; I was glad of my boots. Silver was at least considerate with my tether and didn't pull on it. We trekked easily by Silver's directions, so as not to weary the hands prematurely, with Silver occasionally calling them to slow down so as to accommodate himself and of course me. We got to where we could clearly see the top of the tower above the bushes, and stark and black it looked to me with broken shards of metal at the top, a sort of cream stone lower down with windows that were mere slots of emptiness through which it was all too easy to imagine alien eyes watching. A heavy-scented broom and some of the shrubs being in flower mingled their spices and made the place almost attractive. I could hear Silver purring, not with content but excitement.

The crew were all excited now, and caught between rushing on regardless of their leader, and huddling together to await him, for we were scores of paces behind even the stragglers, those who had been wounded. They tried to roar in an undertone with limited success.

That was when there came a cry from one of the crew

who had gone slightly off the trail. The others ran in his direction.

"He can't ha' found any treasure, for 'tis all in the tower," Silver remarked. "Let us see for ourselves what 'tis that causes sich a commotion."

It was certainly something very different from treasure, as we found when we also reached the spot. At the foot of what was a bush of almost tree height, and half-covered by green moss, lay a kzin skeleton with a few scraps of belt on the ground and a few fragments of fur remaining on the bones.

"He were one o' the brotherhood," said Rraangar, who was bolder than the rest and had gone up to examine the scraps of belts. "Leastaways, he carried a cutlass. Ye can see the mark o' one in the sand."

"Aye, aye," said Silver. "Like enough; you wouldn't look for a priest or a lordling here, I reckon. But where is his cutlass now? Or his *wtsai*? Or a needler?"

"Well, who might he ha' been?" one of the crew asked.

"Whoever it were didn't die natural," one of the crew observed. "Or the weapons would ha' been here too."

"Ahh, well, those who went on trips wi' K'zarr did tend to die. 'Twere natural enough to die wi' K'zarr in the offing," Silver said thoughtfully. "And if K'zarr were living, this would be a right hot spot for all of us. K'zarr wouldn't like it that others than him were lookin' for his treasure."

"I saw him dead with these here deadlights," Rraangar said. "Skel showed me the body. It were K'zarr, sure enough, wi' a snarl on his face and his eyes open to face the Fanged God, or more like the hell demons."

"Aye, sure enough, K'zarr be dead and gone below," said

the one with the bandages. "But if ever sperrit walked, it would be K'zarr's. He died bad, did K'zarr."

"That he did," another put in. "Now he raged and now he hollered for the rum, and always he sang o' death and blood, in that cold, cold voice of his. I dreams about that voice, so I does, like a stab of a *wtsai* made of ice, so it were, a stab in the ear through to the brain. And bad dreams they be, bad, bad dreams."

"Come, Heroes, stow this talk," cried Silver. "K'zarr is dead, and he don't walk lest we let him. And he don't walk by natural daylight, and there's little night on this cursed planet, so if K'zarr walks, he walks a world away. I'll be the Hero what lets K'zarr walk, once we're back in space, and he will dance, not walk, and he will dance to my tune, Heroes, and my tune only. Be sure of it!" roared Silver. Yes, I thought, there was no doubt about it, the others were miserable, wretched petty criminals, unworthy of the name of Hero. But Silver was something more.

I recalled the terror with which I had seen the ghost of K'zarr on board the *Valiant*, a horrible joke of Silver. It must have amused him to bring a ghost of K'zarr back to life to obey his orders. What the crew made of the macabre gesture I could not imagine; maybe they had never seen him, perhaps only the senior ship's officers knew of Silver's strange tastes. Or maybe it was an afterthought that he had arranged to replace *Valiant* by K'zarr and it had never happened before. Perhaps he was planning to use the thing to terrorize the crew later. Who could fathom the working of Silver's mind? I knew I could not.

"Not far to go now, Heroes, on to the treasure!" Silver waved the way ahead, but in spite of the warmth of the sun and the staring daylight, the pirates no longer ran separate and (despite Silver's orders) shouting through the bush, but kept side by side and spoke in whispers. The terror of the dead pirate had fallen on their spirits.

We were mounting a light hill. The tower stood on the top of it, like a medieval fortress holding the high ground. We could not see the base of it, for it was covered by the thin foliage still, but it loomed up over us. There was no sound but the thin wind whistling through the broom and the bushes, making the flowers tremble. I was hot enough to sweat, and often brushed it out of my eyes. My spirits were low and I was half-sick with fear of what would happen. The crew were less than happy, too.

"I don't feel too sharp," the one with the bandaged head said. "I have a pain in my skull despite that medicine."

"The Doctor told you to rest," I pointed out to him.

"Aargh, 'twere all that talk o' K'zarr what done it," he protested, looking at me and brooding.

"Ah well, my son, you praise your stars he's dead," said Silver.

"He were an ugly devil," another one cried. "That blue in the face, he were."

"That were how the rum took him," another added. "Blue! Well, I reckon he were blue, right enough."

Ever since they had found the skeleton and started this train of thought they had spoken lower and lower and were almost to whispering by now.

CHAPTER TWENTY-FIVE

The crew had advanced until we were almost within sight of the great gaping doorway into the tower, and Silver and I were some little way behind when the voice called out to them. Silver froze instantly. The crew screamed in response and fell back. The voice spoke in kzin, but I recognized it. I had heard it before on the memo pad and on the ship. A thin, cold voice like an ice dagger in the head. And there was a figure there too, some big kzin body, dark against the tower, calling out. The crew cried out again and came past us in panic. Rraangar fell to the ground and moaned; the others looked too frightened to move.

"'Tes K'zarr," one of them cried out, his voice trembling.

Silver recovered first. "'Tes some foolery; K'zarr is dead and where he went nobody comes back. There's a livin' breathin' creature ahind this, kzin or man, ye may lay to that."

I realized that the computer I had brought back from the ship was a better explanation than ghosts. Someone on my side had decided to frighten the crew. For almost any kzin, the experience of fear tended to be destructive in itself: it was part of the penalty they paid for not admitting fear so that when they did feel it, it was worse. Marthar must have downloaded the ghost Silver had made, and programmed him to speak and move like the evil old pirate. I was not at all surprised that it had frightened the pirates; it had caused my own heart to stop for a few seconds.

Silver's courage had come back as he spoke, for no doubt he had recognized his own creation. He must have wondered how it had come down to the planet, but this was a lesser matter than his genuine fear of the original kzin. Maybe K'zarr had feared Silver, but what need K'zarr fear after death?

The same cold, cruel voice broke out again. "Dar'marGra, Dar'marGra!" Then with an oath, "Dar'marGra, fetch aft the rum!"

The pirates stood rooted to the ground, their eyes starting from their heads. Long after the echoes of the voice died away, they still stared in silence, dreadfully.

"That fixes it," said one. "Let's go."

"They was his last words," moaned Rraangar. "His last words above ground."

Still Silver was unconquered. I could see he was taken aback, but he had not yet surrendered.

"Nobody on this here planet knows of *Dar'marGra* save us," he muttered. Then he made a great effort. "Shipmates," he cried, "I'm here to get that stuff, and I'll not be beat by man nor kzin nor devil. I was never afeared o' K'zarr when he were alive, and, by the powers, I'll face him when he's dead. There's billions not a thousand yards from here, nay, trillions! When did ever a Hero of fortune show his stern t' that many vrin for fear of a boozy old spacer wi' a blue mug—and him dead, too?"

But there was no sign of reawakening courage in his followers; rather, indeed, there was growing terror at the irreverence of his words.

"Belay there, Cap'n," said the one with the bandages. "Don't you cross a sperrit."

They would have run away had they dared. I think that in facing physical danger or even death, they would have shown the usual bravery of the Kzin, but confronted with a mystical danger, they caved in. Silver, however, had pretty well fought his weakness down.

"Sperrit? Well, maybe, maybe," he said. "But there's one thing not clear to me. There was an echo. Now no being ever saw a sperrit with a shadow, well then, what's he doing with an echo to him, I should like to know? That ain't in natur', surely?"

The argument seemed weak enough to me, but you can never tell what will affect the superstitious, and Rraangar was, to my surprise, greatly relieved.

"Well, that's so," he said. "Ye've got a fine head upon yer shoulders, Silver-Captain, and no mistake. 'Bout ship, companions, I does believe we been takin' a wrong tack on this. There's someone around is tryin' to get us afeard by playing old K'zarr at us. 'Tes some sort o' recordin', I'll be bound."

There was enough truth in this to depress my hopes more than a little. If the pirates were not to be intimidated by the ghost of K'zarr, then my friends were wasting their time.

"Well, here's where we get to find out just how real this

ghost is," said Silver, looking into the wood. "For here he comes. Nay, messmates, I'll be the one to face him down, you'll see. Stand back a little." Silver released the rope around my neck and motioned me back too.

And sure enough, a tall, thin kzin came towards Silver. K'zarr was here. There was no mistaking him. I checked but there was no hint of transparency, he was as solid as Silver so far as I could see. He grinned at Silver, a battle signal from a kzin. From his back he drew a cutlass nearly as long as he was tall. He swung it idly in one hand and looked at Silver. His eyes glowed. There was something red and shining in them. It didn't faze Silver.

"So, Silver, the smooth one, the Hero, the lordling. The subtle one, eh, Silver?" K'zarr snarled softly. "Would you take up a cutlass against me and see which of us goes to hell, you for the first time, me for the third or maybe the fourth now? For they lets me out o' hell, they does, to walk the world o' mortals. Now then Silver, go draw yer cutlass and have at me if you dare."

Silver stared at him, puzzled. "You ain't K'zarr," he told the figure. "You talk too much. And no, I'll not match cutlasses wi' ye."

With that, he drew the blaster from his belt, and fired it at the figure's body.

A needler fires slivers of steel accelerated in a magnetic field, and they can do a lot of damage, even to a kzin. But a blaster is something else. It fires fast spinnning toroids of plasma and, like smoke rings, they maintain their shape for a time; unlike smoke rings, they travel very fast and are very hot. Most of the energy is kinetic in the spinning and, although one of them has little actual matter in it, it is hot, fast matter and it shears through the chemical bonds which hold matter together. So anything made of ordinary matter evaporates in a fraction of a second. They are really for use in space, in air the stability forces are weakened, and it is lethal only over a range of a few hundred paces, but in space, the range is measured in astronomical units. I have seen videos of blasters used against matter, and it is impressive. Sometimes it is used for mining, and I have seen solid rock bubble and melt in a second and then turn into a gas that explodes all around it. I have never seen it used on fuzz. I had no idea what it would do; maybe go right through it.

The cutlass K'zarr held was a real one, that is, it was made of steel, so it whitened instantly and then evaporated in a burst of heat that knocked me back. The body of the pirate was fuzz, pseudomatter, and it just ablated. Bits peeled off and flew away like dust and I could see something like a skeleton revealed. The skin came off, then the body tissues, front and back. Then the skeleton, though it looked different from an ordinary skeleton; the bones were thinner and didn't join up in the usual way. I was watching this in fascination, not afraid so much as awestruck. Silver grimaced as the thing slowly vanished, and the crew looked on.

Eventually there was nothing left except steaming earth and a faint dust in the air. Silver switched off the blaster and blew on it to cool it. It was too hot to stick back in his belt, so he held it loosely.

"By the powers, that was something new, I'll be bound," said Rraangar.

"Yes, I have heard of it, but never seen it used like that

before. But the ship had the stuff, and I was learning to program it. It's programmable matter, d'ye see? Ye can make it do all sorts o' things. Make it look like a ghost, if yer mind works that way." He looked down at me thoughtfully. He was making the connection with his own experiments and the thing we had just faced. We must have got into the command center in order to restore *Valiant*, and we would have seen his version of K'zarr. And Marthar was not here, or at least, not in plain sight. But she would know about K'zarr's ghost even if she had not seen it. Making and controlling a robotic thing made of pseudomatter would have been a fun job of programming, with a little help from *Valiant*. I could see it and Silver could, too. He knew who his real enemy was. He also knew two other things. The first was that Marthar could make a robot that was faster even than a kzin, and could have won in a fight with cutlasses. The second was that there was a lot of fuzz about the place, just needing to be organized. It would take a while, but K'zarr or something even deadlier would be back.

The crew were excited and immensely pleased by Silver's easy victory. All their confidence had been restored and they were jubilant.

"Ah, Cap'n, that were masterly, so it were. Now there is nothin' twixt us and the treasure, ain't it so?"

"The sooner we gets there the better, 'tis true. So onward to the tower, Heroes!"

Silver picked up the other end of my tether and pulled me towards him as the rest of them trooped off towards the tower.

"Peter, I know who I was fighting back there, and your

little friend is a hard fighter, and happy to cheat. Now I think it would be good if you could let her know betimes that I am on your side and saving you from some very hungry kzin, wi' no sense, no judgment but wi' large appetites."

I looked up at him. He waited patiently, as relaxed as a cat, with all the time in the world.

"That's not what you told the crew," I said. "The question is, who are you lying to?"

He sighed. "There's no answer to that will please you, is there? There's loyalty to friends, to ideals and then there's self-interest. The last is the on'y one ye can rely upon. That's all I'll say. Now, come along, I don't want to have to pull on this here rope."

I followed him as he limped after the treasure hunters.

There was no sign of my friends in the tower. We walked through the huge arch of the entrance to hear only the babble of the crew above us. I took some comfort from the silence. The birds had flown, and I was relieved that they had found a way out. It must have been Bengar leading them via the discs. He and Marthar must have joined them and led them to safety.

We climbed the ramp to the next level, where we found the pirates looking in amazement at the same scene we had observed in the memo pad. There were tables around the walls, saddles on poles sticking out below them, and many of the metallic bars stacked in pigeon holes above the tables. There was one difference: instead of those terrifying snakes which had been lying on the tables, there were things that looked like coal scuttles or waste bins, and the snakes were attached to them, one on each side. At the moment, the snakes were flaccid and still.

The bins had a section cut out of them; they were thick, about two inches of metal or something that looked like it, and even thicker where the snakes joined them. The crew were staying well away from them, looking nervous.

"Ah, someone has made some changes since last time," Silver remarked, and he picked up one of the bins and looked at it. He turned it upside down, and it became clear they were helmets of some sort, the cut-out section allowing room for the muzzle of a kzin. The snakes dangled helplessly below them. They looked harmless, but I could not erase the memory of two of them hunting for the burnt kzin's eyes and burrowing into them, blinding him.

"A much better arrangement," Silver commented, looking into the helmet. "Rraangar, be so good as to put this on your head while sitting on that saddle."

"Not I, Cap'n," Rraangar was vehement. "I ha' seen wi' my own lamps what they things did to old Gra-Prompyh, so I have."

"D'ye not want the treasure?" Silver demanded. "We needs to know which o' these is valuable and which not. We need to search for an index, some way of saving us to have to try every one o' these things. Look, there be millions o' them. And many o' them worthless, I'll be bound. We wants them that 'as engineering content, so we does. And since we doesn't read the script over them little cubby holes, we needs to learn it, or find some shortcut."

"Not me, Silver-Captain," said Rraangar, obstinately. "Ye are the one to do the job. Likely none of us could make any sense o' what may be in any o' these bars anyway."

"Why not try it on the man-kit first?" one of them suggested, and my stomach knotted with fear.

"Fair enough," Silver agreed. "Peter, little monkey, just you sit on this here saddle and we'll see if the thing fits ye well enough. I be certain sure 'tis safe, else why should they be here? It has to be your friends made the changes, after all. And they would not want their little kit damaged, now would they?"

The reasoning didn't convince me. But what choice did I have? They could easily force my head into the thing. And if the snake things reached out into my brain through the sides of the helmet, well, I would probably be dead and at least no longer a hazard to my friends. My voice trembled, but I agreed.

"Very well, Silver. At least I can show you that a human being has less fear of the unknown than kzin Heroes."

They scowled at this, except for Silver, who merely looked judicious.

"If no harm comes to ye, then I'll try it myself, so I will. But I am sure it will not. Now sit ye down, and I'll lower it gradually, and ye can say what it is that happens."

He took the rope from around my neck, and threw it on the floor. I sat down, trying not to show fear. It wasn't easy, with that image before my mind. But at least I would show them.

The saddle was too big for me, but it seemed to adapt. I put my hands on the table before me. Silver placed one of the bars in the slight indentation in the table, and turned to look at me with the helmet in his hands.

"I'm thinkin' it will be harmless, Peter, but if it be not, then I shall be sure to tell any that cares how ye were a brave man-kit and put to shame some of the warriors. Now, talk while ye observe, that others may follow ye." And he slipped the helmet over my head, the cut-out section over my face and mouth. It was far too big for me, but the metal part came over my eyes so I could see only blackness and hear little. The helmet too seemed to be adapting itself to me, as had the saddle.

"Tap on the table if ye can still hear me." Silver's voice sounded odd to me inside the helmet; it echoed strangely, but I obediently tapped a finger.

"Now the connections are going to the bar, now they have joined up. Tap again if there is anything happening."

Nothing did happen at first, so I waited. Then the blackness lightened. At least the snakes seemed content with the connections to the helmet and weren't trying to eat into my brain. I tapped.

"Tell us what is happening, Peter," Silver's voice echoed boomily.

"There's a light come on. Can you hear me?"

"Aye, clear as a bell. Just ye let us know what comes."

I looked at the light, a sort of pale blue. Then something like icons appeared, a bit like a computer screen or a phone. What they meant I had no idea. There was a faint humming noise, which seemed to have been there for a while but got loud enough to register. I told Silver about the sound and the icons. I stared at one of the icons and it changed. It went through a series of contortions, but at no stage did it look even remotely familiar. I looked at another, and it started changing too. Then it became a bucket helmet with the snakes attached to a bar, and as I focused on it, the snakes withdrew and the glow faded.

I felt the helmet lift, and, blinking, saw the room again.

"Those connections withdrew o' their own accord, less ye had something t' do with it," Silver said, eyeing me with a thoughful look.

"I think it was the disconnect icon. I think I told it to stop, though I didn't mean to," I admitted.

"Ah, then we know how to stop the thing. Worth knowin,' I think ye'll agree. Let's start it again and see what these other icons do, shall we?" And he lowered the helmet again, and again it seemed to close in on my head and face, leaving my mouth and nose clear.

Again, the blue light came on, the icons showed and the humming started, quite a sweet noise, I suppose. I was making progress; I at least knew how to get out of the thing. Now to figure out what some of the other icons meant. It had to be fairly straightforward, surely? The icons were in a horizontal line, and the one at the extreme left was the disconnect, so I looked now at the one at the opposite end. It looked like a spoked wheel. As I focused on it, it started to turn slowly. The blue light dimmed and then came back much brighter, and underneath the icons, some sort of a script, I think. At least it looked a little like the markings on the discs, rather like a speech waveform. It lasted some seconds, then faded. I was getting interested, and had quite forgotten to keep Silver and the others informed of what I was seeing. He reminded me. "What now, young Peter?"

"There is an icon which I think is the start button, and I pressed it by looking at it. And then it showed me some sort of script, I think, and now it is a picture of something. Oh, I think they are alive. A bit like fish, dancing underwater. Only very, very slowly. Perhaps I can speed it up." I glanced up at the spoked wheel icon and willed it to turn faster, and it did. The fish danced faster too. I willed it to slow down and again, just wanting it to happen seemed to work. The helmet seemed to have its own intelligence; it could sense what I was looking at and somehow could work out what I wanted. I wondered if I could make it go backwards and discovered I could. I told Silver I had some degree of control over the video or whatever it was I was watching.

Looking at things like dolphins or fish dancing is not particularly exciting and they didn't seem to be doing anything else, so I looked at the other icons. There were about a dozen of them altogether. One of them changed colors. I could drive it through orange and red, so the fish were warm glowing red ghosts against a black background, and on until it was all black. Maybe it was showing me infrared pictures my eyes couldn't detect. I then went right through the other way to violet colors and got a brief headache before I went back to the middle region of silvery fish on a blue-green ground. That was another icon learned. My spirits lifted. I was getting good at this; I was communicating with artifacts left behind by an alien race, perhaps a million years ago. Maybe much longer.

I found I could zoom in and out using another icon, but after that it got harder. I reported my findings to Silver and the rest of them. Being useful to them might have some advantages, I thought, between my experiments with the remaining icons.

One of them produced sound. I was at too high a frequency at first, and it was first a hiss, then a high-pitched howl, and I found it deafening, and discovered that part of the icon turned the sound levels down or up. When it was at a tolerable level, it sounded like whale song, which might have gone with the fish or dolphins, I suppose. We have dolphins on Wunderland, and some had served in spaceships.

I found another icon, which seemed to have something to do with smell, but since my nose was outside the helmet, it seemed a bit strange. Silver couldn't smell anything, he said.

There were other icons I just gave up on; some senses I didn't have perhaps.

I think the dancing fish were beginning to bore Silver. They certainly had little interest for me, but I suspected that this was some sort of test pattern to allow the newbie to figure out how to use the icons. So I had to figure out how to get on to the main menu. I explained this to Silver, and he seemed satisfied that I was trying. The truth is, I was enjoying it. Perhaps part of it was relief that I wasn't having my brain invaded by snakes and part was the feeling that the more I learned the more useful I would be to the pirates and the less likely they were to eat me in a few bites. But some of it was just the fascination of learning new stuff.

"Should we mebbe try another bar?" Silver's voice boomed hollowly.

"No, I still haven't figured out how to get this one off the introductory sequence," I told him impatiently. I suspected I'd have to go through the whole process again with any other bar, as turned out to be the case.

I looked at the wheel icon again and noticed that there were symbols on the edges corresponding to the spokes, although what they meant I had no idea. As I watched them, they changed, passing through a lot of different symbols, including one that looked to be the speech waveform script. Ah! That gave me an idea.

CHAPTER TWENTY-SIX

I exited the system and Silver removed the helmet. I discovered I was hungry. I had been under the thing for hours, and I told them I needed a rest and some food. The kzin hadn't eaten for some time either, so we went down the ramp and outside, where the kzin started hunting. They were as efficient as Marthar had been, although they just bit the heads off the animals they found. I had to eat raw scraps, which was not a whole lot of fun, but at least put an end to my hunger. After pointing out to the rest of them that I had value, and was not to be harmed, Silver disappeared for about a short time back into the tower. For what purpose I didn't discover until later. In his absence the team made jokes about taking off little bits of me that couldn't affect my performance with the helmet.

"So long as we don't bite his head off, 'twill do no harm," one of them said loudly to another. "An arm or a leg would make no never mind, so long as we leave enough to sit down."

The others thought this very witty. I didn't, but I just ignored them.

Silver came back and ordered me back up to the helmet. I went with him and the others stayed, lolling about, growling at each other.

"Well, what are you planning now, young Peter," he said genially. "When are we going to find out what is in that damned bar?"

"I think I know how to learn how to read their script," I told him. "When I know, we can see from the writing on the pigeonholes what sorts of things we have."

"That will take too long," Silver said flatly. "We haven't unlimited time."

"Not that long," I told him firmly. "You can get by in a language in only about fifty words. I mean you can't understand much but you can interrogate people and machines with a pretty small vocabulary. And I think I can get to ask it questions."

"Hmmm. That will be a clever trick. Alright, I'll let ye play a little more, but I'm not one as cares for havin' his time wasted, as many a spacer ha' found to his cost. So be sure you aren't going to join them."

I had no certainty that what I planned would work, but it seemed likely to save time if it did, and I told him so. I think that like most kzin, he was inclined to respect people who stood up to him. Up to a point, anyway.

I sat down on the saddle again and Silver sat on the saddle next to mine, his tail hanging over the end. This time I lifted up the helmet myself and put it on. Again the blue light, all over from the beginning, but this time I knew something about what was coming. I sped up the process until I got to the speech or maybe music waveform on the end of a spoke of the wheel icon. I focused on it, and I got a waveform on the screen. I focused on that. There was a sound, something like someone crushing a harp, with twangs and thuds, and the waveform changed color briefly. This was a time sequence, and I sped everything up and did it again. Apart from the fact that time went from right to left, which was the opposite of what seemed natural to me, there was a sort of correlation between what I was hearing and the waveform; there was also a swift succession of scents and a feeling of warmth on my face. There had to be some sort of dictionary here. These things were something like words or phonemes; there had to be a way of making more complicated things of sequences of simpler things, and time had to look pretty much the same to any species that could handle technology, at least at the elementary level. I scanned the icons. Some of them had changed. There was a bar icon which was a uniform gold, and did nothing so far as I could tell. There was a shape which writhed as I looked at it, but again did nothing. And there was one which looked like a star. I focused on it.

The screen on the inside of the helmet oscillated slowly. It showed the sun, then this faded away to be replaced by the script and the sound that went with it, another clashing sound like someone rolling bottles down metal stairs. I repeated it and listened intently. The species which produced noises like that didn't use anything like the human or kzin vocal tracts. The kzin were certainly different from us in that respect, but they could do a good approximation of human speech, and we could do a rather bad approximation of theirs and it hurt the throat after a very short time. But these sounds came out as if they were produced by an orchestra or an organ made to sound like broken glass. Still, it was consistent. I think I had just learned the word for sun, although I could neither pronounce it or write it.

I reached into a pocket and pulled up my mobile phone, just able to insert it in the space before my eyes. I took two pictures of the script and the sun and recorded the sound of broken bottles.

"What are ye up to, lad?" Silver asked. He was genial enough but suspicious.

"I'm making a dictionary," I told him. And I suppose I was, but so far I had only one word in it. Now to get another one.

One of the icons pictured what might be an animal of some sort—something more like an octopus crossed with an eagle than anything I was familiar with. I looked at it hard. I thought perhaps it could be altered, and I found I could make it bigger or smaller, so I made it smaller. All animals grow from eggs, sometimes inside the parent body, sometimes not. Even primitive things like the hydra bud off a parent and are smaller when they start, so growth from small to big might be almost universal. At least it was worth a try.

The picture changed, and the word also. I could make no sense of it, so I scrolled onto the next one. This also seemed to be a dictionary definition in pictures, but I couldn't recognize any of the pictures. The next one was a picture of a bar, like the one I was reading, and the sound quite pleasant, just like a few strings of a guitar being plucked. Not exactly a chord one would hear from a musical instrument, but at least not as complex as the others. I scanned the icons, and again they had changed, but not in any useful way. I pushed the phone up and took some more pictures and recorded the sound. I couldn't do anything about recording the scent, which again was simpler, more like plain soap than anything else. I dimly sensed some sort of correlation between the visual appearance of the "word" and the sound and the scent. I moved on.

After a few hits and a lot of misses, I had six more words in my dictionary. There was a certain amount of guesswork in it, but I think I had words for river, mountain, one, two, three, and planet. I thought hard. There seemed to be no particular pattern in the waveforms for the different words, except the ones I had got were all less complicated than those I hadn't understood. This carried over to the sounds and scents as well. I tried to make the animal icon even smaller, and eventually I got it to an egg shape. After that, things went faster. I found out how to get into a sort of child's primer, the equivalent of Peter and Mary and Spot the Dog, I suppose. It wasn't a whole lot of help, because these creatures didn't seem to have lives enough like human beings for me to be able to tell a pet from a threat, assuming they had pets anyway. But at least I had pictures of the aliens, or at least some aliens, not all the same species. Which were Peter and Mary and which was Spot? Impossible to say, and were they proper names or were they the names of the species? It was all a bit like the River Avon. The Englishman had asked a Welshman what the river was called by pointing at it, and the Welshman said *Avon*, which was the word for *River*, and the Englishman thought it was the name of that particular river. There was also Torpenow Hill in England. Successive waves of settlers had left it with a name that meant "Hill Hill Hill Hill." We'd all thought that was very funny when the teacher had told us this in kindergarten, but now it wasn't funny at all.

I went back to one, two and three. They were just dots, or so I thought at first, but then I realized there were things like brackets in violet around them and I guessed that I was looking at the thing they used to denote sets, much the same as mathematicians do. So I focused on the set symbols, and that led me into a whole lot of mathematics. This was good because the elementary bits had to have at least the same meaning even if the conventions were very different. I found out the symbol for dot-dot-dot, which was the way mathematicians indicated that you carried on in the same way; {0, 1, 2, 3, . . .} meant the whole lot of counting numbers. So I could read something meaning "And so on," which was quite useful. Of course, what looked like a natural continuation to one person might not look the same to another, so it had a mental *handle-with-care* tag on it in my mind. I had also learned the symbol for zero, which was important, as everybody knows.

I found a sort of thing like a pad and I could select a pointer and write on it, although I had nothing to write. It was possible to draw pictures in three dimensions on this particular pad, but I can't say that it was of use for anything.

I tried to move the *and so on* symbol around and in a blink, everything changed. I had run into some sort of block: the system wasn't going to let me use it as I'd intended, to explore much larger categories of things. It seemed to be asking me to draw something. There was a line of five flashing yellow dots which I decided were question marks, and the drawing pad, if I can call it that. I looked at the first of the yellow dots, on the extreme right, and it stopped blinking; then the stylus moved on the pad all on its own. In three dimensions it started to draw something. It was going very slowly, but might have been the beginning of a tetrahedron. I felt my own terahedron in my pocket and gripped it. The drawing speeded up and finished making a regular tetrahedron, every face an equilateral triangle. Then the yellow light at the right-hand end stopped blinking and was replaced by a tiny gold tetrahedron. The one next to it started blinking faster.

I thought about it. It was pretty obviously an intelligence test. I imagined that the makers of the library and the book readers wanted to ensure that only beings past a certain level of civilization could get access to their information. Maybe there'd be other tests later on; this was the one that let in the babies. I decided not to tell Silver about it. He could damn well figure it out himself if he ever had to. But I was awfully glad that Marthar had cracked it and led me to look up the platonic solids.

I took the stylus up with my eyes, and started to draw a cube. It was hard to get it looking right, but the program wasn't going to let me fail for want of drawing skills; as long as I had the right general idea, it would help. So it straightened out my wavy lines and made my parallelogram for the square side seen at an angle much straighter. I drew nine line segments in roughly the right position for a cube seen sideways. When I finished, the yellow light stopped blinking, although it went more orange every half-second. Then the program showed me what I should have done: it drew a square, then it made six copies, then it assembled them in three dimensions, gluing them together. When it had done this, the second yellow light flashed brightly once, then turned into a little golden cube.

Then the middle light started blinking. I had to do an octahedron. I started off by making a square. Then I made a triangle with each side the same as the side of the square. Then I copied the triangle four times. Moving them around so they were attached to each side of the square went quickly. Then I had to move them out of the plane, rotating them about the edges joined to the square until they met to make a pyramid. I copied the pyramid, turned one upside down and fitted the square bases together. The resulting octahedron was moved to replace the middle yellow light, and I gave a sigh of relief.

"What are ye up to now, lad?" Silver's voice echoed around inside the helmet.

"I'm learning how to use some tools which should help me get ahead much faster," I told him. He grunted.

There were two more to do, and I had to recall the dodecahedron. It had twelve faces, and each was a regular pentagon. I made a pentagon, and copied it twelve times. I wasn't at all sure of the angles, but I glued five to a sixth and then copied the whole lot. It was just a matter of assembling the things so the ends joined together, and the program helped me finish the fourth. Nearly finished!

An icosahedron has twenty faces, each a triangle. I made twenty equilateral triangles, and started to glue them and the program just finished the job for me. I think it had decided that I'd made it sufficiently clear I knew the answer, so it didn't want to waste anymore time. I was quite grateful; it would have taken me a long time to get the fitting right because there were so many edges and I had only a vague recollection of the angles between adjacent faces.

Once the thing was finished, the test vanished and I was back on trying to use the *and so on* symbol. I had passed the test! I was a member of an intelligent species, just like the builders of the library, although there could well be more tests ahead, perhaps of other things besides intelligence.

As I had guessed, I found I could use it to get more information related to what I already knew, which meant that I went a lot quicker. If I concentrated, I could pick up an icon and move it, so I made the dot-dot-dot into an icon, copied it and moved it around. It meant I could focus on something and get more information about it. Then I found the periodic table of elements. It was amazing! It looked almost exactly like ours. Well, of course, it would have to; it was there in the universe. It was mirror-inverted, but easily recognizable. I took a lot more pictures and sound recordings. Then I discovered that if the dot-dot-dot icon was located near the thing I wanted to know about and put in different places, I could go off from a word I knew in different directions. In another hour, I had over fifty words learned, including the names of hydrogen and carbon and oxygen; I could have gotten every element in the universe, but didn't bother. Who wants to know what the aliens called Molybdenum?

Every so often, I explained to Silver what I was doing and he grunted. I don't think he was convinced this was going to pay off, but he could see I had a plan and was prepared to give me some rope.

What I was looking for was something like the Dewey decimal classification. The problem I had was that I needed to know how to recognize when I had it. At least I now had some words that had to do with science.

I iconified the sun and the planets, put the dot-dot-dot symbol to the left of them, and put the set brackets around them. Then I iconified the lot and focused on it. I got a word and a sound (and a faint scent) which I reasoned had to be the word for *astronomy*. Or perhaps *planetary astronomy*. It was a complicated set of chords, and didn't sound so bad. I recorded it. Then I did the same with some of the elements and, with any luck, would get something like the word for *chemistry*. Then I did the same with the counting symbols and paused. Was I going to get the word for *mathematics* or the word for the natural numbers? I needed an operator. I entered the symbol for two and the symbol for one and made a copy of it together. Would it fill in the gaps? No. I put the dot-dot-dot in various places. Nothing. I looked at the icons. One was pulsing slowly. I focused on it and suddenly two other symbols I had never seen before came up in my line between the *2* and the first *1*, and another between the two ones! I had learned three things: how to ask a question and the symbols for *plus* and *equals*. This was a triumph, and I told Silver very excitedly. I took a picture and showed him. He was unimpressed, but could see I thought it was progress. I hadn't told him my plan yet, but he could see I had one, and I think it made him slightly worried that I was doing something he couldn't wholly fathom. Silver liked being in control.

I made the symbols for the numbers with the dot-dot-dot and put them inside the set brackets, then I put the symbols for *plus, equals* and *times* (which last I got by something so obvious I leave it to you to work out) next to them, and put the whole lot in set brackets. Then I iconified the lot and looked at it. The resulting word probably meant something like *arithmetic*, or maybe *number theory*. I recorded it. Then I went back to some of the words I got previously and iconified them. They turned into little inscriptions on colored discs. I put them to one side and carried on. I was building up abstractions now, quite quickly. It was all done by sets, which made sense. To the aliens, unless I was horribly wrong and had gotten hopelessly confused, the word for *cat* would be the same as that for a couple of particular cats, together with the dot-dot-dot symbol and set brackets. The word for *animal* would be the word for *cat*, the word for *dog*, the word for *tiger*, all with the dot-dot-dot and more set brackets. Except I doubted they had cats and dogs. I suppose that would give me something rather smaller than the class for all animals, perhaps something like mammals, or maybe a smaller sub-grouping again. It was hardly a definite translation, but at least I knew, or thought I knew, how to get abstract names. And I could stack the whole business. Once I had names for *astronomy* and *chemistry* and *physics* and *biology*, I could stack them together and get the name for *science*. Or something in the same general area, at least.

I exited the system once more and took the helmet off. It had been exciting, but very tiring. It had taken me many hours to get this far, and Silver had gone exploring some of the time, as I could tell by his silences. He was outside, but came when I called him. I showed him the recordings I had made and explained what I had done. He was quite pleased, though not as impressed as I had hoped he'd be. I left out all reference to the intelligence test.

"Well, Peter," he said after some thought, "ye ha' done well enough; 'twould ha taken a lot longer t' get this far had any o' the crew tried, to be sure. Us kzin are mainly not so infected wi' curiosity as you monkeys. And it has t' be said that monkey curiosity pays off in some surprisin' ways. I might ha' done it faster meself, but I had rather not have me head buried in one o' they helmets with the crew wandering around. I likes t' know what's happenin' in my immediate environs, so I does. Has kept me alive before now, so it has, and may again. But ye ha' done well, and what ye plan may well work out. So back wi yon hat and get back to it."

"Silver, I am exhausted. I have worked for eight hours at least, with only a short lunch break. I need to sleep," I told him. He was an ungrateful swine, I decided. "I'll work better after a good sleep. It will give my subconscious a chance to work at it; maybe throw up some ideas when I wake up again. It often happens that way with schoolwork, which is very much what this feels like."

That was true in some ways, but this was a whole lot more interesting than any schoolwork I had ever done.

"Aye, mayhap. And then again, we need to get on. And then again, maybe a little extra time for my little trap to spring would be as well. So all right, ye may sleep, but ye'll do it wi' the noose around your head, and wi some o' the crew within call, I'm thinkin'."

He motioned me to lie down, and went to summon the crew with a roar. For some reason he wanted them all together in that room. It was certainly big enough. I heard the crew coming up the ramp, and then I fell asleep as if hit with a log. Learning is a strenuous business, and sure takes it out of you.

I awoke with no new ideas, but after a walk outside in the sunshine and a bite of the weird-tasting fruit for breakfast, I was looking forward to getting back to work. I felt like a proper scientist, studying an alien language and being able to translate some of it already. I suppose the aliens had made it as easy as possible, it wasn't like finding a washing list in Babylonic cuneiform and not knowing if it was a short story, a poem, or random scratchings. At least I had pictures, and some of the things I could recognize. It meant that the aliens had eyes, and also that they expected other things to have eyes although not with the same window of sensitivity as mine. They also expected something like ears and a nose, although my own nose didn't pass any great deal of information. I thought it odd that there was a scent for a word like sun or planet. But then, they must have had something like our brains, or at least expected them. I recall that at school, the definition of an *organism* was something that has sensors, effectors, and computing power to link them. This applied to complicated machines as well as plants and bacteria, although the computing power was pretty simple in those cases. I guess that the embodiment of the computing power need not be anything I'd recognize as a brain, but plants that grow towards the sky and send out branches have mechanisms that make sure the branches don't grow so as to overbalance the plant. This involves a primitive sort of computing, realized by fluid flows of various nutriments. So brains needn't look much like brains, and of course *Valiant* had a brain that was a string of quantum computers. So the aliens had made some reasonable guesses as to what might try to make sense of their libraries, although why those horrible snakes, I could not imagine. You'd have to be awfully keen to learn to take those things into your brain. Maybe some alien species would be grateful for the extra sensory power, but I wouldn't. It made me sick even to think of those horrible things burrowing into my skull. When I said this to Marthar, much later, she laughed and said that was pretty much how the pirate crew looked at my using the helmet. All those horrible ideas crawling into my brain and contaminating it. A truly ghastly thought, for a pirate.

I went back to work. I had gotten terms for the sciences and mathematics, or some of them anyway. I wanted to do some more mathematics, basically because it was easier, and I had found out how to draw lines, and I drew the Pythagorean Theorem with squares on the edges of a right-angled triangle. The system took a while to get the Theorem, but I found that by making the squares into icons I could get the idea of area, and then I could label the icons and write out the theorem. It gave me a symbol, which I guessed meant that it could prove it, and when I focused on it, it did the old decomposition of a square with four triangles around the edges and then the same square decomposed into rectangles and squares. It seemed to think a proof was a process of moving things around, not just rewriting strings of symbols. I suppose their idea of a proof was different from ours, but it made some sort of sense. That and a few simple Euclidean theorems gave me the word for *geometry*, or at least Euclidean geometry. That led me to a word for *mathematics*. Or near enough, at least.

Then I got animals, and built up until I got *zoology*, then some plants to get *botany*, and then I got *biology* by combining them. Or again, something reasonably close. It was a lot more logical than the human way of doing it, or at least what human beings thought they were doing.

Then I made my great discovery. I could reverse my building-up process and dig down instead. One of the icons at the very beginning, which I had not made any sense of, allowed me to decompose a word into a network of nodes, each node being labelled, and also the arcs joining the nodes being labelled by little flags. I could take a new word and break it up into, its component meanings. The networks had another structure too, it came in layers, but I didn't find out what that meant until a lot later.

I needed to move into something like *soft*, something involving the social sciences. And how did I find out what *poetry* looked like? Or *music*? Or *painting*? Or *dance*? Did the aliens have anything remotely like these activities? All human cultures did, and it came as confirmation of some people's theories that the kzin did too. Something about the abstraction process which was fundamental to probabilistic learning, that being the sort of learning that was forced by evolution, or so it was claimed. I hadn't got that far to follow the mathematics yet. Certainly kzin told their young stories. Certainly, they played, although their maturity was usually more pronounced than with human beings; the kittens played, but very few adult kzin did. But then I don't suppose most adult human beings did either. As Marthar had put it, most grown-ups ossified. I hoped I never did. If I felt it coming on, I decided, I'd start on the immortality drugs that very moment. I drummed my fingers on the table and thought. Music. Playing. If only there was a way to play some music at it. But of course there was, if it could hear me. It could certainly detect where I was looking. I lifted up the helmet so I could see my phone and started searching my apps. There was a Sibelius symphony I had collected, there was a whole lot of guitar music, and some Bach, which Marthar had loved. Right. I would give it the Bach *'Cello Suites* and see what it made of them.

The music certainly seemed to puzzle it, it started to try to turn them into writing, and eventually gave up. But at least it could hear the music. It was strange to think of the centuries and the light-years that music had covered to be playing at an alien computer intelligence. Then I gave it some more classical music that had come a bit later. The Beatles and Elvis Presley. I played the videos at the screen, not having the faintest idea if the thing was able to make sense of the images. They were made for human eyes, with three basic colors, and even some Earth and Wunderland animals had more or sometimes less. But eyes had evolved at least three times on Earth, quite independently, as well as on the Kzin homeworld and many others. So eyes of some sort were credible, even if they were cameras hooked up to a computer.

Eventually I stopped. It seemed to have listened and perhaps watched in silence. Then it seemed to be hesitant. It used the symbol I had worked out that was something like a question mark, although there was not just one of them, but a whole platoon, all slightly different. Then it gave me a word, flashing. I tried to analyze it. I got some examples of the components and focused on them. I think it was something like a symphony orchestra or a rock band, but made up of tendrils of seaweed, but they might have been a bit more active than seaweed. And it made a noise like the ocean, only maybe a bit more regular. I played the Sibelius, and it seemed to feel this was more like it. I'd always associated the piece with wind over vast forests, but it was closer to the alien music if that's what it was. I checked some more samples, and they were totally different, some maybe a bit like Chinese music, but most like nothing on Earth. Or on Wunderland, either. At the same time, I quite liked some of it. It was kind of eerie, but interesting.

This was all fascinating stuff, but not really what I wanted to know. I showed the helmet a video recording of a science fiction movie that had hit the network only a year ago. After seeing a sample, the helmet paused, filled the screen with a whole lot of question marks and gave me a new word and a noise that sounded like a waterfall with growls and howls breaking through. It was certainly not a simple thing. Trying to analyze the components gave things like video clips, most of them quite unrecognizable as anything I had seen, but one looked like animals running around a desert. Not so much real animals, as something like cartoons, and the animals changed into other sorts of beasts as they went. It looked like something you might have nightmares about.

About this time, I noticed the bar icon. It had changed.

There was a thin black line which had moved a small distance from the right; to the left of it was the golden color, to the right it was violet. Of course, I recognized the significance straight away. I concentrated on the thin black line and moved it with eye movements until it was right in the middle of the bar. The picture changed. I was watching something like one of the videos. I paused it, and interrogated the helmet. It seemed to confirm my worst suspicions. I did some more analysis and checked my guesses. When you get pretty much what you expect, you conclude that you've got it pretty well sussed out. I thought for a moment, then exited and took the helmet off.

I looked around. Silver was there, and most of the crew, looking at me as if I had two heads.

"I think I know what is on this bar," I told them. "I'm not really sure of anything, you understand, but it looks to me as if what you have here is something halfway between an opera and a video soapie. It would take about a month to play the whole thing, and frankly I doubt you'd get much out of it."

CHAPTER TWENTY-SEVEN

"What in hell is a soapie?" One of the crew asked in bewilderment.

Silver explained. " 'Tes one o' they stories the bards tell, on'y played out, like strollers, and stored on video so ye can download it if ye've nothin' better to do wi' yer time. An epic, like."

I knew the kzin had their own epics in plenty, but this news certainly did not please the pirates.

"Ye mean the whole bar is nothin' but a sort of storybook?"

"Well, 'tes no great surprise," Silver said expansively. He had his head tilted and his eyes wide open. "And it tells us somethin' important, which is that these here aliens what left the records is type-one intelligence, as the humans call it."

This was true, but not at all surprising. Theory says there are seven possible types of intelligence, where intelligence is the ability to model the universe in order to make conditional probabilistic predictions. All the intelligent lifeforms we have met have been type one, except for a few tales of encounters with a type four, the so-called *Outsiders* who sold "We Made It," the manual for the hyperdrive which Dimity Carmody translated. And all our computer intelligences have been based on our own type, of course. To a type-one intelligence, the universe at our scale looks like a four-dimensional manifold, spacetime, invariant under the Lorentz group, although it takes some time to figure *that* out. Time flows along a line to type-one intelligence. Other types structure the universe in quite different ways. I know about this from school, as I suppose most people do these days, but apart from possibly Silver himself the crew didn't have much by way of education, and this meant little to them.

"Well, 'tes but one bar, there be millions of others," said Rraangar. This cheered them up.

"Aye, find us one wi' some technology on it, something we can sell and make a mort o' money," another said.

"Come with me," I told them, and led the way out of the room and down the ramp. They all followed me obediently. At the moment, I had them under control, but it wasn't going to last and I hope Silver was ready for what was to come.

We went out through the great arch and fifty paces beyond, then I turned and pointed to something I remembered having glanced at before. At the time, it meant nothing. Now, it meant a lot. Over the arch was a pattern that was faint but still recognizable to the eye that had seen a lot of similar things in the past two days.

"What is it? That pattern o' lines?" the Kzin with a bandage on his skull asked, mystified.

There was a set of eight traces that must have been twice the height of a Kzin, and many times longer. Each trace was the waveform-like script.

I pulled out my phone and scanned through my homemade dictionary. "That one. Do you agree it's pretty much the same as what I recorded?"

"Aye, it be similar, I grant ye. Be it some kind o' writin', d'ye say?"

"Yes. And I know what it means, roughly at least. It says *literature*, Or maybe *drama*," I told them, waiting for the wave to break.

They were puzzled rather than angry.

"What the man-kit is tellin' us is that the whole tower be full o' nothin but storybooks," Silver said heavily. "Somethin' like the *Te-vaarar* or *Lord Chmeee at the Pillars*. Nothin' of any interest to us, or anyone else wi' a grain o' sense."

This caused a buzz which turned bitter. "Ye ha' nothin', ye ha' brought us here for kit's nonsense, Silver, and ye need t' pay for it wi' your ears!" one of them screamed. Others snarled. I had, I thought, heard a lot of kzin snarling lately.

They pulled out their *wtsais* as one and turned savagely on Silver, who was standing next to me and picked me up and threw me behind him in one move.

"Avast there, companions," Silver said quite mildly. "By the lore o' the brotherhood, ye've no sense at all. All it means is that we are at the wrong tower. 'Tes a small matter. We jest ha' to find the right one."

"Which might be a world away, and us wi' no more than our legs, Silver!" another screamed and moved slowly forward, the others following him.

"Ah, but there you be wrong, Tar-Marrak. D'ye have such little faith? Sure, and ye can kill me and add my ears to your ring, though some of ye will go down first. And then where will ye be? Stranded, that's where. And me the on'y one can get ye off. No, I ha' put my brain to some use, while ye ha' been fillin' up on rum, ye sots. I knows how to get away from here, I does, an' ye does not. So suppose ye all put those *wtsais* away and listens t' me for a little while."

"Ah, we're tired o' listenin' t' ye, Silver, what good has it done us?" one cried.

"What good has it done ye? Why, ye're alive, are ye not? Which is more than can be said for those what didn't listen, they're rotting away now, in various places, I'm thinkin'. And if ye won't listen now, why, 'tes here where ye'll rot. On cruel red dirt under a violet sky and a green sun is where ye'll lay your bones, that I promise ye. For there's no way out save the one I know of. An' ye follow me, I'll lead ye to the true tower, aye, and the pinnace. Then home we go, companions, back into space where the stars are yer allies, and there's many a world will welcome a spacer wi' more money than he can dream of. More money than the whole world ye will be standin' on is worth."

This made them pause. They growled, but they slowly sheathed their *wtsais*.

"Then show us how to get away from this damned place, for there's nothing here for any of us," Rraangar growled

"Oh, well, when we ha' made more money than there is in the whole rift, maybe we'll be back to take these things. There be a market even for this rubbish, I'm thinkin,' but I agree, 'tes not worth much. On'y a few billions, maybe. Small pickings in comparison wi' what we shall find wi' a small amount o' lookin,' I fancy. So back up into the tower, my fine Heroes, up to the third level. For I ha' been using my skull, so I has, as ye shall see."

I had no idea what he meant, except that he was planning to use the discs. How he knew which ones to use I had no idea.

The crew slowly went back to the tower and up the ramp to the third level, passing the second level where I had been learning so much. I suppose Bengar had done much the same as me, during his long time of solitude, and he had learned how to use the discs; maybe he had found out how to read the writing on them.

The crew went first, and Silver and I followed them. I was apprehensive; I feared that Silver knew something I did not, and the possibility he knew where my friends were was frightening. I hoped they kept a good guard, but they might easily assume that nobody could follow them by means of the discs, and Silver seemed to think he could.

We climbed up the ramp and they milled about on the third level, unsure where to go next. Silver calmly took his phone out of a pouch and pointed it at the wall.

"I knew that the ghost o' K'zarr were an artifact, d'ye see, and I knew that there was someone about the place what could travel betwixt the towers. And it had to be by means of the discs, did it not? And the on'y question was, which one. So I put a few little spy cameras where they would be inconspicuous, but keep watch for me. And there ye see it, young Marthar herself, as I suspected." He turned his phone so they could see what he was watching as he downloaded history from the spycam. I craned around and saw a tiny Marthar prowl confidently into the second room.

The crew cheered, they would never have thought to do anything like this, and their confidence in Silver seemed to have been restored.

"And now we need to see what the camera in this room saw a little later," Silver said confidently, and pointed his phone just inside the open doorway, on the wall. I could see nothing, but spycams were tiny. You could find them electronically with a scanner, but searching by eye was a waste of time unless you had years in which to do it and a powerful microscope. Again, Silver turned his camera in triumph towards the crew, so they could see the diminutive Marthar step confidently onto one of the discs towards the back and vanish. The crew cheered and rushed towards the disc. My stomach churned.

"Belay that, me hearties, we need a little care. Who knows what we may find on t'other side? Best go armed and go careful, I says. Me and the monkey goes first, and then ye follow, wi' yer *wtsais* at the ready. I misdoubts we can go more than one at a time, but follow me briskly arter a count o' five pulse beats atween ye."

Which would give him time to kill them all one by one if he so chose. But I knew Silver would do no such thing until it was clear that he had no choice. And then he would dispose of the rest of the pirates without thinking twice about it.

Silver shouldered his way through them, picking me up with no trace of effort. "Back, messmates, and do not step on the wrong disc, or we'll never see ye again." The pirates looked at their feet cautiously. Then with me over his shoulder, Silver stepped directly on to the disc that Marthar had travelled by, holding me casually with one arm, the other holding the great cutlass he had drawn and ready. The helmet I had worn was dangling around his neck, held by the snakes, which he had tied into a bow.

We came into a world at sunset; it was cold and getting darker. Some of the brighter stars were shining in the sky, visible through one of the huge windows. I had never been here before, and I prayed that it was a waystation and that Marthar had long gone where Silver couldn't find her. Silver looked around, grunted, stepped off the disc and put me down carefully. He picked his way towards the door, and I followed him. I turned at a slight movement from the corner of my eye, and the kzin with the bandage was standing on the disc. He stepped off and followed us towards the doorway. We trooped down the ramp, passing the second floor, which presumably held rooms of alien bookreaders, the others following us slowly. Silver led us all out to look at the word over the arch. I stared, but in the failing light it was impossible to read. This one seemed to have weathered more. It looked older, though possibly less damaged at the top than the first tower.

"Can't make it out at all," Silver said. "I thinks we're going to have to go inside and find out what's in this tower, and Peter, 'tes as well I bought that helmet, for ye may have t' help us here."

"Look, Cap'n, there's another tower o'er yonder." One of the crew pointed and, sure enough, another tower loomed high against the darkling sky. It was many miles off, its base lost in vegetation, which seemed thicker and darker here. The ground was less red, but just as untouched by man or anything that might have grown crops deliberately. Silver took his phone, squinted at it and took a picture of the faint markings. Then he set the phone to clean up the image and emphasize the script. Then he held it out to me, and I looked at the word. It was just possible to see it now. I checked through my dictionary. It wasn't there, and I said so. He just nodded thoughtfully.

We went back into the tower, and up the ramp, the crew going first, me next and Silver at the end. He had sheathed his cutlass, as the crew had their *wtsais*. There was no threat that a weapon would save us from. I shivered.

Upstairs, the second floor was much like the first tower: there were tables and seats like saddles on horizontal poles, and more helmets, these of a different style. They were more like crowns, and the snakes conspicuously absent. They hummed faintly when Silver picked one up for a closer inspection.

"I thinks we'll stay wi' what we have, Peter. Here's a metal bar, one o' they heathen books. Sit ye down again and have a look at it. Wi' luck, it's a treatise on how to make those black discs, for we'd have trillions could we set someone to making them." He spoke to reassure the crew, and perhaps himself. I knew the odds against the first book tried being anything useful in the short term were millions to one.

I sat down at the table. Silver took a bar at random and set it down and connected the cables as I slipped on the hemet. I got the usual starting sequence and a set of icons, most of which were the same. When the title came up, I recognized the word I had just seen on Silver's phone, which saved me having to try to draw it. I focused on it and isolated it and turned it into an icon. Then I had to analyze it into components and examples. I studied the examples for a long time, trying to work out what they had in common. They all had some sort of things in swirling motion, some of them loose-robed living things, some like suits of armor with rings of silver assembled into tubes that bifurcated and bifurcated again. And they all moved, sometimes in a stately pageant, sometimes stamping and getting sparks, sometimes in a sort of conga line of interweaving threads made up of what might have been intelligent beings or programmed machines. I sat back. I suppose I knew roughly what these things were doing, and hence what the word meant. Silver wasn't going to like it, and the crew would like it a lot less.

I now knew how to advance the time on the thing. No doubt it had some sort of search function, but I didn't know how to use it. So I went about a quarter of the way through and looked at the video. There was some of the strange music, and figures gliding through a snow-storm. I jumped forward to halfway through and saw black shapes like canines baying at the moon and jumping into the air as if trying to devour it or catch non-existent frisbees. And finally I fast-forwarded to just before the end. There was a chain of tall figures, etiolated giants, in a long line running in parallel across a featureless plain. And behind them another, running and half-kneeling at the same time. I exited the helmet, removed it from my head and looked around at the expectant faces.

"I found the word on the front of this tower, and I ploughed into examples. Then I watched some of what is on this bar, and it confirmed what I had thought, pretty much. This tower contains records of examples of dance. There are lots of different things dancing, but that's what it is."

Silver sagged. The others looked murderous.

"I thinks I'd like to see this for meself, young Peter. Not that I think ye'd lie to me, not successfully. But I believe in seeing for meself where possible. Now give me the helmet and tell me what needs to be done to use it to see the contents o' the book." Silver had said he didn't trust the world about him not to take advantage if he were absorbed under the helmet, and I suspected that the crew might take the chance to slice his head off with his own cutlass, but they stood about and watched him carefully as he disappeared into the device. He spoke, his voice clear enough, asking for instructions. I told him to wait for the icons to appear, then to look for the one that resembled a golden bar held horizontally. There was, at the extreme right of it, a vertical black thread, I shouted at him with his ears covered by the helmet. If he focused on the thread and moved it to the right, he would do a fast-forward to that location. I waited for some minutes, and the crew waited with me.

"Aye, right," Silver's voice came again. "Now tell me how to get this thing off of me, for it's grown tight on m' head."

I told him about the eject icon, and a moment later he took the helmet off.

"Well, very interestin; very interestin' indeed. I think ye ha' the right of it. 'Tes about them animules, prancin' around, wastin' their time and ours."

The crew growled again. "So another waste, Silver. Another step towards nothin', or nothin' what any sane beast would waste time on. When are we goin' to get some treasure, instead o' this here faffle? Dancin' is for kits again."

"Ye have a point, Tar-Marrak, ye have indeed. So we have to try again, so we do."

"And this time ye have no idea which disc the kit used to get from here, for 'tes clear she just passed through, and so we are lost, Silver!"

"Well, we have several options, my fine fellows. Not good ones, no, I'll grant ye that. But we ain't done yet, no we ain't. I says we have another tower not too far away, and I says we tries for that before the night falls. For when it falls, 'twill be a long time before sunrise, I'm thinkin', and I'd like to be away before then, d'y see. For it be a long, cold night acomin', and ye may lay to that."

They growled at the backs of their throats, but none could meet Silver's steady eye. I looked at him and noticed something different about his appearance, which had troubled me a little before, without my seeing what it truly was. Naturally, Silver had a white bib like an orca, silver against the mahogany fur, but he had dyed it. Now it was starting to grow out. And the other fur on his belly and shoulders was also growing out, he had dyed that too. Underneath, it was red. Blazons of red fur were, not always, but often, a mark of the Riit Clan.

So began the long trek. We were headed into the gloom of approaching night, which didn't make for optimism or cheer. Silver had to carry me on his shoulder, or I would have held everyone up. As it was, we slowly fell behind the seven pirates, who grumbled all the time, but so low we couldn't hear the words. The terrain was rocky and gray in the red of the slowly setting sun.

"Peter, I have t' ask somethin' of ye, to spare your life an' mine." Silver whispered to me, easy enough since my head was close to his.

"Yes?" I asked cautiously.

"Well, 'tes like this. I reckons the chances that we shall find anythin' useful in this third tower t' be rather poor. Likely we shall find 'tes full o' poetry or history or some such useless rubbish. An' if so then they will run out o' patience, I'm thinkin'. So it would be as well if ye were t' gi' them a little hope, d'ye see. Gammon them along a little, that is what I asks o' ye. 'Twill add a few hours to our lives, I'm thinkin'."

"What use will that be?" I asked, scornfully. "A few hours for a lie? Better to die with honor."

"Ah, well, ye may take it so, but much may happen in a few hours. Who is t' tell? Mayhap your friends may catch up wi' us by then and take a part. Wouldn't ye prefer t' live and play wi' your little kzinrett friend again? And there be little dishonor in gammoning such fools as these, ye might think of it as a war stratagem, lettin' the enemy deceive hisself, a mere tactic t'use agin scum what would kill out o' rage rather than for advantage."

Silver wheedled well. And revealed himself in the process, I thought. If you were at war with the whole world, then lying and deceiving was just a tactic, to be used judiciously. Most kzin would be fooled by it, because most kzin disdained to lie, which made them all the more vulnerable to someone who didn't share that value.

"What makes you think they'd trust me?" I asked. Kzin

knew well enough that most human beings had a rather lesser sense of honor, and they despised us for it. I was inclined to agree with them, but then I had been brought up with Marthar, who was of the Riit. And she, I knew, would despise someone who lied to gain advantage, even when their life was at stake.

"Ah, that be a difficulty, I grants ye. But ye have spoken up wi' a rare sperrit in the past, d'ye see. A good tactic that, for it causes people t' trust ye."

I was disgusted with Silver and told him so. "I don't tell the truth so that people will trust me. I tell it so as to keep my own self-respect."

Silver sighed. "Ah well, there's different styles o' self-respect, d'ye see? No, I don't suppose ye do. Ye're young, and ye thinks ye has the world sorted out, and that there be sich things as justice and fairness in the universe. Well, ivery bit o' justice ye find in this world has been put there by some strong being who could impose it by force against th' inclinations of weaker ones wi' more use for mercy than justice. The universe itself has no use whatever for either o' they things. 'Tes a war, Peter, a war wi' intelligence on one side and a cold, indifferent universe on t'other. And 'tes survival is what counts. And in the end we all loses, so we does. At the end o' things, we're all i' the way to study a long silence. But I'll fight for as long as I can, I'll not go easy into the long night. An' ye may lay to that."

"You'll betray any principle to save your worthless life?"

"Oh, aye, indeed I will," he said comfortably. "For 'tain't worthless to *me*, d'ye see? For without it, there ain't a me t' consider the matter. And what's a principle that ye should be so fond o' them? 'Tes no more than some rule the rest o' the world would ha' ye follow, for their benefit, not yourn. What's honor? A puff of air. Who hath it? He that died a week ago. What did it profit him? Not a dot. He lies cold, whether he hath it or no."

"At least he died for what he believed in," I said grimly.

"Maybe. Or maybe for what someone else believed in and cozened him into," Silver said wearily. "Me, I believes in not dyin'."

We loped on in silence after that. Silver had a slight wobble in his artificial leg, and we were slowly falling behind, but every so often the crew would pause for us to catch up. They didn't greatly trust their leader. No more did I, and with reason. If handing me over would prolong his life a few minutes, no doubt he'd do it. When we were close enough to speak easily, Silver would wave his cutlass cheerily and urge them on again, speaking as to friends and colleagues despite their grim looks.

CHAPTER TWENTY-EIGHT

It took an age, but eventually we stood outside the third tower, the light eldritch and withered. The sun had set, and there were stars in the eastern sky. The world had no single moon, but it had a faint ring of rubble, a million tiny moonlets, which made a faint haze against the blackness. It was still too light to see the purple nebulae, but we could see the brighter stars in it. In another day or two of shiptime, it would no doubt be dark enough for the nebulae to be visible. It was cold, and I shivered.

The archway was a great dark hole and the space above it almost as black, and there was no sign of the writing I had hoped for.

"A little dark for clear vision, let's see if a phone will help again," Silver said, and he pointed his phone at the dark space over the great arch, and used the camera. He tried various settings to see if he could read the writing, but announced that it was hopeless. "We'll have to rely on young Peter t' tell us what is in this place. And we'll have to see what the discs look like, too. I have an idea o' how we may leave by them and do some more exploring, should that be necessary t' find the treasure. 'Twill surely be necessary t' find the pinnace, o' course. But I has good hopes o' learnin' more o' that afore long."

He spoke with his usual optimism, though he got black looks from the crew, who were close to another mutiny.

We went in, the crew using their phones as torches to illuminate the darkness of a crypt at midnight. I wondered what the creatures had been who were in it last, what they had looked like, how they had moved. It was hard to believe they had been much like either men or kzin. The sheer size of the place suggested something massive. It gave a weird tingle under the skin to think of them, all long gone, with only their ghosts to watch. And perhaps they did indeed do so. There might be guardians of some sort, robotic no doubt, and there to ensure that no harm came to their legacy. I had seen no sign of such things, but that meant little.

We went up the stairs to the saddle room, or the reading room, if you saw it more as a library, which I suppose it was. It was unlike any data repository I had seen before, of course. These days books were obsolete, and you got your information from a computer that lived in a big black box kept in liquid nitrogen, but I had seen pictures of old-fashioned libraries, and Marthar's father had one. But not like this.

Why was everything kept as a separate book, with similar subjects close together? I suppose it was portable, you had only to pack up a few of the metal bars and a friendly bookreader and you could take it away with you. And of course, centralizing everything made it vulnerable; I had learned at school how a weird sort of desire for uniformity had made human beings centralize their economic systems at one time. It meant that when disaster struck, the whole thing would fall apart; it was complex but brittle: poor design. Most empires of the past had collapsed in a heap because of such poor design; but then they hadn't been designed, they'd just grown for the most part, under the influence of people who had a desperate need to control. *Control freaks*, they called them, I thought. Much of history had been a battle between the control freaks and the people who liked being controlled on the one hand, and people who wanted to be free on the other hand. Neither side won for long. Fortunately, we now knew what government was *for*, those poor people had not. Obviously the builders of the towers had known enough to keep everything distributed and probably duplicated or triplicated. And it was easy to copy information, so if a whole tower fell, at least the contents could be copied again by machines. If an asteroid hit this world it would no doubt destroy a good deal, but not everything. The history of Earth told us that, before scrolls and then books were made, when a civilization fell, everything was lost. Homer's Greeks had had no conception of the civilizations that had gone before them.

I thought of these things as I sat on the saddle and took the helmet from Silver. "Now let him find out what there is to be known, while I check upstairs for something," Silver told the crew, and winked at them. I suppose they thought he was going to bug this place as he had the first tower, and maybe he was. He had some parting words for me which came with a certain menace: "And Peter, no declaring what ye' find until I be back, d'ye hear?" Then he left us.

I could at least do that for him, I supposed. I wasn't prepared to lie, but I didn't have to blurt out the truth either.

I chose a bar at random, placed it in the indentations in the table and then put the helmet on. The cables flexed and must have connected, although I couldn't see them. I could almost feel them sucking information out of the bar.

The usual blue light came on, so everything was working still; I set the age setting to egg to make it as simple as possible, and skipped the standard introduction. I went too far and had to go back, what I saw was just incomprehensible. The word at the top looked like the symbol for what I had decided was *mathematics*. This was promising, but it surprised me a bit. I had noticed that the emotional stuff had been what we met up with first, and as we had travelled east, it had become more austere and abstract. I had expected to find this was *music*. Well, it was and it wasn't. I vaguely thought there would be no sound with *mathematics*, since it is a written language, not a spoken one, at least in human and kzin. But the beings who had made the technology on this world didn't seem to think that. It was puzzling. There was something like music; it had to be. At the egg level it was just like drum beats. The pace was much, much slower than I was used to. They say that the basic drum-beat frequency is an approximation to the human heartbeat, which explains why kzin drumming is usually slower, but much more variable than human music. It is also much quieter because kzin ears are incredibly sensitive, save when they dance on drums in wild ceremonies or before battles.

Marthar and I had sometimes played duets together, I on my guitar and she on drums, which were really more like a wooden xylophone than human drums. I don't say it was good, but it was fun. Once Marthar and I had gone to a concert, where Dimity Carmody had played the solo part in the Elgar 'Cello Concerto. It had moved me to tears, and Marthar to a long silence. Then the orchestra filed out silently, and Dimity had moved forward and played one of the unaccompanied Bach 'Cello Suites. It was received well, but with more subdued applause than the Elgar. She then explained that she was going to finish with a work of her own, called *On a Theorem by Kelangor*. Kelangor, she noted, was in the audience, and she indicated a hulking great kzin with a rich black pelt. If you think mathematicians are delicate souls, you should have seen this one.

I suppose if you take a line from the Elgar to the Bach and kept going for a few light-years, you'd get to her own composition. There was a dead silence for two minutes after she finished. She rose, holding the neck of the instrument in one hand and the bow in the other, and gave a barely perceptible bow.

And Kelangor howled.

It started as a moan which ravaged the auditorium, and rose to a tortured scream, as of a whole wolfpack in anguish. There was a brief flash of compassion across Dimity's face, then she put down the instrument and the bow, turned and walked off. People started climbing to their feet, still silent. The humans who walked past the still keening Kelangor were plainly embarrassed, the kzin gave a respectful nod to him and passed by.

Afterwards we sat together in a shop that sold drinks for both our species and talked of the concert. Marthar had said in a forlorn little voice, "I could never do that, could I?" and she had looked at her paws with the claws on the ends. I suddenly realized she was not just forlorn, she was grief-stricken. I tried to comfort her. "I expect they could make a special thing like a 'cello for you," I told her. She nodded, somberly.

"It wouldn't be the same," she said, still hurting.

We had gone on to discuss why so many mathematicians had an interest in music and she explained it to me: "It's all about patterns, seeing them and making them. You realize I won't be able to do any algebra for a month now? Some of that music will be running through my head, and I won't be able to see anything else while it is."

"Perhaps it will be good in the long run," I told her. "It might be good if the part of the brain which does both gets a rest from one and plays with the other for a while."

She cheered up. "Yes, maybe that's why Dimity does it," she decided. "Different sorts of patterns may be a good idea. And you don't need hands and fingers to do mathematics, thank the stars. You know, you are quite a clever little monkey, aren't you?"

"Why did Kelangor howl?" I asked her.

She looked down. "He was expressing an emotion you humans don't have a name for," she explained. "The grief you feel when you realize you have omitted to do something very important, because you didn't see it until it was too late."

"I don't understand," I admitted.

"I think Dimity showed him something in his own theorem he had not realized was there."

I thought about it. "I suppose it has something to do with us all living much longer these days. In the old days, you couldn't master music, even one instrument, in less than a lifetime. The same with mathematics. But now it's possible to master much more, because we stay young for longer. And Dimity has lived a couple of lifetimes already. If you keep on learning, you could learn an awful lot, I guess."

Marthar looked at me bleakly. "Yes, you are a clever little monkey. But you haven't thought it through, have you?"

I never really fathomed what she was getting at there.

I was reminded of that conversation by the weird stuff I was seeing now. It looked as though these creatures didn't cut the world up the way humans and kzin did. They were more like the Jotok, who also didn't see mathematics the same way at all. They could do it, and they could understand ours, but I don't think many human beings could understand theirs, though I bet Dimity could. But this stuff looked like some weird combination of mathematics and music all together. And the mathematical part of it was different too.

I didn't know much mathematics, as I've already admitted, and certainly a lot less than Marthar. We'd done the basics of course. I knew about groups and metric spaces and measure spaces; I guess everybody does that in primary school. We've known about those things for centuries. And q-groups and q-manifolds, which aren't commutative, and which you need to do any serious *Hard*. But I knew I was not going to be well equipped for the really tough stuff I would need for *Soft*, but then, I was going to be using it, not really understanding it, which is a whole lot easier. I mean, you can train yourself to follow the rules without understanding how people had worked them out. Just as well, or I was doomed.

The thing about mathematics is that it is basically natural language only with very high precision. So you get strings of symbols coming up, and rules for rewriting one string to another; even stupid old early computers could do that without any understanding of what the strings meant. But these creatures didn't seem to use strings, they used networks instead. There were lots of little circles with symbols, and lines joining them in different colors, with flags on the lines and symbols on the flags. And you could trace a path through it, and hear music of some sort. I turned up the age from basic egg to something slightly more advanced, and the sounds and the networks got hideously complicated. Not that it made much difference: I couldn't even understand the egg-level material. They somehow transformed the networks according to some sort of rules presumably, but I never found out what the rules were. Perhaps the rules were encoded in networks, too. It was hard to see how to get started.

I had been puzzling over these things for a long time when Silver came back and asked how I was progressing. I told him I didn't know for certain, but thought I was halfway between music, mathematics and a sort of algebra done with networks instead of strings. He left me to get on with it, but I think it cheered him. If I was right, this definitely counted as treasure. If nothing else, the Jotok would recognize its value, even if many human beings and kzin were too stupid to see it. I didn't envy his having to convince the crew that this was valuable. They knew computers were important, but they probably thought computers could do mathematics. Well, maybe some of them can these days, in a routine sort of way, just as they can compose tunes and paint pictures. But they still aren't very good at it compared with an expert human being or kzin or Jotok. It's not like chess or Go. Computers can beat any human being or kzin at those things, but they don't even do it in an interesting way. All the important part of the program is just stolen from a living brain anyway. And nobody has figured out how to do that with music or painting, still less mathematics.

At last, after three hours or more, I gave up. This was much too hard for me. Marthar might have got somewhere, but I couldn't; I just wasn't smart enough. I took the helmet off and sighed as I uncrossed my eyes. Concentrating for that long wears me out. Marthar can do it for a whole day at a time, and Dimity Carmody can probably keep it up for a week without sleep, but I'm just an average sort of person and I know my limitations.

"Well, what is it this time?" Rraangar demanded. He was not in a good mood.

"It's some sort of mathematics, I think."

He roared with rage. "That's no use," he growled at me and Silver alternately.

"Rraangar, you are an ignorant fool. How can you expect

to understand an alien technology without it? This is the key we have in our hands. Maybe we should sell it, and maybe we should save it for ourselves so that any technology we find has to pass through us; a nice way of steady earning even if others find this world and loot it. Their loot will be useless without the key, and we hold the key, right here, ye damned eedjut." For kzin, this was about the mildest insult in their vocabulary.

The crew looked at each other. They wanted to believe they had something valuable, but they suspected Silver was fooling them and taking advantage of their ignorance.

"The humans on Earth would give trillions for this," I told them positively. More positively than I felt, actually. But if I was right at all, it was true. The possibility that it was some art form halfway to mathematics, but without its utility, haunted me a bit. I could recognize structure and pattern when I saw it, and anything with that amount of structure had to have some kind of value, surely?

The crew seemed to have more faith in me than in Silver. I don't know why.

"I need something to eat," I told them. "That sort of brainwork uses a lot of energy." This is true, the brain uses more energy than all the muscles put together. On the other hand, it's a lot easier to use muscles; we haven't really evolved to use our brains a whole lot. Not for thinking, anyway. It definitely hurts the head, which is why most don't do it, I suppose.

They argued a bit with each other, but weren't too sure of what to do, and in those circumstances, anyone with a clear idea of what they want tends to get it. So we all went out into the plain outside the tower. It was barely any darker than it had been when we went in, so it was light enough for them to go hunting.

"Well done, young Peter," Silver whispered to me. I suspect he felt I had made it all up, and that it was really something useless that I had found. He'd put a good spin on it all the same.

"I didn't lie about it," I protested. "It isn't much like our mathematics, but it's more like it than anything else. I'm fairly sure that there's something pretty much like mathematics in there somewhere." Of course, if aliens came to Wunderland and looked at a music score they might jump to the same conclusion. Not that there were many old-fashioned music scores around these days. It was impossible to make a synthesizer follow one of them, they left too many gaps which a human being could easily fill but a computer program could not.

"No, no, I'm sure you wouldn't lie," Silver soothed me. "It were a good job o' work though, makin' sense o' the malarkey."

We were interrupted by the crew, who came back with some animals they had killed, and they threw me one of the smaller ones, of which I managed to eat at least a little. While gnawing at their prey, they had been arguing with each other about the possible value of mathematics as treasure. I think they would have been happier with lumps of gold.

"Silver, if what ye say is true, then we need to fill up a pinnace wi' these here bars, and get back into space. So we wants to know, how are we to get the pinnace?"

"Let's be taking a look at the discs, then, me hearties, and see what we can be makin' o' them. One flight up, so it is, and afore too long we'll be out of here." He radiated optimism, but there was something strained about it, I thought. And the kzin were much better at reading each other than I was. They looked at each other with something savage in their glances.

We all trooped up the stairs, Silver and I in the lead, and we entered one of the rooms. Silver flashed his phone at the wall.

"Ah, we've had no visitors, not since I put the bugs up. At least, not from this room. Let's try the others."

We went from room to room, and none of them repaid the effort. The crew began to mutter.

"Let's try to see if we can fall back on another plan," Silver said with a cheer I was almost certain he didn't feel.

We returned to the first room, and Silver walked around looking at the discs, motioning me to accompany him. The crew were half in the room and half out.

"Now there be writin' on these discs, which will tell us where 'tes we are headed for, should we step on them, I'm thinkin'. And we have a man-kit here can read the heathen tongue, so we does. Now if he can tell us where the place is on the planet where we came from, I thinks we can return the quick way, and save ourselves a deal o' time and trouble, and when we get there, why, we can discover whether someone has been since we left, which I'd take to be like enough, and we can follow her back whence she came; follow her enough and she'll lead us to the pinnace, I've no doubt of it."

It was an ingenious plan, and might have worked but for one thing.

"But Silver," I said, "I cannot read these things. I've no

idea what they mean in terms of location, and no way of finding out. I suppose if there is a geography tower it might be possible to learn it, but we're in a mathematics tower. There's no way I can help."

I had said it in a loud, clear and definite voice, and I saw Silver crouch into himself, suddenly looking old and hunched. It took a second for the crew to absorb what I had said, and then they snarled with a blood-curdling ferocity.

"Ye ha' lost us, Silver, ye ha' been the death of all here! But ye shall lead the way to the mist demons, damn yer eyes!" Rrangaar shouted and drew his *wtsai*. Silver drew his cutlass in an instant.

"Aah, ye're after promotion once again, are ye, Rraangar? 'Tes a pushing kind o' kzin ye be, to be sure. Why, which o' ye has the stomach to face me down, then?"

But it was all of them, lending each other courage; seven of the huge beasts came forward, *wtsais* raised. Some would fall, but Silver couldn't stand against the lot of them, and then it would be all over. What they were doing was not intelligent; they were maddened with rage at being lost, and someone had to die for it.

There was only one thing to do. The Doctor had said to cry out when we needed help, so I did, at the top of my voice: "Marthar! Help!"

And Marthar flashed into existence on one of the discs, a blaster in her right paw and a needler in her left. She took one look and blasted Rraangar into gas and bubbling gobbets of cooked meat, then took a narrow look at Silver and decided to save him until later. Silver prudently moved behind me and sheathed his cutlass. Marthar gave a scream that echoed around the room and jumped forward. She used the blaster twice, and the remaining crew fled. Bengar appeared on the same disc she had left, and stepped after her, then Orion also appeared and looked around, then the Judge and finally the Doctor appeared and advanced into the room. Everyone was armed to the teeth. They all looked at Silver.

"Well done, Heroes and others! Well met, again, Miss Marthar. Ye got here just in time t' save young Peter and me from a bloody end, I'm thinking." He looked as unconcerned, as amiable and as friendly as he ever had.

CHAPTER TWENTY-NINE

"Bengar just shot up halfway to space before I could get after you," Marthar said. "He saw Silver and decided to get me away, and I suppose it was the sensible thing to do really, though I was a bit mad at him at the time."

"How did you know to come when I called? It was like magic," I said.

"We'd been listening on your communicator, which happily you kept around your neck. So we knew where you were and that Silver was hunting for the pinnace. At least, we had an idea of where you were, until you walked to the third tower. We had to do a bit of work there to find how to get to it by disc, but Bengar soon worked it out for us. I was planning to get you out as soon as we could, without giving Silver another disc to use."

"Well, thank you for saving my life. I'd like to give you a hug for it, sometime when you don't look quite so dangerous. What happens now to the rest of the crew?"

Marthar shrugged. "They can stay here; there's only four of them left. I don't suppose they want to, but I'm not giving Silver another chance to rat on us. I wouldn't trust him an inch."

"Well, he did keep me alive," I argued.

"Sure he did, but only because playing both ends against the middle is the way he operates. Oh, maybe he liked you, you sort of grow on people; there's something nice and simple about you, on the surface at least. And you've got some sense of honor, and Kzin can admire that. But he'd have turned you over without a moment's hesitation if he thought it would do him some good. He kept you alive as a trading chip, something to use to win our good opinion. It doesn't work on me."

"He said something about being distantly related to you," I told her.

"Yes, I heard that." Marthar was thoughtful. "Probably just another lie. It surely doesn't make me kindly disposed towards him."

"What are you going to do with him?" I asked her. I didn't know quite how I felt about Silver, now. There was something appealing in his very badness. He was at least consistent.

"Not up to me. I'd leave him here, although he might manage to blow up all the towers with something valuable in them out of sheer malice, so perhaps just killing him would be best. But Daddy and S'maak-Captain and the Judge and the Doctor are talking about it now. S'maak is up on the *Valiant*, so he's at a bit of a disadvantage because of the light-speed lag—three seconds. The Doctor made a promise, Daddy feels he must honor it, S'maak doesn't, and the Judge doesn't know. But I think your friend Silver is going to be taken back to Wunderland and tried for piracy.

Daddy won't let S'maak-Captain just execute him, though I would."

"I think there's something in this claim he's related to you; you're both ruthless when it comes down to it."

"Just as well I'm on your side, isn't it?" Marthar replied with a toss of her head. "We're kzin. He's a bad guy. I only kill the bad guys, and then I kill 'em quick. Saves complications."

I never see the world in such simple terms myself, but I could see that it would be useless saying so to Marthar. She was one of the good guys, she would never doubt that. I suppose Silver thought he was one of the good guys, perhaps the only one. It must have been lonely being Silver, I thought.

"Was I right about the third tower having mathematics in it?" I asked.

"Dunno. We can talk to Bengar about it. He thinks he knows where the engineering stuff is, but it should be easy to check if the science and engineering material uses the same things as was in your bars. It certainly counts as treasure. All of it does really, even the literature stuff with all those soapies. You know, it's a funny thing, but stupid creatures of all species seem to want to waste time on stories. I can't see it myself. It's not as if there aren't interesting things going on in the universe beside who ends up mating with who. At least the Jotok don't worry about that sort of thing, though they have stories too. It's all a bit strange."

"I think it's a part of type-one intelligence. After all, a scientific theory is a sort of story," I argued. "A story is just a sort of theory of what matters. You don't have to buy into it if you don't want, but it sort of organizes things, don't you think?"

"Most of them only organize things that don't matter, if you ask me," Marthar said impatiently. "Let's go and find Bengar and start getting organized about where to get the best treasure. I want to find out how those discs work; they're cool. If we can take the secret of those things with us, we'll make squillions."

So we went to find out more about the treasure from Bengar.

Bengar was with some of the loyal kzin and the Andersons, and was proudly showing them the home he had made for himself in his tower. He was proud of the little farm he had made, which Marthar and I had already seen, and he showed us all how he had set up a base in one of the rooms with the bookreaders. He also showed us his map.

"See, this is the planet, wi' the towers marked on it. This here is the tower we are at. It has all sorts o' science stuff in it, but mainly about living things, so not very interestin'. This is the tower ye landed by, and that's all stories and sichlike an' so completely useless, save for kits and those wi' time drippin' from their claws. Savin' yer presence, My Lady, young sir, for ye may both be young, but ye be Heroes both, never a doubt of it. Now this one," he continued, pointing at another, "this be proper science, so 'tes, about physics and maybe some o' that there chemistry. Far beyond what a poor spacer can grasp, d'ye see, but vallyble, very vallyble, I'm thinking. Oh, Bengar he has his use, don't ye think?"

Bengar had changed, much for the better, with company, I thought. He was still gangly and showed the signs of his privations, but he had been given the oxygen and glucose drips, and it made him more formidable.

"You learned a lot, Bengar," Marthar told him, and he glowed with pride. He obviously set a high store by what Marthar thought of him.

"Ooh, aye, so I did, warrior lady. Some of it was luck, like when I got desperate on account o' the cold and took a disc at random. Fortunate for me, it led to a tower in the sunlight, and right pleased I was to have the warmth agin. But then I found how to read these curly wriggles, not well, but well enough. Some o' they discs go places where no one would want to go, other worlds maybe. But most o' them lead to other towers like this one, and I kep' a record, so I did, and I knows where all the best bits are. And happy I am to pass it onto ye all, for I know when I have a good berth, so I does, and I hopes to be goin' to a proper world right soon, when we departs this hell planet."

"It won't be long now, Bengar. S'maak-Captain says the first lander is nearly ready, and the second one well on the way. A third is being started soon, too," Marthar told him. "As soon as we can load up the landers with the good stuff, we'll be off. And you are coming with me back to *Ka'* . . . Wunderland. I need a servant I can trust."

Bengar glowed again. "Ah, I be that, ye may be sure of it, warrior lady!"

"We shall need the mathematics if we are to understand the physics and the engineering," I pointed out. "And there are an awful lot of these bars. How will we know which are the best ones?"

"I imagine there's a lot of redundancy in them," Marthar argued. "It wouldn't make sense to leave only one copy of everything. Not if you plan to leave a legacy for posterity, given that posterity might not arrive for a billion years. Think meteor impacts and tectonic events."

Bengar became expansive. "Aye, to be sure, and there be machines on the higher levels; and some in a basement which be harder to get to, but I been down there in one tower. And some o' them be making new bars, as soon as ye take one away. So there be enough for everyone, I'm thinkin'. And I learned t' read from a sort o' kit's book that had a great many pictures in it."

This sounded promising. "Do you have it with you?" I asked him. There was a sort of introduction in every bar, but a bar that aimed at teaching you to read would certainly help.

"Ooh, aye, so I do, there be dozens o' them, and I brought them here by hand, so I did. And there be a great many different ways o' readin' them too, some for one species, some for another. Some o' them assume you has a head, and some does not. Some supposes what you got claws and some what ye ha' tentacles. Some supposes you got one brain, and some that ye ha' no sich thing, maybe for creatures wi but a few nodes, like they insects. I suspects they could gi' ye a kind o' brain transplant to make sure ye're smart enough to read it. I hopes nothing like that happened t'me, but I think 'tes what happened t' Gra-Prompyh, I reckon they snakes was tryin' to make his brain fitter for the readin' which is nothin' proper for kzin or man, I believes."

"Yes, that was disgusting," I agreed.

"And obviously not necessary," Marthar said. "Still, it couldn't have happened to a more deserving kzin. I suppose we shall find out quite a bit more about the aliens that built the towers and filled them up with all these books. The information must be somewhere other than those silly stories."

"Ooh, aye, in this very tower, my lady. I can show ye if ye will wait a moment. Did I not say that here be all the life, science stuff?" He loped off up the ramp and returned with a curious collection of boxes. He rummaged in them and brought out some cables that looked uncomfortably like the snakes, and some shiny smaller boxes. Then he started joining things together.

"See, the thing is, some species would be like they insects, and 'twould be the hive that had all the sense, not the indiwiddles. So they needed t' provide for a sharing device what allows a whole lot t' see and hear what is goin' on in a bar. And this does it, 'tes a sort o' helmet for a crowd o' beings, which is just what we is at present."

The arrangement made a kind of three-dimensional projector, and when he plugged the snakes on the bar, the familiar blue glow came again, but this time in a hemisphere a yard across. We could see the same sort of thing as I had seen in the helmet, but we could all see it at once.

"There they be, so far as I can tell. But mayhap these things are some other species, mayhap we be lookin' at some other aliens from a different world. For it don't look much like this one, I must say."

We saw a landscape, something like a city set in a forest, and with creatures moving around in a kind of dance. I found the zoom icon and focused on it, but nothing happened. Perhaps it needed a team of people to make it work. We watched it for a minute or two, silent. It was strange and hard to make any sense of what we were seeing and hearing, but they were definitely no species I had ever seen before. It would take years of hard work for anyone to get much from this.

Marthar got bored first.

"Well, I daresay a xenologist would be able to get something out of it, but I can't. So let's see, pull out that map again, Bengar. I want to make a list of places to plunder when the lander gets here."

So we made a list with Bengar's help, while the rest, who had been very quiet, as if knowing they were out of their depth, retreated back to get a meal from Bengar's farm.

At Marthar's request, the lander came down the next day to Bengar's tower. S'maak-Captain brought it in, and insisted on taking the pinnace straight back to the *Valiant*. I think he much preferred to be on his ship, and I must allow that I felt safer with it under his command. He had been grave, and very civil to Marthar and even me.

"It seems you have taken charge of the gathering of the spoils, Miss Marthar," he said, with what I would have sworn was a twinkle in his eye. He had seen Marthar rescue me, for Marthar had carried a camera into battle, and I think he liked her style. He and Marthar had pretty much the same idea of how to deal with Silver, too. Altogether it was practically a love-fest in comparison with our first meeting. I had to own S'maak was one of the good guys, though a bit severe for my tastes.

"We need to fill it up, and the Andersons can carry everything to the *Valiant*, and then come back for another load. There's a lot of this stuff, and Bengar is showing us more things we need."

"I had anticipated you might need some mechanical assistance, Miss Marthar, and I have a cargo of robots which should help with the loading. They can be left for the next lot. And in a day or two, you will have two landers on the job. I should wish it done as soon as possible, for I have no desire to linger in this vicinity. Space is big, but I would not want to run into any more pirates, and it cannot be ruled out so near the rift. I want to get back to Wunderland at the earliest moment compatible with your convenience, and also that of your Sire, of course."

"Thank you, S'maak-Captain," Marthar said, and flipped an ear coyly at him. If I didn't know her better, I should have thought she was flirting with him. But, of course, he was much too old for her.

S'maak had gone back into space to be with his beloved ship, and Orion, the doctor, the Judge and Silver had come out to watch the loading. The Andersons took possession of the craft itself and supervised where things were going inside. The lander had not been constructed for passengers, or if it had, there had been some serious modifications. There were about a dozen compartments, and first we loaded a whole lot of bookreaders, including the communal one that Bengar had shown us, and a dozen copies. Altogether there were a hundred helmets like the one I had worn, and Marthar had tried one out to make sure it would work on her. From outside, I could see it changing shape to accommodate to her skull, something I had felt happening but had never seen before. I suppose it must have happened on Silver, but I can't say I had noticed. She seemed satisfied without spending too long doing any reading, but she confirmed that she had the same icons I had seen, and could manipulate them at least as well as I had. I told her about the intelligence test and the five platonic solids, and she nodded smugly.

"Who wants to go back to school when we can play with these things all day?" she demanded in triumph. I suspected that her father would have some opinions on that.

Silver was fascinated by the three-dimensional communal helmet, and set it up so as to see it in operation. "Why, 'tes a wonderful thing, to be sure, and what wi' the Doctor willin' t' speak for me, an' the sheer wonder o' what we has here, why, I might even get a pardon, so I might."

"Silver, you are a scoundrel, but you cared for my daughter's friend, and he is my friend also, so I shall speak for you too." Orion told him in a growl. Orion glanced my way and gave an ear flick, and I wished I could flick my ears too, because I wanted him to know how honored I felt. Young Peter Cartwright had somehow made friends with Royalty. Oh, I suppose Marthar counted too, but somehow I didn't feel much in awe of Marthar, not even when she loped around with a blaster and a needler stuck in her belts. Her father seemed to find her present dress amusing, but he said little.

We filled two compartments of the twelve with the helmets and some bars. Then a few of us crammed into the lander to shift it to another tower, and the others were guided by Bengar to get to the same place via discs. It was only a flight in air, and we had only a few thousand kilometers to go, so nobody minded being squashed up for the half-hour it took. We went to the third tower, and this was where we had to get the robots out, for there were hundreds of bars to be loaded and it would have taken days by hand. The robots unfolded themselves endlessly, so it seemed, and stomped out of the lander one after the other. Bengar and the others were already there, of course, and were pointing out what was to be loaded. I hoped this was really useful mathematics and not just some weird game, although I suppose mathematics *is* a weird game for some mathematicians who do it for fun, and don't give a damn if it is useful or not.

Valuable or no, we filled all the rest of the compartments with the bars, clearing a lot of space in the tower. Marthar took lots of pictures of where the bars came from, and the writing over the storage spaces, and printed out copies of it to put on our compartments. It was a bit like plundering a library and a bit like doing archaeology. Silver had helped stow everything, although the Doctor and the Judge mostly spent the time chatting and smoking. Then we stood well back as the Andersons lifted the lander and headed back to space and the *Valiant*. It had taken us a long time, so we went back via disc to Bengar's tower and ate and slept until the next ship day. Well, the human beings slept, and the kzin napped in that way they do.

The next day was more of the same. This time we did the physics tower, or what informed opinion had decided was physics. The Doctor had looked at some of it and agreed with Bengar, and Orion had too. I was prepared to take their word for it. Getting the lander to come to a different tower was easy enough; we all went there by disc and signalled it, and the lander, after going back to collect the robots, arrived just outside with Bengar aboard. Helping with the robots was easier for Bengar than anyone else, because he could travel about on the discs without thinking about which one to step on. We started the robots out and ordered them to start loading. We were getting pretty good at this by now. The Andersons had, with help from *Valiant*, unloaded the lander, and *Valiant* was busy stowing its cargo in herself. The ship now had rather a lot of room. What had been crew quarters could be used if we ran out of space, but we would run out of time long before that.

Silver darted about, all friendly and helpful, wanting the labels explained to him, and copying them to his phone.

"Never too late t' learn, never too late," he said. "We must document it all so the arky-ologists will not be angry wi' us for makin' it hard t' work out where everything comes from, d'ye see?"

Marthar looked at him. "I suspect him of planning something," she said to me quietly.

"Planning what?"

"Something. I don't know what. But that one is going to be trying something on sometime. Bet your life on it."

CHAPTER THIRTY

We had three more days of it, with two landers for some of it on a permanent shuttle service to the *Valiant*. We loaded thousands of tons of the bars with some other things, including a strange robot that, according to Bengar, was capable of making new bars. We got it from the tower of engineering, which we looted very comprehensively, so I hope it wasn't the only one there. Keeping records of where everything came from and went to was a chore, but Silver was very helpful, taking lots of pictures on his phone and printing them and sticking the results over the compartments in the landers and even going up to the *Valiant* to ensure that they were preserved in the storage bins there.

We thought we had cracked the problem of the discs, or at least Marthar did. It was difficult to tell, but it did look as though we had designs for them that might work. You had to create them in pairs with some sort of quantum entanglement between them; it might turn out that nobody could build the things because there doubtless would be tools to be built first to build the tools you'd need, and so on, five levels deep. Or maybe fifty-five. Still, if we could make it work, it would be worth all the money on Old Earth tied up in a sack. Which would be a big sack. We could make all of Wunderland rich, not just us.

Marthar and I looked around. "I don't suppose you could say we've finished," she said. "But I think we've got enough on the *Valiant* to keep a whole planet busy for a few hundred years. The next thing to worry about is getting everyone back on board the ship. Then S'maak-Captain takes us home, while we work on the next serious problem."

"What's that?"

"How to spend all that money. If we can make anything much work, everyone on Wunderland will be able to buy their own planet. Those discs alone could do it. And I've a fair idea of the principle, although you can understand the principle of a computer without being able to build one, unless you made it out of brass gear wheels. We ought to be able to make something that works like the discs, even if we have to make it out of the equivalent of brass gear wheels."

I wish I had Marthar's confidence, but she knew a lot about *Hard*, and the discs certainly came under that heading. I thought we should be working on understanding the easy bits on the way home, not thinking about what to do with the money, and said so.

"Oh, of course we shall. We've all got heaps to do, and we'll do it. But there are big organizational issues: we have to start off in a small way and make enough money to reinvest it in another project, and then get enough cash from that to go onto the next project, and so on. Until we can buy a few solar systems. The first thing to do is to work out what the starting project is; it has to be something Daddy can finance with his own money. Not Riit funds, we want to own this ourselves."

I hadn't though that far ahead. "Well, it will be nice to be rich, I suppose," I said slowly. And it occurred to me that neither ARM nor the Riit Clan would like so much power concentrated in other hands. We might have to go a long way away.

"I can tell you now, rich won't be the word for it. And I suspect you won't like it much at all. Anywhere there is money, there are parasites; in this case there's going to be an awful lot of money so they'll be huge parasites. Governments and whole planetary systems I expect. The problem isn't going to be making money—the problem will be keeping it, or at least some of it. And I'm a bit worried about Daddy. He's seen super-rich, at least the records of what it was like in the old days. And I'm pretty sure he doesn't want it. I suspect he doesn't want me to be rich either. Bad for the character or something."

"Will wealth spoil Marthar?" I teased her. "Does power corrupt, and will it corrupt you?"

She took this seriously. "It's a good saying, that one; some of you humans are quite perceptive. About power corrupting, I mean. I don't know if power corrupts, or if people who are power-hungry start off corrupt and some of them get power and it sort of comes out in them in a way which wasn't obvious until they got it. I suppose I shall be a controlled experiment, shan't I?"

"Are you sure you aren't already a little bit corrupt?" I said in a tease she didn't recognize.

She was silent. "I don't know," she said very quietly, as if to herself. "I can see that I might be quite horrible in some circumstances. I think if I were an empress I might be one of the really, really bad ones. I'm really not very kind. On the other hand, my name is Riit."

"You're kind to me," I told her, a little bit frightened.

She looked at me in silence. "Yes, I'm kind to you. You'll always be my Peterkin, at least I hope so. After that episode with the implant, I know what it is to just let go, to let the animal reign. I don't want that, and yet I do. And I think it might be awfully addictive."

"You are strong, Marthar. You are capable of frightful things. I saw what you did to Vaarth, and I saw you burn those pirates down as if they were just weeds. But I think that deep down there, you are kind and decent and honorable."

"Well, I suppose a human being isn't the best judge. You humans do it differently from us. We are not kind. But deep down you are utterly ferocious on a level we kzin can't reach. All the truly frightful things you can't face, you let your subconscious handle. That's how you beat us. Only you don't see it. You won't let yourselves see it. You fool yourselves into thinking there's something nice at your core. But down there in the id, you have a monster lurking, little Peter. You can't see it, but I can."

Marthar talks some silly nonsense at times.

We got everyone loaded into the two landers, and waved farewell to the treasure planet. We went over the third tower and, down below, we could see some figures moving around near it. A telescope showed that the pirates were there, hunting. There were only three of them. The fourth had gone—very likely dead; possibly they had fought. They looked up at the lander and waved, hopelessly. But we weren't stopping.

Back on the ship we were badly undercrewed, but S'maak had set up some automation systems with the help of *Valiant*. It was a temporary measure, but would get us at least into the Wunderland system. Or so we hoped.

We had to go slowly to the edge of the system where spacetime was flat enough to engage the hyperdrive. It took a lot longer than it had coming in. Not that Marthar and I were bored, nor any of the others. All of us were learning, with Bengar as a sort of coach in the early stages. We wanted to be able to use anything important we had got, and that meant recognizing it. I was the one who concentrated on trying to understand the mathematics. It was horrible. I'm not all that good at human-kzin mathematics; it would be unlikely that I'd be able to break the code of this totally alien set of ideas in a language that made no sense. We needed Dimity Carmody here. I persevered. You have to, don't you? Once you've set your hand to something, you must never give up or you feel cheap. You're allowed to change your strategy though, and I scrolled through some Jotok mathematics in case it was any help. They had invented something like networks instead of strings, and rules for rewriting them, or redrawing them. It came from being compound animals, I suppose. They were called digraph-grammars, and humans had also invented something similar, though not pushed it as far. They made a certain amount of sense, but although

I could follow the rules and apply them, I never really got the semantics of the things—what they *meant*—which is the important bit, I guess.

At least we had established that it *was* mathematics. The engineering and science bars were chock full of it. So it had to be useful and not just a game or a pure art form. I found that comforting, and it made me persist through some horrible frustration at my own lack of ability.

We weren't going straight home. The *Valiant* was headed for another system just outside the rift itself, a new colony called Tamburlaine in the human starmaps. It had a place where we could refuel, which was important because we had used up a lot with the landers doing all that ferrying, and the ship was a few kilotons heavier now. Also we had used up a lot of metals in making the new landers and hadn't wanted to stay to reclaim the scrap of the old ones, though we did recover the green lander. So the first stage was getting out of the treasure-planet system, which took an age.

We finally made the transition to hyperspace, with all that entailed and after only a few days, we came back to our familiar universe with a bright star in the distance. Now it was the slow drag in normal space to get us to Tamburlaine.

I think the thing I liked best about being back on the ship was the regular day-and-night cycles. *Valiant* turned the lights down at night and up again in the day, so you could actually tell which was which, unlike the treasure planet. The other thing I liked was talking to *Valiant*, who was even helpful with the Jotok mathematics. She could tell me about it in simpler terms than the web references, all of which seemed to assume I already grasped a whole raft of stuff I didn't.

It took us almost a week to arrive at the heart of the Tamburlaine System from the outer limits because we were moving slowly to conserve fuel. There was a human naval base there on the fifth planet, or in orbit around it. We took a lander down to the surface while *Valiant* was organizing the refueling, and Marthar and I wandered around.

This was the second alien planet I had stepped on, and it was certainly very different from the treasure world. There were very few kzin here, and a lot of human beings. To tell the truth it was rather dull. Any big city looks very like any other, and although this was big compared with Munchen, and the buildings were higher in the sky, I can't say it was fun. We didn't need anything special by way of clothes or drips; the oxygen levels were high and the climate warm where we were. We did some shopping. I didn't have any money, so Orion changed some platinum blocks into local currency and gave us both what turned out to be plenty for eating and shopping. I think the local kzin had never seen an intelligent kzinrett before, which meant that there was not a lot of shopping to be done from Marthar's point of view. And the kzin traders seemed to want to talk to her, just to check that she *could* talk.

We had been invited out to dinner with a local kzin nobleman who wanted to be nice to Orion, and Marthar was invited too. She insisted that I go as well, which made me more than a little uncomfortable. Marthar seemed entirely happy with the prospect. I think she was intending to show the backward natives what a modern kzinrett kit was like and was looking forward to shocking them rigid.

It was held in something that was, I suppose, the local equivalent of a palace, though it covered less ground than Orion's house in Thoma'stown. But it rose for seven or eight stories, big ones of course. They even brought me some cooked meat, which they detest for themselves.

I was seated on a huge chair made for kzin, at an enormous table, next to a gray-furred kzin with an artificial eye and a lot of scars. He turned to me.

"You arrre the ship's, uhh, pet, is that rrright? What is the worrrd? Mascot, rrrright?"

"Not exactly, Noble Hero. At least I hope not. Actually Marthar is *my* pet." I can't say I really felt that, or anything like it, but the air of easy patronizing annoyed me.

He flipped his ears several times, the equivalent of a belly laugh from a human being.

"Sssso, you have adopted a Riit kzinrett, iss it sso? And does she behave herself well in public?"

"Not always," I told him. "I've seen her do things to those who annoyed her which would make your fur curl to think about."

He laughed again, this time with sound effects as well. "Aahhrr, I would not want the currrly fur, better I do not know, isss ssso?" And he nodded and turned to the kzin on his other side. Later, thinking it over, and when I knew a bit more about outworld kzin, my blood ran cold when I thought of the risk I had taken in saying that. But the best kzin like a bit of bravado, if you can judge the right mood and moment for it.

Orion caught my eye and winked and twitched an ear. I

am sure he heard the exchange and was amused by it. I hoped that Marthar hadn't heard any of it and that Orion wouldn't mention it.

After the dinner, where neither Marthar nor I disgraced ourselves further, despite Marthar's unusual volubleness—perhaps to prove she could be—we all went back up in the lander to find chaos. *Valiant* had been disabled again, although it had been only temporary, and she was now putting in more patches to ensure it couldn't happen another time. Silver had escaped in the pinnace. There was, of course, absolutely no point in looking for him; he had a whole planet to hide on. He had not only managed to switch *Valiant* off for several hours, he had used the time to fill the pinnace with as many bars as it could carry, and two helmets, one of them a multi-user system, which meant he could read what he had stolen and show it to other people. Of course, he didn't have much of a fraction of what we carried, the pinnace wasn't big enough, but he had been very careful in his selection.

"At least he didn't take anything to do with the discs," Marthar said with relief. "Did he take any mathematics?"

"Ye-es. He did. Nothing I haven't copied. I think he must plan to sell something. Just a fighting fund so he can get back to the treasure planet and really rifle it, I expect. I think he was looking to see what would make decoding the script possible, so he'll know what to steal and where it is. Oh, I've found something new on my phone. This wasn't here before."

"Don't say he's left a note," Marthar said with a resigned

air. "I bet it is. It's the sort of thing he would do, the old villain."

"Yes, that's exactly what it is, only it's addressed to both of us. Come and look at it."

The letter wasn't long, and of course it was an audio-video recording. The screen cleared as I ran it, and the face of Silver looked out at us, his head on one side, and his eyes open wide.

"Hello there, me young kits. This is me farewell message to ye, and thankee for the company on this last voyage, though ye were mostly locked up wi' the bars and suchlike to tell the truth. Still, ye were as civil as someone in my delicate position could reasonably expect, and so were the Doctor, and your Sire, young Marthar, which I take very kindly, indeed I do, and I'd thankee for passing it on to both o' them. As to S'maak-Captain, the less said the better in that quarter, and he a spacer like me. I told him I'd come back to dooty, but he never said a word and looked like he'd swallowed some grass.

"I ha' given the matter a deal o' thought and I think the risk of the hot needle a little too great, so I'm leavin' shortly to save the good Doctor from goin' agin his conscience to save me, for it's a tender little thing and I would not wish to harm it; and he bein' the kind what would dance to whatever tune it played. I also remember the rest of the Riit Clan. And for another reason, this locality be more my sort o' territory, bein' so close t' the rift, like.

"So be brave me hearties, and be so good as to remember kindly now and again, your old spacer comrade and one time tutor, one: Silver."

"Typical," Marthar said tartly. "Leaves out all the